HOUSE

On the

HILL

OTHER BOOKS AND AUDIO BOOKS
BY ANNETTE LYON:

Lost Without You

At the Water's Edge

HOUSE

On the HILL

A Novel

Annette Lyon

Covenant Communications, Inc.

Cover art: woman portrait © William Whitaker; *Spring Logan Temple* © Al Rounds.

Cover design copyrighted 2005 by Covenant Communications, Inc.

Published by Covenant Communications, Inc.
American Fork, Utah

Printed in Canada
First Printing: February 2005

11 10 09 08 07 06 05   10 9 8 7 6 5 4 3

ISBN 1-59156-685-1

Dedicated to the memory of my grandparents,
August and Frieda Miller Luthy,
who lived in Logan and raised their family in
a small adobe house on Main Street—just like the one in the novel.

Also to my late grandfather-in-law,
Keith Jensen,
who opened his heart to me as one of his own
and was one of my greatest sources
of encouragement to keep writing.

Acknowledgments

This book would not exist without the late Nolan P. Olsen's *Logan Temple: The First 100 Years.* I am indebted to him for his work in compiling such a wonderful history.

Thanks to Patricia Record of the Logan Public Library for her aid in my research.

I have continued to be fortunate in having a wonderful editor, Angela Eschler, who works herself into the ground until we're both happy with the final result.

Finally, my close writing friends proved invaluable in helping this story become the best I could make it—Steph, Lu Ann, Michele, Jeff, Heather, and Lynda. I can always count on you, and for that I am continually grateful.

CHAPTER 1

Logan, Utah—August 1877

A heavy cough from the other room forced Lizzy Sullivan to lay aside her journal. She swung her legs to the floor and hurried to six-year-old David's side.

"I thought you were asleep," Lizzy said, reaching for the spare blanket at the base of his bed. She wrapped it around her little brother as he coughed again. "You're going to catch cold."

"I already have a cold, Lizzy, remember?" David attempted a laugh and started a new round of coughing. She sat down and held him until the attack subsided. The doctor had warned the family that David's condition might develop into pneumonia, but no one talked much about the prospect as if fearing to tempt fate.

"I couldn't sleep," David whispered. His eyes looked particularly haggard tonight. Lizzy felt his forehead. He was very hot, but he shivered and his hands were cold.

David peered around her to where candlelight spilled out of her room. "Didn't Mama tell you last night not to stay up late?" He gave her a weak grin.

Lizzy's parents had been after her to go to bed early, saying she was too tired in the mornings and that they couldn't spare the extra candles. But with the rest of the family away at Grandmother Pearson's funeral, Lizzy had made an exception. She stayed home with David because he was too ill to travel, and since no one else would be using any candles over the next couple of days, an extra for herself wouldn't be missed.

"All right, I'll go to bed. But not until you're asleep." Lizzy wagged a finger at her brother.

"Could you get me a drink of water first?"

"Of course."

Lizzy made a move to stand, but David went on. "And I don't think I'll be able to fall asleep unless you read me something . . . please?"

His puppy-dog eyes tugged at Lizzy's heartstrings. "If you insist." She picked him up and carried him into her room. After she set him down, David scooted to the far side of the bed—his usual spot for listening to Lizzy read. She climbed in next to him, and he snuggled into the crook of her arm. He closed his eyes as if going to sleep. Brushing David's hair out of his face, she felt a pang of sadness.

Brother Sorensen had helped administer to David again before her family left. She didn't see what good it did. The first blessing hadn't made a difference either. She wondered if her own doubts were part of the problem; perhaps she shouldn't be around during the blessings. But David always insisted that his sister hold him, so she had, pretending to believe but instead resenting God for allowing her brother to be so sick.

Perhaps, she thought as David seemed to drift back to sleep, her own faith had been stronger at David's age. But she had lost it some-where in her twenty years. Lost it somewhere wasn't exactly true. Lizzy could list the dozens of small moments that had compounded the problem. The first memory came from when she was ten years of age and had broken her foot the day before the school picnic. She prayed all night for her foot to be miraculously healed as her mother's had been on the journey to Zion. But by morning Lizzy's foot was swollen and purple. Instead of racing to the picnic, she watched from the window as her classmates skipped along the road to school without her. Ten years later Lizzy could see the silliness in expecting such a prayer to be answered, but she still remembered the sting of disappointment all the same.

At age twelve Lizzy had lost the necklace given to her by her best friend, Joshua. At the time the necklace was her most prized possession.

"It's for you, Beth," Joshua had said, using his pet name for her. He'd adopted it years ago to distinguish Lizzy from his sister Elizabeth, who also went by "Lizzy." He'd put the necklace around her neck. "It's only made of glass, but I think it's pretty."

"It's beautiful," Lizzy had said, fingering the beads. "Look! The sun makes it sparkle. I'll pretend they're diamonds." She wore the necklace to church meetings, parties, and community dances. Until the day it was lost. One day after church Lizzy had put it on her bedside table, and in the morning it was gone. She must have prayed a dozen times for help finding it, but to no avail. Lizzy still wondered if her cousin Jimmy had taken it as a prank and then forgotten about it, as was his nature. Her fingers went up to the golden chain around her neck, another gift from Joshua on her sixteenth birthday, which she wore always for safekeeping.

As she looked at her innocent brother, she tried not to remember the most painful incident, the one that had started her doubt in the promises of her family's faith. It had happened when she was only six years old—when she was still so believing, so trusting. Just like David.

Shortly after Lizzy's third birthday, Richard Jr. was born. Another brother, named for her grandfather Josiah, had died at birth, but Lizzy had been too young to remember him. Even so, she could never forget Richard's chubby legs as he crawled around the house. As he grew, she loved being a second mother to him, toting him around, feeding him, pretending he was hers, even with only three years' age difference between them. By the time Lizzy was six, Richard was constantly running and getting himself into trouble. That was also when he contracted polio.

At the time, Lizzy knew that if she prayed hard enough, her faith could heal her brother. Sometimes she knelt at her bedside and poured out her six-year-old heart. Other times she went into the trees by the house, like she had learned that Joseph Smith did, and prayed there. She was so sure back then that it wasn't a question of *if* Richard would conquer his illness, only *when*.

But he died.

Even as a young woman, Lizzy couldn't help but shudder at the feelings the memory stirred inside her. Sorrow at losing her brother. Confusion over why he died when she had prayed as she had been taught to do. Guilt that her faith wasn't strong enough. And anger at a Heavenly Father who would take away her brother—at a God who left her parents clinging to each other at night, crying with great, hacking sobs that sent fear through Lizzy's six-year-old heart as she stood by the doorframe and watched them grieve.

Though only moments had passed, Lizzy knew that if she let herself, she could think about such things all night. But no matter how she reasoned, the fact remained that never had one of her prayers, big or small, been answered. At least, not any she had been aware of. She didn't count the prayers recited almost from memory, whether over dinner or with the family, where she asked for ambiguous things like peace, well-being, and protection from affliction. With a shake of her head to clear away the thoughts, she looked again at David, who opened his eyes.

"Can I have some water now?"

Patting David's leg, she smiled. "Of course."

She kissed his cheek, then headed down the dark stairs. Descending into the kitchen, she was glad the moon was almost full, sending light across the floor from the windows. As she ladled water into a metal cup, she eyed the stove. Mid-August was a mite early in the season to be warming water bottles for bed, but David could probably use one tonight. His feet were always cold, even with thick socks.

Lizzy opened the heavy stove door and looked inside. A few glowing embers from supper remained. She poked at them, and sparks flew out, satisfying her that she could coax some flames. The wood box produced kindling and a few sticks, and she set to lighting the stove, once again glad she had stayed behind to care for David. The trip to Salt Lake City would have been more than he could endure. Even so, she regretted not being able to support her mother during the funeral. Lizzy's mother had been very close to her own mother, and Grandmother Pearson's death would be hard on her.

Lizzy blew gently on the embers, and the kindling caught fire. She sat back on her heels and sighed, remembering how hard her mother had prayed for a miracle to preserve Grandmother Pearson's life. Uncle William had written regular letters to keep the family abreast of Grandmother's health. He recounted the priesthood blessings she received, the long nights he and his wife spent at her bedside, the days when she seemed well enough that everyone believed she would resume her usual habits and be preserving bushels of peaches by fall.

But as Grandmother had declined in health over the last month, Lizzy's entire family lived with daily anxiety, waiting for Uncle William's next letter; then the final one arrived, saying Grandmother had passed on.

Lizzy poked the fire, then stared at it while it greedily ate the fuel. What good were prayers and priesthood blessings if Grandmother died anyway? God didn't seem to care about His children. At least not anymore. Her parents and others had told her story after story, recounting miracles on the plains. But was her family now unworthy, or their faith suddenly weak? Did He even notice when they cried out to Him? When they *died?*

What about Richard Jr.? David? They were too young to be unworthy. What about her?

A heavy breath escaped as she shook off the thoughts, closed the stove, and filled a pot with water. She wiped her wet hands on a dishrag, then tossed the cloth aside and grabbed David's glass of water. Heading upstairs with only the moon lighting her way, she wondered if he would fall asleep before the water was warm.

"Here you go," Lizzy said as she pushed the door farther open with her toe. It creaked on its hinges.

David took the cup, drank the water down, and smacked his lips. "Thanks."

"You're welcome." Lizzy set the cup aside and arranged her quilt around David. She glanced at the gable window where the curtains swayed. The night breeze wasn't all that cold, but Lizzy closed the window anyway. No use taking chances at David getting a chill.

She leaned over her bookshelf, which stood next to the bench her father had made for her birthday four years ago. The bench was placed under the window and had quickly become one of Lizzy's favorite spots to read or dream of the future—mostly of the possibility of living with Aunt Louisa in New York and attending school there. And perhaps meeting a dashing young man who was dark and handsome and full of mystery.

The bookshelf beside it had since been filled—then stuffed—with books which she had read and reread until some covers held on by mere threads. Someday, she hoped, she would have loads of bookcases chock-full of books. In the meantime she would make do with the ones she had, plus the new volumes sent from her wealthy aunt on birthdays and Christmas.

She traced the spines with her finger. "What do you want to hear tonight, David? Poetry? A novel? We never did finish *Roderick Random*."

"Poetry."

Lizzy withdrew her poetry anthology from the shelf. "There's Blake, Wordsworth, Shakespeare . . ."

"Tennyson."

Lizzy grinned. "That was my next guess," she said as she flipped to the red bookmark. David requested Tennyson often enough that Lizzy kept "In Memoriam," his favorite poem, marked. It was long, and Lizzy secretly hoped that David would be able to sleep before she finished it. She decided to check on the water around the twentieth section, then settled beside David. He closed his eyes as if already expecting a restful sleep to come.

The rhythm of the poem lulled David into even breathing sooner than she expected, although he was not quite asleep as Lizzy reached the eighteenth part of the poem. "'A looming bastion fringed with . . .'" Her voice trailed off. She lowered the book to her lap, then sniffed the air, coughing at the smell.

David opened his eyes groggily. "What is it?"

"You rest for a moment. I'll go check." She tucked the quilt around him and hurried down the stairs.

As she entered the kitchen, she gasped at the sight of flames climbing up the kitchen wall. The curtains were completely devoured, and little was left of the shelves as the fire spread upward. She flew to the counter, where she grabbed a bucket of water and aimed for the base of the fire. The water sizzled and steamed, but did little else. Thick orange ribbons still climbed, growing every second. The heat made her step back. A dense haze filled the room, and she coughed, covering her mouth to breathe. Hurrying up the stairs two at a time, her eyes stung from smoke. She burst into the room and grabbed David, quilt and all.

"What's the matter?" David asked, trying to sit up in her arms as he coughed.

"There's a fire in the kitchen," Lizzy said, trying to sound calm. "I want to take you outside for a few minutes while I put it out."

David stiffened, and his pale face grew even whiter. He pulled back. "But Mother said the night air isn't good for me," he said, as if that were the only concern.

"She'd approve this time," Lizzy said, covering his face with the blanket and heading down the stairs. Halfway down she had to put the sleeve of her nightdress over her own nose and mouth. The air felt heavy as she raced through the hot kitchen and out the back door.

They reached the wooden bench by the barn, and Lizzy set David on it. Without a word she scurried to the barn door, where she found two buckets, then raced to the well to fill them. When Lizzy reached the house, she discovered that the fire had spread over the entire wall and now licked the rafters. She emptied the buckets onto the fire, but there were no visible results.

Without a backward glance she returned to the well at full tilt, fighting panic. *It can't be that bad,* she reasoned as she refilled the buckets. *I can save the house.* But the very thought felt hollow.

As she went from the well to the fire and back again, she wished there was time to get Brother Sorensen's help. But with his farm nearly two miles away, it would be far too late before she could get there and back.

With a deafening crash, a corner of the roof collapsed, making a gaping hole. The jolt to her concentration sent one bucket flying out of her hand. She covered her eyes as sparks flew into the air, then she lowered her arm, gazing at the fire as it engulfed the house. Though she was breathing quickly, her heart beating double-time, Lizzy suddenly couldn't take another step. She could do nothing but stare as her home was destroyed.

It was hopeless. She knew that now. If only she hadn't been alone. If only the family had been home. Papa and Mama, her cousin Jimmy, and the boys would have helped put out the fire. Matthew or Aaron could have even run for help to the Sorensen farm. With the family home, there might have been a chance. She stood rooted to the ground, transfixed by the bright colors making their way around and over the only home she knew.

Lizzy's fingers grew weak. The other bucket dropped to the ground, and water spilled onto the dirt and around her bare feet. Her hands covered her face, head shaking in disbelief. She peered through her fingers as white smoke rose into the black night, spiraling above the house. When flames reached her gable room, sparks jumped out of the window onto the maple tree.

"My books!" she cried in despair.

With a swipe at the ground, she filled her hands with rocks, screaming as she threw them with all her might. She collapsed to her knees in sobs, then looked to the dark sky, pounded the muddy ground, and cried, "God, how can You do this to me?"

"Lizzy."

She felt David's touch and looked around. Her brother's hand emerged from the folds of the quilt. He held out the anthology. "You still have this one."

CHAPTER 2

Lizzy and David retreated to the safety of the bench next to the barn. With David in her lap, she sat in a daze, hardly able to see clearly for her tears. David laid his head against her chest and pulled his knees up. The touch of his icy toes and burning head brought Lizzy out of her stupor. She tore her gaze from the fire and blinked her tears away, knowing she had to focus on David.

Through her fatigue and smoke-muddled brain, she tried to decide what to do next. Nothing more could be done about the house tonight. The barn, standing as far away as it did, was probably in no danger from the fire, so the cow and chickens, though spooked, were safe. Sleeping on the hay crossed her mind, but with David's weak condition she didn't dare spend the night in a drafty barn. There was only one thing to do. Lizzy wrapped the quilt tightly around David, stood up, and headed for the road.

"I can walk," he said.

Lizzy sniffed hard, tears streaking her cheeks. "No, you can't. Mama would have my hide if I let you do that."

So she walked toward the Sorensen farm, carrying David and stopping along the way to rest when her arms grew tired. Tears continued to run down her cheeks. The Sorensens would take them in, she reminded herself stoically. They would. And later, when the family returned, they would all draw together and work hard to rebuild their lives. They could take care of themselves, and someday they would all look back with pride at what they had accomplished in the face of tragedy.

Lizzy's thoughts kept drifting to the fire, and more than once she gritted her teeth and forced such things from her mind. She and

David needed to get help. That had to be her first priority, not wallowing in self-pity.

It didn't take long before her bare feet were so numb they seemed like stumps of wood. She wondered why her feet were so cold when the breeze blew warm. Surely David's feet were blocks of ice too. She was glad the moon was nearly full. It provided her with enough light to make her way along the road without stumbling into holes or over rocks.

More than once she had to pause and shift David's form in her aching arms, then continue along the road. Trying not to shiver, she held him close, bracing him each time he coughed, then holding him even closer.

When they reached the Sorensen home, Lizzy walked to the back porch and set David down. She wiped at her eyes, then rapped on the door. She knocked several times before someone finally answered the door.

"Sakes alive, what's all the fuss about at this hour?" It was Sister Sorensen's voice. The elderly woman fumbled with the doorknob, then the door opened a crack. She peered out, then flung the door open the rest of the way. "Why, Lizzy, what is the matter? Never mind. Come in, come in." David took Lizzy's hand as she ushered them inside. Their neighbor closed the door behind them and retied her dressing gown around her plump middle.

"I'm sorry to bother you, but—" Lizzy began, emotion choking her voice. "Our house caught fire."

"Land sakes!" Her hands flew to her mouth in shock. "What about the rest of your family? Where are they? Is anyone hurt?"

"No one else is home," Lizzy reassured her. "They're all in Salt Lake City."

Sister Sorensen pulled them to her. "You poor things!" She released them suddenly and turned toward the stairs. "I'll get Samuel and Joshua up right away." Lifting her hem, she hurried up the stairs, arms pumping with each step.

"Thank you," Lizzy called after her. "Although . . . it's probably too late for them to save anything." Her throat grew tight, but she refused to let more tears fall.

Pausing at the top of the stairs, Sister Sorensen wagged a finger toward Lizzy. "Now don't you be talking like that. There's always hope. You two go find a seat in the kitchen." She tossed her graying braid over her shoulder and disappeared into the darkness.

Lizzy and David sat on the bench at the kitchen table and waited quietly for Sister Sorensen to return. Moments later, two sets of feet sounded on the stairs, followed by the door opening and slamming shut.

Sister Sorensen came into the kitchen soon after. "I hope you didn't bang on the door too long before I answered," she said as she brought her abundant self into the kitchen area. "I'm afraid my hearing isn't what it used to be. And you know Samuel. Sleeps like a rock. Joshua's not much better. But I got him up first, and then Joshua woke Samuel all right."

Lizzy tried to smile. Joshua would drag his father out of bed if need be. He would do anything for her. She wondered absently for the thousandth time what had really happened to her glass necklace all those years ago.

When Sister Sorensen disappeared into the pantry, David leaned against Lizzy's shoulder and closed his eyes. Lizzy felt tuckered out too, but she couldn't rest. Instead she stared at the wall, only dimly aware that she should be embarrassed to be seen wearing nothing but her nightgown. She kept stroking the spine of the poetry book that lay in her lap as images of her other books came to mind. She could list each title, see each cover, almost smell their paper. Yet they no longer existed except as black ashes that would fly away with the next breeze.

Lizzy picked up her book and held it close. Her eyes watered. She couldn't fully comprehend what had happened—and wasn't sure if she wanted to yet. The reality of what it would mean hurt too much. She thought of the rocking chair her father had made, her mother's heirloom quilt, the twins' wood carvings. She shook her head. *Not tonight.* Lizzy bit her lips together and blinked rapidly so the ache inside her wouldn't show. Somehow, if she could look strong on the outside, she felt sure she could feel that way on the inside. And if she ever needed to be strong, it was now. David would rely on her more than ever in the next few days.

Sister Sorensen emerged from the pantry with sliced bread and cheese, then set to fixing up a makeshift bed on the floor while Lizzy and her brother ate.

It wasn't long before David slept on the blankets beside Lizzy. She couldn't sleep yet, and instead sat beside him and stroked his fingers, then looked up at her neighbor. "Thank you for taking us in tonight," she whispered in an effort to keep her tears back. She did not want to cry until she was alone. Yet it felt like agony to hold in the tears.

"You know you're welcome here. When your family gets back, they will be too. And you can all stay here as long as need be. Although . . . well, never mind."

"Is something wrong?" Lizzy asked, her brow furrowed. She didn't want to be a burden.

Sister Sorensen stood and wiped some remaining crumbs from the table. "Nothing's wrong, dear. It's just that our George and his family need to stay with us a spell. They'll be arriving from Idaho in another couple of days. He and Ida have six children, so we'll be a bit tight when your folks return, but we'll manage. Don't worry your pretty head over that." Sister Sorensen bit the inside of her cheek. "I don't suppose we could get word to them, could we? I suppose Samuel could leave in the morning for Salt Lake . . ."

"There's no need for the trouble," Lizzy said, picturing Brother Sorensen telling her mother what had happened, assuming he even found them. "They'll be back soon."

Long after Sister Sorensen had returned to bed and Lizzy's candle stub had burned out, Lizzy still sat awake by David. She wouldn't think into the future—to when her family would return, when George and Ida's family came, about where she would be living in six months. It was too painful. But she couldn't keep from reliving her fight against the fire and the moment the flames reached her bedroom. She wondered how the stove had started the fire and whether she could have done more to stop it.

She wrapped an old but warm quilt around herself and stared out the window at the bright stars. Through her watery vision, the stars twinkled more than normal. Tears fell freely, and she was grateful to be alone. The back door opened, and she quickly wiped at her face. A heavy set of footsteps trod up the stairs. *Brother Sorensen,* she thought. He probably assumed Lizzy was asleep. She waited for the second set of feet to go up.

"Beth, are you all right?" Joshua suddenly asked from behind.

She didn't turn around, but nodded a couple of times. Joshua stepped lightly, though still making a floorboard creak as he came around and sat beside her. She kept her face down so he wouldn't see her tears.

"Father and I tried our best . . ." he began.

Lizzy nodded again and whispered, "I know. Thank you." She finally looked up at him. His eyes were shiny too.

"I'm so sorry, Beth," he said again. He reached for her hand, but instead of taking it, Lizzy collapsed into his arms, burying her face in his shirt as she wept.

* * *

It didn't take long for David's condition to take a turn for the worse. The morning after their arrival at the Sorensens', Lizzy was sure he had pneumonia. For two days she stayed by him constantly, despite appeals for her to get some rest too. She refused to leave David for any length of time, until Sister Sorensen put her foot down and nearly dragged Lizzy outside for some air.

"Let's the two of us go on a stroll," she offered when they reached the front porch.

But Lizzy shook her head. "I need to be close by in case David needs me. I'll just sit on the step for a spell." Lizzy rested on the stoop of the Sorensen home and looked at the gown she wore. It was too short for her, and the middle had more room than she needed, but it was all she had to wear for the time being. She sighed and looked into the yard.

When Lizzy noticed the clothesline, memories of happy days at home came to mind, like last summer, the day it hailed as she took down the dried laundry. Cousin Jimmy, larger than Lizzy in body but childlike in mind, had been terrified of the mild storm. He refused to even put his hand outside the doorway to let the balls of hail fall onto his palm. So Lizzy had gathered some of the ice balls for him. "It's called hail," she had told Jimmy, holding out her hand.

Jimmy had looked out at the yard, where white pellets were bouncing around like water on a hot skillet. His brow furrowed in confusion. "But I thought it was hot down there."

As Lizzy remembered the day, and his misinterpretation of the word, she smiled to herself and hugged her knees.

"That's the first time I've seen you smile in the last couple of days," Joshua said, coming from the stables. "What were you thinking about?"

Lizzy shrugged. "Somehow I never thought that I would wish for such simple things."

"Like what?" Joshua asked, sitting beside her.

"Like taking down the laundry." Lizzy smiled wanly. "That must sound silly coming from someone who hates keeping house."

"No, not at all."

Joshua was sitting awfully close to her. Lizzy looked at their legs, nearly touching, then back at Joshua, whose gaze focused on the fields in the distance. She had heard gossip about Joshua's supposed designs for marrying her someday, but he had never given her any inclination that he cared for her beyond friendship. She could admit that once or twice she had wondered what it would be like to really have him for a beau. But each time she quickly dismissed the thought. After all, such things more often than not led to marriage, and she didn't want that unless the man resembled something a bit more . . . Well, something a bit more exciting than Joshua Sorensen. And he didn't exactly fit with her plan of living with her aunt in New York and getting an education—and the possible men she might meet there. Why was it that Lizzy couldn't muster the excitement over local boys that her friends had? Most of them were married or engaged to be, and several were already mothers.

Not that Lizzy had anything against marriage. If she could find someone dark-eyed and mysterious who could recite poetry by the light of the moon . . .

She shook her head at the thought and brought her mind back to the present—and Joshua. A match with him would please both of their families. And she had to admit he would be a good husband to the woman he married. He would provide for his family and be faithful in the Church—he would have the faith to balance her doubts—and he would always be kind. But if Lizzy ever married, she would need more than reliability. She would have to feel for her husband the passion found in one of John Donne's poems.

Or she would have to hear from her suitor the words like those in an Elizabeth Barrett Browning sonnet. Words that made Lizzy's heart pound: "I love thee with the breath, smiles, tears, of all my life!" Joshua wasn't that kind of man—he would never say those kinds of things.

She patted his knee and smiled. "Thanks for being such a good friend right now," she said. "I should check on David." She stood and went inside. Joshua probably didn't have any romantic notions, but then again, there was no point in sitting together on his front step and giving the occasional passerby something to discuss over the next quilting bee.

* * *

The next afternoon after the midday meal, Lizzy walked back to her family's homestead. Her parents would be returning from Salt Lake, and she felt she had to be there to meet them. She trudged down the dusty road alone, wearing a dress loaned her by one of the Foster girls from the ward. Lizzy wore a pair of loaned shoes as well, but they were too big and flopped as she walked.

Brother Sorensen and Joshua had put out the remaining hot spots the day after the fire and had gone each day to feed and water the cow and chickens. Lizzy had avoided going with them, needing to be alone when she saw the house for the first time.

She thought that she had prepared herself to see what would be left of it, but when it came in view, she involuntarily sucked in her breath and covered her mouth. At night with the bright flames, the house had looked, in an odd way, alive. By daylight everything had changed. The house had died. Its tall silhouette against the mountains no longer existed. Instead, black beams stuck out of the dark rubble as if someone had jabbed them into the ground. She could see the barn, which should have been blocked from view by the house, but it looked a lighter gray than usual behind the stark black of charred wood.

"'And day brought back my night,'" Lizzy quoted Milton aloud. She had heard that the line referred to Milton's blindness, but as she stared at her home and remembered fighting the blaze, the words took on a whole new meaning.

Somehow she covered the rest of the distance, then stepped carefully off the road as if treading on sacred ground. She walked around back, where she saw her two buckets still in the dirt by the well. After looking up to where her gable room used to be, she hugged herself tightly as her eyes dropped to the black piles. She guessed which heap her belongings had fallen into.

She stepped into the rubble, half expecting to feel warmth in the ashes. Leaning over, she found a charred scrap of leather and picked it up. A corner from the cover of her Milton. She rubbed the piece between her thumb and fingers to remove some ash, then slipped it into her pocket, her eyes moist.

She left the ashes and slowly walked around the house, each new sight piercing her very center and sending another tear down her cheeks. Her throat constricted, but she couldn't stop taking in every detail. She had to see everything. After one complete circle, she stopped where the kitchen wall used to be. She saw the cast-iron stove easily enough. If she hadn't already known the fire started there, she would have figured it out by just looking at the remains, as there was little left of anything in that area. She ran her hand along a beam, feeling the wood's shiny black blisters from the heat. Taking a step back, she surveyed the entire area, wondering why her family was inflicted with such a loss on top of the death of her maternal grandmother and David's poor health.

Lizzy imagined her family coming home and seeing the ruin. A pit suddenly formed in her stomach at the idea. After a quick glance at the sun overhead, she rushed down the road. She had to reach the bend before her family did. They had to know beforehand. A row of trees would block the view until the buckboard rounded the corner. If she met her family there, she could tell them about the fire before they saw evidence of it.

She hurried toward the bend, holding her skirt up, glad that it was too short. But more than once her oversized shoes came close to pitching her face-first into the dirt. She finally stopped and took them off, feeling strangely like a schoolgirl as she carried them and ran barefoot. Her feet hit sharp pebbles, but she hardly noticed the discomfort until she rounded the bend and could see down the stretch of road. Catching her breath, she assured herself that there was no sign of a wagon or even dust clouds in the distance. Suddenly aware of her smarting feet, she checked the bottoms and wiped them clear of pebbles and briars. As a young girl she had regularly gone without shoes, but in the interim, her feet had clearly softened. She hadn't expected them to hurt so much.

Lizzy found shade under a tree that offered a good vantage point of the road. She sat down, wishing absently for a book to read. The realization that all but one of her prized books no longer existed tore through her again, and she closed her eyes against the pain. The hot afternoon sun beat onto the dirt road, and a light breeze kicked up, making the trees' shadows dance. After several minutes she picked up a stick and began tracing designs in the dirt as she had often done as a little girl. She felt lost, wishing she knew what the future held, wishing she could simply go home and crawl under her quilt with a story. If only her mother's comforting arms were around her. A tear fell into the dirt and muddied her design.

How could she explain what happened when she didn't know herself why the stove hadn't contained the small fire she started? Would they blame her? Her stomach felt uneasy, and her heart beat heavily with anxiety. In some way the fire was her fault. She thought through every action of that night. Coaxing the embers into flames. Adding fuel to the fire. Putting water to heat on top of the stove. Wiping her hands on the dishrag . . .

She closed her eyes and pressed her palms into them. How could she have been such a fool? Of course the dishcloth had caught fire.

Warming a bottle for David was an unselfish act, wasn't it? she demanded of whatever powers might be listening. Why wasn't her home protected? Why couldn't the dishrag have fallen to the floor or the countertop when she tossed it aside?

Now that she knew how the fire began, how would she tell her parents? How would the twins react, and what would Jimmy say? She knew he would probably have the hardest time of anyone comprehending the loss. Like her, this home was the only one he had any recollection of, as he had forgotten nearly everything that happened prior to his childhood accident when he'd fallen off the barn roof.

Jimmy's mother, Lizzy's Aunt Louisa, had left her six-year-old boy in the Sullivan family's care after leaving the West. Jimmy's father and sister had died on the way to Zion, and when it was clear that Jimmy wasn't right in the head, Aunt Louisa could bear no more. She went back to New York to her husband's wealthy family, saying she hadn't the ability to raise such a boy alone. Lizzy's mother had said more than once that she believed her sister always intended to come for Jimmy. But she never did, so he grew up with the Sullivans as one of their own. Lizzy's mother refused to judge Aunt Louisa, always believing that something on the trek to Zion had broken the woman, and that Jimmy was better off with his people—in Zion.

Lizzy bit her lip. How could she help Jimmy understand why she couldn't read stories to him anymore? Perhaps Aunt Louisa could send more books from New York, Lizzy thought hopefully. Since everyone knew Jimmy loved to hear books read to him, Lizzy always wondered if Aunt Louisa's gifts were really for her son's sake. Perhaps it was a way of telling her son she loved him. Maybe it was all she had the strength to give. Lizzy wondered why Aunt Louisa had given up when her mother hadn't, and who she was more like.

If the fire weren't enough of a trial to test her faith, there was David, whose health had grown worse each day since. Lizzy threw a pebble disdainfully. To have him getting even sicker after being exposed to the cold just piled on the agony. She had done as much as she could to protect him and to fight the blaze. It wasn't her fault that fate had delivered such a hard blow.

The sound of clopping horses' hooves and the jovial sparring of the twins was Lizzy's indication that her family was approaching. She scrambled to her feet and hurried toward the noise. When they came into view, she waved her arms and called out to them so they would see her and stop.

As usual, Matthew, Aaron, and Jimmy stood in their seats, fighting to win their game of who saw home first. It didn't matter that any view would be impossible before that final curve in the road. At twelve years, the twins might want to be treated like men, but they certainly acted like boys. Jimmy, thanks to his adult size and strength, generally managed to win the game by shoving both boys aside. With his childlike mind, he cared as much or more than the twins about winning the game.

"Mama! Papa!" Lizzy cried.

"Lizzy? Is that you?" Abigail Sullivan called. As the buckboard rolled to a stop, she leaned forward. "Lizzy, what's the matter? Where's David? Is he well?" She looked to the side of the road in search of her son, then climbed down.

"We're both fine," Lizzy said, catching her breath.

Her father jumped off the buckboard to join them. Lizzy's stomach flip-flopped. She could hardly bear to tell both of her parents at the same time. Her father had built the house himself. She could only imagine how many memories were tied up in it; far more than she had. They were already mourning one loss; this would be more than they could bear.

"Where's David?" Richard Sullivan asked, repeating his wife's question.

That question would be easy to answer. "At the Sorensens'."

"What is he doing there?" Abigail asked. "Is he worse?"

"Well, he's—"

"And what are you wearing?" Abigail took a deep breath, stopping the flow of questions.

Lizzy stared at her hands.

"I'm sorry," Abigail said. "You got me worried that something had happened while we were away."

This was the moment Lizzy had dreaded. Somehow, she felt that the fire wasn't real, wasn't permanent, until she said the words. Her tongue refused to move, and her toes dug into the dry road. She closed her eyes, then plunged in.

"Something did happen, Mama." She looked up at her mother, then her father, and she bit her lips together to keep tears from falling. If even one tear broke free, she wouldn't be able to stop the torrent. She searched her parents' faces as her mind searched for words. "I'm so sorry. I don't know how to tell you—"

"Hello there, Lizzy," Jimmy interjected from the wagon. "What are you doing here? Why did Uncle Richard stop? I wanna go home."

Lizzy swallowed a lump in her throat. "Just a minute, Jimmy," she called over her mother's shoulder. She sniffed. Not a good omen; it meant that full tears would follow close behind. Taking a step closer to her parents, she tried to speak quietly so Jimmy and the twins wouldn't hear yet.

"The other night . . ." Lizzy's voice trailed off. Her mother reached for Lizzy's hands and squeezed them gently, her eyes full of trust. Lizzy had to look away.

"Go on," Abigail said. "What happened?"

"There was a . . ." Once more her voice failed her, and she had to force the words out of her mouth. "A fire."

Both of her parents gasped. The worst out, Lizzy could now rush on, her eyes burning. "David and I got out just fine, and I tried to fight the fire, but I couldn't do it alone. We spent the night at the Sorensens', and we've been there ever since."

Abigail's jaw went slack. She dropped Lizzy's hands, then picked up her skirts and sped to the edge of the bend.

"Aunt Abigail, that's not fair!" Jimmy cried. "I always win. You didn't even tell us you were playing." He braced himself with one hand on the side of the wagon and jumped down, reaching the spot seconds after Abigail. Lizzy's mother stopped and covered her mouth at the sight that met her eyes.

Jimmy didn't notice the farm at first because he was busy turning back to the twins and yelling, "Aunt Abigail won. But I'm going to beat you two . . ." His voice stopped, however, as he turned to look at the house. "What is *that*, and where is my house?" he bellowed.

Abigail, normally the first to put an arm around Jimmy in comfort, walked forward, not even hearing him as she took in the sight of her home. Lizzy fell into step with her. Richard and the twins followed and stood at the bend, stunned, while the women moved ahead.

"Mama, it's all gone," Lizzy said. "Everything except the barn. It's all gone."

Abigail broke her gaze away from the house long enough to acknowledge her daughter. Then she put her arm around Lizzy's waist.

"It will be all right," she said, gazing once more at the wreckage.

"But Mama, everything is gone," Lizzy said. "Everything."

Abigail's eyes smarted with tears. She sniffed and wrapped her other arm around her daughter, then pulled her close in an embrace. "No, not everything. We have you. You and David. You're safe."

CHAPTER 3

Sitting tall, Abe Franklin rode his new mare toward the Franklin farm. A pony trailed behind on a rope.

"This is it, Shadow," Abe said to his horse as he saw the house at a distance. He paused and gazed at the structure before continuing. He hoped his father was home this time of day; five years ago, before Abe had been sent away, this was the hour of the midday meal.

Abe had imagined this day for years. This was when he would return to his childhood home and show his adoptive parents that he was a man. He was a hard worker and could accomplish whatever he put his mind to—everything Brother Franklin thought Abe, a "Lamanite," was incapable of.

Brother, Abe thought. *Balderdash*. Since when had his adoptive father been anything like a brother to anyone?

Abe had spent the years from age eight to sixteen with the Franklins, even taking on their family name. The four years before that it was the Hutchings family who'd purchased Abe to "save" him. Although he had been four years old at the time, Abe didn't remember what had happened. Years later he'd been told that his Shoshone mother fled her husband with another man. To increase the speed of her flight, she'd traded her son to the Hutchings family for a pony and two blankets. He often wondered what happened to his mother. Did she escape the wrath of her husband, his father? Where was she now? Did she ever regret giving him away?

By the time Abe turned eight, Brother and Sister Hutchings decided that Abe wasn't a good enough worker and didn't fit in with their other seven children, so they "gave" him to the Franklins to raise in exchange for a pair of oxen.

As Abe sat astride his horse, he let out a disgusted breath. *You'd think Brother Franklin would know an eight-year-old boy can't do as much work as a pair of oxen.* But apparently the man expected just that. Brother Franklin whipped Abe frequently, as if doing so would make him work the equivalent of three boys his age.

Abe gently nudged his heels into the mare's flanks and moved forward. No point in postponing something he had planned for five years. As he drew closer to the house, he remembered Brother Franklin's words the day Abe was forced to leave.

"I've fed, clothed, and educated you for eight years," Brother Franklin said. "I've given you the truth about God, something few people on the earth have. I even gave you my good name. And what have I received in return? A slothful, ungrateful, stupid boy."

The words cut deep into young Abe's heart. He always did his best, but it was never good enough. As he opened his mouth to speak, Brother Franklin interrupted.

"I've been biding my time for months. And now I can git rid of you. The law says I've done my duty. You're sixteen now. It's time for you to leave and be on your own."

"Why are you sending me away?" Abe asked. "What have I done?"

Brother Franklin snorted. "It's not what you've done. It's what you *haven't* done. You haven't been a son, a part of this family."

"I tried," Abe began, his heart aching. "I truly—"

But Brother Franklin wasn't listening. "I've spent money and time on you for as long as my duty required. And now I'm finished."

Sister Franklin crossed the room and took her husband's hands in hers. "Abraham's our only child, my only son," she said. "Please don't send him away."

Brother Franklin pulled his hands away and pushed his wife to the side. She fell against the wall with a cry.

"You hush, woman. This is none of your concern."

"Mother!" Abe took a step toward her, but Brother Franklin grabbed his arm and yanked him back. "You listen to me, boy, and listen well. I'll let you take the red pony and the clothes we purchased for you."

Abe looked from one parent to the other. His mother had brought her hands to her face, and she was sobbing.

"Nothing else?" Fear and loneliness settled over him. Where would he go? Where would he find work?

Brother Franklin swiped a metal cup from the table and emptied it in a single gulp. He drew his sleeve across his mouth. "You have one hour before I pull out my belt and give you the whipping of your life, so I suggest you get moving."

He shoved the cup into Abe's chest, all but bowling him over. Abe caught his balance on a chair as Brother Franklin reached the door, then left the house and strode across the yard.

His mother waited just a moment to make sure her husband was gone before rushing to Abe's side. She put her hands on either side of his face and wept.

"What will become of my boy?" she cried. "How will I go on without my son?"

Abe covered her hands with his and tried hard not to let the welling tears fall. "I'll be fine, Mother. You've raised me well. I'm a hard worker. You'll see."

She threw her arms around his neck. "I'll miss you so much."

The two stood in the kitchen crying together for some time. Abe knew as well as his mother did that resisting Brother Franklin was useless. Abe had several scars on his back to prove it and had no mind to get more.

His mother finally pulled away, once more gazing into her son's eyes. "Abe, I want you to take the books from the kitchen shelf."

Abe's eyes smarted, and his throat tightened. His mother had taught him to read with those books. Some of his happiest memories were sitting at her side with a book between them.

"Will Brother Franklin allow it?" Abe asked hesitantly.

She nodded. "He's been threatening to burn them anyway. From now on he wants only scriptures and hymns in the house."

She fetched a burlap sack, then took him by the hand and led him to the small bookshelf. "Put them in this," she said. Abe sat before the books for several minutes, trying to decide which to take with him and which to leave behind for his mother—assuming they wouldn't be thrown into the stove as kindling. Each book had memories attached to it, and choosing between them was like selecting which family members to leave behind.

"Take them all," his mother said as she knelt beside him. "I want you to have them."

Abe held out a yellowing copy of *Rasselas*. "Mother, you keep this one," he said, pressing it into her hands. It was the first book they'd ever read together and one they had a tradition of rereading every year. Each time through the book they had sat on the porch swing, watching the sun set in the western sky and discussing at length Samuel Johnson's story about finding happiness.

His mother's brow furrowed, and she caught her breath. She shook her head, then looked up, her eyes welling with tears. She reached for Abe's hands and put the book into them. "Of all the books, I want you to have this one. It will help you remember to go in search of your own happiness."

He held onto it tightly, his eyes burning. "But, Mother, I—" Abe's voice caught.

"Take it," she said. "Please."

He couldn't answer. Instead he fell into her arms for a final moment as mother and child.

Not an hour later, Abe's meager belongings were tied to the pony, and he was ready to leave.

"Good-bye, Mother," Abe said, sitting on the pony. "I'll miss you."

"Not as much as I'll miss you," she answered, then blew him a kiss from the porch.

Brother Franklin returned for the farewell moment. "After tonight," he said, "I expect not to see you again unless it's to return my pony and make restitution. Now git."

Abe and his mother didn't dare exchange more words as Brother Franklin stood there angrily, waiting for him to leave. Abe nudged the pony with his heels and moved out. As he left the farm, he looked over his shoulder and saw his mother one last time; she was waving a handkerchief. The sight tore Abe's heart.

"Remember," Brother Franklin called loudly, "I expect restitution."

The words struck Abe harshly as he rode into the distance, the farm growing smaller behind him with each passing minute.

Restitution? For what? Abe thought as the pony took him away. He hadn't done anything wrong, except for not being capable of doing the work of several men at once . . . and of course, not accepting Brother Franklin's church. That last part was a burr in both their skins. Brother Franklin never ceased preaching and threatening and insisting Abe believe in the Book of Mormon and Joseph Smith. But Abe wouldn't listen.

Why would he consider turning his life over to the God of a man so horrid he would feed his dog more food than his son? *No,* Abe had thought many times over the years, *I can do without that well enough.*

Restitution. Brother Franklin expected Abe to make restitution. He squared his jaw. *Very well. If that's the way he wants it. Someday I will earn enough money to pay him back for every morsel of bread he ever fed me. And he'll get his miserable pony back, too.*

Now, five years later, Abe was returning. He rounded the house and rode to the barn. After dismounting, he tethered up both animals and looked about. The place was much like he remembered. There was the porch swing. It was just as it had been so long ago when he'd sat reading day after day with his mother. A stirring in his heart made him wish he could live here again, at least with her. Boardinghouses couldn't really be called home no matter how nice they were, even the clean, well-kept one he had found in Logan. It didn't have the warm touch of a home, the warmth of past memories.

"Mother!" he called. He wanted her to see his horse, a sign of his success.

The back door creaked open, and Sister Franklin peered out with a curious expression. When her eyes fell on Abe, a look of shock and joy broke across her face. She gathered her skirts and raced to him.

"Abe! Oh, Abe!" She threw her arms around him and kissed his face, then held him back and looked him over. "You're so tall! Where have you been all these years? Are you eating well? Do you need anything? Why didn't you tell us you were coming?"

Abe laughed at her torrent of questions. "I'm fine, Mother. I came to repay Brother Franklin all the money he spent caring for me—and to return his pony."

Sister Franklin noticed the horse for the first time. "This is yours?"

Abe nodded with pride. "I just bought her."

"She's beautiful." Sister Franklin stroked the tall horse's neck in admiration.

The back door opened again. "What's going on out here?"

Abe straightened. His heart quickened, and he swallowed hard. Facing the reality was a bit tougher than the imagination. "Hello, Brother Franklin. I've come to repay my debt."

Without a word, Brother Franklin sauntered across the yard, his boots heavy with each step. His steely eyes took in Abe's appearance—worn hat, linen shirt, work pants, boots.

"So you're wearing your hair like an Indian, are you? I thought we civilized you."

Abe's hand went to the nape of his neck, where his black hair was pulled into a ponytail.

Sister Franklin turned on her husband. "Is that all you have to say to him after all these years? He's a man of means. You should be proud of how he's turned out."

The comment took Abe aback for a moment. Since when did his mother ever speak back to her husband? Abe rummaged through his saddlebag and removed a cloth sack tied with twine. He hefted the coins inside. "Here you go, Brother Franklin. This should cover my room and board for the eight years you cared for me." Brother Franklin all but snatched it away, as if he didn't even want to touch the hand of the boy he had indentured. Abe refused to show any reaction to the gesture. This was *his* moment, not his "father's."

"As you can see," Abe went on. "I have returned your pony. He's in good health. I believe my restitution is complete."

"Not quite," Brother Franklin said gruffly. "I've been without that animal for five years. You owe me for its lost work. And now I've got an old animal. It wasn't young to begin with. Five years is a long time in a pony's life."

Abe's cheeks flushed hot. He stepped forward, voice rising. He was a man now, he reminded himself, one who could stand up to Brother Franklin. But the years of intimidation and fear had left their mark, and Abe had to force himself to confront the man. "What do you expect me to do? Give you my own horse? Since you forced me out of your house, I've spent every day working and saving enough to prove you wrong, to show you that I am not lazy or ignorant. And all you can say is that I owe you a younger animal?"

Abe's mother folded her arms at her husband, indignant. "Even you can't deny that Abe has done more than necessary to repay any supposed debt."

"This is none of your business, woman," Brother Franklin said gruffly, then lifted a hand. Abe flinched, but his mother just pushed it aside.

"Don't you go threatening me," Sister Franklin said, jabbing a finger in her husband's chest for emphasis. "This most certainly is my concern. I made the biggest mistake of my life letting you send my son away, obeying my husband because I thought I was supposed to. No more. This time you are plain *wrong.*"

Brother Franklin stared at his wife as if he didn't recognize her. Abe had to get control of a smirk threatening to show itself on his face. Apparently his mother had toughened up in the last five years. He hardly recognized her. Perhaps losing her son had been the catalyst.

Her outburst softened Abe's anger. He put his hand on his mother's arm. "Don't worry," he said. "He can have the horse if he needs it that much. I can easily buy another one." The statement wasn't completely true; it would take a long time for Abe to save enough for another horse. But Abe wouldn't give Brother Franklin the satisfaction of holding one more debt over his head.

The two men stared at each other, neither willing to look away first. Sister Franklin finally broke them apart. "Abe, come inside and eat. We have plenty."

"I'd love to, but only if I pay for the meal," Abe said. Brother Franklin grunted in approval, then turned to go back inside. Abe went on. "I can't stay long. I'm leaving for Logan in the morning."

Sister Franklin faced him, upset. "Why so far away? And so soon?"

"They need more workers for the temple up there, and they're paying good money."

As they reached the door, Brother Franklin opened it and scoffed, "You couldn't work on such a construction, nohow."

Abe couldn't help but grin and break the news. "Actually, I've spent a year working on the Salt Lake City Temple. Logan is simply in greater need of workers right now. Maybe I'll do mortar work. Or labor at the lime kilns. I don't know yet. But you'll see—I'll have another horse soon. And a whole lot more."

CHAPTER 4

One afternoon, a week after the fire, as Lizzy worked in the kitchen, Abigail came in from sitting with David. Strands of hair had escaped from the knot at the nape of her neck, and her eyes looked tired as she rubbed her forehead and pulled out a chair.

"How is he?" Lizzy asked, punching down the dough for rolls.

Abigail shook her head and sat at the table. "If anything, he's worse. I hate leaving him, even when he's asleep, but there's so much work to do."

"You need to rest," Sister Sorensen said, coming in the back door with a bucket of water for washing dishes. "Lizzy and I can take care of things in here for now. You go lie down for a spell."

Lizzy wiped her fingers on a dishrag and sat beside her mother. Abigail's hands came to her face and she whispered, "I'm afraid, Lizzy. I'm truly afraid. He's so weak and pale. And burning hot . . ." Her voice trailed off.

Lizzy nodded, knowing that nothing she could say would help. If only David hadn't been outside the night of the fire. If only the fire hadn't happened. If only, if only, if only. She had done her best that night, wrapping him in the quilt and walking two miles to find shelter. Why hadn't David been blessed for her efforts? *Why indeed.*

She wondered again why the fire had to steal her home, why God hadn't stopped it from happening. Such a small thing—the dishcloth could have simply slipped to the floor. An inch one direction, and her home would still be standing.

Instead, her family had lost everything. With disdain, she blew a stray wisp of hair from her eyes. Why did she allow such thoughts to enter her mind? They brought only frustration. But even so, she couldn't stop hoping that someday she would find a glimpse of the faith and love of God everyone else around her seemed to have. Especially David.

David. With a sniff, Lizzy shook her head. Her mother had lost three children. Josiah, then sweet Richard, whom she remembered as if he'd died last week, including the overwhelming pain she saw in her mother's eyes. Just two years ago the same wound was ripped open when baby Hannah died days after her birth. The loss nearly tore Abigail apart. Lizzy glanced at her mother. Would she have to face a fourth burial, another tiny coffin—this time for her sweet son so hopeful about every day of his life?

Putting a hand over her mother's, Lizzy said, "If anything will get him well, Mama, it will be you."

"And, of course, the priesthood blessings he's received. We must always have faith in them," her mother said.

Lizzy lowered her chin and didn't respond. David's blessings *hadn't* helped. She admired her mother's faith, but Lizzy knew the blessings would not somehow start working now, no matter how much she hoped for the best.

"Mama, you look tired. Go lie down."

Abigail's eyes misted again. She squeezed Lizzy's hand in gratitude. "Thank you, Lizzy, but there's something else I need to do first."

Abigail stood and left the room, Lizzy watching until her mother was out of view. Then Lizzy sighed, feeling helpless and angry.

Sister Sorensen turned from putting water to heat on the stove. "This must be so hard for your family. No one as young as David should be so ill."

"No one as good as he is should be," Lizzy said sullenly as she returned to the bowl of dough.

Jimmy suddenly came in the back door and headed in the direction of the parlor. Lizzy hurriedly extracted her hands from the sticky dough and moved to block his way. "David is sleeping. Why don't you play here for a while?"

He pointed toward the parlor and protested. "But I wanted to draw on the slate I left there. Please?"

Sister Sorensen went to a cupboard and produced another slate and piece of chalk that she kept for her grandchildren. "Here you go, Jimmy."

He eyed her suspiciously for a moment, then reluctantly took the slate, found a seat, and began scribbling. Periodically, he wiped at his art with the heel of his hand and started over.

Lizzy ripped off chunks of dough and formed rolls as she thought of David's blessings. She shook her head. If only making David well were as easy as placing a drop or two of oil on his head and pronouncing a handful of flowery words. She thumped a roll onto the cooking tray a bit harder than necessary. The rolls would turn out the same regardless of how much of her own frustration she inflicted on them.

She covered the rolls with a cloth and left them to rise one last time, then turned to peeling potatoes for the stew. Ever since the fire she couldn't help but think of all the times her faith had failed her. Her daily mundane chores provided plenty of time for such thoughts, miserable as they were.

She knew people who claimed to have been miraculously healed after receiving a priesthood blessing. That number included many relatives and neighbors. And her mother. According to the story, it was through a priesthood blessing that her mother's foot healed almost instantly, allowing the family to continue their journey through Nebraska.

Lizzy hadn't experienced anything remotely like that. She recalled receiving a blessing when she had scarlet fever at the age of eight. As far as she could tell, it had done no good. Back then she had truly believed that the blessing would make her well quickly, and had been crushed when she wasn't able to go to the corn-husking party the next day. Eventually she recovered, but it was a long, drawn-out illness. She suddenly noticed the similarity between that disappointment and the one with her broken foot two years later.

Those were silly things, she told herself. A corn-husking party and a school picnic are hardly things that Deity would bother about. Bringing faithful Saints to Zion was another matter. The thought made Lizzy's brow furrow, and she looked up for the slightest moment, inadvertently cutting her finger. She brought it to her mouth and sucked hard, the sudden pain somehow feeling like an outward manifestation of her inner thoughts.

So why didn't God care about an eight-year-old girl and a corn-husking party? She supposed such things didn't have eternal signifi-cance—except for her continual loss of faith. But the party had been important to her. At the time, nothing mattered as much. *If God cares about a measly sparrow,* she wondered, *wouldn't He care about the heart's desire of a young child?*

Perhaps God heals only the most righteous, she thought, returning to the potatoes, this time taking greater care with the knife. That would explain why she hadn't been healed either time. After all, she hardly fit the category of "most righteous." It would also explain her mother's miracle on the trail, since Abigail Sullivan was a righteous woman by any standards.

But then, David certainly qualified as "righteous." Better than anyone else Lizzy knew. Yet he lay at the edge of death.

"How do you like my picture, Lizzy?" Jimmy's voice brought her back to the present.

"It's very nice," she said absently.

"What part do you like best?"

"That part," Lizzy said, pointing with the tip of the knife at a section of wavy lines. She couldn't come close to guessing what the picture was intended to represent, and didn't want to speculate in case she was wrong.

"These are books," Jimmy explained. "And those crookedy parts are the words you read to me. I'm getting better at reading. Been practicing lots. Sister Sorensen lets me read *Pilgrim's Progress.* It's hard, but I'm already on page ten. Can you read it to me later?" Jimmy let the slate fall to the table with a clang and waited for an answer to his question.

Lizzy hesitated, then nodded. "Let's do it tonight when I have some time. Right now I have to help with dinner." But she didn't really want to read, not now.

He rubbed out his picture with his sleeve. "Watch this." With great effort, he dragged the chalk across the slate, his tongue sticking out the side of his mouth in concentration. "See? I practiced this too." He held up the slate, pointing to where he had scrawled *Jimmy,* although the tail of the *Y* went the wrong direction.

"Very good, Jimmy," Lizzy said, managing a smile. "You've improved."

"I know." He grinned, then turned back to his writing, and Lizzy watched him for a moment. Sometimes she envied Jimmy. He was never bothered by anything for long. The simplest things gave him intense joy. And everything in the world around him brought out genuine wonder and awe. If only her life were so simple.

Carrying a small wooden box, Abigail returned to the kitchen. She opened the box and took out a large serving spoon, then began polishing it with a cloth. Lizzy's gaze fell on the spoon, and her eyes went wide. In excitement, she abandoned the potato and knife and leaned closer to get a better look.

"Mama!" Lizzy gasped. "Are you polishing . . . is that Grandmother's silver?"

Abigail looked up and smiled, holding up the spoon for her daughter to see. "I brought it with us on the trip to help with the funeral dinner. Aunt Rebecca didn't have enough serving silver." Her finger traced the floral design on the handle. "Who knew that taking these to Salt Lake City would preserve them."

Abigail sniffed, her eyes misty. Lizzy knew her mother was probably thinking about her trip to Zion, carrying the small wooden box across the plains for her mother. The silver had spent more than two decades in Salt Lake City, and it was two years ago that Grandmother Pearson had passed them on to her eldest daughter, Abigail. The small box held only a few serving spoons and a pair of sugar tongs, the last remaining items from her family. Of course, with Grandmother Pearson's recent passing, the silver had taken on increased meaning.

As she placed the spoon into the box and pulled out a second piece, they heard a moan from the parlor. Abigail made a move to stand, but Lizzy shook her head.

"I'll go check on him," Lizzy said.

As Lizzy entered the parlor, David wiped his eyes.

"How is my big brother feeling?" Lizzy asked.

David didn't smile at her joke. Instead, he looked over, face pale. When he spoke his voice trembled. "Being sick all the time is mighty bothersome."

"I know it is," Lizzy said, crossing the room. She sat beside him on the edge of the sofa and stroked his hair. "I wish I could take it away. But I think you're getting the best of the pneumonia. It'll be gone soon, just you wait."

But what illness will strike next? The thought jumped into her mind before she could stop it. David's constitution had never been strong; if he wasn't suffering from one thing, it was another.

He clung to her hand and closed his eyes. Tears leaked out onto his pillow. "My head hurts," he said. "And my throat is dry."

"I'll get you some water," Lizzy said. "And then I'll sit with you and hold your hand for as long as you need me to."

David opened his eyes. "Can I sit in your lap instead?"

She leaned down and kissed his burning forehead. "Of course."

* * *

Joshua stopped by the parlor and peered around the corner. There, near the fireplace, Beth sat with David. He appeared to be sleeping, but she still hummed to him. Joshua leaned against the doorframe and watched, enjoying the sight. Having Beth nearby of late had been a dream come true for Joshua. It wasn't long before afternoon walks became a daily habit for the two of them—something he looked forward to more than he would admit.

Beth looked up and noticed him. She smiled, sending warmth through Joshua's body.

"Care to go for a ramble?" Joshua asked quietly so as not to wake David.

She gave a nod, laid David on the couch and adjusted his covering, then crossed to Joshua's side. "Shall we?" she asked.

He put out his arm. Beth put hers through it, and together they went outside. They strolled along the same path every day, one that was tree-lined and provided shade from the afternoon sun. Joshua tried not to think about how their walks wouldn't last, that someday—probably quite soon—the Sullivans would leave. They heard a bird twittering in a pine tree above them.

"I wonder if he's calling to a friend," Beth said, craning her neck in search of the bird. "Sort of like you used to call me with that ridiculous peacock cry."

"Ridiculous? I don't recall you thinking that at the time," Joshua retorted with a laugh.

"True," Beth said. "Although I always wondered if that's really what a peacock sounds like. Maybe that peddler who taught you the call didn't really know."

Joshua considered for a moment, then agreed. "You're right. I've never seen—or heard—a peacock before. But you must admit, whenever you heard my call, you always knew it was me."

"No confusing it with any other sound, that's for sure," Beth said. She found the bird she'd been searching for and pointed. "There it is. Funny how something as simple as a noise can remind you of the past. I had forgotten about your call until now."

"I hadn't thought of it in ages," Joshua said. Even as he said it, he knew he hadn't forgotten anything else about his friendship with Beth. It was both a blessing and a curse.

They reached an old, broken-down fence where they often stopped to rest and talk before turning back or continuing their walk. Joshua put a foot on a low beam that hadn't broken and rested his arms on a fence post. Beth stood beside him, and together they gazed out over the Sorensen fields and beyond.

A knot twisted in Joshua's middle, and although he fought the urge, he felt he had to speak. "How do you imagine your life five years from now?" he asked, knowing exactly how he imagined his own, or at least fantasized about it.

Beth leaned against a beam in the fence. Her face turned up to the sky, and she watched the clouds as she thought. "I'd still like to go visit Aunt Louisa and go to school in New York," she began. Joshua already knew that part, but he didn't think it was likely to happen. At least, he hoped not.

"And then what?" he asked. "I don't suppose that would take five years."

"Perhaps I would come back and be a teacher. I heard about the Brigham Young Academy getting started in Provo. I'd love to be the first female teacher there."

When Joshua answered, he tried to keep his feelings from betraying him. "You don't see yourself staying in the valley then? It'll be awfully lonely around here without you."

Beth's chin lowered. "I hadn't thought of it in those terms before," she said quietly. For a moment she stared in thought at some tree roots. Just as quickly, she perked up and shook off the dismal mood. "Of course, if I did leave, I'd come back to visit periodically. You won't be getting rid of me that easily, you know."

"I wouldn't dream of it," Joshua said, trying to match her smile. "So—so you don't see marriage in your future?"

"Perhaps," Beth answered. "If someone dashing and mysterious comes along who sweeps me off my feet."

"Who woos you by the light of the moon and whisks you away into a life of bliss?" Joshua asked with just a hint of sarcasm.

Beth laughed at his apparent attitude toward romance. "That wouldn't hurt."

"Sounds like a book," Joshua said, unable to keep some irritation from his voice.

"I suppose it does," Beth said. "But what's wrong with that? Can't a girl dream?"

Joshua couldn't answer right away. He had tried to read some of Beth's favorite stories to impress her, but the effort resulted in one thing—the knowledge that he didn't live up to the ethereal man of Beth's dreams. That man was dark and brooding and exotic. Joshua was homespun and about as clear and obvious as a summer sky. In his heart, he felt sure that Beth's ideals weren't something that would make her truly happy. But was that something he could convince her of?

"Let's go back," Joshua said, hoping to change the subject. The discussion hadn't gone where he'd hoped. But he knew Beth well enough after all these years that the course it took wasn't all that unexpected either. It had been silly of him to hope for something else, even after all their time together recently. He pushed away from the fence and headed for the pathway home.

"Could you teach me the peacock call sometime?" Beth asked, falling into step beside him.

Joshua couldn't help but smile. "Of course," he said. "But you can't use it to call anyone but me."

* * *

George Sorensen and his family of eight arrived the next day, and to Beth it made the house feel as cramped as a barrel of pickles. A person was likely to trip over any number of children at all hours, and meals had to be staggered so everyone could sit. At night every room had people sleeping in it, many on the floor. The women helped in the kitchen, and Richard kept the boys and Jimmy busy with odd jobs that had piled up. But despite the cooperation from everyone, the situation clearly would not be tolerable for long.

One evening Richard and Abigail sat in the parlor, waiting for the children to come for family prayer before retiring for the evening. The room had been unofficially designated as the Sullivans' private area—where they slept and where David rested during the day. It was the only place where the Sullivans had any semblance of private time. Abigail held David now, already dressed in his nightclothes.

"Do you think Joshua will ask her soon?" Richard asked.

Abigail glanced at the door to be sure no one heard. "Not yet. I don't think he'll do anything until he's confident about her feelings."

"Then again, he might see our family's situation as a good time to ask," Richard said. "She's been with him an awful lot since the fire."

Abigail brushed off the hint. Little else could be expected of best friends living under the same roof after a family tragedy. It was natural for Lizzy to be with Joshua. Regardless, Abigail also nursed a hope that Lizzy might start seeing Joshua in the same light he surely saw her in. She wished Lizzy would live in this world rather than the one inhabited by imaginary people and stories. If her daughter could find a man who was the spitting image of one of the dashing heroes of her books, there would be no doubt about her accepting his hand. But Joshua might prove too familiar and practical for someone with such overgrown romantic notions.

David lifted his head. "I like Joshua. Do you really think he'll be my brother someday?"

"I don't know," Abigail said. She bit her lip and smiled. "He would be good for her."

"And good *to* her," Richard added.

With a sigh, Abigail brushed hair from David's eyes. "But if Lizzy doesn't accept, it would break his heart."

They heard footsteps on the stairs and quickly stopped talking as Lizzy entered the room. Abigail began moving the rocking chair back and forth. She hoped Lizzy didn't notice the shift in mood as her daughter sat on the sofa beside the rocker and settled an afghan across her lap for warmth. They waited in awkward silence for the rest of the family to arrive. The twins stormed in, with Jimmy barreling behind as usual. The three knelt down in preparation to pray, but Richard gestured for them to sit.

"Before our prayer, we have some items to discuss," Richard said. The boys scrambled a moment, finally settling on the floor with their legs tucked under them. Abigail thought it a wonder they ever stopped moving long enough to sleep.

"I have some somber news," Richard began.

Abigail felt an ache in her heart at the sight of Lizzy's head coming up with a start, her eyes wide with worry as if she hardly dared imagine what else might have befallen the family.

"Papa . . ." Lizzy's voice caught and trailed off.

"I found out that President Young has passed away."

Lizzy sank back into her chair, a queer mixture of sorrow and relief crossing her face.

As for her own heart, Abigail couldn't help but mourn for the prophet she had followed since her baptism. Her eyes teared up again at hearing it mentioned once more. Of course, Lizzy had never seen President Young, so it was natural that news of his death wouldn't cause the same grief it did in Abigail. But for her daughter's sake, she was grateful that it was nothing more devastating than that.

Abigail dabbed a handkerchief at her eyes, her mind casting back over the years. Although she had heard about Joseph Smith—sometimes by those who had known him personally—the only prophet she had ever known was Brigham Young. It had been his counsel she followed to leave her home and gather in Zion. Now she felt as if she had lost a dear friend.

After the news settled in, Richard went on. "We also have several issues facing our family. The most pressing is finding a new place to live. You all know that Doctor Brown was here earlier to check on David." Richard turned to Abigail. She adjusted the blanket spread over David, lowered her gaze, and nodded for her husband to continue. "David's pneumonia isn't getting any better while we're here. He needs rest and quiet, and he can't get that here anymore."

Abigail noticed Lizzy shifting uneasily on her chair. She looked ready to cry out in frustration. Abigail could sense a resentfulness behind Lizzy's eyes as she clenched her jaw and stared at the floor. She wondered what her daughter was thinking.

"Secondly," Richard continued, "we have imposed on the Sorensens' hospitality far too long. They are good people to help us as much as they have. But I know it hasn't been easy for them, what with trying to care for their own family." Richard glanced around the room and took a piece of paper out of his vest pocket. He put on his reading glasses and unfolded the sheet. "With that in mind, I have something to read to you. It's a letter from Brother John Parry, the master mason for the temple here in Logan."

He cleared his throat, then began to read. "'With the pace of temple construction increasing, the demand for skilled masons has also increased, but we have been unable to find enough skilled workers to accomplish the required labor. From your work on the Logan tabernacle, you have a reputation as a seasoned mason, and, as much of the temple will be of the same stone as the tabernacle, your experience would be twice as valuable to the work. If we cannot find enough willing men, I will have to begin searching outside of Cache Valley for laborers. We pray you will accept the call to work full-time as a mason on the Logan Temple.'"

"Full-time?" Lizzy asked. "But your work on the tabernacle was only a tithe. Surely Brother Parry can't expect you to abandon the farm every day. Perhaps when the weather is cooler and the crop is in—"

"This wouldn't be a tithe," Richard explained. "Brother Parry's letter also says that I would be paid for my work. Not a king's ransom, by any means, but a decent wage. Three dollars and fifty cents a day. It's more than some of the less-experienced masons currently working on the temple earn, according to Brother Parry." He put the letter back into his breast pocket, then went on. "After receiving this letter, I went to Brother Parry's home and talked with him—explained our situation. He's found us a solution. Turns out that the Joseph Webster family lives right close to the temple and have offered to let us stay with them. They have a spare room and a loft. It will be cozy, but we'll get by, and we'll be able to start saving some money toward a new home."

Now it was Abigail's turn to shift in her seat. She eyed Lizzy, knowing that her daughter would have a difficult time coping with what her father was telling them.

"A new home?" Lizzy asked, her voice raising a notch. Then she calmed herself. "You mean we'll save to *rebuild* the house." She put on a tentative smile. Abigail's heart pricked at the sight. "Of course, we won't have to stay with that family for long . . . " Lizzy continued, making plans.

How can I explain? Abigail thought with aching heart. She had to be honest. "We can't afford to rebuild. With winter coming on, even if we had the money, we couldn't start until spring, and even then it would take a long time. Years, most likely. It's one thing to build when there's only a husband and wife and a child or two like your father and I did before. But now we have a large family to worry about, and one very sick little boy. I'd like to think we will rebuild . . . someday. But for now we need to work on getting David well and the rest of us sheltered and fed."

"We won't rebuild?" Lizzy asked, looking from her father to her mother and back again. Her eyes were shiny, making Abigail's well up with tears too.

"I'm so sorry, Lizzy."

Lizzy dropped her head into her hands. Her shoulders began shaking. "Why is God taking everything from us?"

Reaching over, Abigail took both of her daughter's hands away from her face. She leaned down to look in Lizzy's eyes. "The Lord gives more than He takes away. And it's good to remember that nothing truly belongs to us anyway. Everything is His. We knew that when we came to Zion and covenanted to give everything to the Lord."

Lizzy ripped her hands away. She stood and threw the afghan to the side, her voice raising to a high pitch. "You knew that when *you* came to Zion," she said, pointing to her parents. "What about me? I was born *here!*" she said, pointing to her own heart. "The only home I've ever known is burned to the ground. *I* never promised to give up everything I care about." She covered her face and ran, through the kitchen and out the back door.

The screen slammed shut behind Lizzy, and she dropped to the back step in tears, grateful for the darkness of the night that gave her grief some privacy.

* * *

Joshua was coming down the stairs as Lizzy raced outside. He peered into the parlor where her family sat around the room, somber. "Is something wrong?"

Richard cleared his throat and put on a weak smile. "We won't be imposing on your family for much longer," he said. "In a couple of days we'll be leaving you."

Joshua glanced toward the kitchen. He could hear crying. Richard answered the question Joshua was about to ask. "But that's not entirely why she's upset."

Richard and Abigail exchanged glances, and Abigail answered, her voice shaky, "She learned that we won't be rebuilding the house."

No wonder she's so distraught, Joshua thought. *That home's the only one she's ever known.* The Sullivans shifted in their seats, and Joshua realized he was intruding on a family gathering. He excused himself and went through the kitchen toward the sound of sobbing outside. He stopped at the door, which stood open a crack. Beth was now standing, leaning against the side of the house, moonlight spilling over her shoulders and making her look like an angel. *A grief-stricken angel,* he thought compassionately.

Joshua suddenly wanted to comfort her, hold her, to once and for all tell her what was in his heart and promise to make her happy. He put an arm out to push the door, but paused. If she didn't feel the same way, would she shut him out completely? Would their friendship be lost? His hand dropped to his side. *Not yet.* He would tell her after he found a way to win her heart.

What if I bought the Sullivan farm?

The thought jumped out at him and began swirling in his mind. Yes. He could rebuild the house for Beth. If nothing else proved his love for her, that would. Surely he could find work that a man with a wife and children couldn't do—work that might require being away from home but which would pay more. And he would save every possible penny. He could do most of the work on the house himself. It might take a few years, but what did that matter if Beth would be his at the end?

With renewed determination, Joshua pushed on the kitchen door. He wouldn't tell her anything about his plans tonight. Now she needed the friend of her old school days at her side.

He took a breath. "Are you all right?" he asked quietly as the door creaked open. She looked over, her eyes red. Joshua ached at the sight. "Your parents told me about the house."

"Oh, Joshua," she said, turning to throw her arms around his neck. "Can anyplace else ever be home?"

He held her close. "You'll have a home again," he said. "I promise."

CHAPTER 5

The Sullivan family was packing to leave. At noon, Joshua helped Richard and the boys load their meager belongings in the wagon. Joshua and Beth had spent more time together in the last two weeks than in months previous, and he cherished every memory they'd made. He and Lizzy might make promises to visit each other, but he knew that they would most likely drift apart—unless he made an extra effort not to. And that would be difficult if he was trying to buy a farm and build a home on it.

He watched the twins and Jimmy go back inside. When Abigail came out with a final armful of clothing, Richard by her side, Joshua decided the time had come to approach them with his idea. He stepped toward them. "Brother and Sister Sullivan, I know this hasn't been an easy time for you. But I was wondering . . ." He gave an awkward cough. "Are you still not planning to rebuild your home?"

Richard sighed. "I don't see how we can anytime soon. I'm afraid we won't have the resources for several years."

"In that case, I think I might have an idea that could . . . well . . . help build your resources." Joshua straightened his posture, steeling himself. "I have a proposal to make."

Richard and Abigail eyed each other. Richard nodded. "We had a feeling you might."

"You . . . you did?" Joshua hadn't expected that Beth's parents would guess his plans. "I don't have a lot of money saved up, but I think it should be enough for a down payment. I would make monthly payments, with interest of course—" He stopped short when he noticed the Sullivans' confused expressions.

"Joshua, exactly what *are* you proposing?" Abigail asked.

"I want to buy your farm, of course. If you're willing. In time I'd like to build a house and settle down."

"The farm? You want the farm?" Abigail's hand flew to her mouth. She laughed aloud, which brought new life to her weary eyes.

Joshua looked from Abigail to Richard. Abigail was still laughing, and Richard was unsuccessfully trying to keep a smile from the corners of his mouth. Joshua could feel his face turning red, including his ears.

"I'm a hard worker. I promise to take good care of the place, especially knowing how much it means to you—"

Richard held up a hand to stop Joshua's effusion. He let out a rumbling chuckle. "You don't need to convince us of all that, Joshua." He glanced at his wife. As if the tension inside her had finally snapped, Abigail began another round of uncontrollable giggles. "We thought you were proposing . . . something else."

A look of understanding dawned on Joshua, and his already-flushed face darkened two shades.

"Oh." He stared at the dirt at his feet. "Well—I—uh—that *had* crossed my mind as well, but . . ." His voice trailed off, and he coughed again. "Will you consider my offer?"

Richard nodded. "Let's sit down and discuss the terms. I think Abigail will agree with me in saying it would take a load off our minds to know that our farm would be in good hands."

Abigail nodded eagerly. "It would be a blessing to pass the farm to you."

Relief flooded through him. "Thank you, Brother Sullivan, Sister Sullivan. You won't regret this."

"You won't either," Abigail said. She stepped closer to Joshua and touched his arm. "Perhaps you will still win the wife you've hoped for." She glanced toward the house. "I know Lizzy would love to live on the old farm again."

Joshua flushed and nodded, his hands deep in his pockets.

Before more could be said, a buggy came into view, driven by a stocky man with a brown beard, his head and face rimmed with hair. Brother Webster had agreed to drive part of the family so David could lie down for the trip. Joshua's heart fell at the sight. In a few more minutes, Beth would be gone. He wished he could prolong the day, as the prophet Joshua had done. Only instead of pushing back the sun, he would delay Brother Webster's arrival a few hours—or weeks.

Brother Webster hopped down and approached Richard. "Brother Sullivan, I presume?" he said heartily, pumping Richard's hand. As he did so, the family came out to join them. Richard introduced each as they emerged, putting an arm around Jimmy as he began. Abigail turned toward the house to get David.

"This here is Jimmy, my nephew. He's like a son. Then there's Lizzy and our twins, Matthew and Aaron. Matthew's the dark one, Aaron's the towhead."

Joseph greeted each of them, then turned to Joshua. "And you are—?"

Joshua offered his hand. "Joshua Sorensen."

"Oh, so you aren't part of the Sullivan family."

"Uh, no," Joshua stammered, hoping no one could tell his hopes for the future actually lay in that direction.

Brother Webster laughed. "For a moment I thought I'd get another strapping worker to help bring in the harvest. But it's sure nice to meet you anyway." They shook hands, and Joshua tried to smile casually.

Richard nodded toward the house. "Here comes my wife, Abigail, with David."

She came out cradling David in her arms. "Thank you for coming for us, Brother Webster," she said in the quiet voice she was accustomed to using around her son.

"It's my pleasure. And please, call me Joseph. Brother Parry mentioned that your son was ill. Let's hurry and get him to the house so he can rest. It's not a long trip, but it'll still be a little difficult with him feeling unwell."

Leaning forward in his mother's arms, David asked, "Are we going to pass Temple Hill?"

"Nope," Brother Webster said with a shake of his head. "It's not far from the house, but I wasn't planning on taking that road. Thought it was a mite steep for someone not feeling his best, like yourself."

"Could we please? I'd like to see the work on the temple."

Richard and Abigail exchanged looks. Brother Webster shrugged. "If you think it's not too much for him, it's fine by me."

One more look at her son's pleading eyes convinced Abigail. "He does get his heart so set on things, and it might be awhile before he gets out of the house again. I suppose a few extra minutes won't hurt."

"Thank you, Mama," David said, and snuggled into her arms.

Patting Richard's back, Brother Webster said, "It'll give you a chance to see where you'll be working, too."

The Sullivan wagon seated Richard and the boys, while David rode in Brother Webster's buggy with his mother and sister.

Joshua stepped closer to the buggy. "Good-bye, Beth."

"Don't say that, Joshua. It makes it sound like we're moving across the country. We'll be on the other side of the valley, that's all."

"I know," Joshua said with a shrug. "But we won't see as much of each other, all the same. And I've enjoyed having you around so much lately."

She smiled. "It has been nice."

"I'll miss you." Joshua's voice was growing hoarse. He hoped it wasn't giving away his real feelings.

"I'll miss you too." Her eyes brightened. "I know. Let's write letters. It'll be the next best thing to our long talks. I'll write as soon as we're settled."

Joshua's heart made a little jump. Maybe Beth cared for him more than he'd thought. "I'll wait for your letter," he said, then reached for her hand and squeezed it. "So if you won't let me say good-bye, what should I say?"

"How about 'until next time'?"

"Until next time, then."

* * *

As they drove away, Lizzy couldn't help but look back, first at Joshua, then once more in the direction of her home, or rather, what was left of her home. The rubble wasn't visible at this distance, but she could almost see it in her mind's eye. She didn't shed tears; none were left, though it would have been a relief to let some of the hurt out. She squeezed her eyes shut, remembering. In another month, the leaves of the maple that had shaded her bedroom window would have been readying for the change to bright orange and yellow.

The passengers of the buggy remained quiet. But where Lizzy and Abigail lacked in conversation, Jimmy and the younger boys made up for in noise in the back of the wagon. Lizzy could hear Jimmy boisterously singing off-key, while Matthew and Aaron kept elbowing each other and insisting the other had more than his share of the seat.

A coughing fit shook David's body, making him grimace. Abigail lifted him to help ease the attack. He coughed harder, spitting up blood. Lizzy quickly produced a handkerchief and handed it to her mother, who wiped the blood from his face.

As Abigail handed the cloth back, Lizzy noticed a few spatters of blood on her mother's hand and began to wipe them away. Her mother's fingers closed around her own, and Lizzy looked up questioningly. Abigail looked suddenly helpless. Ever since the fire, Lizzy had marveled that her mother had kept careful control over her feelings. At times she had wondered if her mother had any trepidation about the move, any concerns about what the future would bring. But now, at least, her mother's eyes couldn't hide her fear for her son.

"He'll be well soon, Mama," Lizzy said, though rather unconvincingly, as she didn't believe it herself.

"If the Lord desires it, he will be," Abigail said, her voice implying that she had accepted that the Lord's plans might not coincide with her own. With a gentle touch she pushed David's sweaty, matted hair away from his eyes as if caressing a newborn baby.

They rode in silence for some time. As they pulled onto Main Street, Lizzy noticed a cozy two-story house on the left. It was adobe, painted white with green shutters. She must have seen it dozens of times, but today she couldn't take her eyes off the friendly house. It seemed to wink at her with its small windows, one on either side of the front porch. When she could no longer see anything but the gable and chimney, Lizzy turned back around. She closed her eyes and envisioned it, even picturing what the inside might look like. If she had to pick a house to replace her own dear home, that would be the one.

"Who lives in the white house we just passed?" Lizzy asked.

After a quick glance over his shoulder, Brother Webster said, "Oh, that would be Sister Ellen Mills's home. She's a widow. Lives there alone. She's been making clothing and socks for the temple workers. Wonderful sister."

"I love her home," Lizzy said, craning her head to see it again.

"I'll have to introduce you to her someday," Brother Webster said.

Several minutes later, when they reached the top of Temple Hill, Brother Webster pulled on the reins, and the horses slowed to a stop. "Here it is. Temple Hill."

Gingerly supporting her son, Abigail helped David sit up. He smiled. "It's going to be big, isn't it?" he said, gazing at the outline of the foundation and the number of workmen using shovels and pushing wheelbarrows.

Brother Webster hopped out and met Richard, and Lizzy gently lifted David out and carried him so he could get a better view without having to walk. Jimmy also stood up to jump out of the wagon. "This isn't where we're stopping, Jimmy," Richard called to him.

But Jimmy pointed at the temple lot. "But I want to go see it. That's a special place."

"Come watch by us," Richard said. "We don't want to bother the workers."

When Jimmy joined Richard, he put his arm around his nephew. "You're right, Jimmy. This *is* a special place. We can't stay long today. But don't worry. You'll have lots of chances to come back."

Grinning, David hugged Lizzy. "I can imagine just what it'll look like." He turned to Brother Webster. "Will it have towers? I think it'll have towers. And lots of trees around it."

"You might be right," Brother Webster said, then chuckled. "Actually, we don't have official plans yet. Brother Angell was appointed architect a few months back, but so far the only thing we have to go by are the heel marks President Young made where the corners of the temple are to be." At Richard's surprised look, he simply shrugged. "I know it sounds crazy. But it'll all work out. The Lord has had a hand in this for a long time, and will to the end."

Joseph gestured toward the site. "As you can see, they're starting to excavate the hole for the baptismal font. They finished digging the foundation and have been filling it in with gravel for more than a month now."

Richard nodded absently, then cocked his head to one side, a bit perplexed. Lizzy noticed her father's confusion and looked closer at the trench for the foundation. It was six or seven feet wide and two feet deep at most. She didn't know enough about construction to know what her father was wondering about.

"Aren't they planning on making the foundation any deeper?" Richard asked. "That seems rather shallow for such a large building."

Brother Webster nodded, a knowing smile cracking his face. "You aren't the first person to say that. But you see, the ground of Temple Hill is basically gravel. President Young says it's that way all the way to the bottom, that there's no point in trying to dig for solid rock. We wouldn't find any. He says that a two-foot foundation is all that's needed to support the temple. So we're going by what he said."

He turned around and walked with them eastward toward the other side of the street, with Richard glancing over his shoulder at the foundation as he went. Lizzy followed, still carrying David. Brother Webster pointed. "That there will be the cookhouse, where the temple workers' meals will be made and served. And to the right is the stone-cutting shed, where I hear you'll be doing much of your work."

Richard nodded, and the group spent a few more minutes looking around. But when David began coughing again, Lizzy headed back to the buggy.

"I'm fine, Lizzy," David insisted.

"No, you're not," Lizzy said. But a lecture wouldn't convince him that he wasn't well, so she added, "Besides, I need to rest. Will you keep me company?"

David tried to free himself of her arms. "If I can walk the rest of the way."

"You will do no such thing," Lizzy said with a laugh, and had to hold him tighter.

Richard came up and felt David's forehead, then called for Jimmy. "Are you ready? We need to go." Jimmy nodded reluctantly. "I think we're ready," Richard told Brother Webster and followed Lizzy to the wagon, Jimmy in tow. The men each clucked to their horses, and the group began rolling forward again.

A few minutes into the drive it was clear that David's brief burst of energy had only drained him. As the carriage bumped along the road, sometimes hitting stray rocks, Abigail held David closer, trying to absorb the extra motion as he whimpered.

"It hurts, Mama," he said, his voice scratchy.

"How far is it from here?" Abigail asked Brother Webster, keeping her voice cheery in an attempt to hide her worry.

"It's just around the next corner. See those poplars? Planted them myself at the edge of our land."

They soon stopped in front of the Webster home, a small brick house with two narrow windows flanking each side of the door. A pleasant, brown-haired woman stood on the porch, looking about the age of Lizzy's mother. She wore an apron dusted with flour.

The group in the wagon left their seats much more quickly than Lizzy and her mother did.

Jimmy poked his nose into the buggy window. "Look, Lizzy," he said pointing excitedly at Sister Webster. "She looks like you do after making bread. I'll bet there's some in there!"

Richard gently took David, who had nearly fallen asleep in the short distance from the temple lot. As they approached the house, a sheep dog raced around the side, barking wildly at the intruders. Richard gripped David tighter and raised him out of harm's way as the dog lunged toward them.

"Sophie, come here!" Brother Webster hollered. The dog stopped in its tracks, but kept eyeing the strangers and growling suspiciously. Brother Webster called to her again, this time more sternly. The dog reluctantly walked to him, but continued to watch the family's every move. Brother Webster held onto the collar and patted her. "It may take awhile for Sophie here to get used to all of you. She's a bit protective of the family." He looked to Abigail, who had worry written across her face. "Don't you mind Sophie, Sister Sullivan. I'll be sure to tie her up for the time being. She won't be causing any trouble with your little ones."

"Thank you," Abigail said, eyeing the dog as she stepped toward the house. Sophie barked a warning and tried to lunge forward, but Brother Webster calmed and led her away, presumably to tie her up. Everyone headed inside, where Sister Webster welcomed them on the porch with a warm smile.

"If you'd like, he can sleep on our bed in the room right off the kitchen," Sister Webster said, nodding toward David. "I'm afraid your room isn't quite ready."

"Thank you. The road was rather hard on him," Abigail said as she followed Richard inside. The boys hurried in, eager now that they could smell cooked potatoes and fresh bread.

Lizzy paused before going in. She hugged her arms to her chest to keep out the chilly autumn breeze that had just picked up. She looked the small house over. *How large is the Webster family?* she wondered. How would both families live together? And when would her family have their own home again?

Her gaze turned upward at the rows of trees that framed three sides of the house. The long arms of their branches seemed to reach out protectively to the home, their leaves rippling cheerfully in the breeze.

A knot formed in Lizzy's throat as she looked away. What she wouldn't give for one more night in her cozy room upstairs, her maple tree watching over her window, swaying in the night wind and whispering secrets as she fell asleep.

"Are you coming?"

The friendly voice tore Lizzy from her thoughts. She hadn't realized that Sister Webster had returned to the front porch. She held the door open for her last guest.

"Yes, thank you." Lizzy picked up her skirts and crossed the distance. She smiled at Sister Webster as she entered the house. "I was just admiring your trees. You have so many."

"You'll have to blame my husband for that. I suppose you could call trees an obsession of his." Sister Webster chuckled as she closed the door. "Every year he must plant some more. Once he ran out of room near the house, he started out back. At least he's planted fruit trees, too, so those are practical."

Lizzy laughed as they walked through the front room into the kitchen area, but she felt a sinking in her stomach. Only now did she realize the hope the trees had sprouted, the hope that she might feel at home here, that the Websters were a family after her own heart. And while Sister Webster was very kind, she apparently didn't share the same affection Lizzy had for trees. That fact said volumes about their potential for being close friends.

Sister Webster showed Lizzy into the kitchen area. Although it was relatively spacious, it seemed cramped with two families squeezed in. A table with benches ran along one wall, which appeared to be the family's regular table. A second, slightly shorter table looked out of place, and Lizzy assumed it had been brought in especially for the Sullivans. It ran along the adjacent wall under the window over-looking the backyard. It didn't quite fit in the space, with three or four inches sticking out into the doorway that led outside.

The children in both families prattled on with excitement, and the noise was deafening. Lizzy crossed the room and sat at the end of the bench by the outside door, where she could see the entire group.

Brother Webster held up his hands, and the talking subsided. "I think it would be fitting for some introductions." He stood and stretched out his arm. Sister Webster came to him and nestled into the crook. "Of course, this is my lovely wife, Laura." Sister Webster smiled and nodded. "And those two chatterboxes over there are our girls Mary and Sarah. Mary is ten, and Sarah is almost eight. And next to them are Sam and Leroy, six and five years, and the carrottop by me, with the food all over his face, is Wyatt. He'll be two in a month. Nearly lost him a couple of times, though. We call him our miracle baby."

Brother Webster didn't elaborate on Wyatt's miracle status. Instead he gave his wife a squeeze and sat down. He nodded to Lizzy's father, who took the cue and stood up awkwardly from his seat in the corner, narrowly missing bumping his head on a plant hanging above him. He repeated the introductions he had given at first meeting Brother Webster, with a few additions here and there. He called Lizzy the "clever" one in the family because of her reading. She forced a smile. She reached into her pocket and stroked the book corner she had found in the rubble.

"Now that we have introductions out of the way, let's have a blessing over our meal." Brother Webster bowed his head. Lizzy glanced at her father, then looked away and closed her eyes. Her father should be presiding at his family's meal. But only in their own home. And this *wasn't* their home. The reminder was disheart-ening.

Sister Webster made sure everyone had plenty to eat, refilling plates and passing rolls down the tables along with a crock of freshly churned butter. Lizzy had to admit that Sister Webster was an excellent cook. Her own rolls never tasted this good.

When they heard a gasp coming from the bedroom, Lizzy and Abigail both dropped their forks and ran to check on David.

"What's wrong?" Abigail asked, reaching him first.

"Do you need some water?" Lizzy asked from behind her mother.

But David wasn't looking at them. Instead, he gazed on the wall opposite and pointed. "Look at that," he said in a voice hoarse from coughing.

Abigail and Lizzy followed his gaze to see a framed sketch of the Savior hanging on the wall. They glanced at each other, then back at David. Abigail took his hand. "What about it?"

"Isn't it the most beautiful picture you've ever seen?"

Sister Webster appeared at the door, a concerned look in her eyes, and Abigail soothed the worried woman. "He's fine. David was just admiring your drawing."

Sister Webster eyed the sketch. "My son Peter drew it for me. He made several of the Savior, but that's my favorite one. He was an excellent artist."

Lizzy arched a brow at the word *was,* but before she could ask anything, David bit his lip, drawing everyone's attention. Abigail's brow furrowed. "Are you in pain, dear?" she asked.

"Not much, Mama," he said, shaking his head. "I was just wondering if . . . if while we stay here, if I could look at that picture sometimes."

Sister Webster nodded. "Of course you can, David. Whenever you want to look at it, just come in here and sit on that bed and take a good long look. I do all the time. That's why I put it where I'll see it first thing when I wake up each morning. It's been a great comfort, especially in the years since Peter passed away." Her voice lowered. "Maybe we could sit and look at it together sometime."

David smiled. "I would like that."

The rest of the evening was filled with trying to get the remainder of the days' chores completed and the Sullivan family settled. The Webster home had two bedrooms downstairs and a small loft. The

Webster girls and little Wyatt would be sleeping with their parents, leaving the second bedroom for the Sullivan family. David slept in a cot Sister Webster had borrowed from a neighbor. The twins and Webster boys would take the loft. David napped in the Websters' room while Lizzy set to making up the beds.

Lizzy's and Jimmy's beds consisted of layers of blankets and quilts on the floor. She supposed that Jimmy should sleep by the far wall, and she would sleep under the window. That would leave room for David by the door so his mother or Lizzy could reach him easily as well as check on him during the day.

As Lizzy smoothed out the quilt on David's cot, she hoped that he would be able to sleep well with all the extra noise. Matthew and Aaron were boisterous all by themselves, and adding Jimmy to the mix only escalated the noise level. But if dinner were any indication, the Webster children could hold their own as well, so David would be lucky to get any rest during the day.

Lizzy finished by arranging pillows on each person's sleeping area, then surveyed the cramped room. As the only daughter, she had always had her own bedroom, and although it was small, it had been hers. Here she would be lucky to ever have a moment's peace. She wished for a nice long read. What she wouldn't give for a few minutes of solitude with George Eliot.

She had been hearing voices from the Websters' bedroom for several minutes and knew David must have woken from his nap, so she headed for the other room. Abigail sat at his side with a small tray of food. David sat against some pillows and drank a cold, thick glass of milk. His eyes no longer drooped, and his cheeks had a slight tint of color. Sister Webster stood at the foot of the bed, pleased to see her youngest guest faring better.

"How are you feeling, David?" she asked.

David swallowed his mouthful of roll and smiled. "Good. I was really hungry."

"I can believe it. You slept most of the day away," Sister Webster said with a smile. She gave his foot a squeeze through the covers.

"I'm just glad he's got his appetite back," Abigail said. "He hasn't eaten like this in weeks."

"What about his fever?" Lizzy asked from the doorway.

"It broke."

They heard a burst of laughter as the boys came through the back door. It appeared that the Webster and Sullivan children were having a jolly time getting to know each other.

"Hey, Ma, are there any rolls left?" Sam called.

Sister Webster chuckled as she headed for the kitchen. "I think I could spend all day feeding those children, and they would still never have their fill."

As she went through the doorway, a shaggy form raced past her knees and jumped on the bed. Abigail gasped and placed her arm across David's chest to shield him from the animal. But instead of growling and barking as the dog had at their arrival, Sophie curled up on the bed against David and panted, tongue hanging out. Sister Webster hurried back into the room and reached for the leather collar.

"The children weren't supposed to untie the dog. I'm sorry, Abigail," she said. "She's always trying to get in the house. She knows she's not allowed."

"If it's not too much trouble, Sister Webster," David quickly said, "could she stay with me for a couple of minutes? I like her." The dog put her head on his lap as if agreeing to the arrangement. When David scratched her behind the ears, her eyes glazed over with pleasure. Abigail hesitated, clearly not liking the situation at all.

"I suppose she could this once. If you don't mind," Sister Webster said.

The blood drained from Abigail's face as she looked at the animal, then at Lizzy, who understood. Her mother still didn't trust Sophie, but she also didn't want to deflate her young son's hopes. And the dog did seem to be behaving. Lizzy smiled encouragingly.

"This may sound silly, but after seeing how she acted toward us earlier today, I worry about what she might do to my boy," Abigail said tentatively.

"I understand. If it's any reassurance, Sophie's never bitten anyone. She's certainly not the friendliest dog, but as they say, her bark is far worse than her bite." Sister Webster glanced at David and the family pet. "This is rather strange behavior for her, I must say. I've never seen her act like this. Usually she prefers to be on her own. She tries to sneak into the house for food, not attention."

David considered the dog as he scratched it behind the ears. "I think she was lonely out there by herself. She probably wanted to see what the house is like." He paused for a moment before continuing. "I understand, Sophie. It's hard sometimes when you can't do what you'd like, isn't it?"

Lizzy's heart ached at his words. She thought of all the times his brothers had gone out to play and explore, all the shopping visits to the stores on Main Street, all the fishing trips to the river—things David missed more often than not due to illness. He rarely complained, making it easy to believe he didn't mind being sick. But his brief words hinted at frustration and pain that she could only guess at.

She sat beside him. "I think you are just the friend Sophie needs now," she said. *And she is the friend you need too,* Lizzy finished silently.

CHAPTER 6

Before the sun was up and anyone else was awake, Abigail got out of bed and threw on a shawl. She put a hand on David's forehead, grateful that it was cool to the touch after another feverish week. After adjusting his covers, she reached down and kissed his forehead. Before leaving, Abigail glanced over at Jimmy in his makeshift bed on the floor, limbs sprawled in all directions. She turned her gaze to Lizzy and sighed. It had been too long since Lizzy had worn one of her customary grins or laughed—a laugh everyone was helpless to resist. If Lizzy laughed, everyone else laughed too.

Abigail quietly padded through the house and slipped out the front door, which closed with a click behind her. At the edge of the Webster property she stopped and picked a bunch of wildflowers. Yesterday, hearing of Abigail's intended outing for this morning, Laura Webster had insisted she take some with her. Abigail placed them on the seat of the wagon, then hitched up the horse. Soon she was on her way, headed northeast toward the cemetery.

In a strange way, Abigail was glad to be staying on the other side of the valley now—closer to her destination. Before, living on the west had made it much harder for her to visit the graves of her babies. Not that the distance was really so much greater, but between daily chores, David's illnesses, and everything else, somehow just getting to Main Street for essentials—an occasional trip to Christiansen's People's Store—took more time than she had. Traveling a dozen more blocks to the cemetery wasn't an option. Twice a year she faithfully made the trip, at Easter and at Christmas, when Richard made a point of hitching up the horses to the buckboard and taking Abigail there himself.

As she drove, her mind traced the years. She remembered vivid details of the journey from Salt Lake City through the canyon, climbing the mountains upward and then down to Logan. She thought of building her home, and of the addition they built later. She remembered taking Jimmy into her home, her first child to care for. Then came the birth of each of her seven children, and the burial of three. Tears welled up and tumbled over. She wiped at her cheeks so she could see the road.

When she reached the cemetery, Abigail stepped to the ground, tied up the horse, and held the wildflowers in her hands as she would a precious vase. She did not walk far before reaching a large stone marker, several feet tall, that read, "Pioneer Plot." Abigail looked out on the grassy area behind the stone, wishing with everything in her heart that she knew exactly where her two baby boys lay. Back when their tiny wooden caskets had been laid to rest in the old cemetery, she could kneel before their final resting places. But as the city grew and encroached on the cemetery, it needed to be relocated, and the graves of Abigail's little babies had been moved here to the new cemetery in one large unmarked grave, along with the remains of forty other early settlers.

Abigail divided the makeshift bouquet into three parts. She laid a group of flowers on one side of the stone marker for her first son, Josiah, named after her father. He was born when Lizzy was not yet two years old and had died minutes after his birth. Abigail remembered well his tiny whimpers, his cheeks that should have been pink but were tinged blue.

She laid a second bunch of flowers on the other side of the marker, this one for Richard Jr. His death had been even harder to bear than Josiah's. He had lived for three years, long enough to talk and play and get into mischief, and to be one of the greatest joys Abigail had ever experienced. Little Richard had died just a year before the move to the new cemetery. More than once Abigail had wished that if she *had* to lose her son, that he would have at least lived long enough to get a proper grave in the new cemetery.

Instead, all she could do for her two boys was her own simple ritual. Twice she kissed her hand and blew the kisses onto the grassy area. She gripped the last bunch of flowers as she walked a distance away to the corner of another section in the cemetery, where the plots were tiny. This section was saved for babies. Her husband had created the small stone himself.

As she walked toward the marker of her lastborn, Hannah, Abigail gazed toward the spot where the temple would someday stand. She was anxious to receive the blessings of the temple and to have her children sealed to her forever. The St. George Temple had been dedicated just a few months before, the first in Utah and the first since Nauvoo. She wondered if the Logan Temple would be completed before the one in Manti. The grand temple under construction in Salt Lake City would probably take longer.

She stopped before Hannah's grave, her little girl who had passed from life five days after birth. At the top was the image of a dove, and below it the words, "Another little angel before the heavenly throne." Abigail closed her eyes tightly for a moment. This wound was still fresh, more raw than the others. Hannah had died only two years ago. Abigail had had more than a dozen years to grieve for her sons. She choked slightly as she put the flowers down, said her farewell, and traced the words at the bottom and whispered, "My little angel, how I miss you."

* * *

Richard prepared for work Monday morning. Knowing that Richard had many of his own masonry tools, Brother Quayle sent over a list of what to bring along.

"Do you have everything?" Abigail asked.

"There isn't much according to the list," he said, pulling out the paper once more. "A six-inch chisel, a four-inch mallet, and an ax," he read aloud. He glanced outside the door, where his bag rested on the ground. "I haven't forgotten anything."

"Except this." Abigail handed him a scarf around. "In case it gets cold." She rose up on her toes to kiss him good-bye.

Richard nodded. "I'll see you this afternoon for dinner." He took a deep breath, picked up his tools, then headed across the yard. When he reached the road, he turned back to wave at Abigail, still standing at the door.

The walk to the temple block warmed him, and when he arrived, men were already bustling about at their various duties. He expected to see more workers around the foundation, but instead they were concentrated on the east end, where stone walls were already rising, but it was too far off-center to be for the temple proper.

"Hello."

Richard turned to see a bearded man approaching, his hand extended. Richard shook it. "Good to see you again, Brother Parry."

"Brother Sullivan! I heard you were coming in yesterday. Follow me."

Brother Parry led Richard toward the construction site. "We're working on the temple's annex first," he said, stopping in front of the structure Richard had been looking at. "When it's finished we'll use it to feed the workers until the cookhouse is done." Brother Parry pointed east across the street to a small square structure.

"There's the stonecutting shed." Brother Parry began walking down the street, the cookhouse on their left. He gestured to a building which stood farther south of the cookhouse. It was long and narrow, probably a hundred feet long and no more than twenty wide. "There'll be fires in there each morning to help you warm up, and the south side is open, so the sun shines there in the afternoons. Hopefully that'll help, since it can get mighty cold in this area, from what I hear."

"You *hear?* I didn't realize you were new to Logan."

Parry nodded. "Moved from Bountiful just a couple of months ago. Been working hard ever since, I can tell you that. I must say it was a relief when you responded to the call. It's been mighty hard to find willing men to work regularly. I've had to start looking south of Salt Lake to find masons. We've had so much trouble finding brethren to work on the temple that we've been getting help from Indians."

"Indian workers?" Richard stopped short in surprise.

Brother Parry turned around. "Yup. Quite a few of them." He pointed out a pair of darker-skinned men who were mixing mortar for the annex walls. "Like those two brothers over there. I think the food and clothing attract them to the work, and that's fine by me.

They've been good, regular workers. If we can keep getting their help, we'll be ready to roof the annex by Christmas."

Richard picked out several other Indian laborers that he hadn't noticed before. They looked far different from the Indians he had seen on their journey from Winter Quarters so long ago. For one thing, they wore the same shirts and pants provided for other temple workers. The Indian brothers at the mortar wore their long black hair tied into a ponytail. He noticed another worker who was probably also Indian, but his clothing didn't match the others.

"Is that fellow one of the local Indians?" he asked, nodding toward the young man.

"Nope," Brother Parry said with a shake of his head. "Well, he's Shoshone, sure enough, but white on the inside, as they say. Raised by Mormon folk back in Salt Lake City."

As Richard turned away, a tightness came to his middle without warning. He had to consciously remind himself that those men were no relation to the ones who pillaged their wagon train so many years ago. But walking past them brought back the urge to guard cattle and gather the children close.

He quickened his pace to catch up to Brother Parry. Ironic that these Indians, who knew nothing of the gospel, were more willing to labor on a temple of God than many of the people who would actually be using the building. But then again, food and clothing could be powerful motivators for the poor, while more comfortable folks could easily deny the request when it meant leaving family for two or three weeks at a time. The other man, the one from down south, looked too young to have a family. He'd probably come up to Cache Valley for the money offered to full-time men.

When they entered the stonecutting shed, the workers were pounding mallets against chisels, shaping the sandstone blocks. At seeing the two men, they paused in their work, and Brother Parry introduced them to Richard.

"This here is Brother Robert Parker, and over there is Brother Lewis Smith." Both men looked up and nodded greetings, then returned to their tasks. "Their wards sent them on a rotation schedule, so they'll be replaced by other men in a couple of weeks. The work isn't complex, but there's plenty of it. Right now we're just cutting the blocks to size."

Brother Parry walked over to a finished stone that was less than two feet across, and rubbed his hand along one edge. "See, we want the outside surface of the stone to be perfect." He leaned to the other side of the stone and pointed. "The inside doesn't matter as much, since it'll have carpentry and plaster covering it anyway. That's the side I've been having the unskilled masons learn on. I'd like you to do the outer edges."

"I'd be happy to," Richard said, squatting down to look at the piece. "Sandstone is soft, as stone goes. Good for learning on." He picked up a piece from the floor and rubbed it against uneven chisel marks on the back of the block, smoothing the rough parts. "There. Much better." He put the stone down and looked outside the cutting shed where several loads of rock were being stored. "Where do you get the rock from?"

Brother Parry jerked his thumb in a northeasterly direction. "The Green Canyon Quarry is about five miles or so down the canyon. The Brethren selected it more than a year ago for the temple. Workmen have spent all summer down there. First load arrived the second week of June, and it's been coming right along ever since."

After Brother Parry excused himself, Richard went to work. His chisel and mallet felt comfortable in his hands, and he hardly noticed the chill of the morning air turning warm as the sun beat into the open end of the shed.

A few hours later when the cookhouse triangle sounded, the men set down their tools. Richard wiped his sleeve across his forehead, then rotated his shoulder and stretched out his fingers. He put on his coat and headed back for dinner. Most days he would probably eat with the other men, but on his first day, Abigail wanted him to come home for the meal.

She apologized when he arrived. "I'm sorry the rest of the family already ate."

"I understand. It's all but impossible to hold off a meal when young boys are waiting, isn't it?" He gave his wife a peck on the cheek and smiled at Laura Webster. "Sure smells good, though."

He had developed quite an appetite for the chicken fixins with potatoes and the fresh bread with strawberry jam that Laura had stored that summer. His wife dished up his meal, then she and Laura set to cleaning the kitchen and washing the rest of the family's dishes as he ate.

"Tell us about it," Abigail said as she scrubbed a plate.

"Seems they've been working all summer in preparation," Richard said, and began relating much of what he'd learned from the other brothers in the stonecutting shed. "There's a wood camp, rock quarry, and a lime kiln. They've already decided they need a second kiln, and right now we're building the temple's annex." Richard took a big bite out of his roll.

"What's the annex for?" Laura Webster asked, wiping the table down with a rag.

Richard had asked the same question of Brother Parker as they'd worked. "For offices, the furnace, a reception area, and such. It's also how you'll enter the temple. Brother Parry says the annex will be ready for roofing in a few months. At least, if he can keep getting Indian help, but that shouldn't be a problem."

A crash sounded as a plate hit the floor. Abigail stooped to clean up. "I'm so sorry, Laura . . ." As she picked up a piece, she let out a cry and inspected her hand.

"Are you hurt?" Richard asked.

"A bit," Abigail said, her voice wavering. "I'm so sorry, Laura . . ."

Laura knelt down beside Abigail and began cleaning up. "Don't you worry over these old stoneware things. They've been mismatched for years anyway. Broke one myself not a year ago. Why don't you go take care of that cut?"

Abigail nodded, pale-faced, and left the kitchen.

For a moment, Richard watched her go. "I'll be back to finish up in a minute," he told Sister Webster as she stood with the dish fragments. "You're a mighty fine cook."

"Then I won't clear your place just yet," Sister Webster said, smiling at the compliment.

Richard found Abigail sitting on the rocking chair in the front room, staring at the fireplace. To her hand she held a white cloth stained with blood. Richard pulled up a chair beside her.

"Abigail?"

She blinked, as if coming out of deep thoughts and back to the present. "The cut's pretty deep, but it doesn't hurt too much," she said, eyes belying her practical tone.

Richard clenched his hands together, unsure how to approach the subject. He had a good idea what was bothering her, but since they hadn't talked about it for years, he had thought her feelings might have changed.

"The Indians really are good workers," he tried. "They've been a blessing for the temple."

"That makes no difference," Abigail said in a brusque tone. "Those—those *people* should not be allowed to build a house of God." She couldn't even bring herself to call them by name.

Richard dropped his head and sighed. "Abigail, the young men I saw today had nothing to do with Edward's death. They weren't even born then. And the Indians responsible lived hundreds of miles away from here. Even the fathers and grandfathers of the temple workers couldn't have had anything to do with it."

"That makes no difference," Abigail repeated. She stared at the mantle, eyes glistening.

Richard said nothing for another minute. He wondered what, if anything, he could say to help. "Brother Joseph loved them. He sent missionaries to them."

Abigail finally turned to look at Richard, tears streaking down her cheeks. "Louisa's husband died because a group of those savages scattered his cattle."

"I know, Abigail, I know."

"And then their baby died. He wasn't there to care for them. They didn't have milk or meat," she said, as if Richard hadn't been present for the events. "Louisa almost died too."

"I remember."

"Indians are savages. You know that as well as I do. If those men you saw today had been on the trail all those years ago, they would have done the very same thing to my family." Unaware she'd dropped the rag, Abigail stormed outside.

The front door slammed shut, and Richard stared at it for a moment. He had always admired his wife for her forgiving and compassionate nature. He knew no one else who came so close to showing true Christianity as did Abigail. Except in this one area.

CHAPTER 7

The Webster house was in a flurry. The Sullivan twins and Webster girls had so much energy anticipating today's circus that they had already gotten through their chores and had to wait for breakfast.

"Is it time *yet?*" Mary wailed.

"Not yet," Sister Webster said, stirring the oatmeal. "We'll be eating soon enough."

"Why don't you boys wash up?" Abigail asked as she counted plates. "Your faces are filthy. I expect you to look decent for the cornerstone dedication."

The boys groaned as if Abigail had pronounced a prison sentence on them. "I forgot about that," Aaron said.

"But we were all washed for church yesterday," Matthew added. "Why do we have to clean up again today?"

Abigail picked up a basket to gather the morning's eggs from the chicken coop and wagged a finger at them. "Because this is an important day. You'll always remember September nineteenth, 1877, as the day you witnessed the cornerstone dedication for a temple of God. It's something you'll tell your children about. No one is going to the circus until after the dedication."

"We'll suffer through it," Matthew said with a grin, then jumped on Aaron and wrestled him to the floor. Sam and Leroy Webster joined in as best they could for being smaller than the Sullivan twins.

"And don't go rumpling your clothes, either," Abigail said, heading for the back door. "Go wash up now. And comb your hair. The two of you look like stray mutts."

As she headed for the henhouse, Abigail smiled to herself. Watching her boys with excitement in their eyes gave her a measure of joy, even if she wished they looked forward to the dedication with a fraction of the excitement as they did the circus. Granted, twelve was young to understand the magnitude of what would happen on Temple Hill that day, she reminded herself as she put eggs into the basket. But even at eight and ten, the Webster girls seemed to grasp it better, if only because they practically lived where the shadow of the temple would one day fall.

Matthew and Aaron didn't understand the importance of their father's work now, but she imagined that someday they would remember it with fondness. Perhaps they would even forget they had attended the circus on the same day.

Then again, maybe not.

With the eggs gathered, Abigail returned to the house, pleasantly surprised to see her daughter setting the tables. "Thank you, Lizzy," she said, hoping that perhaps Lizzy would be her old self again soon.

"You're welcome, Mama," she said over her shoulder. "I didn't want you to be late for the procession."

"That's very considerate of you," Abigail said, putting the basket of eggs on the counter to be washed later.

Lizzy grinned and shrugged. "I'm excited to go too. I've never seen a parade before, or most of the Church leaders, for that matter."

"Well, it won't exactly be a parade," Abigail said, checking on the oatmeal. "People won't be lining the streets to watch. Everyone will be going up to Temple Hill."

Lizzy smiled and nodded in understanding, then continued her work. During breakfast, Abigail kept eyeing her daughter, who seemed in good spirits, something rare of late. What a relief that Lizzy seemed more like her usual self. She hoped that going to the circus would help too, and was grateful for Richard's temple wages that made it possible for her children to go.

It wasn't long before they were walking toward Main Street, where the procession would begin. From there they would climb back up the hill to the temple block with the rest of the crowd. Abigail and Richard had agreed to let David come to the cornerstone dedication, but he lacked the strength to go all the way to Main Street and then walk back up the hill to the temple. While the pneumonia had mostly passed, David was still tired from the battle. So Richard decided he would carry David from the house and meet the family at the dedication.

Everyone else reached the intersection of Main Street and Center around eleven thirty. Quite a crowd had gathered; as Lizzy looked around, she saw mostly strange faces and many people dressed in their best clothes. Hundreds of people had traveled to the city for the event, and more poured in on every street, some heading straight to Temple Hill, others joining the group that would form the procession.

Shortly before noon Logan's brass band began to play, giving the signal for them to line up. The band came first, then the temple architect, workmen, and choir. Lizzy's family managed to secure a spot close to the priesthood leaders. They hoped to find Richard and David before the rest of the throng converged behind them on the hill. When the Apostles and patriarchs approached, Abigail shushed the family as a reverent quiet descended over the crowd and the leaders of the Church took their places. Other priesthood leaders lined up behind them, and everyone else was encouraged to follow.

When the crowd gathered together, the band began to play, and everyone headed up the hill to the southeast corner of the temple site. Lizzy couldn't help but walk in time to the boisterous music. Brother Webster hummed along, and Jimmy decided to join in by belting out a rather off-key version of the melody. When Matthew and Aaron burst out laughing, Jimmy looked over and grinned, then sang even louder.

As they neared Temple Hill, however, Abigail whispered to Lizzy, asking her to quiet Jimmy down; Lizzy had a way of influencing Jimmy more than the rest of the family. Matt and Aaron generally encouraged him in the other direction when it came to noise. Lizzy took Jimmy's hand, stood on her toes, and leaned toward his ear.

"Jimmy," she said rather loudly.

He looked over and stopped in surprise. "Lizzy, are you listening to me sing?"

"Oh, yes. And it's very good, too."

"I can sing even louder. Listen."

Lizzy jumped and put her fingers to his lips. She shook her head. "Not now, Jimmy. You can show me how loud you can sing later. It's time to be very quiet and pay attention. Can you do that? Do you think you can be quieter than anyone else?"

Jimmy nodded intently. "I can, Lizzy. Just watch." He pretended to button his lips with his fingers and didn't make another sound. Abigail gave Lizzy a grateful smile as they gathered around the southeast corner of the hill. They secured a spot close to the front. Richard and David arrived a moment later, finding them in spite of the large crowd.

Abigail reached for her son and wrapped his blanket tighter. "Thank you for remembering the quilt," she said to her husband. "Are you feeling well, David?"

David nodded. "I'm fine. Papa carried me all the way. I can walk now."

Just then the band stopped playing, and the choir lined up. A small group of men also took their place, including Brother John Parry, architect Truman Angell—who went by his middle name, Osbourne—and several of the Twelve. It would be their job to help put the first stone in place. When the President of the Twelve, John Taylor, came forward, all turned to hear him. He was now the Acting President of the Church since the death of their prophet less than a month before. A large stone, measuring six feet by four and a half, rested by the corner of the foundation behind him, and identical stones waited by each of the other corners, lying east to west, ready to be tipped into place on cue.

As President Taylor opened the meeting, Lizzy looked around, amazed at how many people had traveled to attend. She watched President Taylor, wondering how it felt to shoulder a responsibility like leading the Church. Someday he would be sustained as the prophet, just as President Young had been. He was a man of significance, and she was glad she had the chance to see him up close.

Although he was getting on in years—Lizzy guessed he was somewhere near seventy—he didn't seem frail. She liked the bright white of his hair and wondered what he would look like if he grew his beard long like President Young had.

When President Taylor finished his remarks, he stood aside and gave the signal to Brother Parry. Assisted by several men, Brother

Parry pushed the stone so it fell nearly flush with the ground. Brother Angell helped the men shift it into exactly the right place.

"Very good," President Taylor said. The men lined up again, and President Taylor launched into a speech about the temple and what wonderful things lay in store for it. Lizzy looked up where the temple's walls would one day stand and tried to picture what it would look like. She wondered what kinds of things would happen inside.

After Franklin D. Richards gave a dedicatory prayer, President Taylor addressed the gathering again. "We will now be favored to hear from the choir, which will sing, 'Come All Ye Saints throughout the Earth, Your Cheerful Voices Raise.'"

Several minutes later, as the choir finished, Jimmy began squirming. Apparently forgetting about his buttoned lips, he murmured, "Is it over yet?"

Matthew seconded the sentiment. "When can we go to the circus?"

Abigail pointed at the corners of the temple foundation. "There are three other stones to be laid. Be patient." But even as she gently chastised the boys, her worried glance at David revealed her fear that this was too tiring for him and that they might need to take him home early.

"Will the procession please reform and follow us to the southwest corner?" President Taylor called over the crowd.

"How are you feeling, David?" Abigail whispered.

David looked up with a weak smile and squeezed her hand. "I feel really good."

"You aren't too cold or tired?"

"Don't worry, Mother. I can always rest later. I don't want to miss this. After all, I'll never have another chance to see a prophet."

Abigail wanted to contradict him, to insist that he would live plenty long and have other opportunities to see leaders of the Church if he so chose, but at that moment, President Taylor stood to conduct the next portion of the meeting. This time the Presiding Bishopric laid the stone in place with the necessary help from Brother Angell and Brother Parry. Presiding Bishop Hunter spoke, followed by a prayer and another song by the choir.

For the third time they regrouped, then marched to the northwest corner of the temple to repeat the dedicatory process. As the family took their place in front, Lizzy noticed a young man standing about five rows behind them and to the left. He seemed about her age or a little older. His long, black hair was tied in back, and his skin was a few shades darker than she was used to seeing. Except for his clothes, he looked like an Indian.

The young man watched the ceremony with a certain level of detachment, almost like he had come out of curiosity. Then as if he could feel her gaze, he looked over at her. A smile broke over his face, and Lizzy flushed, quickly turning away. Her mother followed Lizzy's stare and started in surprise, then inched ever so slightly away. The action made Lizzy realize that there was more room around the boy than anywhere else in the crowd, and she wondered if it was because he looked different.

Following the third stone's placement was another talk, prayer, and song, none of which held Lizzy's attention. Instead, she kept stealing glances at the boy behind her. Between looks, his dark hair and eyes didn't leave her mind, and the memory of his smile made her cheeks warm.

President Taylor directed the group to gather and march to the northeast corner for the laying of the final stone. A few children around them could be heard murmuring in complaint.

"Mother, haven't they done enough talking already? I'm dying to get to the circus," a young boy of nine or ten whispered rather loudly.

"Joseph, this is an historic moment. You will listen and keep quiet, or you will not be going to the circus at all."

"But it's already been so *long*."

His mother patted his shoulder. "I know it's hard to sit still and listen. But years from now you'll remember that you were one of the few who witnessed the cornerstone dedication of the Logan Temple. You will never forget it."

"I'll remember how long it was," he said with a moan.

His mother ruffled his hair. "Hush now."

The last stone was laid by the First Presidency of the Seventy and several elders quorum presidents. After President Rockwood spoke, Horace Eldredge offered the prayer, making special mention of the masons. More than one member of Lizzy's family paid close attention to his prayer, and Lizzy cracked her eyes open to look at her father, his face lined with concentration as if he were trying to commit the words to memory.

She listened more carefully then: "We pray that these cornerstones may be immovable," Brother Eldredge prayed. "May the masons who have charge of the erection of these walls connect this cornerstone with the others already set and laid in such a manner as no workman ever need be ashamed of . . . "

After the choir sang again, Jimmy clapped his hands. "Circus time!"

Lizzy grabbed his hand and pulled him to her. "Hush, Jimmy."

"You mean it's not circus time?"

"Not yet."

Jimmy gave a long, audible sigh. While Lizzy was embarrassed, she could sympathize. The meeting had already run a bit long. Little did she know that seven more speakers would follow. President Taylor began talking again, and Lizzy glanced behind her. But she did not see the young man anywhere. She even raised up and looked around, but to no avail.

A bit disappointed, Lizzy turned back as Wilford Woodruff stepped forward to speak. At first her thoughts kept returning to the young man, but at some point during the speech she began listening, and what she heard suddenly began to impress her.

"If our eyes were opened so that we could see those around us who are witnessing these proceedings more intently and anxiously than we are," Elder Woodruff said, "where we now behold one, there would be hundreds of thousands. The hosts of the spirits of men rejoice when the foundation and every stone of the temple is laid; for they well know, in their prison homes, that their salvation depends upon these things."

Lizzy looked around, as did several other people in the congregation, as if she might see the spirit beings Elder Woodruff spoke of. She glanced at her mother, whose eyes had misted. She was probably thinking about those she'd left behind on her journey to Zion, many of whom had passed away years ago. Lizzy sighed, wishing she could feel what her mother felt for the gospel, even for a moment. The words were beautiful, but she didn't have the stirring in her heart that her parents talked about.

Some of Elder George Q. Cannon's words paralleled Elder Woodruff's. "Every foundation stone that is laid for a temple, and every temple completed, lessens the power of Satan on the earth," he said, his voice rich and firm, "and increases the power of God and godliness, moves the heavens in mighty power in our behalf, invokes and calls down upon us the blessings of eternal Gods and those who reside in their presence."

Lizzy looked behind the Church leaders at the foundation of the temple while the speakers' words repeated themselves in her mind. Could a building really have power like Elder Cannon said? Were thousands of angels really gathered here as Elder Woodruff claimed? She glanced around, wishing she could see such things, then sighed. Perhaps her mother could see them. Or David. She just didn't have a connection to heaven that way.

* * *

Abe left the cornerstone ceremony early and headed for the big top. He had money in his pocket and intended on having some fun before returning to work tomorrow. As he sat in the big top and watched animals parading around, he heard a loud voice.

"Look, Lizzy. Popcorn."

Abe turned and saw the girl from the ceremony, the pretty one with big brown eyes. So her name was Lizzy, he mused. She was surrounded by younger children tugging at her sleeve.

"Can we get some?" a boy of maybe twelve begged. The other children chimed in. "Please, Lizzy?"

"Everyone sit down first," she said. Rather noisily, they all found seats as Lizzy consulted the coins in her hand. "I'll see if I can buy some popcorn."

"Can I have my own bag?" a tall young man asked. Abe's brow furrowed. The speaker looked like a young man, but he acted like a child.

"Me too," another voice piped up. "I don't want to share with him." This one jabbed a boy—presumably his brother—in the ribs with his elbow.

Lizzy grinned at their excitement. "If I have enough money, I'll get each of you your own bag, including you two, Mary and Sarah. Your parents were kind enough to give us some extra money." She flagged down the vendor and asked how much for five bags of popcorn. When she counted out her coins, her face fell. "I'm afraid some of you will have to share," she said. "Three bags, please."

Easily climbing over two benches, Abe reached the aisle and took the steps two at a time. "Four bags," he said when he reached her. "I have enough for one more."

She turned and seemed to recognize him. He wasn't sure, but he thought the tips of her ears turned pink. Shaking her head, she said, "Oh, I couldn't—"

"Of course you could." He dug into his pocket for some money, paid the vendor, then handed the group one more bag, which the girl named Mary promptly let her younger sister have, then scooted a bit closer to the boy Matthew, gazing at his popcorn.

"W—would you like some of mine?" he asked, holding it toward her.

"Yes, thank you, Matthew," Mary said, blushing. "You're a real gentleman."

Abe suppressed a smile at the sight.

"Thank you," Lizzy said, drawing his attention back to her.

He made a slight bow. "It was my pleasure, Miss . . . ?"

"Sullivan. Elizabeth Sullivan." She gave a small curtsy. "But it's usually 'Lizzy.'"

"Nice to meet you, Miss Sullivan. I'm Abraham Michael Franklin. Friends call me Abe."

"I don't think I've seen you before today. Are you new to the area?" Lizzy asked.

"You could say that," Abe said. "I grew up mostly in Salt Lake City, and now I'm here for work."

"Mostly?" she asked, sitting on the bench and moving over to make room for Abe. "Where did you live before that?"

Abe hesitated. His childhood wasn't something he discussed with strangers, but it was pretty obvious to others that he wasn't a run-of-the-mill white man. "I'm Shoshone," he explained. "I lived with my tribe until I was four, when a family adopted me."

"You're adopted?" Lizzy asked with clearly increasing interest.

"I know, it's not all that common in these parts." Abe paused, not really wanting to share the unpleasant details. But somehow this Lizzy girl seemed different than the other Mormon girls. He eyed her for a moment and decided to tell her part of his past, just to see what her reaction would be.

Abe grinned. "Apparently my mother was trying to flee my father—with another man. My father threatened to kill both of us. As she fled through Salt Lake City, she found a family to take me. They paid a pony and two blankets for me, if I remember correctly."

Lizzy leaned back and sized him up, deciding whether to believe him.

Abe raised a hand in the air as if making a promise. "It's the truth. As you Mormons would say, I was born Lamanite, raised a Gentile. But that's not because my father didn't try to convert me."

"You were never baptized?"

Abe shrugged. "Nope. And that's the irony. My father always said he took me in to save a heathen. Never did work. Pity. I suppose I'll never be saved now."

Lizzy laughed, and he grinned at her reaction. After a few more words they watched the circus for a few minutes, then he looked over, a playful smile toying at the corners of his mouth. "Aren't you embarrassed at being seen with a heathen?"

She returned his look and replied with a challenging tone, "Should I be?"

"I doubt your parents would approve."

"Should that matter?"

Now it was Abe's turn to laugh as they turned back to watch, but he couldn't keep himself from smiling for the rest of the circus. This Lizzy was powerful different. Different like a breath of fresh air.

CHAPTER 8

Lizzy was pleasantly surprised to have Abe accompany her on the way home, and she noticed that Mary Webster made a point of walking beside Matthew. "Thanks for sharing your popcorn with me," Mary said, lowering her eyelashes.

"You're welcome," Matthew answered, then turned to Aaron and continued their nonstop chatter about the circus. Aaron declared that the bird act was his favorite, while Matthew insisted that the acrobats' tricks were more exciting. Jimmy was undecided between the horse riders and the monkeys, but admitted he liked all the colors the clowns wore.

Lizzy and Abe walked several feet behind the group, quietly laughing at Mary's futile attempts at gaining Matthew's attention. They also discovered a mutual liking for books and began comparing favorite titles and authors. To Lizzy's horror, Abe had never read Charles Dickens or Mark Twain.

"I'm hoping that my aunt in New York will send me some new books soon, maybe for Christmas," she said. "And if she does, you can borrow them."

"And you can read anything in my *meager* library," Abe offered, pretending offense at her shock over his incomplete literary training.

"If you don't have Dickens or Twain, then what *do* you have?" Lizzy countered with a teasing grin.

"Mostly books my mother gave me before I left home," Abe said, suddenly sober. Distracted by his sudden mood change, Lizzy missed her step, and their shoulders brushed together. She flushed and was grateful when Abe went on. "Do you like poetry? I have a couple of poetry books."

"Oh, I do," Lizzy said, her eyes lighting up. "Tennyson is my favorite."

Abe squinted in thought. "Don't think I have any Tennyson. But I've got a volume with Milton."

"I love Milton," Lizzy said with a clap of her hands. "I've read *Paradise Lost* several times, although I'm afraid my parents would be shocked if they knew that I enjoy the parts in hell a lot more than those in heaven. They're so much more interesting."

Abe kicked a rock and asked with a twinkle in his eye, "What about Shakespeare? You've heard of him, haven't you?"

"Of course I have," Lizzy said. "I had a book of his sonnets that I've read more times than I can remember." She didn't mention the fact that she hadn't read any of Shakespeare's plays, although she had seen one performed once; she didn't want to sully his opinion of her. The thought of her dog-eared book of sonnets brought a twinge of sadness, and she realized she had high expectations about Aunt Louisa's continued generosity. Of course, even if Aunt Louisa gave the books to appease her guilt over leaving Jimmy, Lizzy wouldn't look the gift horse in the mouth—especially not now.

The group came to the lane that led home, and the younger ones turned down it. Lizzy slowed her step. "I suppose this is where we say good-bye."

Abe stopped, but before saying good-bye he asked, "So this is where you're staying?" and nodded toward the house in the clump of trees.

Lizzy looked over her shoulder. "Until we find a place of our own. We don't know how long that will be." She sighed. "Well, thanks again for the popcorn. And for walking me home."

Abe tilted his head and touched his hat. "My pleasure. Could I see you again sometime?"

"You'll have to if I'm ever going to read any of Spenser's work," Lizzy said, grinning as she brought up one of Abe's favorite writers.

"Your parents won't mind?" Abe asked, glancing at the house.

Lizzy answered a bit too quickly. "Oh, you don't need to worry about them."

Abe's eyebrows rose. "Are you sure?"

"Sure I'm sure," she said with an awkward laugh.

Abe folded his arms and studied her. "But I'm a heathen. From what I've heard, Mormon folk don't like their youth mixing outside the faith in case it leads to the altar."

She couldn't tell if he was joking. All the same, she dismissed the idea with a wave. "There's no need to worry about that. I plan on going to college in New York, perhaps becoming a teacher myself. I don't plan on ever marrying, unless—" Lizzy almost clapped a hand to her mouth; she had almost described the man she envisioned for herself—and that man strongly resembled Abe.

"Oh really?" Abe cocked his head. "That sounds like a challenge."

Lizzy laughed. "I wouldn't be placing any bets if I were you." She turned and headed down the lane, moments later slowing her steps to steal a glance over her shoulder. Abe still stood at the end of the lane. Moments later he waved, then turned and walked away. Lizzy couldn't stop smiling.

She didn't notice that Mary had waited for her and set to walking beside Lizzy. "How do you do it?" she asked in a conspiratorial whisper. "I saw you walking with that boy back there. How do you do it?"

"How do I do what?" Lizzy asked, tearing her thoughts away from Abe.

"How do you get boys to notice you?" Mary looked back toward the road. "Abe likes you. I can tell."

Lizzy glanced in the direction Abe had gone. "You think so?" She thought of Matthew, the object of Mary's affections, and wondered what helpful advice to give. He didn't look at girls that way yet, and even if he did, the two were both far too young to be thinking of courting. Not that she and Abe would ever court, she quickly reminded herself.

"How can I get a boy to notice me?" Mary asked again.

With an arm around Mary's shoulders, Lizzy said, "At your age, the last thing you need to worry about is catching boys' eyes. That will come soon enough"

"Not for *years*," Mary said of the lifetime she envisioned between her current age and her courting years.

"If I were you, I would enjoy being young. You know, the older you get, the more responsibilities you'll have. Extra chores, less time for play."

Mary considered. "I suppose," she said, clearly unconvinced. She watched Matthew walk around to the back door. When she couldn't see him anymore, she sighed. "But sometimes the heart can't wait for the years." With another sigh filled with of the woe of ten years' maturity, she followed the rest of the group into the house.

When Lizzy came through the door, Jimmy and the twins were in the parlor, relating every detail of their afternoon. In the final analysis, the highlight for Jimmy had apparently been the popcorn. He even kept the bag to show everyone.

"You had enough money for popcorn?" Abigail asked as she threaded her needle.

Jimmy tucked the bag into his pants. "Only for three bags, and there were five of us. But an Indian boy bought us another one. So I got one all to myself."

Lizzy held her breath. Her mother's face drained, and Abigail seemed particularly intent on her mending. "What's this Jimmy is telling me, Lizzy?"

"It was nothing, Mother. Just a boy I saw at the cornerstone dedication who happened to be at the circus as well." Perhaps mentioning the services would cast Abe in a better light, she reasoned. "He offered to buy an extra popcorn. He's nice."

"How old is he?" her mother asked.

"My age, I think," Lizzy said, noticing increased worry cross her mother's face.

"And he's an Indian?" Abigail's lighthearted tone sounded forced.

"Born, but not bred. He was adopted by a Mormon family in Salt Lake City as a child."

Abigail nodded. "I've heard of some families doing that. It has often led to problems. Some Indian children have betrayed their adopted families in the worst ways imaginable. I hear one killed his mother." She paused. "But I suppose if he's a member he might not be like that."

Lizzy didn't say anything to correct the assumption and instead stepped toward the bedroom. "I'm going to see David. I promised to tell him about the circus." She walked out of the room, her heart beating hard, a heavy feeling inside. She hadn't outright lied to her mother, but she had willfully let her believe something other than the truth. But if her mother knew the truth about Abe's Church membership, Lizzy knew she wouldn't be allowed to see him again. She knew how strongly her parents felt about relationships outside the faith—and how much her mother distrusted Indians because of something that happened on the way to Zion, something her mother rarely spoke of. Lizzy didn't know the details, except that Indians were responsible for the death of her uncle and cousin.

When she entered the room, David lay on her parents' bed instead of the cot, with the dog at his side again. When he saw Lizzy, his face lit up. "You're back! Tell me all about it." He patted the bed beside him. The dog's tail thumped in reaction to David's excitement.

"I thought Sister Webster didn't want him in the house," Lizzy said. She scratched the dog behind the ears, winning a few thumps of her own as reward.

Sophie settled her head onto David's leg and closed her eyes. He kept on petting her. "I overheard Sister Webster telling Mama that Sophie can come inside as much as I want while we're here. She thinks it might help me get well. Mama says Sophie seems gentle enough now, so she agreed."

David's face always lit up at the sight of Sophie, and he seemed to have much more strength the past week. "I think Sophie's already helping you get well," Lizzy said, brushing some hair out of David's eyes. Sweet Sister Webster, sacrificing her house to dog fur and dog smells in the name of helping her little patient.

"Mama promised that if tomorrow is good weather I can go outside and watch Sophie play. I hope it isn't too cold." David pulled his blanket higher. "Were there any animals at the circus?"

"There were *loads* of animals."

His eyes grew round, his little mouth opening into a small circle. Lizzy spun tales about the circus, painting each act in as much detail as she could to re-create it for David. She couldn't remember everything; she missed some of the clowns and trapeze artists, she realized later. But after all, she had been a bit distracted by Abe. But David didn't seem to notice anything amiss in her narrative.

When Lizzy finished, he snuggled into his covers. "Thanks, Lizzy. Now I can close my eyes and see the whole thing." He yawned.

She decided it was her cue to leave. As she stood, her mother called from the sitting room.

Lizzy looked over her shoulder. "Yes, Mother?"

"Could you come here for a few minutes, please?"

She kissed David's forehead and scratched Sophie behind the ears, then closed the door. "What is it?" she asked, hoping her mother would ask her to do some chore, but having a sinking feeling that the conversation would be about Abe.

Abigail didn't give Lizzy any tasks. She sat on the rocking chair, gently pushing herself back and forth with one foot as she darned a pile of socks. Lizzy looked around. They were very alone. The children had all scattered to enjoy what little good weather was left before they would be cooped up in the house during the winter months.

"Please sit down."

Lizzy complied, her stomach twisting slightly as she waited for her mother to continue.

"What's this boy's name?" she asked.

Lizzy ran her fingers along the polished grain of the seat. "Who?" She knew full well who her mother referred to, but wanted to make her meeting with Abe seem as harmless as possible—as innocent as it was, she reminded herself.

"That Indian boy at the circus. What's his name?"

Lizzy wanted to say again that she had first seen him at the cornerstone dedication, but she resisted. "Abe Franklin."

"Which ward does he attend?"

"I don't know," Lizzy stammered. She had never lied to her mother before. Her hands dropped to her lap. "Mother, that's not entirely true."

"You *do* know which ward he attends?"

"He has never been baptized."

"Humph. So his name is Abe, is it?" Abigail said. She poked a sock rather harshly with a needle, as if it were merely his name that bothered her. "Lizzy, I forbid you to see him again."

"Please don't do that, Mother. What is so horribly wrong about seeing him? I've been so lonely since the fire, and now that I might have a new friend, you want me to never see him again?" She sat on the edge of her chair, leaning close to her mother as she pled her case. Abigail didn't seem to notice. She kept jabbing the sock with the needle, drawing the thread through roughly.

"You just met him. It should be simple to end a friendship before it ever takes root."

"But *why?* We could become good friends."

"He couldn't be *just* a friend. He's a boy."

"Why should that make any difference? Joshua Sorensen is a boy. You never worried about my friendship with him."

"Of course I didn't." Abigail began talking blindly, her thoughts spilling out one atop another. She sewed quick, nervous stitches as she spoke. "For one thing, Joshua isn't an Indian. He comes from a faithful Latter-day Saint family. And if you would have opened your eyes years ago, you wouldn't be the last person to figure out that Joshua loves you. He told us himself that—"

Abigail's voice cut off suddenly.

"What did you say?" Lizzy asked. Her hands gripped the edges of the chair, and her heart began pounding.

Abigail's gaze locked on hers, then fell to her work. "Nothing. Just that Joshua is a good man." She stammered something about needing to check on David, then excused herself.

Lizzy stayed behind, stunned at the information her mother had just dropped in her lap.

Did Joshua Sorensen really love her?

CHAPTER 9

Lizzy could not stop thinking about Joshua and her mother's words. As she sat at David's bedside one afternoon, reading one of Brother Webster's books aloud but not hearing the story, she recalled her assurances that she and Joshua would still see each other and write often. How wrong she'd been.

She missed him and meant to write as she had promised, but the revelation about his feelings haunted her. What could she say in a letter now that she knew his true feelings? Each time she had tried to put pen to paper, her mother's words repeated themselves in her mind, making it impossible to write to him as a friend. Her words were invariably strained and horridly proper, and the result was stilted and trite. She tore each attempt into shreds. Wincing each time at the waste, she eyed how many more sheets of stationary remained and knew she couldn't go on like that.

Lizzy released David's hand to turn a page. The paper was crisp, and when she opened the book the spine still cracked. Yet the volume was quite old. It didn't take long for Lizzy to see why it was in such remarkable condition—the book wasn't particularly interesting. No wonder her mind wandered. She heard a movement behind her and glanced over her shoulder. Abigail stood in the doorway, having just returned from errands.

"He's doing better today," Lizzy told her mother. "He ate most of his dinner."

Abigail eyed her small son and the shaggy dog beside him, now a common feature of the room. A smile curved her lips. "I'm glad. I think he'll be over it soon."

"Was there any mail?" Lizzy asked absently, turning back to her book before hearing a response. The family didn't receive much mail, and Lizzy didn't expect today to be any different, though her mother had been expecting a letter from Aunt Louisa.

"Yes, actually." Abigail paused awkwardly. "This arrived for you." She held out an envelope addressed to "Beth Sullivan."

"For me?" Lizzy noticed her mother's hesitance. She took the envelope and felt a thin, hard object inside. But it was the writing that sent her heart suddenly beating. She would recognize Joshua's handwriting anywhere. And he was the one person who called her *Beth*.

"I think I'll go find a quiet place to read this." She knew her mother would understand her need to be alone. Lizzy stopped at the door and turned around. "Thank you, Mama."

"You're welcome, Lizzy."

Abigail watched her daughter go, then leaned against the door-frame and folded her arms as she sighed. She had wondered all the way home from the post office whether she had made a huge blunder in mentioning Joshua. After all, the boy had only hinted at how he felt toward Lizzy. Perhaps she had read too much into his words.

Then Abigail remembered the "Indian boy," as she mentally referred to him, and shook her head. She hoped and prayed that her comments about Joshua hadn't ruined his chances with her daughter, that she hadn't all but pushed Lizzy into that Indian boy's arms. Granted, such thoughts were rather hasty, but one couldn't be too cautious when it came to matters as grave as matrimony.

* * *

Lizzy walked through rows of poplars at the side of the house, wishing that she could seclude herself in her old bedroom where she could lock her door tight and sit by the window to read Joshua's words. But these trees would have to do, she reckoned. At least they would provide some privacy. She sat on the ground with her back to the house and leaned against a thick maple trunk. She stared at the unopened letter. What had Joshua written?

Would he be hurt at not hearing from her? She couldn't bear it if her closest friend were angry with her. Would he suspect that she knew of his true feelings? Or would he profess them?

With shaky fingers, Lizzy opened the letter, which was several pages long. The object she'd felt fell out, and Lizzy laid eyes on a key scarred from fire. It was from the box Joshua had given her for her birthday a year before. She ran her fingers across the blackened metal and wrapped them around it, then thumbed through the pages of the letter. The first was written in neat script, but the last sheet was a mess. Lizzy smiled to herself. *How like Joshua.* His handwriting had never been all that good, even in their early school years. He could make it look neat enough when he really tried, but if he was rushed or excited, his penmanship turned into hen scratchings, and the reader had to squint to make out his meaning.

Not two sentences into the epistle, Lizzy was laughing aloud. His letter was nothing but good old Joshua. He told of his plans to find his own place soon, and how his mother insisted he learn a few house-keeping skills he would need as a bachelor. He related every detail, such as making the stove too hot and scorching everything he tried to cook.

Then he described the goings on of the Sorensen house, still full with his brother's family. His nieces and nephews had gotten into scrapes that closely resembled mishaps Lizzy and Joshua had experienced at the same age, and she couldn't stop smiling while reading about them.

All in all, his letter contained everything Lizzy could have asked for. She could almost hear Joshua's voice as she read his words, could almost see his gestures as he told a story—including the crooked smile that appeared whenever he laughed.

My brother George has heard about a place in central Utah, called Scofield, where there is a lot of coal. He's going down to help get the mine set up and, with any luck, make some good money. I'll be going down there with him for the next few months to build their house while Ida and the children stay here. I am counting on getting letters from you so I won't get too homesick.

Lizzy leaned her head against the tree trunk and sighed. She knew that even with Joshua in town they wouldn't see as much of each other as they used to. But having him actually out of the area, a couple hundred miles away, made the loss more profound. She felt determined anew to keep up her end of the letter writing.

Joshua didn't mention the key until the last paragraph, where his writing was scarcely legible.

Beth, you know I tried to save your house. I'm sorry I couldn't. I've been back several times trying to find something that you might like to keep, something that made it through the fire. I found what was left of your keepsake box and discovered this inside. I had hoped to find your necklace, but had no luck. I know what I did find isn't much, but I hope it helps.

He closed the letter asking for her to reply soon, then signed it, *All my love, Joshua.*

Lizzy swallowed hard, knowing that the final phrase meant more than she was supposed to be aware of. The letter fell into her lap, and she stared at the tree branches above her, now growing bare as their colored leaves had fallen to the ground. She would have to write to Joshua, but what could she say?

She looked over a few passages again, reread the account of the stove and chuckled. If she kept the letter at her side, she should be able to keep her tone like his. She would simply have to erase her mother's words from her mind. After all, her mother might be mistaken. She looked at the key. Joshua knew her well. It was so like him to send it to her, knowing it would be a comfort. She would keep it safe around her neck on the golden chain.

That evening as she dried dishes, Lizzy's thoughts wandered from Joshua's letter to Abe. She wondered if he would ever come by like he had promised—and what her mother would do if he did. Their friendship would be entirely harmless. What could a few friendly chats about books hurt? After all, she had nearly exhausted the Webster family's library, such as it was. But her mother had forbidden her to see him again.

The dishrag in Lizzy's hand drooped a bit. She stacked the stoneware dish on top of the others, letting out a deep sigh as she did so.

"My poor Lizzy."

Lizzy turned to see her father leaning against the doorframe. "Hi, Papa. I was just finishing up in here."

He came into the kitchen. "I know the move has been harder on you than anyone." She tilted her head down so her father would not see the sudden tears forming in her eyes. "Mama said you got a letter from Joshua," he continued. "I'd wager that didn't help your feeling homesick any. It must be mighty strange not to have your nose in your books. Even Jimmy's started to complain about not hearing you read to him lately. He misses it."

"So do I," Lizzy said, almost in a whisper. At times in the past, Jimmy's begging for her to read to him had been an annoyance. Today she would give almost anything to share one of her own books with him.

"I told Brother Webster about the dilemma, and the two of us did something about it."

Lizzy's head came up. "You did?" A flutter of hope went through her middle.

A smile spread across his face. "Come with me."

Lizzy followed her father outside, where he picked up a lantern from the ground and led her to the barn. He pushed the door open, where Brother Webster stood inside, trying hard to conceal a grin.

"If you'd be so kind, please open this," he said, pointing to a package wrapped in brown paper and string.

Lizzy took a step forward and sat beside the bundle. She slowly opened the parcel, holding her breath and hardly daring to hope for what she wanted to find inside.

"Oh, Papa!" Lizzy's hands flew to her mouth. She threw her arms around him, kissed his cheek hard, and squeezed him again. Richard stumbled back a step, then laughed and held his daughter tightly. Inside were four books: *A Tale of Two Cities, Little Women,* a poetry anthology, and Milton's collected works.

"Thank you, Papa. You too, Brother Webster," she said, pulling back and picking up her books. She held them close and took a deep breath to smell the paper and leather. "You have no idea how much this means to me."

Richard smiled. "I think we might have a little idea. We got these special from Salt Lake, and we've written to your aunt and asked her to send a few more as an early Christmas present."

Lizzy's eyes widened. "More? I can hardly wait." Sitting down on the hay bale, she flipped through one book and then another. Where to begin? She would start *Little Women* over again with Jimmy. They had just begun it when the family left for the funeral. She would let Abe borrow the Dickens book if they ever managed to see each other again. And she would go through Milton's works immediately.

The next few days were the happiest Lizzy had experienced since the fire. She had less time with her books than she would have liked, but being able to read her own volumes, even a few minutes at a time, made all the difference. The prospect of getting more only added to her joy. She often propped up a book so she could read while doing chores, or carried one place to place as she walked. She quickly finished Milton's works and began the poetry book, and Jimmy loved every minute that Lizzy read to him from *Little Women.*

Amid all this, however, one concern hung over her head—the need to finish a letter to Joshua. She had put the key on her chain, and it rested under her dress every day in safekeeping. And his letter was always close at hand, tucked inside a book to mark her place, reminding her of their promise to write.

* * *

Abigail peeled potatoes in the kitchen while Laura Webster churned butter. They worked in silence save for the rhythms of their respective work, but soon Abigail's thoughts plagued her long enough that she couldn't keep quiet.

"Do you remember what Richard said about the temple workers?" she asked.

Laura looked up from the churn, hesitating. "What part do you mean?"

"About the . . . the Indian workers," Abigail said, not looking at Laura. She focused on cutting a deep eye from a potato.

"Yes, I heard what he said," Laura said in a noncommittal tone.

"What do you think of it?" Abigail stopped cutting for a moment and braced herself for Laura's answer. Abigail struggled with the wisdom of Church leaders in using Indian workers for the house of the Lord, but at the same time Richard was right—these men had nothing to do with her brother-in-law's death. Then why did she feel so hostile?

"I'm not sure how I feel about it," Laura said. "I don't think I'd feel all too easy walking around the temple block with them there, to be honest, and I'm a mite ashamed to say so. It doesn't seem too Christian, does it?"

"They *are* heathens," Abigail pointed out.

"True, but they haven't caused any problems in these parts for years."

Abigail grabbed the next potato and began hacking at it nervously. "Do you think it's true that they're descendants of the Lamanites?"

Laura shrugged. "I suppose."

"And if Lamanites really were cursed . . ." Abigail's voice trailed off. She couldn't quite get herself to say that these people deserved to be treated poorly because of the sins of their fathers, even if she wanted to.

Laura sighed. "The way I see it, when the temple is dedicated, it won't really matter who built it."

"Yes, I suppose so," Abigail said, dropping a potato in the bowl and picking up the next one, settling into her work silently. She wasn't the only one with reservations. But that thought didn't exactly give her peace.

CHAPTER 10

One evening after both families had retired, Lizzy sat up finishing the last of her poetry collection. When she set it aside, she wasn't tired and didn't want to go to bed quite yet. Sometimes she enjoyed staying awake a little later than everyone else; it gave her some of the solitude she craved. She was tempted to start *A Tale of Two Cities,* but it was in the corner of the bedroom, and she couldn't get it without waking the family. Her eyes wandered, and soon her gaze landed on the writing table by the window. Sister Webster had frequently told them to help themselves to any paper and ink they wished.

She crossed the room and settled herself in the chair. After pulling out a few sheets of paper and the pen and ink, she wrote, "October 4, 1877, Webster Farm, Logan, Utah" at the top. After "Dear Joshua," she stopped, staring at the page and all the space below which she would have to fill. She unfolded his letter and read it for the hundredth time, then laid it on the desk. She swallowed hard and began.

First she answered Joshua's questions about the Websters and work on the temple. She wrote about the circus, although she didn't mention Abe. She soon was engrossed in her tales, and to her surprise, she easily filled three pages. She wrote, "Love, Beth" at the bottom, then blew the ink dry. She folded the letter, then sealed and addressed it. Tomorrow she would go downtown with Sister Webster, who had said something about needing to sell eggs and buy flour and material, and mail the letter.

The following morning Abigail was scrubbing at the laundry tub in the backyard when Lizzy approached to mention her plan.

"Mama, Sister Webster is going downtown today, and I was wondering—"

"That's right," Abigail interjected. She stopped and, keeping her sudsy hands from her face, brushed some hair out of the way with her arm. "The bottle of Lester's Liniment is gone. I need to give Sister Webster some money to buy another."

"Could I get it?" Lizzy asked. "Sister Webster is ready to go, and she said I can come along."

Abigail shook her head and returned to work. "Let her buy the liniment. We need your help today. The men and boys are out working on the hay harvest, so I need you here to do their other chores."

Lizzy glanced at the barn. She would probably be clearing out the cow and horse stalls, cleaning the chicken coop, feeding all the animals, and then some. She couldn't work as fast as the boys could, who were used to the tools and had done it so many times they could practically do it sleeping.

"But I was hoping to mail a letter to Joshua," Lizzy said. She held it up for her mother to see. "It's been over a week since he wrote. You said yourself I really needed to answer him."

Abigail paused over the laundry tub. She blew out heavily and looked over at her daughter. "You're right about the letter. It's about time you sent it to Joshua. But there is no reason that Sister Webster can't mail it for you."

"But—"

Abigail wiped her hands on a nearby rag and turned to face Lizzy. "Your father insisted this wouldn't happen, but I told him it would."

"What do you mean? Don't you want me to write to Joshua?"

Abigail placed a fist on one hip. "I mean that ever since your father and Brother Webster bought those books, you have been all but invisible around here. You take twice as long to do the simplest chore, and you sneak off at every possible chance to read. I need your help, Lizzy. So does Sister Webster. We all do. The men and boys aren't here today, and Sister Webster is already going to town, and now you want go mail a letter that someone else is perfectly capable of doing for you."

Lizzy hesitated. She really wanted to go herself. What if Sister Webster forgot? What if the letter got lost? Of course, Lizzy also wanted to get away and spend a little time at the stores on Main Street. It sounded horribly selfish when she thought of it that way. But her mother was treating her like a child. Lizzy imagined her old friends having to bow to the whims of their mothers. The idea was preposterous; they were ladies of their own homes now.

It wasn't as if Lizzy was unwilling to work for the family, but she felt the need to demand some respect. She stood taller and said, "Mother, I am informing you of my plans, not asking for permission. I will not be gone long, and upon my return I will do whatever work is needed. And I will buy the liniment for David as well." With that she spun on her heels and walked away.

"Elizabeth Sullivan! Get back here this instant."

Lizzy ignored her mother's voice and walked into the house. As the door shut behind her, she felt a tingle in her middle. She had never spoken to her mother that way before, had never defied her like that. On one hand, it felt good to take control, to stop acting like a timid child. At the same time, she knew her words and actions had hurt her mother, and for that she felt guilty. But it wasn't as if she were the ideal daughter; she disappointed her mother often enough, she realized, and couldn't spend all her time trying to be perfect.

Shaking her head, she went into the bedroom. She knelt beside the side table drawer and withdrew several coins from her parents' money jar, enough to pay for the liniment and postage. With a swipe at the wall hook, she grabbed her shawl and wrapped it around her shoulders.

"I'm ready, Sister Webster," she called, heading for the front door where her hostess was waiting. "Let's go."

The two women headed west for Main Street. Sister Webster had prepared a cold afternoon meal for the family ahead of time so Abigail wouldn't have to cook while they were gone.

As they walked, Sister Webster filled the silence with lighthearted chatter. "Mary and Sarah both need new dresses for winter, if you can believe it," she said. "They've outgrown their old ones, and with Sarah nearly as tall as Mary now, we can't just hand Mary's dresses down anymore. Not that I would want to this year—Mary's dress is a sight. It's in no condition for a body to wear. I have mended that thing until it's practically one big patch."

Lizzy nodded and smiled, but wasn't in a mood to chat. She could still hear her mother's stunned voice calling her back, and couldn't help but relive the moment over and over. Would she do it again? Did she regret it? She couldn't answer those questions, because each had at least two possible responses, and her final one was simply that she didn't know.

When they reached Main Street, they crossed the road and walked past several stores. Lizzy ran her hand along the worn wood of the hitching posts outside each store and looked through the windows at the harness shop and the furniture store, which had an awning on either side of the doorway. Lizzy had always enjoyed looking at the wares and smelling the different aromas—wood, leather, spices. They came to H. J. Christiansen's People's Store, where Sister Webster opened the door. Smells wafted out, and Lizzy thought of the lemon drops she and Joshua used to buy as children.

Sister Webster shifted her egg basket from one arm to the other. "I'll be a few minutes in here. After you mail your letter, you know where to find me."

"I need to buy some liniment for David," Lizzy said, stepping forward. "And besides, I'd like to look around." She enjoyed wandering around stores, eyeing the fabrics and picking out her favorites—imagining dresses made from them. Sister Webster turned toward the doorway as a young man came out. He reached over and held the door open for them, and Sister Webster hesitated when she glanced up and saw his long black hair and brown skin. She ducked inside and began talking with the woman behind the counter about prices for her eggs.

Lizzy's eyes flew open. "Abe!" The name choked out before she could stop it. She looked to Sister Webster, hoping she hadn't heard. If she did, Lizzy's mother would be sure to hear about it, especially since Sister Webster herself wasn't entirely comfortable with the idea of Indians working on the temple. But she was engrossed in her bartering and hadn't noticed. Lizzy's mind raced. So did her heart. She tried to not look directly at Abe, and instead focused on a knot in a plank. She took a step into the store.

"On second thought," she called to Sister Webster, "I think I could use some air. I'll take a stroll outside."

Sister Webster turned around and nodded. "Are you feeling well? You look a bit peaked."

"Oh, I'll be fine," Lizzy said, putting on a smile quickly. "Nothing some fresh air won't cure." She promised to meet back at the store soon and ducked outside, then motioned for Abe to follow. They hurried down the street, out of sight of the store's windows. Lizzy stopped abruptly and turned around. Abe nearly ran headlong into her but caught himself on a hitching post instead.

"Hello again, Miss Lizzy," he said with a tip of his hat. Her face broke into a huge smile.

"How do you do, Mr. Franklin?" she said with a curtsy. She was acutely aware of her cheeks burning, whether from hurrying away from the store so quickly or from seeing Abe again, she didn't know. He had nice eyes, she suddenly remembered. She had never seen any quite so dark.

Abe glanced over his shoulder and gestured behind them. "What was that about?"

"Well . . ." Lizzy turned around slowly and started walking. Abe followed as Lizzy mulled over what to say. "I need to mail a letter," she said abruptly, hoping to change the subject. She grimaced, turning over the letter so Abe wouldn't see Joshua's name and hoping he wouldn't ask about it.

"I'll walk with you," Abe said, continuing down the street with her. When Lizzy didn't say anything else, he spoke up. "So who is the letter for?"

Lizzy hid the envelope between folds of her skirt and tried to sound casual. "An old friend."

Abe nodded, then glanced over his shoulder at the store. "So what happened back there?"

She stopped and looked over her shoulder, hoping they had gone far enough down the street that Sister Webster couldn't see them. "I didn't want Sister Webster to see me talking to you, or she'd tell my mother. Mother doesn't want me to see you again."

Abe's mouth went hard. He shoved his hands into his pockets and began to nod. "Oh, so that's it. I thought you said that it didn't matter what your parents thought."

"I didn't realize there would be a problem. It doesn't matter to me, but you have to understand—my mother can't see that there's no need to worry about a friend who is . . ." She let her voice trail off, not wanting to say the words.

"Oh, I understand." Abe looked beyond Lizzy, avoiding her eyes. His voice was stony. "It's not everyone who can trust a heathen Indian. Don't worry. I won't be bothering you any more." He tipped his hat and moved to turn away.

On impulse, Lizzy reached for his shoulder. "Don't go. My *mother* doesn't want me to see you. That doesn't mean *I* don't."

Slowly, Abe turned to face Lizzy, one eyebrow raised. "What do you mean?"

"It means I'd like to be your friend. It means that I'd like to read those books you promised to lend me. And I've got one for you that's just waiting for you to come for it."

"What about your mother?"

"She would have a fit if she knew," Lizzy admitted. "At least at first. It would be better if I could get her used to the idea. We might need to see each other . . ." Lizzy searched for the word. "Privately."

Abe nodded, an odd glimmer in his eye. "Are you sure you want to go against her wishes? Wouldn't it be a *sin* or something?"

Lizzy smiled ruefully. "I'm not known for being a perfect daughter," she said. "Can you come tomorrow? Meet me in the grove on the east side of the house. I'm the only one who ever goes out there. You can bring me one of the books you told me about, and I'll lend you the Dickens novel I just got."

"How's two o'clock?"

Lizzy couldn't suppress a wide smile. "I'll see you then."

Abe tipped his hat and walked away with a casual gait as if he and Lizzy weren't planning anything, as if he hardly knew her. Lizzy watched him go, a fluttering sensation inside. Her thoughts were already on tomorrow afternoon. After all, she would get to read a new book by an author she had never read before.

And even better, she would get to see Abe again.

Lizzy took a step toward Christiansen's Store, her hands clasping in excitement. The envelope crinkled, and she remembered the letter. Laughing at herself for being so flustered, she hurried to the post office, then back to the store. Sister Webster came out just as Lizzy arrived.

"All set?" she asked.

Sister Webster nodded. "I'll have to show you the fabric I picked out for the dresses—light blue calico for Mary and a really pretty brown for Sarah."

"I'm sure the girls will love them," Lizzy said, reaching for the flour. "Here, let me carry that for you."

"Thank you," Sister Webster said, surrendering the sack.

The conversation as they walked back home was similar to their last, but for a very different reason. Once again Sister Webster did most of the talking, and Lizzy remained silent. Only, instead of feeling guilty for her actions toward her mother, she thought of Abe and wished she didn't have to wait till tomorrow to see him again.

When they reached the Webster farm, Abigail was waiting for them on the front step. Her arms were folded, her lips set into a straight line. Lizzy cleared her throat and braced herself as they stepped off the road and into the shade of the Webster trees. She shivered at the temperature change.

"Abigail, you should go to Christiansen's soon," Sister Webster said. "They have some wonderful material for a very reasonable price. Come see what I bought."

"I'll be right in," Abigail said, her voice terse.

Sister Webster looked from Abigail to Lizzy and must have sensed the tension, so without another word, she entered the house. Lizzy stayed outside, knowing her mother wanted to speak with her. But instead of a lecture, Abigail simply held out her hand.

"May I have the liniment and any remaining money please?"

The liniment.

Lizzy's stomach dropped. She had completely forgotten about it. If the envelope hadn't reminded her to go to the post office, she would have forgotten that too. "I—I—forgot," she stammered. "I'm so sorry, Mama." She held out the coins and dropped them into her mother's palm. Abigail looked at the money, then gave her daughter a final, stony look before walking back into the house.

CHAPTER 11

The following morning, Lizzy went about her chores quickly and without complaint. Her mother remained in icy silence for the most part, speaking only when needful. But Lizzy worked harder than normal for two reasons: first, to be sure her work would be done by two o'clock so she could meet Abe in the grove, and second, to soften her mother's anger.

Working at an increased pace also meant getting tired much more quickly. So by the time Lizzy had milked the cows, separated the milk, gathered the eggs, and cleared the breakfast dishes, the day already felt as if it had twice as many hours as normal. And the time continued to drag on. The hours would have been easier to bear if she and her mother could chat during chores as they normally did. Instead, Lizzy kept looking out the window to study the angle of the sun, still hours away from its zenith, and knowing it would be even longer before she could escape to the grove and meet Abe.

With her chores done early, Lizzy helped Jimmy practice his handwriting on a slate. "It's been so long," he said. "I hope I remember how to write my name."

"I'm sure you do," Lizzy said, glancing out the window for at least the hundredth time. Jimmy's mouth pinched tight as he dragged the chalk across the slate to create each letter. Finished, he smiled widely. Looking at the result of his efforts, he turned the slate so Lizzy could see it.

"Look!"

"Very good," she said with a pat on his back. "Now practice the rest of the alphabet."

Jimmy wiped the chalk off with his fist. "And then maybe we can write a whole story." He eyed his slate and scrunched up his mouth. "Only it might not all fit."

Lizzy worked with Jimmy for what felt like an eternity. She constantly checked the time and resisted the urge to go out into the grove. Finally Laura and Abigail came to the kitchen to prepare dinner. She sent Jimmy off to practice his *b*'s and *d*'s and put on an apron. Lizzy went to the cupboard, stealing yet another glance out the window. The sky was no longer bright blue. A layer of gray clouds covered it, masking the sun and making it difficult to sense what time it was.

As Lizzy began chopping vegetables, she pictured Abe's smile and got a flutter in her middle, followed by a knot as she thought of what would happen if her mother were to find out. Her hands fumbled, and she dropped a bunch of carrots onto the floor.

Abigail stooped to help Lizzy collect them. Their hands touched, and Lizzy looked up, afraid her mother would chastise her.

"I'll do it," her mother said. Her voice had a hint of tenderness, although it was still distant. "You look unwell. Go lie down."

Lizzy hardly knew what to say. She wasn't ill. Tired, perhaps, but not ill. "I'm fine, Mama," Lizzy said, taking the carrots and returning to the counter.

Standing up, Abigail nodded. "You—I mean, I—" she stammered, and she had to pause before continuing. "What I mean to say is thank you for working so hard today. After dinner, I'd like you to go out for some air—and perhaps some reading time."

Lizzy turned to her mother in surprise and gratitude. "Thank you, Mama."

Abigail cleared her throat nervously, then nodded and headed toward the stove to work on the meal. They said little else during the preparations or while the families ate. The strain between them was still very real, although lessened.

Inside, Lizzy could hardly contain her excitement. Her mother had practically handed her the perfect excuse to escape to the grove.

After the meal, Abigail was about to dismiss Lizzy from helping with the dishes when she peered out the window and shook her head. "I don't know if you should go outside after all, Lizzy. It looks like rain."

"I'll be fine," Lizzy said, surprised at her own abruptness. She wanted nothing to stop her from seeing Abe, but she didn't want another quarrel with her mother, either.

"I suppose it wouldn't hurt to go out, provided you come in the moment it starts raining."

"I will, Mama," Lizzy said, unable to conceal a smile.

Abigail glanced at the clock on the wall and shook her head. "On second thought, I want you back here in an hour. If you stay out longer you're sure to catch cold, and I need your help with the mending anyway."

"I'll be back before three o'clock. I promise," Lizzy said, then rushed to the bedroom and retrieved two books, one to read while she waited for Abe and *A Tale of Two Cities* to lend him. As she hurried outside, she hoped no one would notice which books she carried. She was leaving with two books, and if Abe brought her one to read, she would also be returning with two. As a precaution, Lizzy put the Milton on top rather than the Dickens.

She went as deep into the grove as she could, wishing that it were twice as large so she would be able to hide completely from the house. The sky was dark and cloudy, making Lizzy wrap the shawl around her shoulders a bit tighter. If it didn't get any colder, she would be fine.

It was fifteen minutes before two when she left the house, so Lizzy had to wait. Had the ground not been so damp, she would have sat down to read. Instead she walked in and out among the trees, gradually getting closer to the other side where she had a good view of the road. She opened her book, thinking she could immerse herself in it and pass the time quickly as she so often did. Not today. She tried. Three times. But she never finished more than a page without looking up and searching the road for a dark-haired figure that might be approaching.

Impatiently, Lizzy put the books under one arm so she could blow on her hands and stomp her feet. It was getting colder already. After pacing the length of the grove to keep warm, Lizzy turned back toward the road. It had to be two o'clock by now.

Finally, in the distance, she made out a form. She stopped and waited, her stomach jumping inside her. He noticed her too. Abe lifted his hat and waved it. She waved back, holding back the urge to call out his name. She knew better than to risk that. Instead, she glanced at the house just to make sure no one had come out.

When Abe reached her, a grin on his face, he held out a book. "Here it is," he said. "As promised—*Pride and Prejudice*." A dark lock of hair fell in his eyes, and he brushed it away. Once again Lizzy was struck with how dark his eyes were; she felt she could almost get lost looking into them.

She looked at her hands to break the spell, and produced her book. "*A Tale of Two Cities.*" As they swapped, their fingers touched, a thrill shooting up Lizzy's arm. But Abe's eyebrows furrowed, and he took her hand and held it tightly.

"You're cold," he said, placing the book under his arm and his other hand on top of hers.

"I've been out here for a while," she said sheepishly, halfheartedly trying to reclaim her hand. She would have been quite content to leave it in his for hours; never mind that her other one, holding the books, still felt like an icicle. Never mind that if anyone saw them it would create a stir, if not a scandal.

Abe put her arm through his own, his other hand still covering hers to keep it warm, and this way they strolled into the long rows of trees that Brother Webster had planted many years ago. "So this is where you live," he said.

"Not for long, I hope."

"Don't you like it?"

Lizzy shrugged with indecision. "In some ways I love it. The trees, the farm . . . the house is nice. But it's not *ours*. I can't pick flowers or plant a garden . . ."

"You couldn't do any of those things now anyway," Abe pointed out. "It's nearly winter."

Lizzy laughed. "You know what I mean."

As they strolled among the trees and talked, Lizzy lost track of the time. Her right hand was comfortably warm under Abe's, but gradually her left hand felt cramped and cold around the books. That was when she felt a heavy drop of water hit her head. Abe looked up and watched a few more drops, big ones that splashed in his palm. The sky was nearly black, and thick clouds rolled across the sky. Thunder sounded in the distance.

"You'd better go," Abe said. "You'll be drenched if you don't."

"What about you?" Lizzy asked. "How far do you live from here?"

"Don't worry about me." He glanced down at the book. "How long will it take you to finish that one?" he asked, a knowing smile playing across his features.

Lizzy grinned back. "Till next Thursday at two o'clock." She felt sure she could get away to meet Abe again by then, even though she knew the book would be finished long before that.

Abe brought Lizzy's hand close to his face and kissed the top of it, damp with raindrops. Lizzy caught her breath at the thrill of his touch. If her mother knew a boy had just kissed her . . .

"I'll see you Thursday, then." He tipped his hat as he always did before leaving, tucked the book under his coat, and ran away as raindrops fell harder.

The fingers of Lizzy's left hand covered her right. Despite the cold, she could still feel the warmth of Abe's kiss. With a sigh, she turned away, knowing that she had better get inside.

The ground was already getting muddy. As she picked her way between the trees, her shoes were soon covered and the hem of her dress soaked. Lighting flashed brightly in the sky, and a clap of thunder made her jump. She hugged the books to her chest and raced through the grove toward the house, not caring if her boots turned black from mud.

As Lizzy ran, she saw Brother Webster standing at the far end of the grove. She tried to stop quickly, but slipped in the mud and barely caught her balance against a tree branch.

"Brother Webster!" Hardly a sound came out, she was so out of breath. A look behind her confirmed that where she and Abe had been standing was in full view from that spot. She absently covered her hand. "How long—"

"Long enough," he cut in.

"Please don't tell Mama. He's a friend, and we're just lending each other books. But Mama's afraid of him because he's an Indian and not a member of the Church, and—"

Brother Webster raised his arm, and Lizzy's profusion stopped. "Your mother will find out sometime, Lizzy. You can count on that. I won't tell her today. But I also won't promise to never tell. I hope you'll do it yourself."

"Surely you aren't afraid of Indians, Brother Webster. You can't think my mother is right in hating them?"

"This isn't about love or hate. It's about honoring your parents, about being truthful."

"Please don't tell her."

Brother Webster sighed and slowly shook his head. "I won't. This time. But *you* should." He nodded toward the house. "Let's go inside. Your mother must be worried sick. She sent me out to find you. She couldn't come herself because David's fever is back."

"It is?" Lizzy picked up her skirts and rushed into the house. She hastily dropped her wet wrap and unlaced her boots by the door, then raced inside. Her mother was in the kitchen, filling a basin with water.

"Give me that cloth," Abigail ordered.

Lizzy jumped into action and handed it to her mother. "How is he?" she asked breathlessly.

Without an answer, her mother returned to David's cot, where he moaned incessantly. His face was red, his hairline dripping with sweat. Abigail dipped the washcloth into a bowl of water and squeezed out the excess before responding.

"I'm hoping he just overexerted himself today and that it's not the scarlet fever the Pickerings have." Abigail dabbed at David's forehead a few more minutes in silence, until her husband came in the door.

"I'm home early," he said. "It's too cold to work in the rain—" His voice cut off when he came into the bedroom and saw everyone gathered around David.

"Will you sit with him awhile?" Abigail wearily rubbed her forehead.

"Of course," Richard said, setting his tools down.

Abigail turned to Lizzy. "Come with me." Once in the parlor, Abigail's face changed, showing pain and frustration. "What do you have to say for yourself?"

Lizzy looked at her wet clothing. "I'll take care of the dress. I'll scrub out the stains, and the dress will be good as new. You'll see."

"That's not what I'm talking about, Lizzy. Why can't you see that? I need your help. We have two families living here and one very ill little boy. But I can't count on you anymore. When I wake up each morning I wonder if today you'll be forgetful, or distracted, or simply disobedient. Do you realize that last week you mixed the Websters' laundry with ours? Sister Webster was a mite embarrassed to say the least when her underclothes were mingled with your father's."

Abigail began pacing the room, tears now falling freely. "But that wasn't enough. Yesterday you outright *defied* me. I am your *mother,* and you treated me in that manner."

"You were treating me like a child," Lizzy countered. "I am a grown woman, Mother. And I will make my own decisions."

Her mother's jaw hung open for a moment as she processed what Lizzy had just said. Her brows came together. "You think you're acting like an adult? A woman fulfills her duties before seeking after her pleasures. A woman doesn't abandon her family and her work for an afternoon of fun."

"But what about today?" Lizzy countered. "I worked extra hard today. Does that count for nothing?"

"I am grateful for your dedication this morning. I feared you were working too hard, and that was why I thought you should have a moment to yourself." Abigail stopped and raised her hands. "And how do you repay my gesture? By staying out in the rain—as you said you wouldn't—and staying out twice as long as we agreed."

Lizzy glanced at the mantle clock.

"See?" her mother cried, pointing to the time. "Four thirty. Even without David's fever, I would have needed your help by now. Here, in the house. And when he is unwell I can't take care of everything else that needs attention. It is your duty, just as it is mine, to attend to the family."

Lizzy swallowed hard as guilt, anger, frustration, and hurt all clashed against each other. "I know all these things, Mother. You don't have to talk to me as if I were still a child," Lizzy pleaded.

Abigail shook her head and wagged a finger at Lizzy. "Well, you are certainly no woman, Elizabeth Sullivan. You are acting exactly like a child. And until you can see that, I will have to treat you as one."

"I'm sorry, Mother," Lizzy whispered, shame coursing through her.

"Sorry isn't good enough." She pointed to the books in her daughter's hands. Lizzy instinctively curled her fingers around them.

"No reading for a week." She nodded toward the mantle. "Please place your books beside the clock. I expect them to remain there."

Mother and daughter stared at each other. Lizzy fought the urge to refuse, to remind her mother that she was married at Lizzy's age. But she decided on a compromise. "Certainly I can promise not to open a single cover for a week without putting them on the mantle for supervision."

Abigail looked her daughter over and considered. "No. You have acted as a child and you will be treated as such. Put them on the mantle."

Lizzy hesitated a moment. Would acquiescence win back her mother's trust? Would it show that she was willing to be responsible?

"I promise to do more work around the house and to be more trustworthy," Lizzy said. Abigail's eyebrows went up in expectation, and Lizzy struggled to go on. "And I promise not to read a word from my books until Thursday next." She placed the books on the mantle, titles against the wall.

Lizzy stood, turned around, and walked out, standing taller than usual. She refused to sulk away like a beaten schoolgirl.

"Lizzy," Abigail called after her.

She waited for her mother to speak.

"This package arrived today," she said, placing a familiar brown, wrapped bundle on the fireplace mantle. "But I trust you will not open it until the full week is past."

Lizzy's stomach suddenly burned with anger. Her mother had purposely held back new books from Aunt Louisa until she extracted the promise. Lizzy had an unruly urge to rip the paper off the books and plop onto the sofa with one of them that very moment, wet dress and all. But she wouldn't act the part of the child. She would keep her promise, difficult as it would be with that package taunting her all week, making her wonder if her aunt had sent a few replacements of her old dear books or brand new titles she had never read.

"One week then," Lizzy said in her stateliest voice, in spite of the anger welling inside. She turned to the bedroom when her mother spoke again.

"Yes. One week. Unless I see reason to extend the period."

Lizzy braced herself on the doorframe. She took a deep breath to even out her emotions. She turned around and asked, "Is there anything I can do to help?"

"Get out of those wet clothes before you make a big puddle on the Websters' floor and catch cold. Then I'll let you know."

"Yes, Mother," Lizzy said. She closed the bedroom door, then sat on the bed and let out hot tears.

CHAPTER 12

Lizzy counted each day with impatience, waiting for when she would be able to see Abe again. More than once she was sorely tempted to crack the cover of Abe's book as it sat on the mantle, but she resisted. Next time they met, he would understand why she hadn't read it yet. *Next time.* Just the thought made her step lighter and helped her endure day after day of tension with her mother.

As the week went on, David's health improved little by little. His fever broke on Sunday, and by Tuesday, to everyone's relief, he felt quite well. He even had permission to go outside again, as it was an unseasonably warm early November day, and when winter arrived he would not be allowed outside at all.

Lizzy helped David get dressed and ready. She found a thick sweater and a comforter to bring along to make sure he kept warm. But as they headed for the back door, David stopped by the mirror and stood on his toes to look into it.

"We almost forgot my hair," David said, looking at the unruly mop in his distorted reflection.

"Of course," Lizzy said. She retrieved a comb and a mug of water. "I'm glad you remembered." She dipped the comb in the water, then worked at the tangles. Most of the time David didn't mind the mess his hair became from lying in bed days on end, but going outside was another story. He had to look "presentable," as he told Lizzy, something he had heard his mother say of herself more than once.

Lizzy made a part in one side and smoothed over the wet hair, grateful for every day she combed his hair, because that meant he was well enough to go outside. Every time she drew the comb through his brown locks meant her brother was stronger than he had been. She looked into the mirror and nodded in satisfaction. "You look handsome," she said, then leaned down and hugged him.

"Yes, I do," David said, eyeing his image.

"You look like the healthiest boy in town," Lizzy added, then crushed him in another hug.

"I am stronger. I can feel it."

Lizzy waved the comb at him. "Now don't overdo it outside. We want you to *keep* getting stronger, you know. No wrestling cows today."

David snickered. "I'll try to remember. Mother won't let me do any heavy chores anyway. Not until my 'cheeks are rosy.'"

"Good." Lizzy ruffled his hair affectionately, then laughed at the mess she had just made of it and combed it down again. "There you go."

"Thank you. Now I'm off to find Sophie. I haven't seen her since this morning."

"Not without your sweater," Lizzy said. She pulled it over his head, then handed him the quilt. "There you go."

As she watched him go out the back door, Lizzy felt a small worry creep into her heart. She and her parents credited much of David's recovery to Sophie's love and attention. They feared that David might respond poorly when the family no longer lived with the Websters and had to leave the dog behind.

Lizzy put the comb away and began straightening the cramped bedroom. She had yet to get used to sleeping on the floor or with so many others in the same room. Another quilt folded, she plopped it into the pile on the chair in the corner. "I cannot wait until I have a room of my own again," she said under her breath as she picked up the next worn blanket to fold. Now that the weather was turning cold—the first frost arrived a few days back—every spare covering in the house was being used at night. Today promised to be sunny, but in November, even a warm day could yield a cold night.

The kitchen door slammed shut, and Lizzy heard someone hurry inside. Quick footsteps stopped at the bedroom door. Lizzy turned to see David with labored breathing and a worried look on his face. His cheeks were flushed pink with cold.

"Come quick! Something's not right with Sophie. I think she's sick."

Lizzy dropped the blanket and rushed outside, following David to the barn. There they found Sophie lying on an old blanket in a corner strewn with fresh straw. Lizzy and David crouched down to look at Sophie. The dog lay still, pain etched in her eyes. When she saw David, she whimpered. He stroked her face and back, and her tail gave a brave attempt at a wag.

"What's wrong?" David asked, his question directed at Sophie as much as at Lizzy.

Lizzy ran her hand along Sophie's swollen belly. "I think her puppies are coming. I'll go find Brother Webster."

"I'll get him," David said, and nearly bolted for the barn door.

Lizzy grabbed his arm. "No, you'll exert yourself too much. I'll find him. You stay here and make her as comfortable as you can."

David glanced at Sophie, then back at his sister. He swallowed hard. "Will you hurry?"

"Of course." After a quick squeeze of his hand, she ran out of the barn and into the fields, heedless of mud soaking the hem of her dress. She found Brother Webster breaking down dried corn stalks, with Lizzy's brothers and Jimmy working at his side. By the time she reached them she was gasping for air and had to take a moment before she could speak.

"What's wrong?" Brother Webster asked, abandoning his work.

"It's Sophie," Lizzy said. She had to take a breath between each sentence. "I think it's her time. David's with her. He's really worried."

"You boys finish up here. I'll be back soon if I can," Brother Webster said, then hurried alongside Lizzy to the barn.

When they entered, David let out a breath of relief, his face wet with perspiration. Sophie's head rested on the floor. David sat helplessly beside her. "I've been singing and talking to her. Nothing seems to help for long. I think her pain comes and goes."

Brother Webster nodded as he knelt to investigate. A quick check confirmed Lizzy's suspicions. "She's close," he said, glancing first at David, then to Lizzy. "I don't know if he'll want to be here for this. It will get worse before it gets better."

Lizzy nodded in understanding. For any child living on a farm, birth was no mystery. But Sophie wasn't just any animal, and David was such a sensitive boy. Watching his best friend labor might be too much for him.

"Brother Webster will take good care of Sophie. Let's go inside."

David moved closer to the dog and moved a hand over her protectively. "She needs me."

Lizzy sighed and reconsidered. "Are you sure you want to stay? It won't be easy."

"I know." He jutted his chin into the air. "But I'll be strong. I can't leave her."

So David stayed. He soon learned that Sophie's pains did come in waves, and he soothed her when they peaked.

The minutes dragged by, and more than once Brother Webster got a look in his eye that put a knot in Lizzy's stomach. He had surely seen many farm births and knew the signs to worry about. Sometimes he would give Lizzy instructions, but most of the time they waited on the cold ground, the only sounds being Sophie's whimpers and David's voice singing hymns.

When the first puppy began to emerge and Sophie let out a strangled moan, David's eyes grew big. "Poor Sophie. It'll be better soon," he said, his voice wavering. He tried to stroke her face, but in her pain, she nipped at his fingers.

David pulled back. "I wish there were something I could do," he said in both a surprised and hurt voice. "She won't let me pet her."

David's song didn't continue, and Lizzy wondered if letting him stay was a mistake. Living on a farm, he had seen other births, but never one with an animal he cared for like he did Sophie. He watched her give birth to a tiny puppy—shivering, eyes closed, and very wet. When it let out a pathetic cry, David let out a sob and began petting Sophie again. "You did it, Sophie," he said in relief. "You're a mother!"

Brother Webster remained focused on the dog as the puppies appeared, while Sophie licked them one by one, gathering them close to her. Immediately they started searching for nourishment.

The barn door creaked open, and Abigail entered. "Have you seen David?" She stopped when she took in the scene before her. "What's wrong?"

"Nothing," Brother Webster said, pointing to Sophie with satisfaction. "We've got five healthy puppies."

"And David?"

"I'm fine, Mama."

But his face was drawn and tired. Lizzy coaxed him toward their mother. "Why don't you go inside for a bite to eat? Sophie's fine now."

"Supper will be ready in a few minutes," Abigail said. "Come in and warm up before we eat."

David hesitated. He looked from his mother to his sister, and back to the dog.

"I'll stay with her for a spell, if you'd like," Lizzy offered. "If she needs anything, I'll fetch you."

David made a move to stand from the damp ground. "I do feel tired." He leaned over and gave Sophie a gentle pet. As if in a sign of gratitude, the new mother nuzzled David's foot, and he reached down to scratch her ears. David stretched his cold and cramped legs, then looked at Sophie and the five little balls of wet fur gathered close to her side. He smiled and went to his mother.

"Let's find a quilt to warm you up," Abigail said, and the two of them disappeared through the barn door.

Lizzy turned back to watch the new puppies. She and Brother Webster sat silently. She found her eyes misting and wiped at them.

"It was just so beautiful," she whispered.

"Birth is a miracle."

She shook her head and tried to explain. "It's more than that. It was watching David help her, seeing each puppy recognize its mother right away. Sophie already loves them so much. You can just tell. She knows how many there are, and she makes sure they all get some milk."

"Always amazes me, it does," Brother Webster said after a moment. "It'll be a few years yet before you can understand how a parent feels toward a child, but like you said—you can see it yourself." He shook his head and ran his fingers through his hair, wind-blown from his work in the fields.

For a moment Lizzy tried to imagine what it would be like to become a mother. Would she experience the same attachment to her child in the first moments as Sophie had? Lizzy remembered other animal births she had witnessed, other mothers caring for their young, and marveled at the love of a parent.

The image of her own mother came to mind, and Lizzy had to close her eyes. Memories from the past week resurfaced—the quarrels with her mother, the lack of respect Lizzy had shown, even her simple absentmindedness. She felt ashamed for acting as she had. Her mother was right; instead of behaving as a grown woman, Lizzy had acted the part of the demanding child.

But the worst of it was realizing that—whether her mother was wrong about Abe or anything else—her mother did love her and was trying to protect her out of love. And Lizzy had returned that love with hurt. She turned to look away from Sophie, as if doing so would stop the ache.

Brother Webster stood up, apparently unaware of Lizzy's emotion. He gestured toward Sophie. "If a dog can love her puppies like that, just think how much God loves us. That's something we can't even begin to imagine." He hitched his pants higher, brushed off his knees, and said, "I'd better check on the boys' work."

His footsteps scraped against the barn floor as he left, and his words repeated themselves in Lizzy's mind. Truly, she thought, if a dog could care for all her puppies, wouldn't Heavenly Father cherish all His children? Did He care? Or was it solely the righteous He loved? She had made mistakes—many over the last weeks alone. Again she wondered if perhaps she didn't qualify.

She scooted over and leaned against the wall of the barn, looking up at the shadowy rafters. Tears of confusion and frustration streaked her face.

"Are You there?" she asked the darkness above her. "Please tell me if You are."

Lizzy stayed in the damp barn for a long time with only Sophie and the puppies as company. In the background she could hear the murmur of the family having dinner. If her stomach growled, she was unaware of it. The dusk turned into black until she couldn't make out anything but the shape of the barn door with the moonlight shining on the other side.

No response had come to answer her plea.

"Good night, Sophie," she whispered to the dog. "Take care of your babies. They need you." She stroked the new mother's head before leaving the barn and slipping into the house.

CHAPTER 13

On Thursday Lizzy was in charge of shucking the corn for preserving. Normally the corn had been put up by this time, but with the hectic work between two families, this year they had to wait and had stacked the ears in the fruit cellar. Since the task tended to cause a mess, Lizzy put on a bonnet to keep the corn silk out of her hair and went onto the back porch to work on the pile of ears brought up from the cellar. She knew she could finish the job before her fingers got too cold, and gently rocking the swing, she tore off the greens and silk from one ear of corn after another.

The work didn't require much concentration, and soon her thoughts turned again to Brother Webster's words and the time she spent in the barn with the puppies. Her parents loved her, she knew that. It was something to remind herself of now and then, particularly when they didn't seem to understand her worries, her concerns, her heartaches—such as the house. They didn't seem to grasp why it bothered her that they wouldn't be rebuilding. At least Joshua had bought the farm instead of some stranger. She couldn't bear to think of someone living on it who didn't truly care for it.

But her parents did love her, in the same way they believed Heavenly Father loved them. She put an ear of corn onto the pile with the others and grabbed the next one. Not only did her parents believe in God's love for them, but they loved Him enough to give up everything for Him.

Lizzy blinked suddenly with the realization. Her parents had lost their home of over twenty years just as she had, yet they didn't curse God, doubt Him, or murmur as she had.

She hadn't really understood what that meant before. They too lost everything. Neither of her parents had spent hours pining for any of the many items they had lost. And they hadn't decided to sell the land because they thought the family would be better off someplace else. They sold the land because they needed the money and couldn't rebuild. Her parents hadn't made that decision to spite her or make themselves feel better about anything. They left, surely aching just as she had; and instead of supporting and helping her parents to make the transition smooth, Lizzy had done little but grumble for three months.

She tossed a handful of corn silk into the growing pile and sighed. Complaining wasn't the only thing she was guilty of, she reminded herself. Her mother deserved an apology.

Lizzy looked up at the angle of the sun. She was supposed to meet Abe in the grove in another hour. What should she say to him? At some point she would have to return his book, but it was still on the mantle, and although it had been a week already, her mother hadn't mentioned the books, and Lizzy hadn't dared bring them up. But she would go anyway. She wouldn't stay away after promising to meet Abe again, even if she had resolved to be a better daughter.

After all, she reasoned, she needed to get her own book back, and she would have to set up a way to get his book to him once her mother returned it. And it was not as if one small meeting between friends would hurt. She resisted thinking beyond today, whether she should tell Abe they could no longer see each other. It would please her mother, but did that make it something she needed to do? Couldn't she be a good daughter and still have his friendship?

Perhaps she should tell her mother all about Abe. But Lizzy quickly made that decision—no. That would only cause more problems, more hurt. Lizzy hoped that the past several days had demonstrated her extra effort to be helpful, and telling her mother about Abe would only ruin her efforts to make peace.

Her mother came around the side of the house, returning from errands in town. Lizzy called out to her. "Mama?"

Abigail pulled her bonnet off and turned back. "Yes?"

When had her mother gotten that small gray spot of hair at her temple, Lizzy wondered, realizing how much life was changing. "Could I talk to you for a few minutes?"

"Of course," Abigail said, and headed for the porch swing, where she settled in beside her daughter. "Is something wrong?"

An awkward silence followed as Lizzy tried to steel herself. "I know I haven't been very . . ." She searched for the right word. "Very *daughterly* of late. I've been angry at you and Papa . . . at God too . . . ever since the fire. I'm . . . I'm sorry, Mama. I really am. I just wanted you to know that. And I love you."

Abigail placed one hand over her daughter's. "I know this has been a difficult time for you. In some ways it's probably been harder on you than on the rest of the family, hasn't it?" Lizzy's face turned down. She nodded slightly, not trusting herself to speak. Abigail reached out and lifted Lizzy's face. "Your father and I both love you very much. And we are proud of you. Remember that."

"I will, Mama. I'll remember." She threw her arms around her mother and held her tightly. "I'll try harder to be a better daughter. I promise."

Abigail pulled away and smiled, a hand cupping Lizzy's cheek. "I know you will."

"And not just because of my books." She searched her mother's eyes for acceptance.

"I'm glad," she said, smiling and patting her daughter's hand. "And you've certainly turned over a new leaf this week. You may have your books back."

"Thank you," Lizzy said, trying not to look like a child on Christmas morning. She watched her mother go into the house, then took a deep breath of satisfaction. Things were on the mend between them. She could do what was needed to live up to her mother's expectations, to be the help the family needed. Perhaps she could even soften her mother's feelings toward Abe.

Lizzy hurried to finish husking in time. Much of tomorrow would be spent putting up the corn, a task she despised, but she would not say a word of complaint. At least it wasn't summer, she told herself. Canning in the heat was almost enough to do a body in. Doing it in November would be far more comfortable. The mess from shucking cleaned up, she casually found her woolen shawl and escaped to the grove, gratefully not needing any of the excuses she had invented for this walk in the chilly afternoon.

When she arrived, Abe was already there. He leaned against a tree, and his head came up at the sound of her step. A smile broke across his face, and Lizzy couldn't help but grin back.

"Have you been waiting long?" she asked.

Abe shook his head. "Not at all." He eyed the sky. "But when it snows we'll have to find a different place to meet." He rubbed his arms to warm them, and Lizzy laughed.

"I hope that by the time it gets really cold Mother won't mind inviting you in."

Abe replied with a grunt, as if he would believe that when he saw it. He held out *A Tale of Two Cities*. "That's a good book, although it makes me glad I didn't live during the French Revolution."

"I'm glad you liked it," Lizzy said, taking the book.

"So what did you think about *Pride and Prejudice?* I suppose you know why I picked it for you. Of course, there's Lizzy's name, but her personality reminds me of you, too."

She glanced up, but then looked away, avoiding the dark brown pools of his eyes. Her finger twisted the shawl. "I didn't get a chance to read it."

Abe's eyebrows raised, and he leaned forward, sensing her hesitation. "Why not?"

Lizzy dropped the ends of her shawl and sighed. "My mother and I had a quarrel, and . . . and I agreed to put my books away for a week."

"Did she find out about our meeting?"

"No, it wasn't that," Lizzy said as she began strolling through the trees. "I really upset her . . . in other ways. I'm rather good at that," she said with a self-deprecating laugh. "But we talked today, and everything is better. Hopefully it won't be too long before I'll get to read all about this Lizzy."

They reached the edge of the Webster property and the road and kept going to be out of sight of the house and others' prying eyes—a danger in good weather like today. "So tell me about the Lizzy in the book. Why does she remind you of me?"

"For starters, she has a mind of her own," he said with an awkward smile. "She's a strong woman, the one who holds everything together in her family. And then, of course, there's the part where she ends up with a man her mother can't stand." When Lizzy looked up at him in surprise, Abe suddenly flushed at having revealed quite so much. "But mostly it's because she has a mind of her own," he finished lamely.

Lizzy grinned as much outwardly as to herself. Abe was thinking of her in those terms. "So I've got a mind of my own, do I? I'll take that as a compliment, although some might not."

"Do you see it as a compliment?"

"I can think of few higher compliments."

They walked some distance, talking and learning more about each other.

"You told me before that you grew up with a Mormon family, is that right?" Lizzy asked as they rounded another bend. "How is it, then, that you aren't one of us?"

Abe shrugged. "My mother insisted that I shouldn't be baptized unless I truly believed. I came to live with them when I was eight, so I could have joined anytime. But . . ." His voice trailed off.

"I shouldn't have pried," Lizzy said, suddenly realizing how rude her question might have seemed.

"Oh, I don't mind. Only . . . it's not something I've ever talked about before."

"I'm sorry," Lizzy said, waving her hand. "Truly, you don't have to talk about it."

Abe slowed his step and looked at Lizzy. "I don't mind telling you. Somehow I doubt you'll think me evil for not having faith, even if you are a dyed-in-the-wool Mormon girl."

"Who happens to enjoy secret meetings with Lamanite Gentiles?"

"Something like that," he said with a laugh. But then he grew quiet and continued walking along the dirt road. "Do you have doubts about anything?" he asked her suddenly.

She looked up at the sky, pale blue with gray clouds. "Lots of things," she said, thinking back to the day the cornerstones were laid. "Did you hear Elder Cannon speak at the ceremony?"

Abe shook his head. "There were too many speakers with too many names. I don't remember who spoke before I left."

Lizzy chuckled, but grew serious as she remembered Elder Cannon's sermon, one of the few she had paid attention to. "He said that the temple would diminish Satan's power on the earth." She stopped in her tracks and turned to Abe. "Do you think a building can really have that kind of power?"

"I'm not even sure Satan's a real being," Abe answered with a shrug.

Lizzy sighed and kept walking. "My father is a mason. I know that he'll take Elder Cannon's words seriously. With each stone he works on, he'll believe he's decreasing the power of evil." Lizzy frowned, berating herself for not having the simple faith David did.

"It all *sounds* so wonderful, doesn't it?" Abe said.

"Exactly!" Lizzy said. "But is it true? I've always been expected to accept every teaching without question, as if doubting a thing would make me the prodigal daughter."

They walked in silence for a moment, gravel crunching under their feet.

"Have you ever told your parents how you feel?" Abe asked.

"In a way." Her head tilted to the side in thought. "But I don't think they realize my concerns are real. They take it for granted that I'll always be part of the Church and believe as they do . . . Sometimes I wonder how life would have been outside the Rocky Mountains instead of in the middle of Zion."

"My father assumed the same thing about me. Surely if he brought me into his home I would become a *saint* like him." Abe's eyes clouded, and his voice lowered. "But I've never even prayed. Know why?" He looked at Lizzy, who nodded her encouragement. "Because of my father. He never saw me as a true son. Tried to mold me into the person he thought I should become—from doing chores the way he decided was the only correct way, to attending the church he believed was the only true one. I watched how mean and low he was with my mother and how different he was with Church 'brethren,' acting pious and saintly . . . Made my stomach turn."

He paused, but Lizzy didn't speak since Abe seemed so caught up in thoughts and emotions from the past.

After a moment, he continued. "Brother Franklin insisted I was evil and full of the 'natural man' . . . and often at night tried to whip it out of me. I still have scars on my back from his efforts."

"Oh, Abe . . ." Lizzy's hand came to her mouth.

"When all his highfalutin preaching didn't work, he threw me out." Abe shoved his hands into his pockets. "Fact is, the way I saw it, any God who thought Brother Franklin was a good man wasn't for me."

"What about your mother?" Lizzy asked. "It sounds like she's different from him."

"She is. Her God was a very different kind of person," Abe said. "She believed in a Father who loved His children and watched out for them. But I couldn't reckon how to accept her God without accepting Brother Franklin's, being as they're both part of the same church. Her God never protected either of us." Abe kicked at some rocks. "I never have found the being she believed in."

"Me neither," Lizzy said quietly. Abe was voicing so many of her own thoughts that she felt certain they were kindred spirits. "My parents believe in the same Father in Heaven as your mother—one who nurtures and guides and loves His children. I tried to believe. As a child I prayed all the time. I just took it for granted that everything I'd been taught since I was knee-high to a milk stool was true. Can you guess what happened?"

"Only too well," Abe said with a pained smile.

"Not once has one of my prayers been answered. If God truly does love His children, why doesn't He answer my prayers? Or is it that I, Elizabeth Sullivan, don't matter to Him because I'm not as good as His other children?"

Tears prickled the corners of Lizzy's eyes. It was such a relief to talk about these things with someone who wouldn't brand her a heretic for saying them, someone who understood exactly what she felt. She looked up at him. "I'm glad you came."

"Me too." He eyed the sun. "But we've been gone a long time. We should probably turn back."

Lizzy agreed reluctantly, knowing that she might already be missed at home. Soon they reached the crossroads where they had said good-bye the first day they met.

"Should I come again next week?" Abe asked, facing her. He took her hands in his.

Lizzy considered. Finally she shook her head. "Let's not meet for couple of weeks. Just to be on the safe side." Lizzy glanced over her shoulder. "Brother Webster saw us last time. I'm afraid he'll tell my parents. If I don't see you for a while, he might think I've changed my mind."

Abe thought a moment too, then came up with an idea. "I'll come by Thursday after next, then each Thursday after that, at the same time. If you can come, just tie a cloth to a branch of that crooked tree over there. If I don't see it, I'll know you can't."

"I can't make you come all the way out here week after week not knowing—"

Abe raised her hands to his lips and kissed her fingers. "I want to come. And I will."

Warm shivers went up Lizzy's arms. Abe was daring, and it thrilled her. Then he squeezed her hands a final time in farewell and turned down the lane. She watched for a moment, her heart beating wildly.

As she finally turned and began walking home, her mind went through her belongings as to what cloth she could use as a signal to Abe. It should be a bright color, if possible, and nothing that would be missed . . .

CHAPTER 14

Lizzy quickly decided on a yellow dishcloth as a signal for Abe. It was bright enough to be seen from the road, old enough not to be missed, and not so colorful it would attract undue attention from the family. Over the next weeks, and with the aid of the cloth and occasional meetings on Main Street, Lizzy and Abe continued to see each other regularly.

No one in the Webster or Sullivan families seemed the wiser, and Lizzy couldn't have been more thrilled. She did her chores without complaint, and her mother hadn't said a word about books for weeks. Lizzy began to read more slowly, especially Abe's books, savoring the words and phrases, sometimes imagining his voice in her mind. After all their time reading books aloud to each other, she could easily imagine what he would sound like reading various passages.

As if to complete her happiness, Lizzy received weekly letters from Joshua, each as light-hearted and chummy as the one before. She quickly abandoned her awkwardness and hesitation about him, as he never wrote anything to indicate he had feelings along the lines of romance. The last letter before Christmas contained a package. As she tore off the paper, David laughed at her excitement.

"You shouldn't be doing that yet, Lizzy. It's not Christmas for another two days."

Lizzy only grinned as she tossed the paper to the side. Inside lay a case holding a wooden pen with a walnut barrel. Her initials were carved into the side in beautiful script. Lizzy ran her fingers along the smooth surface in wonder. "I hope it didn't cost him too much," she said. She carefully placed the pen back into its case, keeping it safe for her next letter-writing session.

* * *

On Christmas Eve the families trimmed a tree that Brother Webster had found in the canyon. He spent half an hour with an old saw, cutting off six inches from the bottom to make it fit in the house. Abigail watched from the sofa, and Laura Webster sat near the fireplace, her knitting at her feet and young Wyatt in her arms, also watching. Sam and Leroy had made a popcorn garland earlier that day under Laura's watchful eye; after all, she had only one other needle, and she didn't want her sons to ruin or lose it. The popcorn garland was completed without incident, however, and now both families sang carols as they strung it around the tree and hung red and gold balls on the branches.

Lizzy knew that the tree and songs would remind her of times at home, times she would never have again, and she had expected the memories to ruin the holiday. But somehow the usual feelings of Christmas managed to permeate her heart anyway, and she felt uplifted and jolly. After Jimmy placed the last ball on a high limb, she stood back and surveyed the tree with satisfaction.

"It needs one more thing," Brother Webster said, stroking his thick whiskers.

"Oh?" Lizzy asked.

Mary clapped her hands. "I know! It's time for the star! Who gets to put it on this year, Daddy?"

Brother Webster retrieved an obscure box from a corner and unwrapped brown packing paper to reveal a crystal star. Lizzy sighed and gazed at it glittering in the firelight.

"It's beautiful," she whispered, more to herself than to anyone else.

Laura spoke up from her chair. "My sister sent it soon after we arrived in the valley. She had it made especially for us, and it arrived two days before Christmas that year. We've used it every year since."

Brother Webster eyed the faces of the children, one at a time—Matthew and Aaron, then Sarah, Mary, Sam, and Leroy Webster. Last of all, Jimmy and David. They each waited eagerly, cheeks flushed pink with anticipation.

"Let's see . . ." Brother Webster said, drawing out the suspense. "I think I know the perfect person to put the star on our tree this year." He walked to David and held out the star.

David's eyes opened wide. "Me? But what if I break it?"

Brother Webster gave a rumbling laugh. "You won't break it. Come on. I'll help you."

With one arm, he lifted David's thin form and nestled the boy on his hip, then handed over the crystal, hoisting David higher so he could reach the top of the tree. David stretched out his arms to place the star, then adjusted the tilt one direction, considered it critically, and tapped it again with a finger the other way. Satisfied it was placed securely and correctly, he nodded, and Brother Webster set him down.

David gazed up at the star with a faint smile curling his lips. "That's how they found Him," he said softly. "It was the star."

He returned to his mother's arms on the sofa, and everyone else sat down as well, as if on cue. The two Webster girls wrapped one big quilt around themselves and snuggled in close to each other. Sister Webster took the sleeping Wyatt to the other room and returned to her rocking chair, where she picked up her knitting. Brother Webster retrieved the family Bible from the bookshelf and sat down. The room had grown quiet so that the only sound was the crackling fire and the clicking of knitting needles.

"From the first chapter of Luke," Brother Webster said in a soft voice.

He proceeded to read the account of the Savior's birth—the shepherds, the angels singing to herald the birth of God's only Son, the manger . . . When he closed the book, no one said a word, basking in the stillness and warmth.

Abigail sniffed, then broke the silence. "I want to thank the Websters for their love. For opening their home to us for almost four months now. I know it has been at great sacrifice."

Sister Webster seemed about to protest, but Abigail shook her head. "It *has* been a sacrifice, for everyone." Abigail glanced meaningfully at Lizzy, whose eyes watered. Lizzy blinked hard and looked at her hands. Abigail continued, "I must say thank you, both to the Websters and to the Lord, for giving us so much." She stroked David's cheek as she spoke.

When the room lapsed into silence again, Lizzy felt her heart speed up. She also needed to say something. She had given thanks and an apology to her mother a month ago, but the Websters deserved one too. The silence grew thick for a minute until she stood and broke it.

"I know I have been somewhat difficult to live with, especially when we first came into your home," she said. "I apologize for that. I hadn't seen what blessings I have, and instead saw only the things I had lost. So Brother and Sister Webster, thank you for everything. And I am grateful that David is so much stronger now than he was our first day here."

Her little brother came across the room and gave her a big hug, and she held him. Brother and Sister Webster crossed over and hugged Lizzy too.

"I hope you regain everything you have lost," Laura said to her.

"And more," her husband added.

Lizzy's voice grew thick. "Thank you," she said. "Thank you again for everything."

* * *

Christmas morning, 1877, arrived with a fresh dusting of snow. Abigail and Laura made breakfast as Lizzy artfully kept the children out of the kitchen, where their individual gifts were kept. At breakfast, each child would find a present on his or her breakfast plate. The Websters' own tradition included unwrapping gifts by the tree, but they wanted to incorporate some of the Sullivans' traditions as well to make Christmas feel more like home. The two mothers also collaborated on the recipes for the Christmas feast.

When two of the children peeked their heads around the kitchen door for what must have been the hundredth time, Sister Webster nodded to Lizzy, and she motioned them in.

"You're ready?" Sarah asked, eyes wide in hopeful disbelief. "Really?"

Abigail laughed. "Yes, we're finally ready." The children raced into the kitchen, but Abigail held up her hands, and they stopped dead. Aaron, who was last in line, bumped into the others and almost fell down. "Matthew, Aaron, go find your father and Brother Webster. Tell them it's time to eat."

Matthew's and Aaron's faces turned pitiful. "Mama," they began in unison.

But Abigail was firm. "We can't eat or open any presents until everyone is here."

The boys couldn't tear their eyes away from the gifts. The butcher had given the family some scraps of brown paper, and the children had decorated it with paint, using carrots and potatoes to stamp patterns over it. But now they looked at the presents as if they had never seen the paper—or anything so wonderful.

Jimmy pushed forward. "I'll go get them. I want my present fast."

"Thank you," Abigail said, but he was already racing out the back door.

In no time the two families were seated at the tables. Brother Webster and Richard took off their hats, and the former said a prayer of thanksgiving for the blessings of their lives and the blessing of the Christ child. Lizzy could feel Mary and Sarah wiggling in their seats on the bench, obviously not thinking about their father's words, but instead about the gifts waiting inches away.

"Amen," everyone chorused when Brother Webster finished.

The children ripped into their gifts, and soon oohs and aahs filled the room. Lizzy found an anthology of the British Romantic poets in her package, something her parents knew she had wanted for over a year. Mary and Sarah unwrapped matching sweaters knitted by their mother, plus a small doll for each with real porcelain faces and hands. Matthew got a wooden checkers set made by his father, Aaron the harmonica he had wanted since his last birthday, and Jimmy a slate of his own. David opened a gift of carved wooden animals. His face lit up, and he immediately began marching a giraffe and an elephant across his plate. Lizzy smiled to herself, knowing he would enjoy playing with them even if he grew ill again and had to be confined to bed—surely the very reason her parents had exchanged a sack of flour with their neighbor, Brother Howard, for his services in carving them. She glanced at her mother, whose eyes sparkled as much as her children's.

"Look, Mama," David said, his voice filled with excitement. "There's two of each, just like Noah's ark." He held up two elephant shapes.

Abigail wore a grin that nearly split her face. "Maybe when Papa has some time he can build an ark to go with them."

David's attention turned to a second package, which hadn't been there when Abigail had put the other gift in place. Instead of being wrapped in the brown paper like all the other gifts, a pretty scrap of blue calico served as a covering. Abigail turned to Laura, brow raised in question. Laura only smiled back as David opened the gift. Lizzy didn't move as she watched, as curious as anyone what David's other present might be.

David slipped the fabric off the gift and revealed a picture frame. "Oh, Mama. Look!" His eyes were wide as he turned the gift around so everyone could see the sketch that used to hang on the Websters' bedroom wall.

"Laura, we can't accept this," Abigail began. "It's all you have left of your son."

But Laura shook her head. "No, it's not. We have others pictures he made us. That one belongs to David now. We felt that after all he's been through, he's one of Jesus' chosen ones, and probably knows Him better than the rest of us."

At first David seemed to have lost his voice, and his face was pinker than it had been in weeks. He finally whispered, "Thank you . . . so much. May I hang it at the foot of my bed so I can see it when I wake up?"

"Of course, David," Abigail said with a nod, wiping a tear from the corner of her eyes. "Thank you, Laura."

CHAPTER 15

As the snow gradually melted and tulips pushed through the ground, the excitement of spring swept through the community. Everyone seemed to be in a cheery mood and walked with a lighter step. By April, the work on the temple was in full swing again. More full-time, skilled men had been hired since they could work faster than the ward men on rotating shifts. New immigrants began paying off Perpetual Emigration Fund debts as well, which paid more workers and increased the pace of the construction.

Lizzy walked along the road to Temple Hill, carrying a basket of fresh rolls and jam for her father as a special midday treat. When the temple came into view, she stopped to admire the work. Scaffolding covered the outside, and the walls were growing now. Her father had come home from work early a few days because the masons had started using the stone faster than the quarries could provide it. Now the quarrymen were working full-time just to keep up.

She shielded her eyes from the afternoon sun and looked about the scaffolding for her father. At one corner Hugh McKay was working, but he was so far away she couldn't make out what he was doing. Then there was Brother Jensen, Brother Tidwell, and four men she didn't recognize. Her gaze landed on her father at the top of the scaffolding at the southeast corner. He stood to his full height and stretched his back, clearly working out the sore knots in his muscles. He looked around, pleased at the progress on the structure. Lizzy waved, and he straightened further when he caught sight of her, then waved back. She raised the basket high, and he nodded. As he gathered his tools and headed down the planks of the scaffolding, Lizzy looked around.

The aging yellow horse dubbed "Old Jim" was navigating the paths between the stone. Lizzy walked closer to watch this animal that never ceased to amaze her. Without a driver or any reins, the horse knew exactly how to do his job, using the block and tackle to hoist rocks up to the top of the walls. As Lizzy drew closer, now standing beside a half dozen boys also watching Old Jim, she didn't blame the frequent spectators who gathered to watch the horse pulling, stopping, and turning all at the precise moment. The horse maneuvered his way through the stone piled all over the temple block without ever getting stuck, in spite of the fact that the spaces between the piles were barely wide enough to fit the cart's wheels.

"Lizzy!" Richard called as he trotted between stacks of stone and arrived at her side. He lifted the cloth covering the basket and inhaled deeply. "Mmmm. They're still warm."

"They're straight from the oven."

Just then one of the boys beside Lizzy reached out his hand to stroke Old Jim's nose. Richard tried to stop the boy. "Don't touch Old Jim!" he warned. But it was a moment too late.

In an instant, Old Jim bit the boy and punched his rear legs into the air. With a stunned cry, the boy ran off, cradling his hand and yelping. The horse calmed down, then plodded forward.

Richard laughed to himself and shook his head. "I tried to warn him. Did the same thing myself first week here. Thought I could make friends with the old brute. Learned my lesson and haven't tried again since."

Old Jim strained against the ropes, and Lizzy took a few steps back, looking upward as a stone was hoisted to the top of the temple walls. She wondered where it would be placed. She tracked the top of the wall for the next logical spot, where men were waiting to grab the block. From the southwest corner, she noticed Hugh McKay gripping another large stone as he settled it into place. He wiped his hands against each other, grabbed it again, then took a step back toward the scaffolding to get more leverage.

A shrill cry erupted as Hugh's foot slipped between the platform and the wall. The heavy rock still gripped between his fingers, he lost his balance. In stunned silence, Lizzy covered her mouth and watched in horror as Hugh and the massive stone tumbled toward the gravel-covered ground below. He released the stone and clawed at the air, trying in vain to grasp anything. His yells continued as he fell, his voice coming to an abrupt stop with a heavy thud as he hit the rocky ground. The stone landed on top of his chest.

After a split second of stunned paralysis, men sped into action.

"I'll get Dr. Ormsby!" someone yelled and raced away.

Richard scrambled toward Hugh through the maze of stacked rock. Lizzy followed closely behind, heart racing, basket abandoned on the ground. Was he dead? Of course he was. No one could survive such a fall. But they reached the base of the temple to see Hugh not only standing up, but walking toward them. His legs trembled, and his face was pale, but he stood on his own. A wave of shock swept through Lizzy. *He's alive? And walking!* Maybe she hadn't seen what really happened. Maybe he was able to grasp the scaffolding and slow his descent. But she knew that wasn't right. She had seen him fall with her own eyes.

"Hugh?" Richard said, scarcely able to believe what he was seeing. "Hugh, are you all right?"

The brother's eyes rolled to the back of his head, and he collapsed to the ground. John Parry and Lorenzo Hansen reached him first.

"He's still breathing," Brother Hansen announced as Brother Parry raced across the street to the cookhouse. He emerged a moment later with a vial of consecrated oil, but to reach Hugh he had to push his way past the group that had gathered around.

With nervous hands, Brother Parry tipped out a drop of oil, then he and Brother Hansen administered a brief blessing. A deep chorus of "amen" was followed by one of the workers racing toward them across the street, the doctor following close behind and carrying a black bag. At the sight, Lizzy's stomach felt heavy with dread. That kind of fall would be enough to kill a man even without landing on a hard surface or having a stone falling on top of him. Then again, Hugh had been walking on his own a moment ago.

She swallowed hard as Dr. Ormsby navigated the path of moving workers to reach the unconscious mason. The two priesthood brethren backed away to give the doctor room.

Dr. Ormsby knelt beside Hugh and inspected the injuries. "Looks like a couple of cracked ribs," he announced to the waiting crowd.

"And his fingers are cut up pretty good. Can't see anything more from here, but he's sure to have serious internal injuries. Be extra careful moving him." He looked up at several men in front of him and gestured to them. "You. Help me move him to a bed."

"There's one in the cookhouse," Brother Parry said. "I'm sure Sister Kent won't mind us using it."

Dr. Ormsby nodded. "Good. Careful now. Support his whole body and don't make any sudden movements. I don't want any more internal damage."

Minutes later after Hugh was carried away, the remaining workers milled around mutely, unable to return to work. Lizzy stood, shaking head to toe, beside her father. She held onto his arm to steady herself.

"Do you think he'll recover, Papa?" Lizzy asked.

Richard shook his head in amazement as he looked up to the top of the scaffolding and traced the path of the fall. She followed his gaze. The scaffolding was so high that from where they stood, they had to crane their necks to see the top.

"He should have died from a fall like that," Richard said. "But you saw him stand yourself. I think he'll be back to work soon."

Lizzy shook her head doubtfully. "It would take a miracle."

* * *

Eleven days later, Abigail sent Lizzy to the temple with her father's sharpening stone. He had forgotten it two days in a row, and kept mentioning how dull his chisel was getting. Lizzy hefted the metal in her hand as she rounded the final corner. At the sight that met her eyes, she dropped the sharpening stone, which landed squarely on her toe. But she didn't notice the pain; all she saw was Brother Hugh McKay walking toward the temple.

"Mornin', Sister," he said, tipping his hat.

Too stunned to give an answer, she just stared, her jaw hanging open. Seemingly enjoying her reaction, Brother McKay grinned and picked up his step.

"Beautiful day to work on the house of the Lord," he said as he walked on.

"Papa was right," she whispered. "It's a miracle."

* * *

The winter had felt long to Lizzy, although folks said it was one of the milder ones on record. It had been plenty cold for secret meetings with Abe outdoors, and Lizzy welcomed the warmer weather. Only her meetings with Abe and Joshua's letters had kept her content. She wanted to see Joshua again soon—they still hadn't seen one another since saying good-bye last fall—but knew most likely that wouldn't happen until it grew warmer.

During the cold months she had often pictured the two of them walking along roads lined by budding trees. They would talk as they had so many times—not about Abe, of course. She couldn't imagine telling Joshua about him, though she had never held anything back from Joshua before, not even her crush on the school teacher years ago. But talking about Abe was different, although she wouldn't admit the reason—that her mother's words about Joshua still haunted her. Knowing that he just might care for her in that way made it impossible to tell him about Abe.

One Friday evening as Lizzy milked the cow, she held Abe's latest book open with her toe and leaned forward to make out the words. She had put down a cloth to protect the book from the ground and had even wiped off the toe of her boot before using it to hold the pages open.

It would have been far easier—for milking as well as reading—to simply put the book away until Sally was stripped dry. But this way Lizzy didn't feel guilty. Despite how much her relationship with her mother had improved over the winter, she was intent on working hard to please her mother, largely to assuage the little pricks of guilt she felt each time she sneaked out to meet Abe.

She had managed to keep a cheerful countenance and carry more than her share of the work, even though the spring workload increased, from giving the entire house a proper cleaning to getting the vegetable garden planted.

Lizzy finished reading a page and leaned over to turn to the next. Engrossed in the story, she came back slowly to her work at Sally's udder, white sprays of milk going into the bucket at longer intervals.

"Good book?"

Lizzy jumped in surprise and lightly sprayed the pages. "Oh, Abe. It's you," she said, taking the book and wiping the damp pages. She put a hand over her heart to steady it, but couldn't hide her pleased smile at seeing him. She hadn't expected to see him until the next Wednesday at Christiansen's Store.

Lizzy was to bring eggs to sell on Wednesday, one of the regular chores she had volunteered for, as it provided a perfect opportunity to meet Abe without raising suspicions. He conveniently met her at the same time each week, during his midday meal break. At the sound of the cookhouse bell, he'd told Lizzy, he would drop his tools and hurry across the street to be one of the first men in line. He ate quickly, then raced down the hill to Main Street.

They had concerns about their Main Street meetings. For one thing, anybody could see the two of them. Granted, the ground was covered in mud and the air still chilly, but that didn't mean everybody was inside. They might be seen.

"Come here," Lizzy said, glancing around. She scooped the book from the straw-covered dirt and, with a corner of her apron, wiped milk from the pages as best as she could. She took his hand and dragged him through the back door of the barn, rounding the corner that bordered the grove. This was the best hiding spot under the circumstances.

Lizzy leaned against the barn and steadied her heart, which beat from nerves. "So, what brings you here today?" she asked, as if they were meeting in the parlor.

His dark eyes sparkled. "The Petersons are having a dance tonight."

"Really?" In her excitement, Lizzy moved abruptly and caught her hem on a nail protruding from the barn wall. She tripped and fell into Abe's arms, laughing. "I'm not particularly graceful today, am I?" She steadied herself and detached her hem from the offending nail. "I doubt anyone would want to dance with someone so clumsy."

"If that means no one else will want to be your partner tonight, that's fine with me," Abe said.

Lizzy inwardly hugged herself to ward off the chills of excitement, then smiled. The evening air had begun to change, and she could feel the oncoming crispness in the breeze. "I haven't been to a dance in ages." She glanced in the direction of the house and bit her lip. "Mother will *probably* let me go, as long as I finish my chores. I couldn't go to the last dance because David was having a bad day and she needed me here."

"I *must* dance with you tonight," Abe said with determination. He took a step forward, gave a formal bow, and held out his hand. "May I? Just in case I don't see you there?"

Lizzy reached for his hand and gave a small curtsy. "I would be honored."

Abe drew her through the mud and weeds and held her in closed dance position. Lizzy took in her breath. His hand was warm around hers, and she didn't want the moment to end. But at the same time, she knew what many of the older generation thought of the waltz, her mother included. Lizzy remembered her mother calling the dance "vulgar," and others thought it scandalous that youth would touch each other—and even face one another so closely—when they were not married.

Even so, the young people of Logan often managed to convince Brother Lindsay to play a waltz or two on his accordion during dances. At one dance between songs, Lizzy had heard him talking to another brother about how he thought waltzes were a harmless fad, so unlike the predictable cotillions many had grown bored with. Brother Lindsay generally left the dances with a token of the youths' appreciation, a treat of some kind brought specifically to persuade him to go along with their plan.

"No point in admitting that I'd play a waltz without the bribe," he had said. "In some strange way I suppose the young people see the dance as less scandalous if they bribe me—or at least that they aren't encouraging *my* downfall as well as their own." He'd chuckled, then hefted the bushel of vegetables left him that night. "I suppose I'll play two or three waltzes this time."

Abe led Lizzy into a simple waltz step, and a tingle went up her back. She smiled up at him, oblivious to everything around her. Their eyes locked, and they gently moved in circles through the shadows of afternoon sun.

"Lizzy!"

The couple flew apart. "Mother!"

Abigail stood at the back door of the barn, one fist squarely on her hip. Her form was more of a shadow with the fading light behind her, but Lizzy didn't need to see her face; she knew all too well the frown, the raised eyebrow, the tight lips of displeasure.

Rushing to the bucket, Lizzy said, "I finished with Sally. I was about to strain the milk . . ."

Her arms folded, Abigail looked at Abe. "I think you'd better leave."

After a brief nod, he gave Lizzy an apologetic look, then hurried off.

Abigail watched his form as he walked away, then she turned to Lizzy. "Finish your chores and come straight in."

"Yes, Mama." Lizzy knew there was no point in even mentioning the dance. She stole a glance at Abe's retreating form and caught him turning back to look at her too.

Her mother said very little to anyone the rest of the evening, and nothing to Lizzy. Had she banged pots and pans and showed her anger, Lizzy wouldn't have felt so bad. But her mother simply withdrew, hurt etched on every feature of her face.

That night Lizzy lay in bed, unable to sleep. Nearly four months of regaining her mother's trust, four months of working hard every day to give her mother more time to be with David and make her burdens easier, all gone in a single moment. She chided herself for being so careless. She should have gone away from the barn—at least into the grove or even to the road for a walk—when Abe arrived.

But the meetings with Abe were harmless, she reassured herself. Besides, her mother had an unreasonable mistrust of Indians. As she lay in bed, she regretted hurting her mother and felt guilty over the deception, but had no intention of cutting off her ties with Abe.

An hour later, her mother still hadn't come to bed. Lizzy could hear that she sat in the kitchen, alone. Then Lizzy heard the back door open and close.

"Everyone asleep?" she heard her father ask. A few heavy footsteps sounded across the wood floor of the kitchen, then, "Abigail, what is it?"

"What have I done wrong, Richard?" Lizzy heard her mother say. "I thought that in Zion our children would grow up in the Lord."

"What's wrong?" His voice was strained, and Lizzy closed her eyes. A tear squeezed out one eye.

"I found Lizzy dancing—dancing the *waltz*—with an Indian boy today. It must be the same one she met last fall. They are clearly anything but strangers. She has been lying to us, Richard. Lying to me. And he has corrupted her."

Richard's voice took on a soothing tone. Lizzy heard a creak, and she could imagine her father sitting beside her mother on the bench by one of the tables and putting his arm around her. "Don't worry. She's still young. I don't think she has any serious thoughts about matrimony."

"I saw them waltzing together!" her mother shot back, as if that should explain everything.

There was a pause before her father answered, but he whispered his response, so softly Lizzy couldn't make out the words, only her mother's muffled sobs. Lizzy rolled over in her covers while hot, silent tears fell down her cheeks. Her mother talked as if she were a heathen, and Abe the devil himself. She hadn't done anything so terribly wrong.

* * *

On Saturday morning Abigail awoke early, her eyes puffy from crying the night before. She began the morning chores with hopes that Lizzy would apologize.

When Lizzy appeared in the kitchen, she didn't even mention the previous day, and in fact said very little. But she did help with extra chores without anyone asking her to. Abigail noticed Lizzy's increased efforts and appreciated them, but even when her daughter took the egg basket outside, she could not get the image of Lizzy dancing with the Indian out of her mind—dancing face to face, touching so closely, his hand around her waist. She shuddered, hoping Lizzy would admit wrongdoing, ask for forgiveness, and promise to abandon her so-called friendship with the boy.

That night was not much better. Abigail still couldn't sleep. She guessed it must have been around three o'clock in the morning when she still lay staring at the ceiling, her heart breaking. She could hear her husband's steady breathing, see David's form on his bed, and she knew that Jimmy and Lizzy slept peacefully on the floor.

She thought back to her journey across the plains. At that time she had a clear picture about what she expected of Zion. She would be able to raise children away from worldly Babylon, away from persecution and outside influences. Her children would grow in the gospel with unwavering testimonies. Yet Lizzy seemed so far away, and Abigail wondered if she had failed at instilling enough faith in her daughter. Perhaps her daughter had life too easy.

It hadn't been too long ago at Christmas when Lizzy had seemed like a different person—repentant, helpful, grateful for her blessings. Yet something was off-kilter.

Abigail couldn't help but wonder—where had she gone wrong as a mother? Brother Joseph had said one had to be willing to sacrifice anything. Had she not given enough?

Was coming to Zion a mistake? Abigail immediately abandoned the latter idea. She had known in her heart nearly a quarter century ago that coming to Utah was the will of the Lord. Had she taken life for granted recently?

She rolled over and choked back a sob. Perhaps there was some blemish the Lord had yet to purge from her character, something that hadn't been fully cleansed in the refiner's fire. She wondered if that was why she lost her last baby . . . why she had lost her home in the fire . . . and now was about to lose her eldest daughter. Abigail swallowed hard.

The Lord must require more. Very well, she decided. If the Lord required another sacrifice, so be it.

But please, Lord, when I give my offering, bring my daughter back to me.

* * *

Early the next morning Abigail retrieved her small box of silver and sat at the table to polish the few pieces inside before church meetings. With the children of the house still sleeping, the place was quiet—something of a rarity. Richard was out back helping Brother Webster with the milking, and Sister Webster was preparing breakfast. Only Lizzy was awake, and had gone out moments ago to collect the morning's eggs.

Abigail gently rubbed each piece of silver, trying not to think too hard about why she was polishing them. The time would come soon enough. As she thought, the door opened, and Lizzy came inside from checking the chickens.

"Here they are," Lizzy said, putting the egg basket on the table. "I gathered nearly a dozen today. It's as if those chickens know we won't get any use of eggs laid on the Sabbath. If they laid this well any other day, we could buy a new house much sooner."

"Now, Lizzy," Abigail said. On one hand, she didn't want to remonstrate, since this was the most she had heard her daughter speak in two days, but she really couldn't allow such talk.

"I know, I know," Lizzy said. "Eggs laid on the Sabbath belong to the Temple Fund." Lizzy waved a fly away. The house always swarmed with flies, and while they would be far more active in a few months, they still had a way of bothering everyone. "We're already contributing the fifty cents a month they've asked for. They should realize that fifty cents is a much bigger amount for families like ours than for others who have more."

Abigail put the silver down for a moment. "It's not about money."

"I know. It's about 'building the kingdom.'" Her voice wasn't angry or bitter as it might have been months ago, but the comment still held a worrisome tone to Abigail's ears.

She glanced at Sister Webster, who stood over a pot of oatmeal. Abigail's brow furrowed. "I don't understand," she said. "You said yourself at Christmas that we have many blessings, that we've been given so much. Why complain about giving away a surplus of eggs?" Abigail picked up the silver and began polishing again.

Lizzy seemed unsure what to say. "I'm sorry, Mama. The chickens aren't mine. If you feel it necessary to give the eggs to the Temple Fund, that is your choice." She watched her mother for a minute before asking, "Why are you polishing the silver? Are we expecting company?"

Looking up and eyeing her daughter, Abigail hesitated. "I am donating it to the Temple Fund."

"The Temple Fund?" Lizzy's eyes flew open. "But—why? They're all you have left of your mother and grandmother. You carried them all the way—"

Abigail raised her hand to stop Lizzy's speech, fighting the emotion creeping up her throat. She would not cry. "You needn't remind me. I know the history better than anyone. My mother and grandmother loved this silver, but they also loved the Lord. I believe that if Grandmother were still alive today, she would want me to give it."

"But, Mother, a few pieces of silver can hardly make a difference to the temple." Lizzy pulled out a chair and sat down. "They're worth far more to our family than whatever money they would raise. We're already sacrificing money and eggs every month—"

"The silver will mean more to the Temple Fund than the eggs ever will," Abigail pointed out. "The Lord will see our offering."

She clung to the faith that the Lord *would* see and remember this sacrifice. Sister Webster seemed to notice the tension in the room and discreetly left mother and daughter alone, for which Abigail was grateful. Putting down the silver, she took Lizzy's hands in hers. "Oh Lizzy, if you only knew the thousands of people who have sacrificed for the gospel's sake, those who have given everything, even their very lives for your generation—"

Lizzy pulled her hands away. "I've heard all the stories before, Mother. The bloody footprints on the snow, the pain, the deaths."

"Does your heritage mean nothing to you? Haven't you ever seen God's hand in your life? You remember Brother McKay's fall from the temple. And there was James Quayle, the master carpenter. Remember the gash between his fingers? Nearly four inches long, but it healed in days. Don't you have faith that the Lord is watching over us too? He can work miracles in our lives, even for something small like finding the money for shoes if we need it." *Or for bringing a daughter back to the fold,* Abigail added silently.

Lizzy's hands kneaded each other for a moment. "Mother, I know eggs are a small thing, but when will enough be enough? We've already lost the only home I ever knew. We are imposing on another family for who knows how long, living on far less than we need. And now the sugar tongs and silver? *I* never chose to give anything up. Every person who pulled a handcart or trudged through dusty trails *did* choose. They cared." Her voice trailed off and lowered so it was scarcely audible. "They believed."

Abigail's hands dropped to her lap, a pit heavy in her stomach. Her mouth fell open, and she groped for words. Did Lizzy mean what she'd just said? Had Abigail talked so much of sacrifice, of Zion, of the kingdom, that she never got around to teaching her daughter to receive a witness of her own? She finally regained use of her voice. "Is that what this is about, Lizzy?" she said, her voice uneven and pleading. "Don't you believe?"

"You asked if I had ever seen the hand of the Lord in my life. The answer is no. I haven't."

Abigail was stunned into silence. How could her daughter have grown into adulthood and never felt the Lord's hand?

"I know I *should* believe," Lizzy said. "I've lived and breathed the Church all my life. It's in my bones. But do I have the same conviction that you do about the Book of Mormon? About Joseph Smith?" She shrugged helplessly and shook her head. "No."

Abigail rubbed at her forehead, then stared at her hands and tried to keep too much emotion from registering in her voice. Her mind swirled with thoughts and emotions as her daughter revealed things Abigail had never suspected. No, Lizzy had expressed doubts, she reminded herself. *But I never thought they were something to be concerned about.*

Abigail couldn't accept that this was just about faith. It had to be more.

"Is that why you've been seeing that Indian boy? Because you don't believe?"

Lizzy's head snapped up. "No. Of course not. I like him, that's all. We're friends."

"Friends often become much more. Does it mean nothing to you that he isn't a member of the Church?"

"Why should it when I don't know what I believe?" She focused on the tablecloth and smoothed out wrinkles. "What if I send Abe away and everything I've learned since the cradle is not true? What then, Mama? I will have lost a friend for no reason."

But it is true, Abigail wanted to say. Instead her frustration got the better of her. She gripped the spoon so hard that the edge dug into her palm. "Is he only a friend?"

Lizzy shrugged. "What if he isn't? What if someday I marry outside the faith?"

Abigail's throat was so tight she could hardly breathe. "Lizzy, don't talk like that."

"Why not?" Lizzy pulled away, her gaze meeting her mother's. "Abe is a good person even if he's never been baptized. For that matter, he is much better than some I know who have been members all their lives. There's the family renting the Millet farm. Everyone knows the husband beats his wife. And that Brother Penrose. He's as lazy as they come, always expecting the Church to pay for everything he gets without lifting a finger of his own. And the mean old elderly woman around the corner—"

"Elizabeth, stop that this instant. We do not judge others in such a manner."

Lizzy's cheeks flushed, and she shook her head. "I'm sorry, Mother, I shouldn't have said those things. But I won't give up my friendship with Abe just because he's a Gentile."

Abigail's heart beat hard, and she couldn't contain her emotions. "He's not just a *Gentile*—he's also an *Indian!*" She covered her face with her hands as emotions from years past rose to a head. Abigail's sobs came one on top of the other until she clumsily pushed away from the table and stood, stumbling blindly into the bedroom where she collapsed on the bed in tears.

CHAPTER 16

With her feet curled up under her, Lizzy sat at the desk in the parlor and wrote to Joshua using the Christmas pen, which she reserved for his letters. With a heart full of questions and frustrations, she needed someplace to turn with them. Her mother wouldn't bother her, she knew. Not when she was spending time on a letter to Joshua. And not after their quarrel the day before. She dipped the pen in the inkwell, then paused as she remembered the heated words.

The silver. Why did her mother insist on giving it away? Lizzy couldn't understand why, especially now of all times. Why not months ago when the Church first asked for donations? Lizzy couldn't help wonder what the bishop would say about her mother's gift. She suspected that he would convince her mother to keep the silver, considering how much they were already contributing to the temple in money, eggs, and even her father's work. Not to mention losing their home and all their possessions. Surely no one would expect a family heirloom to be thrown into the mix.

Lizzy shook her head. That wasn't the whole problem, she reminded herself, putting the pen back into the inkwell before it dripped onto the page. She had finally revealed to her mother the extent of her doubts, but in a way she wasn't proud of.

Why had her mother assumed those doubts were connected to Abe?

But as soon as the thought crossed her mind, Lizzy knew the answer. It was simple. Abigail had no idea what her daughter had ever felt and thought. She had no inkling that Lizzy's lack of faith wasn't something new, because the two had never discussed it. Ever. Until yesterday, when it all came out like angry bees from a hive—and Abe got stuck with the blame.

Lizzy wiped excess ink from the nib of the pen and continued the letter.

> *Why is it that I haven't the faith that you have, Joshua? Everything has always seemed so easy for you, so clear and understandable. Has it always been so?*
>
> *Mama must think I'm next door to being a heathen for speaking my true thoughts yesterday, but the facts are that I have never known anything but what she's taught me. And those things I know in the same way I learned to read and figure sums at school. They are memorized, not "written on my heart" like I have heard others describe it. I have never known the whisperings of the Spirit I keep hearing about. How can I know if any of it means anything at all?*
>
> *I've done some things over the last several months that have upset my parents, and the worst part is that I'm not at all repentant over some of them. I wish those things hadn't caused the pain they did when they were discovered, but faced with similar circumstances, I can't say that I would act any differently today.*

Lizzy paused. There were plenty of things she regretted, like being disrespectful to her mother, neglecting chores, and murmuring those first months after the fire. But she didn't regret her secret meetings with Abe. Not one of them—dancing behind the barn included. Not that she would mention Abe to Joshua.

> *You must think I'm terrible now too. Do you, Joshua? I don't think I could bear that. Some days I wonder why you have been my truest friend all my life. You are certainly of finer character than I ever will be.*

She paused and reread the letter, then imagined his reaction upon reading it. Sending it to him would risk his respect and affection, something she could not—would not—live without. Three quick rips destroyed the letter, but to be certain no prying eyes would read her words, she went to the kitchen and shoved the fragments into the stove. After watching them curl and burn away, she closed her eyes and sighed. Was there anyone who could fully understand, anyone she could share these troubles with? Abe could empathize, as he had similar doubts about the Church. But somehow she couldn't even turn to him this time, knowing that since he believed—or disbelieved—as she did, his words would only keep the wounds between her and her mother from healing.

Sister Webster walked in the back door, Wyatt toddling behind her and sucking on a lollipop from Christiansen's Store. "I checked the post office for your family," she told Lizzy. "And this arrived for you."

Lizzy's stomach flipped over at the sight of the brown envelope, which she knew contained a letter from Joshua. "Thank you," she said, taking it. She all but rushed into the parlor and once again curled up on the chair by the desk to read it. The envelope was thinner than usual. *Strange,* she thought. Joshua generally wrote nice, plump letters full of family news, his own doings, and sidesplitting stories about work in Scofield.

> *Dear Beth,*
> *The next time you hear from me, I will not be here with George.*

Lizzy's heart jumped. Was he coming home? She pictured him at his parents' house, then remembered that Joshua had bought the Sullivan farm. He did not yet have a home built there, but somehow the thought that it belonged to someone who already cared for it gave her some peace.

> *I'm not sure how consistent the mail will be from where I'm going,*
> *but I'll try to keep writing as often as I can.*

Lizzy's stomach lurched slightly. *Going? Where? He isn't coming back to Logan?* She sat straighter, her feet now on the floor, to read the rest.

> *I need to earn more money if I am to make a start on my own and*
> *build a house on your family's farm . . . which I suppose I could call*
> *my farm now, although that seems odd. I've decided to go up to the*
> *canyon for work—for the temple, wherever they can use me. I may*

end up at the wood camp or at one of the rock quarries—I think
there are at least two, maybe three of those—or even at one of the
lime kilns.

I can hardly wait to see you again, but I suppose I must, at least
for a few more months, so I can earn enough money to build a house
on the farm.

Yours,
Joshua

The letter dropped in her lap. She hadn't realized until that moment just how much she had anticipated seeing Joshua after all these months. He would be gone "for at least a few more months," he said. Did that mean three? Five? No matter, she decided, firmly folding the letter and replacing it in the envelope. She would have to face more time with just letters, and *then* she'd see Joshua again. In the meantime, she would continue to see Abe at least once a week. She smiled to herself. Even she couldn't convince herself anymore that his books were the only draw in their meetings. *Hardly,* she thought.

She took out a fresh sheet of paper and her letter-writing pen to respond to Joshua. But her hand hovered over the inkwell as she thought about what she would write. Not about her lack of faith. Not a complaint about how much she wished he would abandon extra work and simply come home. Generally his letters held so many stories and thoughts that she found it easy to respond. Not today. But she didn't get a chance to even begin the letter before her thoughts were interrupted.

"Lizzy," her mother called from the kitchen.

"Yes, Mama?" Lizzy tucked away the pen and paper, then stood to go into the kitchen.

"Could you come talk with me for a moment?"

The tone of her mother's voice made Lizzy hesitate, although she didn't know why. She stepped into the kitchen warily, then sat on the bench and held her breath. Apparently her mother felt the need to provide a lecture after yesterday's outburst. The tension between them hung in the air. Abigail was writing a letter of her own, presumably to her sister Louisa. Lizzy hoped it didn't include a request to stop sending books.

"Your father and I have discussed the problem of your devious behavior concerning that Indian boy," Abigail said, crossing a *T* before looking up. "Because you have shown yourself to be less than trustworthy, we have decided to give you two choices. Either you cut off your relationship with . . . with *him,* or you will go live with your Aunt Louisa in New York."

Lizzy's eyes shot open in shock. Of all the things her mother could say, this wasn't one Lizzy would have thought of in a lifetime. She couldn't find her voice, but it didn't matter; her mother went on as if she had said nothing more than she wanted Lizzy to buy some seed at Christiansen's Store.

"If need be, you will stay with Aunt Louisa for the next year—or more. However long it takes for you to forget this Indian boy." Abigail signed her name at the bottom of the letter, then blew on the ink, every muscle in her body tormentingly calm.

"How can you consider such a thing, Mama?" Lizzy asked. "You cannot send me away."

"We most certainly can, and we will, if need be," Abigail said, blowing on the ink again to be sure it was dry before she folded the letter. "Come now, it wouldn't be a punishment. You've been talking about going east for years."

"Yes, Mama," Lizzy said, "but I meant for school."

Abigail looked up, eyebrows raised. "Who said you couldn't attend school while you're there?"

"School for one year? What will that benefit me?" In exasperation, Lizzy sifted through every argument she could come up with. "If you are so concerned with my spirituality, why send me away to live in the middle of Gentiles, away from Zion and the Saints?"

Her mother looked up at Lizzy. The thought had clearly penetrated her mother's armor. A flutter in Lizzy's middle gave her an inkling of hope that perhaps her mother would see the logic and change her mind.

"Aunt Louisa may not be living among Latter-day Saints, but she is a good Christian woman. She will see to it that you read from the Bible and attend church meetings. And she will keep a close eye on you." Abigail folded the letter. "Really, Lizzy, you seem to be missing the point entirely. You would not be going to New York as if on some religious quest. Someday I hope you decide to go in search of the truth yourself. But until that day arrives, it is my duty as your mother to protect you from danger at all costs. Don't you see? A person bit by a rattlesnake must be removed from the situation before the wound can be attended to."

"How *dare* you compare Abe to a snake!" Lizzy yelled at her mother. "He is a good man—one of the most honest and hard-working people I have ever met. You don't know beans about him, and I will not hear him be called a snake." She shoved her chair out of the way and stormed toward the bedroom.

"That's not what I meant," Abigail called after her. But Lizzy wouldn't listen and didn't respond when her mother added, "I meant the situation, not him."

Lizzy slammed the bedroom door shut and stared at it, as if she could still see her mother.

New York! For a year? She can't be in earnest.

But Lizzy knew her mother had never been more serious in her life and began pacing the room. Her stomach twisted into knots, wondering what she was to do. Could she keep seeing Abe secretly? No. Now that her parents knew about the relationship, they would track her every move to be sure she wasn't seeing him anymore. They would be worse than bloodhounds on a trail; she had no hope of keeping it a secret.

In that case, could she walk away from Abe and never see him again? Her heart ached at the thought. That idea seemed impossible, too.

What could she possibly tell Abe?

* * *

On Thursday, Lizzy strolled along the dusty road that led to the cemetery. This was the first time she had told her mother that she was going to see Abe.

"Absolutely not," Abigail had said. "I thought I made the terms of our agreement perfectly clear."

"But Abe doesn't know about that," Lizzy explained to her mother. "I must explain the situation to him. It would be cruel not to."

Abigail thought for several moments while Lizzy waited for an answer. She almost gave up and left the room before her mother finally spoke. "Very well. You have my permission to meet the boy today. But it must be brief."

"Thank you, Mama," Lizzy said, and left the room with a sigh of relief. She felt compelled to go explain to Abe with or without her mother's blessing, but she was grateful that the need hadn't arisen.

Now as she walked along the road, the hem of her dress sometimes kicking up bits of dust, Lizzy hadn't decided what course of action she would take. She would tell Abe about her mother's feelings, of course. But would she still attempt to maintain the relationship against her parents' wishes and risk going to New York? When she reached their meeting spot, he looked over and smiled, but instead of feeling warm inside as she usually did, her heart pounded in her chest with dread.

"What's wrong?" Abe asked, taking one of her hands in his.

Lizzy forced back tears. "It's my mother. Oh, Abe, I don't know what to do."

Abe put her hand through his arm, and the two continued along the road. "Tell me what happened," he coaxed.

She had always avoided discussing her family with Abe—it wasn't something that she wanted to contemplate during her time with him, and discussing family life wasn't exactly exciting. Today was different, though. She began with the argument over the eggs and silver, then explained what happened after her mother had caught them dancing behind the barn, and ended with her mother's ultimatum.

"What should we do?" Lizzy finished with a sniff and a quick swipe at her cheeks.

"It's simple," Abe said with an unwilling shrug. "You must promise not to see me."

Lizzy stopped walking and faced Abe head-on, eyes glistening and eyebrows drawn tightly together. "I mean so little to you?"

Abe shook his head. "Just the opposite. This is the only way." He put his arm around Lizzy's shoulders and resumed their way along the road. "Either you get sent off to New York and we never get a chance to be together, or you comply with your parents' wishes—now—and we do whatever we can to regain their trust and eventually change their minds. And then . . ." He looked into Lizzy's eyes, sending butterflies through her stomach. "And then maybe I could officially court you."

If the circumstance weren't so bleak, Lizzy would have thrilled at the thought of Abe courting her. But at the moment, such a thought didn't seem possible. "How long would that take?"

"Less than that year in New York, I'd wager."

Lizzy sighed in resignation. She looked up at his eyes, so dark she could scarcely make out the black of his pupils. How could she go weeks—or months—without looking into them? "I suppose so. But I can't help fearing that it might turn out to be forever." Lizzy sat on a large boulder. She picked some wildflowers beside the rock, twisted them in her hands, then threw them away. "I feel like I have to choose between you and my mother."

"Let's hope it won't come to that." Abe sat beside her and tenderly brushed her hair off her shoulder. At his touch, emotion rose in her chest, and she swallowed hard to keep it at bay. He continued. "It won't be easy, but if we don't do what she's asking now, we may never be together."

Lizzy nodded. A tear slipped off the tip of her nose and dropped onto her lap. She couldn't let them be separated by a continent. How ironic that a year ago she would have considered living with her aunt an adventure—a gift, even.

"What if we see each other around town?" she asked. "I can't pretend I don't know you."

Abe licked his lips in thought. "That won't be a problem for at least a couple of months. And after that, I hope your mother will think more favorably toward me."

Lizzy looked up, confusion written all over her teary face. "What do you mean?"

"I had been considering taking some summer work up the canyon, but now I'm sure about it. I've been earning about two dollars a day as a laborer on the temple, but I could get more in the canyon. Up at the sawmill it could be as much as three dollars."

"You're going to be a sawyer?" Lizzy asked.

"If the sawmill needs one, which I have doubts about. More likely a quarryman. I did a lot of quarry work down in Salt Lake City, and as a skilled worker, I could make at least another twenty-five cents a day up there. I hear they want more men working full-time. I could earn a tidy sum in two or three months, plenty to buy a horse."

Abe shifted, as if he hadn't meant to disclose that detail.

"Why do you need a horse?" Lizzy asked. "I thought you still had a pony."

"I do," he said. "But I need a horse. It's sort of a promise I made to myself." He reached for Lizzy's hand and squeezed it. "I had held off going up the canyon before, but now it seems like the best thing for us."

She put her head on his shoulder and closed her eyes tightly. First Joshua and now Abe. What would summer be like without either of them? "I don't want you to go."

"And I don't *want* to go." Abe reached down and lifted Lizzy's head. "But the quarries have strict rules—no cussing, no whiskey, lots of prayers, and mounds of good religious stuff to read. If I'm willing to abide by those rules, your mother might see past my . . . heritage."

Lizzy brightened. "And she'll see that you really are a good man. She'll have to look favorably on you, won't she?"

Abe grinned. "I'll write both of you letters, and I'll show her how civilized and educated I am. She'll just have to believe that I've never scalped a man."

They both laughed. Abe's eyes looked deeply into hers, and his voice lowered. "Think of this—I'll be earning money for our life together." Abe leaned in and gently pressed his lips against Lizzy's cheek. Her heart began beating wildly, and her breathing stuttered as he pulled back.

Abe smiled and wiped a tear from her cheek with his thumb. "I'll miss you, Lizzy. But remember, it will be worth it in the end."

CHAPTER 17

A month later Abe had hardened muscles from work at the quarry. He reached up and rubbed a knot in his shoulder as he read the notice on the wall of the mess hall. "Reward: The man who gets the old bear will get credit for two days' work."

He laughed to himself and shoved his hands into his pockets. "Good luck," he said to no one in particular.

"What, you aren't going to try trapping it?" Joshua asked from behind.

Abe turned around. "Didn't I say those bears would cause trouble?"

"You sure did," Joshua said as the two headed for the door. "But you also said it would be the *cubs* that Eddy and Cal were keeping as pets. I don't think anyone expected it to be the old ornery one we'd be worrying about. But if somebody doesn't stop him soon, we won't have anything left to eat."

Abe laughed. "I guess the fear of losing food and the promise of two days' credit might be enough motivation for someone to get rid of the animal."

Once outside, the two young men squinted at the glaring sun and looked toward the dirt road where they heard a wagon approaching, likely the one scheduled to bring new short-term workers from local wards. Abe had been asked to train one of the men. Abe knew quarry work well enough; he had done similar work on the Salt Lake City Temple before coming to Logan, and he hoped the man he was to train didn't look on Indians with suspicion, like a handful of the quarry men did.

Not that anyone had caused any real trouble for Abe. But he was very aware of times when people wouldn't talk to him, avoided sitting near him in the mess hall, or whispered among themselves while looking askance in his direction. It was to be expected, and nothing he hadn't experienced most of his life. But it had been a relief when the majority of men at this quarry didn't seem to care about his appearance.

Joshua shaded his eyes and peered at the wagon. "I hope they brought the mail with them."

"Me too," Abe said, although he suspected that he had a greater desire to receive mail than Joshua did. The mail pouch came infrequently as it was. There was just one big bag for all the temple camps—the quarries, the wood camp, and the lime kilns; the bag took its time getting around to all the camps and back home again.

Abe wrote weekly letters to both Lizzy and her mother, four to each so far, but had received only a single letter from Lizzy in return. He hoped it was because of the snail-paced pouch mail. But he still wondered if Lizzy's mother wasn't just tearing up her own letters unread and had started intercepting Lizzy's letters as well.

He knew from previous experience what the rules of quarry life would be like, and he quickly adapted to them. He was secretly glad he wasn't a man of whiskey. Several men he knew wouldn't have survived such a strict lifestyle.

When the wagon stopped, Joshua was called away by someone with a question in the mess hall, so Abe jogged over to find his trainee alone. A middle-aged man, a bit portly and balding, jumped out and glanced at Abe, then stared at him. At first Abe wasn't sure who the man was eyeing, so he checked behind him on both sides to see what else or who else the new worker could be looking at. Abe looked back. The man was definitely staring. *Just because I'm Indian,* Abe thought in disgust.

But then the man's eyebrows arched with curiosity. He turned to get his bag out of the wagon, then walked straight for Abe and held out his hand.

"I'm Joseph Webster."

"Abe Franklin," he said, shaking hands.

"Yes, I know."

Abe took a step back. "You do?"

"We haven't met formally, but some time ago I saw you and the Sullivans' daughter at my farm . . . and since then I've been witness to some spirited discussions about you. I feel I know you all to pieces."

So my skin isn't the cause of the extra interest after all. Abe wasn't sure what to say next. What had this man heard and from whom? Lizzy or her parents? And what did Mr. Webster think of Abe's friendship with Lizzy? Even if he didn't have the same hostile feelings that Lizzy's mother did, Abe doubted that the man fully approved, either. Should he apologize? Try to explain?

"To be honest," Abe said, "I was hoping that my being up here for the summer would help calm things with Lizzy's family. I've tried writing to her mother about it, but I haven't had any luck."

Joseph Webster nodded. "I know Sister Sullivan received at least one letter. Seemed pretty upset about it." At Abe's nervous expression, he grinned. "Don't worry. I don't share her opinion of Gentiles or Indians."

"Thanks," Abe said again. He chewed the inside of his cheek. "Then may I assume you approve of the match?"

Joseph waved his hand. "I wouldn't go that far, my boy. You and Lizzy come from very different backgrounds. I think she'd be happiest with someone who shared her beliefs."

Abe had to bite his tongue to keep from saying that he and Lizzy shared more beliefs than Joseph might imagine.

At Abe's sudden cool look, Joseph added, "But what I think doesn't really matter, does it?" He shot Abe a grin and patted him on the arm. "Let's be friends."

Abe's mouth cracked into a weak smile, and he nodded. "Sure."

Joseph hefted his bag over his shoulder. "Maybe while we're here I can convince you to get baptized. That would solve a lot, wouldn't it?" Chuckling, he headed toward the sleeping quarters as he exchanged a knowing look with Abe—one that said such a prospect was as likely as Abe sprouting wings.

* * *

Joshua emerged from the mess hall just as Abe and his trainee were heading off toward the sleeping quarters. The new worker was shorter than Abe, a bit portly, and somewhat familiar-looking to Joshua. He furrowed his brow and tried to remember when he might have met the man, but came up blank.

"Hey, Sorensen!"

Joshua turned to see Cal behind him. "Cal. Got any plans for catching the bear?"

Cal shrugged. "We'll see. Could you help me tie up a load on the wagon?"

"Sure," Joshua said, once more glancing over his shoulder in the direction Abe and his trainee had headed off to.

I'll have to talk with him sometime and see if we have any common relations, Joshua thought.

* * *

"Not that I have any interest in changing my own beliefs," Abe said one day in mid-June as he and Joseph Webster worked on the stone, "but I've always wondered about you Mormons. You seem to believe a lot of crazy things."

Joseph looked up from his grip on the drill. "Such as?"

"Such as angels appearing to young boys and telling them to start their own church," Abe said, pausing in his work.

"It started with one young boy seeing the Father and the Son," Joseph countered. "And why the sudden interest?"

Abe shrugged and admitted, "Understanding why you believe as you do might help me understand Mrs. Sullivan, too."

They worked silently for a moment, Abe hitting the drill with the hammer and Joseph bracing the drill and turning it between each blow. "It's hard to explain," Joseph finally said, pausing to wipe his head. "If you believe, it's simple. If you don't, the miracles sound like crazy talk."

With a nod, Abe picked up the double jackhammer, getting ready for when Joseph had the drill in place. "In fact, it's all that miracle stuff I can't stomach. I just don't believe that God sticks His hands into men's lives." He pictured Brother Franklin whipping him behind the old barn with a belt, a hundred lashings to purge the natural man out of him. God certainly hadn't intervened then.

Gripping it tightly, Joseph twisted the drill to bore the hole deeper into the rock. This hole would be lined up with several others already bored into the mountain. Tomorrow they would all be filled with powder and blasted. With any luck, the rock would break off cleanly, and they would spend the day shaping and cutting the stone so it could be hauled back to the temple block for the masons to finish.

With all his might, Abe thrust the hammer down, then said, "Thing is, I have yet, in all my born years, to see the hand of heaven in anything. I read something once that compared God to a clock-maker who created a clock, wound it up, and then let it run its course. That sounds about right."

Squinting at the bright sun, Joseph glanced up at Abe. "Tell me. Do you believe in the Bible?"

Abe glanced quizzically from the drill to Joseph and back again as he made his aim with the hammer.

"You know, that big book people read from, especially on the Sabbath?"

The hammer fell, and Abe raised it again, ready to strike. "I may be a heathen, but I do know what the Bible is."

"Do you believe it?"

Abe pounded the drill again, then stopped and considered as he caught his breath. "I hadn't thought much about it. I mean, sure, I guess I believe some of those things really happened." He pulled out a bandanna from his pocket and wiped his face.

"So you agree that at times God *has* meddled? Say, with Moses and the Red Sea?"

Abe removed the drill to check their progress. He cleaned out the hole and inspected it, eyeing Joseph warily. Abe wasn't sure he dared enter into a debate where he knew very little about the subject matter. He surely wouldn't be able to hold his own with Joseph, who likely knew a lot of scripture. "I suppose He has, from time to time."

"But not today?"

"No, not anymore."

"Why not? I don't see what time has to do with who God is or how He works."

Abe picked up the double jack. "Listen, Brother Izatt wants all the teams to have full loads tomorrow, and we have to get this finished today for that to happen." He checked the sun, which was rapidly descending in the western sky. "They'll be ringing the bell for mealtime in less than an hour, I reckon. So let's not argue. Can we both just agree that I don't believe in miracles?"

Joseph put his hands up in mock surrender. "You won't hear another word from me . . . for now."

"Good," Abe said, taking his stance and swinging the hammer in an arc.

Although they continued their work in silence, Abe couldn't help but think about their conversation. Did Moses really part the Red Sea? Did God meddle in men's lives? And if He did, would God bother answering the prayers of one man in the middle of Utah Territory? He remembered Lizzy saying that none of her prayers had ever been answered. Abe couldn't say the same because he'd never offered a prayer in his life.

When the dinner bell rang, Abe stood and wiped the beads of sweat forming on his forehead, then said, "We're almost finished. Just a couple more holes to do in the morning before blasting." He hefted the hammer with one hand and carried the wooden box of tools under his other arm. As he headed down the rock face, Joseph followed behind. They hadn't gone too far when Abe stopped. "On second thought, let's leave our tools here so we don't have to carry them back up in the morning." He placed the box and hammer under some bushes so they could be easily found. Abe took a step down the hillside, but Joseph stopped.

"What's wrong?" Abe asked.

"Let's take them this time." Joseph reached for the tools. "I'll carry them up tomorrow so you won't be bothered by it."

"Why?"

Joseph shrugged. "Just a feeling."

Abe shook his head and laughed as he headed down the hill again. "Don't tell me—this is going to be part of a miracle. There will be a crisis in the mess hall that only you will be able to solve because you have a point drill and a double jack."

"Abe, Abe, Abe. Go ahead and mock all you like," Joseph said with a sigh. "I don't know why I'm taking the tools. Maybe it's for the exercise. Perhaps I'll never know why. But when it comes to obeying that feeling I get from the Spirit sometimes—"

Abe looked over his shoulder at his partner, one eyebrow crooked in disbelief.

"And I *do* get that prodding that tells me to do things. Laugh if you will," Joseph insisted as they continued to trudge down the mountainside. "I have decided never to question them, because if I start doing that, one of these days I won't be listening well enough to hear a really important message."

Abe chuckled. "I don't understand you, Joseph Webster," he said. "But I have to say one thing—you're an honest, God-fearing man. No one could say otherwise."

* * *

The evening meal was typical. Among the twenty or so men in the room, small groups discussed their latest ideas for trapping and outwitting the old bear. One man was excited over the new pet he'd found, a small animal none of the men had ever seen before. It was black with a white stripe down its back. Abe and Joseph listened to the description of the animal, but ate without much conversation. Twelve hours of nonstop work tended to tire a body out.

Suddenly a loud, rumbling noise began, shaking the tables and growing louder by the second. Joseph gripped the edge of his seat. "What in tarnation . . ."

"It's an earthquake!" Abe said, planting his feet on the floor and grabbing Joseph's arm.

Joshua appeared at the door, late for his meal and white as a sheet. "Rockslide!" he cried, then raced to the back of the building and braced himself. Men scrambled away from their tables, hearts pounding, and joined Joshua at the far wall. For several long seconds, the building shook, sending dust filtering down from the roof. Abe held his breath and braced himself.

Finally, all was still. At first, no one moved. Suddenly John Wolfe gained the use of both his legs and his voice. "My team!" he cried and dashed to the door. Abe, Joshua, and some others ran out behind him, looking out to see Brother Wolfe's horses jittery and pawing the ground only feet from the mass of fallen rock. When the slide's movement stopped and the dust settled, the horses took off. Brother Wolfe grabbed the back of the wagon in a vain attempt to hold them, and the horses lurched forward, dragging him across the rough surface of the slide. Rocks smashed into wagon spokes, sending splinters flying through the air.

Men rushed over, trying to help Brother Wolfe find a way to calm the horses. After their initial bolt, the horses seemed to calm down and soon slowed enough for Alexander Izatt, the foreman, to grip the reins and soothe them.

"John?" Alexander called, still stroking the neck of one horse to keep him calm. "John, are you hurt?"

A groan sounded from the rear of the wagon, and Brother Wolfe emerged. He stood up, brushed off his pants, and rubbed the back of his arms, which had struck against the rocks. All the men in the camp stared in disbelief that he was on his feet.

"John?"

"No worries. I'm probably better off than that thing," he said, kicking the wagon and grimacing at a pain in his arm. The two men walked to the side to take a look at the wheels.

Alexander crouched down and whistled, shaking his head when he saw no serious damage to the wagon, at least nothing that couldn't be fixed. "Looks like you both got off just fine." He handed the reins to Brother Wolfe and headed toward the rest of the men standing outside the mess hall. As he strode over to the huge river of boulders that had come pummeling down the mountainside, he removed his hat and wiped at his brow with his arm.

He settled the hat on his head as he reached the edge of the slide and worked his way down the six-foot mound, then stopped and stared. When he turned his head to gaze over his shoulder at the slide, all the other men watching also traced the path of the slide to where it had ended. Alexander stepped off the rocks and began to count aloud with each step.

"One, two, three . . ." At six paces, he reached the mess hall door, where he turned about. "So close . . . it's a miracle any of us are alive."

A miracle? The word took Abe by surprise. *Lucky* had been his first thought. Had the slide been in the hands of God? Abe looked up the hill, where the swath of stones, twice as long as it was wide, began, and recognized the spot where he and Joseph had been working. The area was now buried. He shuddered at what could have happened to him and the other workers had the cook not rung the bell when he did. Or if Joshua had been any later coming off the mountain.

"I left my tools up there," a man named Ralph said.

Abe nodded. "I almost did too—" He stopped, then turned around, catching Joseph's eye. They both glanced up at the mountain and back at the tools resting by their table. Abe took a couple of steps toward Joseph and wagged a finger at him.

"Now don't go saying our tools were protected by Providence. If anything, the miracle is that no one was up there when it happened."

The corner of Joseph's mouth curved. "So you aren't ruling out a miracle?"

Abe stifled a smile of his own. He threw up a hand in protest. "Don't get started on that again."

* * *

"Any luck?" Joshua asked Abe one night late in July before they retired for bed. Sitting on their cots after a hard day of work felt like heaven.

Abe shook his head. He folded up another letter from his girl and put it in his pocket. "Her mother won't budge."

While he and Joshua had shared bits and pieces of their letters and hopes for the girl they each had at home, Abe tended to keep more of the details to himself. Joshua could understand Abe's reluctance to discuss it—after all, Abe himself pointed out that his girl's family didn't approve of the match. Logan was a small place; if Abe told too much, word could easily get out and upset people, particularly those Mormons who viewed relationships between Gentiles and their own suspiciously.

"I wish I knew what you could do," Joshua said. He had hurdles to cross in winning Beth's heart, but at least gaining her parents' approval wasn't one of them. He couldn't imagine the frustration Abe must be feeling. Then again, Joshua hadn't admitted to Abe that the girl writing to him hadn't expressed feelings that matched his own. He wasn't about to tell Abe or anyone else about that part of his angst. All he said was that he had come to work at the quarry, hoping to get a nest egg and a home for his bride.

Abe lay back on his thin pillow. "Her mother trusts her again. At least she thinks so. That's a step, I suppose. But I don't know what else either of us can do. We've tried to show we're trustworthy, that I'm a good person. But unless I can suddenly change my blood and my beliefs, both will always be a problem to her parents."

"But they aren't going to send her away anymore, are they?" Joshua said.

Abe shook his head again. "No, she doesn't think so."

"Well, isn't that something?"

"It doesn't mean that I'll ever be allowed to darken their door."

The two men were lost in their own thoughts for a moment.

Hearing Abe talk about his girl, Joshua's own thoughts turned to Beth. He bit the inside of his lower lip, remembering how carefully he had approached her in trying to decipher her feelings for him. He felt quite confident that she cared for him deeply, but he wasn't sure if her feelings extended to matrimony. He was sure of only two things—he could make her happy, and he couldn't picture any other woman being mistress of his farm. Of his home. Or of his heart.

"Do you believe in signs, Joshua?" Abe suddenly asked.

The sun had set, and dusky light filtered through the windows, creating silhouettes of each other.

"What kinds of signs?" Joshua asked.

Abe breathed out heavily in the growing darkness. "I didn't used to think much about these kinds of things, but something Joseph said has been itching at my mind." He paused for a minute, collecting his thoughts. "I'm wondering if God meddles in men's lives. And if He does, I could use a sign to tell me whether I'm wasting my time trying to get into the good graces of her mother."

Joshua glanced over at Abe, who stared at the ceiling as he lay on his back, hands clasped behind his head. This was the closest they had come to discussing religion. "Have you tried praying?"

Abe turned his head just enough to look at Joshua. "Why would God answer me? I've never uttered a prayer in my life. Now, if I were somebody important, maybe He'd look my direction, but what significance are two people's feelings for each other? There are millions of people around the world with much bigger problems."

"The Bible says God notices even the flowers and the birds," Joshua said. "I'd bet He notices a man with his heart set on a girl—a man who has a great swing with a hammer when it comes to building God's temple."

Abe chuckled and closed his eyes. "I suppose it couldn't hurt to try." He rolled over, which Joshua took as a signal that he didn't want to talk anymore. Joshua took off his boots, placed them at the foot of his bed, and blew out his candle. He lay on his cot and thought of rebuilding the Sullivan home, of coming in from the fields to find Beth waiting for him inside.

Abe was looking for a sign. Joshua's eyes narrowed in thought. Being able to purchase the land had to be a sign that his plans would work out, wasn't it? And then he would be the happiest man in the world.

He looked once more at Abe and prayed that both of them would be lucky in their pursuits of happiness.

For some reason the man Abe trained returned to Joshua's mind. "Abe?" he whispered.

"Yes?"

"Has Joseph ever said I looked familiar?"

Abe rolled back over, eyebrows raised. "No," he began. "Should he have?"

With a shrug, Joshua shook his head. "I suppose not. But he looks familiar."

"You've probably seen him around town. Joseph says he's been in Logan for a long time."

"That's probably it," Joshua said with a yawn. His eyes drooped and he brushed the thought aside. It was time to get some rest.

* * *

A few days later on their last Monday at work, Joshua and Abe were getting a load of stone secured onto a wagon. The late morning sun beat down on them, and they stopped for a drink of water.

"I tried it," Abe said.

Joshua looked up from the ladle and raised his eyebrows in question.

"I prayed about whether I should bother trying to get her mother to approve," Abe said.

"And?" Joshua asked, wiping his mouth with the back of his hand.

"No angels, no lightning bolts."

"It doesn't usually work that way. I'm sure you know that," Joshua insisted.

Abe shrugged. "And you know I'm not one of those deep spiritual men who can hear that 'still small voice' I hear you Mormons talking about. So I asked for a sign. A big one. Something that would tell me whether she's lost to me or whether I can win her."

As they headed back to the wagons to load the stone, Joshua patted Abe on the shoulder. "I hope you get your sign. I really do. But maybe your prayer will be answered in a smaller way."

Over the course of the morning, the sky had been overcast, providing some relief from the sun. But as the morning wore on and the clouds gradually broke, the day only grew dimmer. Joshua didn't think all that much about it until an hour or so after noon. The sun should have been beating on his back, and yet the light was more like dusk and growing even darker. Something in the air had changed, and as other men began looking around, questioning, he knew they had also sensed it.

Birds came flying back to their nests, chirping frantically. A woeful howl came from the camp's dog, and several horses spooked. Joshua even spotted an owl which, strangely, began its flight in what was no longer daylight.

He kept tightening ropes around the load of stone that would be transported down the canyon, but soon he could hardly see his hands. It didn't take long before he could see nothing. When the day became as black as midnight, a hush fell over the workers. Everyone stopped what they were doing.

Joshua gazed at what looked like a nighttime sky, full of stars, yet all around the horizon it looked like a red dawn. And where the sun had been a moment ago was only a pearly, gold ring of fire. He could look directly at it without any trouble.

"By golly, it's a total eclipse," he murmured, breathless. "It's beautiful." He had never seen or imagined anything like this. It made him feel small and insignificant. He gazed in wonder at the heavenly spectacle.

A clattering could be heard from the mess hall, accompanied by a string of unintelligible exclamations.

"By the sounds of it, Cook just broke the camp cussing rule," Abe laughed.

"Several times," Joshua agreed.

"Dinner'll be ready soon!" Philip, the cook, cried out.

Chuckles erupted from the workers as they realized what had happened. He must have thought he'd slept the day away. Philip stumbled out of the mess hall, carrying a lantern in one hand. He ran the other through his hair, which stood on end. His eyes were red and droopy.

"Sorry your supper's late, boys. It'll be ready soon. I am truly embarrassed. This'll never happen again. I must've fallen—"

But the nightlike darkness was already leaving, with the sun peeking out again behind the moon. The men quickly looked away to save their eyes. Slowly, light began to reclaim the day. The cook blinked several times and shook his head, wondering why everyone was still working if the meal was late and why he could see details he couldn't make out before. His brow furrowed in confusion.

"What's happening?"

"It was an eclipse," Joshua called.

Philip's cheeks flushed red. He glanced up at the sky, where the stars were growing less visible by the moment, then back at the mess hall. "So . . . it's *not* time for supper?"

"Not unless you're willing to feed us again tonight," a wagon driver said with a chuckle.

"I don't know about the rest of 'em, but I'll always take an extra meal," his partner added.

"Better not fall asleep on the job again, eh?" another man called.

The cook tried smiling at the humor of the situation, but the tips of his ears burned. He ducked back into the mess hall without another word.

Joshua turned back to the team. "I suppose we can finish tying this on now." But Abe had a far-off expression in his eyes, as if he hadn't heard him. "Do you feel well? You look a bit peaked."

Abe blinked, breaking his thoughts. "Joshua, do you think that was my sign?"

Joshua glanced up at the sky, then at Abe, and began to shake his head. "I—" He stopped. He didn't think so. How often did God create natural wonders to answer small prayers? But then again, Abe had asked for a big sign, and if he had done so with faith . . .

"I don't know," Joshua said with a shrug.

As Abe's face still stared upward, his eyes filled with wonder, and a smile cracked the corners of his mouth. "It's funny. The first time I pray, I get a sign." He shook his head and laughed. "But I made one mistake."

"What's that?"

"I prayed to have a sign about her. Didn't say whether the sign would mean I should *keep* pursuing her or if I should *stop*. So now what do I do? My first real prayer, and I mess it up."

Joshua leaned against the wagon and folded his arms. "If that eclipse was really a sign for you, then I'd say it's a pretty big indication that you're on to something. If I were you I'd keep at it. There's always a chance you two will be together. And if you end up losing her, there must be a purpose in it. There always is when we lose something we treasure."

Abe nodded thoughtfully. "You really think I should keep at it?"

"If you love her as much as I love my girl, you shouldn't give up."

Abe clapped his hands and rubbed them together with purpose. "Then that's what I'll do. Come on. Let's finish this. Maybe if we get done early I'll get a chance to write her mother another letter."

CHAPTER 18

Abe was just days away from leaving the quarry when he received a letter from his mother. The date showed that it had been posted some weeks before, but had just found its way from the boarding-house to the pouch mail and now up the canyon. Ever since his last visit home, she had written more often—every month or two. The five years before that he had received maybe two a year.

As he walked from the wagon to his quarters, he opened the letter and wondered if it held anything interesting this time. He loved his mother, but had to admit she wasn't a particularly skilled letter writer. Her missives were as stiff as a starched collar. But that didn't matter so much to Abe. He knew she wrote because she cared, because she missed him, and, after all these years, she no longer gave a hoot what her husband thought. Abe settled on his cot and read the short letter.

Dearest Abe,
This week I sanded the kitchen floor in a right nice pattern. On Monday Sister Edna Jones is holding a quilting bee. I look forward to it, as I don't have nearly as much to keep me occupied as I once did, and it gets lonesome. The house still feels empty without someone to care for.

He smiled to himself. Apparently Brother Franklin didn't count as "someone" to care for. But Abe knew what she really meant. She missed being a mother. He read on.

Your father speaks of you often. I miss you too.

Abe nearly snorted. If Brother Franklin spoke of Abe, it certainly wasn't in sentimental terms. Cursing Abe under his breath was more like it. But his mother didn't have the heart to say so.

Your father isn't as strong as he once was. It's sobering to think he's getting older.

If Brother Franklin was getting older and weaker, then didn't she have someone to care for? Abe wished he could talk to her right then and find out what she was really thinking; her letters could be so vague.

Tell me about your girl. You haven't mentioned her since your last letter.
    All my love, Mother

Abe reread one line over and over. *Tell me about your girl.*

Should he? For months now he had kept information about Lizzy closely guarded. Of course, he reminded himself, of all people on this green earth, his *mother* would be happy for him. But deep down, would his mother accept him and Lizzy together only if Lizzy managed to drag him into the water? Would she secretly disapprove of the relationship because he wasn't of Lizzy's faith? He had often heard his mother speak in wistful terms of a neighbor couple not of the same faith—of the struggles they faced as a result. "That poor woman," she'd said more than once. "If she only knew twenty years ago what she knows now, she never would have married outside her faith."

Mother would surely wish that Abe looked for a girl with his same beliefs so they would have the best chance at happiness. And if that were the case, could he bear to know his mother felt that way?

Abe folded the letter. He rested his arms on his legs and thought. What could he tell her about Lizzy? He reached under his cot for the box where he kept paper and a pencil. Closing his eyes, he thought of Lizzy, then of his mother. Then he opened his eyes and began to write.

Mother,
    Lizzy is wonderful. She's intelligent. And when she looks at me, she sees more than my heritage. And I love her.

* * *

"He's a hard worker, Abigail," Joseph Webster said, taking a seat on the bench in the backyard. A fortnight ago he had returned from the quarry, and he was still trying to convince Abigail that Abe wasn't the horrible person she had conjured him to be. She didn't appreciate the efforts.

Abigail continued washing clothes in the big washtub and scarcely looked at him. She wasn't in the mood to discuss her troubles over Lizzy. "The Indian boy's ability to work is not in question, Joseph." She turned back to the tub and scrubbed at a particularly stubborn grass stain in one of the twins' shirts.

"Abe's a decent fellow. I saw enough of him at the quarry to know that."

She sighed, set aside the shirt and wiped her soapy hands on her apron, then faced him, firmly pushing a stray wisp of hair back in place. "Joseph, I appreciate your concern, but I am afraid I don't want to discuss my family's affairs."

He raised a hand to appease her, but she only raised her eyebrows, unwilling to be appeased.

"I'm sorry for putting my nose in your business. But I've seen a lot in my day, and I can safely say that his determination to win over Lizzy is mighty strong. It might do well to . . . well, to ease up a bit on her."

Abigail planted a fist on her hip. Surprise and indignation combined inside her. "You don't seriously expect me to encourage Lizzy to marry a Gentile?"

Joseph shook his head. "No, no, of course not. I just have a hunch that . . ." His voice trailed off, and he avoided her eyes.

Abigail's heart lurched at the look in his eyes, the tone of his voice. "That *what,* Joseph?"

He shoved his hands into his pockets and kicked at the dirt with the toe of his boot. "I hate to say it," Joseph said reluctantly, "but I think that the more you try to keep the two of them apart, the more she'll keep running to him."

"Not anymore. You know she hasn't seen him in months," Abigail insisted.

"It's not because they've stopped caring for each other. Abe told me how much they hoped to change your mind, to 'soften you up' on him. They're both grown now, remember."

"If she insists on being with him," Abigail said, scrubbing even harder, "we will remove her from the situation."

"Send her to the States?" Joseph said. He shook his head. "That's a no-good solution, and you know it. The two of them have stuck it out since last September—that's what, nearly ten months? What makes you think another year away will change anything? She may return with as much conviction about Abe as ever."

Abigail wouldn't look at him. "A year can be a long time to a young woman with fickle emotions."

"True," Joseph said. "But Lizzy doesn't seem to be the fickle type. And assuming she was, who's to say she wouldn't meet some truly objectionable fellow while staying with her aunt? Someone who doesn't have the work ethic and decent morals Abe does?"

Abigail paused at her work, then slowly turned away and wiped her eyes. "Do you think I've pushed Lizzy into his arms?" She spoke almost in a whisper. Shoulders slumped, she sat down on the bench and held the hem of her apron to her eyes. Her prayers and sacrifice hadn't brought the blessing she had been searching for. Had she lacked so much faith?

Joseph took an awkward step closer and squatted down to look at Abigail. "He truly is a good man, even if he isn't a member of the Church."

"He's still a savage," Abigail said dully.

"He's more civilized than many men I know," Joseph countered. "Abigail, consider my words. It might do good to let Lizzy see him," Joseph pressed. "And it might do *him* some good to be around your family. Maybe someday he would want to enter the waters and join the Church."

Abigail sniffed with disdain. "Richard wouldn't mind inviting him over. He thinks their friendship is harmless. He'd probably agree with you, thinking that Abe is like a lost puppy we could take care of."

She fought with her emotions. On one hand, she could see what Joseph meant, but she had always assumed that removing any restrictions would only thrust Lizzy and Abe together.

Joseph went on. "Lizzy has been awfully down of late. Seeing him again might help her smile again."

The thought pierced Abigail. Was there nothing else to make Lizzy happy again? Yet even if seeing Abe would cheer up her daughter, she would only spend more time with him, not less. She sighed, trying to be resigned to God's will. If He wouldn't answer her petition, she would have to make decisions as best she could. Deciding which road to take was the hard part. She grudgingly admitted to herself that *if* Joseph was right—and he likely was—then Lizzy would be lost to her forever unless something changed, and soon.

"I'll talk to Richard about it," Abigail said. She would try to swallow her pride enough to invite the boy over—and then she'd keep praying that nothing would come of their so-called friendship.

Just then her husband strode around the back of the house, looking about as if searching for someone. "There you are, Abigail," he called, and trotted over to her. "Joseph, you'll want to hear the good news too." His eyes sparkled.

Abigail's eyebrows went up at the sight of her husband's jovial tone. "What is it?"

"I know it's a little early for your birthday present, but I've got something for you." Richard held a key out to Abigail.

She took it from him, momentary confusion making way for a look of hopeful excitement. "Richard, is this . . . ?"

Grinning, Richard stuck his thumbs behind his suspenders. He rocked onto his heels and then back to his toes. "That, my dear, is the key to our house."

"We have a house?" Her hand flew to her chest, and her voice trembled as she said each word. She squealed and threw her arms around him. Joseph clapped at her reaction.

"But how?" she asked, pulling away and fingering the key.

"One of the masons knows Sister Mills down on Main. Said she's been looking to sell her place. He brought me over to meet her, and together the two of us convinced her that we Sullivans are the kind of people she could trust with her home. She's a bit elderly and feels she's getting too old to live alone. She wants to move in with her son in Salt Lake City. She won't be leaving until she can settle her affairs here, but—"

"But it'll be *ours*," Abigail interrupted, gazing at the key, which she held with both hands.

Richard nodded. "It'll be *ours*."

Lizzy poked her head out of the door, holding it open with one hand. "Mama, where is the—"

Abigail picked up her skirts and scurried to her daughter's side. Lizzy let the door shut with a clang behind her as Abigail held up the key. "This opens our new house."

Lizzy's hands went to her mouth. "Really?" She threw her arms around her mother and the two embraced. "Oh, Mama. You'll have your own home again."

Abigail nodded. "And in the spring you'll be able to plant a garden and tend your very own flower bed." Her eyes lit up once more. "You can even plant tulip bulbs this fall."

"Where is it, Papa?" Lizzy asked.

Richard put an arm around her. "Do you remember that nice white house on the north end of Main Street? Near the railroad tracks?"

Lizzy held her breath. "You mean the one all by itself, with the orchard and the field . . . and the green shutters?" That house had called to her on her trip to the Websters' home so many months ago. And now she would be living in it . . .

* * *

That very day after supper, Richard tended David while Lizzy and Abigail walked down to the small white cottage with the green shutters. After they knocked at the back door, Sister Mills emerged, deep wrinkles etched around her eyes and mouth.

"Sister Sullivan?" she asked.

Abigail nodded. "It's nice to meet you, Sister Mills. This is my daughter, Lizzy."

"It's a pleasure to meet you both. I've been looking forward to showing you around. Come in, come in."

Sister Mills ushered them inside a washroom with a coal stove, then up a few stairs into the kitchen. A plate of oatmeal cookies sat on the oblong table in the center of the room. "Have a seat," she said, pouring each woman a glass of water. She sat at the table with them.

"I've talked a lot to Brother Sullivan about your family, and I feel right good about your taking the place." She smiled, her eyes crinkling at the corners. "And that's saying something, because I'm picky when it comes to my home. But like I said, I felt good about your husband, and I'm guessing that I'll feel the same about the two of you."

She stood and bustled around the room while Lizzy and Abigail nibbled on their cookies. "The inside of the walls are adobe, so the rooms keep nice and warm in the winter, cool in the summer," Sister Mills began. "Took a mighty long time to build. Charles and I must have spent at least six years on it. I remember working on that wall over there just weeks before my second child was born." She pointed to the southern side of the kitchen, where a window over the sink was framed with red-and-white checked curtains. Sister Mills stared out of the window for a moment, deep in thought, as if mentioning her late husband had brought back a wave of memories.

"He promised me glass windows," she said softly. "When we left Nauvoo, he promised me glass windows. And he kept that promise, though it took him ten years to do it." She smiled. "Well, enough of that. As soon as you're done eating, I'll show you the rest of the house."

Lizzy put her cup down with a thump. "I'm ready. I mean . . ." She didn't want to offend, but her excitement and intent would not be delayed long by cookies.

"We'd both like a look around," Abigail said. "If that's fine with you."

"Of course." Sister Mills pushed her chair in.

They began in the kitchen. The wall with the curtains had white cabinets on either side of the window. A stove stood on the north wall. "Stove's a bit temperamental, but I can teach you Maddie's tricks in no time," Sister Mills said, patting its black top affectionately. Lizzy remembered naming their old stove "Louise." She knew Sister Mills was a lady after her own heart.

Sister Mills brought them through an open doorway to the family room and adjoining parlor area. The front door faced west on Main Street. The room was decorated in light golds and browns. The far wall on the parlor side was home to a pianoforte.

"I won't be taking much of this with me," Sister Mills said. "So you are welcome to any furniture you'd like."

"It's beautiful," Abigail said, sitting on a sofa and running her hand over the design in the fabric. "We'd love to have it, but we'll have to pay you."

Sister Mills shook her head, then jabbed a wayward hairpin back into the knot at the nape of her neck. "Don't worry about that. You'd be doing me a favor by taking the lot, including the pianoforte. I can't play it, and neither can anyone in my Geoffrey's family. Though I imagine it would sound a fright if you tried to play it now. Hasn't been tuned in years. Come back this way and I'll show you upstairs."

The staircase began in the kitchen. A thin, narrow door was held shut at the base of the stairs by a small piece of wood, worn smooth with years of use, that rotated on a nail. Sister Mills twisted the piece so it stood vertically, and the door opened. Abigail and Lizzy followed Sister Mills up the stairs, which stopped halfway up at a narrow landing, turned a corner to the left, and continued to the top. The walls were painted a pale pink, and a handmade rug covered most of the wood floor. A large bed was pushed against one wall, where the gable ceiling met the far edge of the bed.

"This is what we always called the small bedroom," Sister Mills said, stepping in and leading the way across the floor. She gestured through the open doorway on the other side. "Over there is the other room, where the girls slept. It's slightly bigger, and it gave the girls more privacy than the small room." They retraced their steps and went through another doorway. "And over here is where Charles and I slept." The far wall in the bedroom had a short door. She lifted the hook holding it closed, and the door creaked open on its hinges. A dusty smell wafted over the women as they stepped inside. The room was cluttered with trunks, some clothes, a broken clock, and other aging items that surely held special memories for Sister Mills.

"The children slept in there when they were young so they were close to us. It's just storage now. I'll probably take most of these things with me." She looked around, sniffed lightly, then put on another one of her big smiles.

"Well, that's all." She headed back down the stairs, Abigail and Lizzy following close behind. Sister Mills led them to the back door, which she opened. "As you can see, the barn out back isn't big, but it's always been enough for us." She looked around the room and wrapped her arms around her middle. "I'll sure miss the place. It holds a heap of memories for me. And I'm sure it will do the same for you folks, as well." With a pat on Abigail's arm, she added, "Maybe it's something about the adobe in the walls. It keeps memories better than plain wood."

CHAPTER 19

That evening, when both families had quieted down for the night, Richard and Abigail sat on the bed, talking. David slept restfully on the cot, and Jimmy rolled over in the corner under his makeshift bed of quilts. Lizzy sat reading in the parlor. Abigail closed the door softly so her daughter wouldn't hear the conversation.

"Did you hear what Joseph was telling me this afternoon?" Abigail asked her husband.

Richard shook his head as he removed his boots. Of course he hadn't heard; Richard came into the backyard with the key after the conversation was over. "What did he say?"

It took a moment before Abigail could put her thoughts into words, and another one after that to get up the grit to say it. "He thinks I may be pushing Lizzy into that Indian boy's arms. By trying to keep them apart, I'm doing just the opposite."

Richard considered the idea. "Possibly. Although I've never known Lizzy to do anything because of what someone else thinks—or doesn't think—about it."

"Joseph said something else, too," Abigail said, studying her fingers. This would be the hardest part of all to admit.

"Oh?" Richard asked and looked over expectantly.

"He said that the boy's a hard worker. A good man." She glanced up at her husband. "One of the most civilized people he knows."

The hint of a smile appeared at the corner of Richard's mouth. "Joseph says he's not a savage then?"

Abigail couldn't answer right away. She just shook her head and wiped at her cheeks. "What are we to do?"

Richard came around the bed and sat beside her. He held her hands in his and looked deeply into her eyes. "It's not up to us. We've raised her the best we could. Her choices are just that now—hers. And I suppose we have to let her make them."

Abigail nodded miserably. He was right. Of course he was. But that didn't make the burden easier to bear.

Richard stroked her hand thoughtfully. "Let's invite Abe to the ceremony."

"What?" Abigail's head snapped up in surprise. John Taylor and several of the Twelve were coming soon to place historical items into one of the cornerstones. "Invite him to a sacred meeting? But he doesn't have the respect for the temple. He—"

With a shake of his head, Richard stopped her. "Proper respect isn't a requirement. If it were, the twins wouldn't be coming." They both smiled, knowing Richard was right. "And perhaps the meeting itself will engender some of that respect. He is a good worker. I saw that myself my first weeks as a mason when he was working with the mortar on the annex. It was hard to miss him because he worked much harder than many other men there. I think he does have a respect for the building—in his own way."

Abigail searched his eyes, finding love and concern. And goodness. Richard was a true Latter-day Saint. Much more so than she, when she couldn't see past the boy's heritage. But thinking that Abe was a decent person and *feeling* it were two very different things.

"Very well," Abigail finally said. She glanced at the door. "Should I talk to her now?"

For an answer, Richard stood and opened the door for his wife. Abigail stepped forward, stopping to brace herself against her husband before going into the parlor to face her daughter.

Abigail went in and sat in the old rocker. Lizzy looked up at her mother and was about to return to her book, when she noticed her mother's worried expression.

"Mama, do you feel well?" Lizzy asked, uncurling her legs from beneath her.

Abigail nodded, steeling herself for what had to be said. "I need to speak with you." She pressed her hands together deliberately. "This has been a difficult summer for you, and yet you have carried yourself well. I . . ." Her voice trailed off. She coughed, clearing her throat. She looked pale, almost ill.

"Mama, are you sure you're well?"

"I'm fine," Abigail said. But she wasn't. She could hardly believe she was going to say the words pounding in her mind. She took a deep breath and braced her hands on the armrests of the rocking chair. "Your father and I have discussed the matter, and we agree that you have shown yourself to be trustworthy of late. In addition . . ."

Why was this so difficult to say? Abigail felt a frog threaten her voice, and she had to cough again. "I have treated you as a child, and for that I apologize. You are a grown woman with the right—the right to make your own choices."

She had said it all. Her body felt weak all over, and she had an unruly urge to take back the words because of what they might mean to her daughter.

A smile threatened to break across Lizzy's face, but she resisted it. "Does that mean . . . ?"

Abigail nodded curtly. "It means that I will no longer stand in the way of who you decide to meet and when."

Lizzy's face broke into a wide grin. The sight would have made Abigail happy if the cause had only been something else.

"I can see him anytime I wish?" Lizzy asked.

Once again a choke threatened Abigail's voice. "You may, without any fear of leaving for the States. I will not set down any rules. However . . ."

Lizzy's face fell ever so slightly. "Yes?"

Her mother lifted her head and raised her eyebrows as if she were the child pleading of the parent. "However, I would ask that you voluntarily agree to a few items to alleviate my own concerns."

"Such as?" Lizzy shifted uneasily in her seat.

Abigail could tell Lizzy was practically holding her breath until she knew what her mother was thinking. "I ask that you inform me and your father before each—each outing," she finished, unsure what else to call the rendezvous.

"Of course, Mama," Lizzy said, her face relaxing.

Abigail raised a hand to emphasize her point. "Truthfully, Lizzy. Will you no longer see him without my foreknowledge?"

With a quick shake of her head, Lizzy tried to convince her mother. "Never, Mama. I promise."

Abigail too relaxed. "I want you to understand that this is not to be seen as an indication that your father and I are encouraging a relationship. We still expect you to marry in the faith."

Lizzy waved off the thought a bit too quickly. "Oh, Mama, you don't need to worry—"

Abigail shook her head. "Emotions are fickle things. Please be careful. If you start thinking about matrimony, I beg you to stop seeing him. Partners in marriage must be equally yoked."

"I understand," Lizzy said.

Abigail was very aware that her daughter was deliberately holding back any reassurance about what she had just asked. A knot twisted in her stomach, and it took effort not to begin a lecture. She remembered both her husband's and Brother Webster's words and tried to have faith that by no longer pulling Lizzy and the boy apart, she wasn't pushing them together.

The last thing she had to say was almost as hard as the first. *Richard's olive branch.* "Further, we have decided . . ." Abigail closed her eyes and took a deep breath. "That you and he may both accompany the family to the ceremony."

Lizzy's head shot up. She clearly hadn't expected this. If Abigail hadn't heard herself speaking the words, she might not have believed it either.

"At the temple block?" Lizzy asked.

"Yes, of course." Abigail could imagine what her daughter must be thinking. Since when did Abigail Sullivan accept a heathen Indian at a sacred meeting? Well, she wouldn't exactly be *accepting* of the situation. *Tolerating* would better describe it. But she would do it for both her husband and her daughter.

Lizzy crossed the space between them and hugged her mother. "Thank you, Mama," she whispered. "I know this isn't easy for you."

Abigail hugged back with a force that surprised herself. She clung to her firstborn, praying as she did so that Lizzy wouldn't be lost to her. "I love you. Please remember that. More than you know. And I pray for you. Every day."

"I love you too, Mama."

* * *

Lizzy went straight to the writing desk and scribbled a note to Abe, inviting him to the ceremony and telling him that the invitation was from her parents.

Who would have thought this would ever happen? Remember what you told me before you left for the canyon? That it might be a way to convince my parents. Brother Webster took a liking to you up there. I think his opinion might have swayed theirs. Regardless of the reason, I cannot wait to see you. I'll wait for you by the tabernacle.

The day of the ceremony the entire household headed for the temple block, except for Lizzy. She parted ways as they reached it and headed down the hill, her step light. If so many people hadn't been going up the hill and slowing her pace, she would have up and run down to meet Abe.

At the bottom, she emerged from the crowd and looked around. There, leaning against the unfinished tabernacle wall, stood Abe. Lizzy's heart pounded in her chest, and she grinned widely. The sight of him smiling back sent a flutter of emotions through her. The last several months had been so lonely without someone to spend time with. It had been nearly a year since she'd seen Joshua, and that emptiness had only been compounded when Abe left for the summer. Instead of closing the gap between them, Lizzy found her eyes tearing up.

Abe's brow furrowed, and he hurried to her side. "Lizzy, what's wrong?"

Shaking her head, she smiled through her tears and wiped at her cheeks. "Nothing. Everything is wonderful. I just learned how much I missed you all summer."

He smiled and stroked her cheek. "I missed you too."

Lizzy turned toward the hill and grabbed his hand. "Let's go find my family."

They climbed up together and joined the crowd around the southeast corner of the temple. They had to stand several feet away from the Sullivans and Websters, but found a spot where they could see the stone box and Church leaders well. John Taylor was at the head with eight Apostles, and a stone box to be filled with important relics, then sealed in a cornerstone. A future generation would open the box.

Behind the men rose one of the temple's corner towers. Lizzy's father had said that the original plans called for the two towers on the east to be taller than those on the west to represent the Melchizedek and Aaronic Priesthoods. Rumor had it that Brother Angell was changing the plans to make the towers the same height so the temple would look more proportional.

Either way, Lizzy knew it would be beautiful. The towers reminded her of a fortress, strong and secure. She gazed up at the soft gray color of the stone with its hint of pink undertones, its perfect lines and sharp corners. She was proud of her father's work, and wondered which stones were his. But Abe had worked hard on the temple too, she reminded herself, and she looked at him admiringly as well.

She took a step closer to Abe, smiling in spite of her mother's constant glances in their direction. Lizzy was grateful that her mother had decided to bend, and wondered what exactly had caused the change. Aside from Brother Webster, Lizzy suspected that her father must have had something to do with it. Perhaps Abe's working for the temple at the quarry helped. And of course the prospect of a home had improved her mother's temperament, too. Regardless of the reason, Lizzy was grateful. But her happiness wasn't quite complete with her mother looking at them that way.

Following a congregational song and a prayer, John Taylor spoke, explaining each of the artifacts to be placed in the box. One of the Apostles, Lizzy didn't know his name, handed Brother Taylor some books.

"Here are two complete sets of the standard works, in both English and Danish," he said. "They reflect a portion of the heritage of the people who will have helped build the temple and who will come to worship therein." He placed the volumes into the box, then took several papers from another Apostle in line behind him. "We will include copies of the *Deseret News, Millennial Star,* and *Women's Exponent.*" He separated each item from the stack as he called it out, then placed them all into the box. A third brother dropped something that clinked into Brother Taylor's hands.

"Here is a collection of coins," Brother Taylor said to the people, then poured them into a linen sack and deposited it into the box. "And finally," he said, accepting a sheet of paper from another brother, "I have here written the names of the leaders of the Church in three local stakes. It also includes the names of the chief workmen on the temple. We expect this box to be opened on the fiftieth anniversary of the temple's dedication. It will help our descendants know about who labored to build this temple of our God."

She noticed her father standing a bit taller. She wondered if his name was on the paper and imagined a future generation opening the box. What would they think when they read the names? What would it be like to have her father's name among them, especially if decades from now, one of his own grandchildren or great-grandchildren was present at the opening?

Lizzy stood a bit taller too, picturing her own children watching as the box was unsealed. But then she bit her cheek. *Would* they be here if she left with Abe? The thought that they might not see the temple was a sad one. She wondered what the city would look like in another generation. Joshua's children would likely be here, she knew. Imagining them was easy—miniature versions of their father, adept at creating mischief yet being true to those they called friends. A pang went through her at the thought of Joshua. She missed him terribly. Was he here? Craning her neck, she looked around, but couldn't find him. This group was significantly smaller than the one that had gathered for the dedication of the cornerstones. It shouldn't have come as a surprise that he wasn't here.

Abe leaned toward her, concern registering on his face. "Are you well?"

A smile returned to her face. "I'm wonderful," she said, and drove all melancholy thoughts from her mind. She was determined to enjoy her first guilt-free day with Abe.

* * *

The Sullivans spent the next several days moving their belongings to the new house, including Lizzy's growing collection of books from her aunt. Abigail, Laura, and Lizzy had spent hours getting the house in working order. On this quiet morning, the family stood outside the Webster home by their wagon, ready to leave for the last time.

"Thank you for everything, Joseph, Laura. You've been so good to our family," Richard said.

"We can never fully repay you," Abigail agreed.

Joseph Webster broke into a smile, his cheeks looking like rosy balls. "It's been our pleasure. We'll certainly miss having you here."

A blur of fur raced around the house and stopped beside David. He leaned down and stroked Sophie's head, his eyes growing misty. "Hey there, girl," David said, his voice betraying his emotion.

Abigail turned to Joseph and Laura. "I don't know if we'd have David today if hadn't been for Sophie. She brought so much joy to him during his illnesses."

The group watched the young boy as the dog nuzzled him, then licked his face. David was sniffing and trying to keep tears from falling.

Bending down, Laura said, "Please come anytime to visit Sophie."

Choking back his grief, David looked up and said, "Thank you, Sister Webster."

But with a shake of his head, Joseph said, "No, that won't do." At David's furrowed brow, Joseph reached down and put his arm around the boy. "Take her, David. She's yours now."

His wife gave him a questioning look, but he shook his head at her concern. "Don't worry about me, Laura. Naturally, I'll miss her something fierce. But I think she needs David as much as he needs her. It would be a crying shame to split the two of them up now."

David hugged Sophie so hard she yelped, then he turned to his parents. "Can I have her?"

Abigail and Richard exchanged glances that left no doubt. David ran to Brother Webster and threw his arms open, trying to encompass the man's ample waist in a hug. "I'll love her forever and take good care of her every day, I promise! Thank you, thank you, thank you!"

* * *

Lizzy didn't see much of Abe for a few weeks, but getting settled into their new home helped pass the time between visits. Sister Mills had left most of her furniture and a lot of other things to replace what the family had lost in the fire, like dishes and cooking utensils. Even so, Lizzy and her mother spent hours organizing the kitchen and other rooms to make it their own. Her father and brothers worked outside, clearing out the barn, then cleaning and repairing what farm tools Sister Mills had stored away.

One afternoon as Lizzy hung freshly starched drapes in the living room, she noticed someone coming down the road toward the house. It was a woman who appeared to be only a few years older than herself. She carried a platter while a little child clung to her skirts and toddled beside her.

"Someone's coming to visit," she called over her shoulder to her mother. A moment later a knock sounded on the back door, and both Abigail and Lizzy went to greet their guest. Abigail wiped her wet hands on her apron and did her best to fix her hair before opening the door.

"Hello," the woman said, holding out the tray. "I thought I'd welcome you and your family into your new home."

Lizzy smiled at the kind woman, and Abigail accepted the platter of biscuits, still warm from the oven. She breathed in the tantalizing aroma. "Thank you so much, Sister . . . ?"

"King," she said. "Helen King. I live just down the way a bit." She ruffled the hair of the curly headed youngster who clung to her knees with one hand and chewed the hem of his white gown with the other. "And this is Andrew."

Lizzy bent down. "Hello, Andrew." The little boy dropped the hem and grinned, showing two teeth poking up from his bottom gum. She couldn't help but think about how most of her schoolmates were mothers now, and wondered if she too would have a little one like Andrew in a few years. "Thank you for the yummy biscuits," Lizzy said to the little boy. "Would you like to come in and have one?"

He nodded, then clung to his mother a bit tighter.

The three women began talking, but soon Abigail turned to entertaining little Andrew. With the experience of a well-seasoned mother, she pulled out wooden spoons, a pan, and some measuring cups, which Andrew thought were delightful fun. The sight made

Lizzy's heart ache. If Hannah hadn't died, she would be a little older than Andrew, she thought.

Lizzy and Helen chatted about a variety of topics—a recent community dance, their hopes for the coming harvest, the temple construction.

"My husband and I decided we both wanted to help with the temple," Helen said. "So he volunteers as often as he can up at the wood camp, and I've been making clothing for the workers." She turned her hands palm up and inspected her fingertips. "But I'm afraid my skills aren't so good. If I keep pricking my fingers, soon I'll have nothing but stubs left."

As they laughed, Lizzy couldn't help but admire Helen's dedication. Lizzy herself was no expert seamstress—and that fact alone would provide a good reason not follow Helen's lead. But perhaps there was another way she could make an offering, be it ever so small.

At that moment, Abigail glanced at the clock on the wall. Her brow furrowed, and she turned to Lizzy. "I hope David's all right after being in the sun so long."

"I'll go check on him," Lizzy said, getting to her feet and crossing to the water pail. "I imagine Papa and the boys could all use some water as well." As she reached for the cups in the cupboard, she mentally calculated how many cups she'd need—*Papa, Jimmy, the twins. And David.* That meant five rather than four. She smiled to herself as she put the glasses on a tray and filled them with lemonade. Not long ago, no one would have expected that this summer David would be counted among those working. Granted, even now no one gave him the hard jobs, and their mother was particularly careful not to overwork him, but David was thrilled to be a contributing part of the family again.

Carrying the tray, she turned around and pushed the door open. "Helen, it was so nice to meet you," Lizzy said.

"Likewise," Helen said, standing and coming over to help with the door. "Why don't you come over for a visit in a few days? My Billie is working in the canyon, so Andrew and I will be all by ourselves."

"I'd like that," Lizzy said. "See you then."

As she carried the tray of glasses outside, Sophie ran out of the barn and rushed to her. "Careful, Sophie," Lizzy said, dodging the dog to avoid a spill.

She entered the musty barn where her father was trying to fix an old rusted plow. The boys worked on cleaning the place to get it ready for livestock. It was smaller than the barn on their original farm, but it would do.

"Who needs a drink?" Lizzy asked. It took only seconds for the boys to surround her and guzzle down their drinks, then give sighs of contentment and clap their glasses back on the tray.

The twins returned to their work, but Lizzy spoke to David before he had a chance to go. "How are you feeling?" she asked. "Mama wants to be sure you're not overexerting yourself. Are you too hot?"

David shook his head. "I haven't felt this good in a long time." Sophie bounded into the barn and nearly knocked him over. He laughed and ruffled her fur. "Tell Mama I'm fine."

David returned to work, but Jimmy stayed behind and twisted a piece of hair between his fingers. "Lizzy?"

"What is it, Jimmy?"

"Uncle Richard says I can take a break. Would you read to me for a while?"

"Sure," Lizzy said. It had been nearly three weeks since she and Jimmy had read together. "But I should make sure Mama doesn't need anything first," she told him. "I'll be just a minute."

When she returned to the house, Sister King had left and Abigail was at the sink. Her mother agreed that Jimmy could use some attention, so Lizzy deposited the tray of glasses on the table and headed upstairs to select a book from her chest.

She returned, and Jimmy followed her to the north side of the house, where they settled under a shady tree. While he listened, Jimmy picked at grass and drew pictures with a stick in the dusty drive. Lizzy had just finished a chapter when she heard someone walking up the drive. She glanced up, grinned at the sight of Abe, and hurriedly marked her place with a thick blade of grass.

"Remember me?" Abe asked with a mischievous grin.

Resting the book against the tree, she stood and brushed off her skirt. She smoothed her hair, which she hoped wasn't sticking out in ten directions, and crossed over to him. "It's been a few weeks, but I think I can recall something about a handsome Gentile in these parts."

Abe laughed, and the two turned to walk around the house. Lizzy suddenly noticed that Jimmy was gone. She heard the back door slam shut. "Land sakes, no!"

"What's the matter?"

Lizzy picked up her skirts and ran, Abe following close behind. "If Jimmy thinks I'm meeting with you in secret, he'll tell Mama."

She ran inside to see Jimmy nodding profoundly and Abigail looking perturbed. "Mama, it's not what it sounds like!" she protested. "I was just reading to Jimmy outside, and Abe came over to say hello." She gestured to Abe, who stood awkwardly at the door. "I was coming to tell you. We hadn't planned on meeting, and we haven't seen each other in weeks, never without you knowing. You have my word on that." Lizzy could feel her cheeks flush, and her heart pounded furiously.

Abigail looked at Abe, then at Lizzy. She finally nodded. "Thank you for telling me."

Lizzy's eyebrows raised. "You . . . you believe me?"

"Yes. I believe you." With that, Abigail went back to work, not having acknowledged Abe's presence.

Jimmy watched the interchange without comprehension. "But Lizzy did bad," he insisted. "Didn't she do bad?"

Not trusting herself to comment kindly on his question, Lizzy decided to leave quietly with Abe. As the door closed behind them, Lizzy could hear her mother murmuring an explanation to Jimmy. She breathed a sigh of relief and leaned against the house.

"I'm glad she trusts you again," Abe said, but his voice seemed a bit strained. Lizzy gazed at his expression, trying to read it.

"Abe? What's wrong?"

He shrugged. "I'm just wondering how much longer we'll have to play by your mother's rules. I'm glad we don't have to meet secretly any longer, but . . ." He shook his head. "We're both grown now, Lizzy. It's time we take the next step." He turned to her and took her hands in his. "I'm willing to leave everything to be with you."

Lizzy's throat went dry. She could hardly breathe, let alone speak. Her thoughts whirled.

"If your people won't accept us being together, then let's get married and go live in California. There's a lot of work out there. I'm sure I could provide well for you and make you happy."

"I . . . I . . ." Lizzy stammered. She had always suspected he had such intentions, but he had never said so until now. Her thoughts were such a jumble that she felt as if a beehive had erupted in her head.

He leaned closer to read her expression. "Well? What do you say?"

Lizzy straightened her shoulders and stood taller, a grin spreading over her face. "If that's the only way, I'd go anywhere with you."

Abe placed a kiss on her forehead as she added, "But let's give Mama a little more time."

He leaned against the wall and sighed. "Very well. I can wait a spell if I get my Lizzy in the end." He stroked the back of her hand with his thumb. "You know, I almost gave up on you earlier this summer when your mother showed no signs of softening."

"You did?"

"Yep. And you know what convinced me to keep trying? A conversation with a fellow I met at the quarry. He had his own girl back home. 'If you love her as much as I love my girl,' he told me, 'you shouldn't give up.'"

CHAPTER 20

The bottom six inches of Lizzy's dress were covered in dirt as she worked in the flower beds in front of the house, but she didn't care. She was planting tulip bulbs and could hardly wait for spring, when their sharp stems would poke through the soil, and blooms of red and yellow would grace the sides of the porch.

Afternoon sun beat on her hat, and Lizzy felt tiny rivulets of sweat running down her hairline. A wisp of hair had escaped its bun, and she pushed it behind her ear, then scratched the itch on her nose.

A horse trotted along Main Street, and at first Lizzy didn't bother turning around. Although they were farther north than almost everyone else on Main, there were enough people passing by that it didn't occur to her to look over until the horse stopped. Then she twisted around and squinted to make out the person silhouetted before the afternoon sun.

The rider slid down, and two steps later Lizzy recognized the gait. "Joshua!" She abandoned her spade and raced across the yard, but stopped before bowling him over. She threw her arms around him, unaware that she was covering him in dirt. "It's been a coon's age since I saw you last!"

Joshua either didn't notice her unclean state or didn't care, as he returned her hug. "It's been much too long. I missed you."

Lizzy squeezed back hard, his arms around her feeling warm and secure. "I missed you too." Pulling away, she put a fist on her hip. "Do you realize it's been a year since we've seen each other?"

"It's good to see you, Beth." Joshua brushed some dirt from her nose.

She flushed, then rubbed at the spot with her apron, realized it was dirty too, and decided she might have just added to the problem. "I must be a sight," she finally said with a chuckle of surrender as she dropped the hem.

Joshua sighed with contentment. "A sight for sore eyes."

They gazed at each other for a charged moment, and Lizzy felt her stomach flip over. When had Joshua's eyes gotten those golden flecks in them? She swallowed and then blinked, breaking the connection. Taking off her hat, she tried to flatten her sweaty, matted hair. "I'm such a mess!" she said, trying to shake the disconcerting feelings that had just erupted in her middle. *Abe.* He was coming to visit tomorrow. Or was it in two days?

For the first time ever, she and Joshua seemed to struggle for conversation, and Lizzy looked around for a topic. "I'm almost done planting bulbs."

"Why don't I help you?" Joshua said, sauntering over to the right side of the porch. He knelt down and began digging into the rich soil before Lizzy could protest. She sat beside him and watched his profile as he worked. His strong arms had become more defined than she remembered—probably a result of working at the quarry.

"Tell me about your work in the canyon," Lizzy said, handing him the next bulb.

"Let's see . . ." Joshua said, his voice trailing off as he thought. Their hands touched and lingered for a moment, and their eyes caught again. He coughed and placed the bulb into the hole he had just made. "Wasn't my last letter after the rockslide?"

"I can hardly believe no one was hurt," Lizzy said.

Joshua nodded in agreement and tightly packed the dirt around the bulb. "Neither could we. I don't think I told you about what the cook did during the eclipse, did I?"

"No, I don't think so," Lizzy said.

Joshua laughed at the memory, then told her about how the cook assumed it was past suppertime. When Joshua finished, he grew quiet and pensive. He turned to her, resting his arm on his knee, then opened his mouth as if the eclipse had reminded him of something.

But he hesitated and turned back to the flower bed before saying, "Do you believe in signs?" His voice was a little too strained for Lizzy to believe it was as simple a question as it appeared.

"I don't know. There are so many things I'm still trying to sort out for myself. I'm not sure what I believe." She stopped, then closed her mouth, still unwilling to admit, especially to Joshua, that she had doubts about the Church. Had he heard those doubts in her words?

As far as she knew, Joshua had never doubted, not once even as a child. The gospel was so clear to him, like a long, straight road stretching out forever—easy to follow and no way to get lost. Lizzy felt as if her road were constantly bending and dipping, and she couldn't see much ahead at all. The journey might be more interesting this way, she thought, but she envied the peace that Joshua seemed to have, the same peace her parents had. He was so good, too good for her, and she was . . . well, at times like these she felt unworthy to be his friend.

Lizzy pulled a few blades of grass and ran her thumb across their smooth surface, then ripped them into tiny pieces and tossed them aside. "Come on. I think Mama has some grape juice inside," she said, rescuing them from whatever awkward moment might have followed.

* * *

The road to Salt Lake City had never felt so long as Abe rode his new horse toward home. He hardly knew which reaction he wanted to see more, his mother's proud smile or Brother Franklin's shock that the gentile boy had done well for himself. The next step would be buying some land and becoming a true gentleman farmer. He smiled to himself. If only he could bring a farm in his duffle bag to show off to his family. Perhaps he could invite them to visit and see his land.

Unless, of course, he and Lizzy decided to leave Utah after all. In that case, good riddance to Brother Franklin and all he stood for. Abe would feel a twinge of regret and sadness at going so far away from his mother, but sometimes one had to make such sacrifices.

He arrived later than last time, at candlelighting. As he trotted into the yard, he could see the yellow-gold glow through the windows, and could picture his mother sitting in her rocking chair as she darned socks while Brother Franklin sat near the fire, his boots beside him as he snored.

He knew the enclosure for the horses would fit his own animal—which he hadn't yet named. Somehow he felt that naming the horse before seeing Brother Franklin would tempt fate, and Abe would lose this animal just as he had lost Shadow last time. He entered the barn and led the chestnut down the center corridor of the barn, unable to stop admiring the horse's strong muscles, fine shape, and deep color. Surely Brother Franklin would turn spinach green with envy. They stopped beside the door, where Abe removed the saddle, bridle, and his own bags.

He unlatched the door to the horse enclosure, which was connected to the fenced area behind the stable. The horse followed Abe and immediately began eating at the feeding trough. Abe patted his neck, then turned to leave when he saw a gray mare several feet off. Shadow.

"Hello, girl," Abe said softly, and approached the horse. "Do you remember me?"

Shadow pawed the ground and eyed Abe's approach. He held out a hand for the animal to smell. Shadow sniffed, then nuzzled Abe's palm. Abe laughed. "You do remember."

He reached up to stroke Shadow's face, but his hand stopped as his eyes filled with dismay. Shadow's halter was far too small for the horse and was digging into her flesh. As Abe investigated, he found several spots, behind her ears especially, with exposed sores, some bleeding, and all clearly painful.

"Some Christian he is," Abe muttered under his breath. "Don't worry, Shadow. I'll take care of it." He tried to unbuckle the halter, but it still wouldn't come off; the leather straps were nearly embedded in the horse's skin. Abe ran into the barn, where he rummaged through his bag until he found a knife, then returned to Shadow's side.

"This is going to hurt," he warned the horse, then continued to speak in a soft, reassuring voice. "We'll get this thing off you. Just wait. Soon you'll be right as rain."

Abe worked the knife carefully between the horse's flesh and the halter, slowly peeling it away. Shadow whinnied in pain, trembling under Abe's touch. She pawed the ground, and more than once reared, but Abe brought her around and coaxed her back.

"I know it's hard, but it'll make you feel much better later, I promise," he said, then once again set to working the blade under a strap.

Why did he do this? Abe wondered in frustration. He couldn't recall Brother Franklin ever being cruel to animals before. Negligent on occasion, but never cruel. Shadow's condition was no accident, Abe knew. But it made no sense.

As he peeled off another strap, he noticed sores by Shadow's mouth. Brow furrowed, Abe turned Shadow's head and checked the other side. Open sores were there too. It was all Abe could do to keep from yelling on the spot. *What kind of man keeps a bridle in a horse's mouth?* he thought angrily. By the looks of the halter, he guessed it must have been some time ago that Shadow had worn a bridle, but she was still suffering from having the metal bit continually in her mouth. She would be useless to ride until she healed completely. And Brother Franklin knew that.

The answer to the torture came to Abe suddenly. He had to stop working so he wouldn't hurt Shadow in his anger.

Spite. That's why Brother Franklin did it. Simple spite. Shadow was Abe's horse, and Brother Franklin abused her as one more way to hurt Abe.

Well, it worked. Abe gritted his teeth in anger and returned to the halter.

By the time it was finally cut off, Abe shook with effort and anxiety on behalf of his horse. The moon had risen, and several bright stars were shining down on them. Abe tossed the ruined halter to the side and breathed out a sigh of relief. Shadow seemed to do the same.

Abe nuzzled the horse, and Shadow nuzzled him back, bringing tears to Abe's eyes. "I'll be back," he promised.

He reluctantly left and headed for the house. Last time he was here, he had called for his mother so she could see Shadow. Then she had invited him inside. But as thoughts of Shadow's pained eyes and bulging sores returned to his mind, he simply burst through the door to find Brother Franklin.

Abe didn't bother wiping his boots on the scraper as he strode into the house. He didn't even say hello to his mother. Instead he went straight to the fireplace, where sure enough, Brother Franklin reclined, bootless and snoring.

"How dare you treat my horse like that!" he bellowed.

In surprise, Brother Franklin jumped to his stocking feet, one big toe sticking out through a hole. His eyes, first registering shock, relaxed when they rested on Abe. "Oh, it's you."

"Abe!" Sister Franklin abandoned her darning and flew across the room. "Are you well?" she asked, looking him over top to bottom and even putting the back of her hand to his cheek to check for fever.

Abe took her hand from his face and held it. "I'm fine, Mother. It's Shadow who isn't."

Apparently the name didn't ring a bell, because Brother Franklin planted his hands on his hips and asked, "Who?"

"My horse. The one I left here because you wrongly accused me of still owing you more." Abe took several strides toward the man and pointed a finger at him. "I have never seen such cruel treatment of an animal in my life!"

Brother Franklin merely shook his head and sat down again. He put his head back and closed his eyes. "Hush, boy."

For the first time in his life, Abe was going to fight back against the man who proclaimed to be his father. He reached for Brother Franklin's arm, and with a yank, lurched him to his feet.

"You will listen to me when I speak."

Brother Franklin was too stunned to respond. He rubbed at his arm and stared at Abe, who continued. "I blame myself for how you've mistreated Shadow. If I hadn't been so all-fired determined to pay you back every penny, I never would have left her here. But all eight years I lived under your roof, you pounded it into my head that I wasn't worth the dirt on your boots, that I wouldn't amount to anything, so last year I felt I had to convince you once and for all that I owed you nothing."

Brother Franklin opened his mouth to speak, but Abe refused to hear him and barreled on. "Well, you were wrong. You always were. Last year I didn't owe you one more red cent. I am worth something. I've bought another horse—that's two I own now—and my new one is even better than Shadow. I've been working hard, and before you know it, I'll have enough money to buy some land of my own." Abe's face was hot as he yelled at his "father," but he couldn't stop, not until he had finished. "And you know what else? I got me a good Mormon girl. And she doesn't care one bit about where I came from or whether I pretend to be pious and holy on the Sabbath." Abe spat out the last word, then spun on his heel and stormed out. His mother chased after him.

"Abe," she called after him. "Abe!"

He stopped, paused a moment to gather his strength—and to be sure Brother Franklin hadn't come out as well—then turned around.

His mother stared at him helplessly. "Oh, Abe," she said, seemingly the only thing she could say. She opened her arms and held him, all but disappearing in his large embrace.

"I'm so sorry," she finally whispered.

"It's not your fault, Mother," Abe said, choking back the emotion brought up by reliving so many horrible memories. "I should have known better than to come back again."

She pulled away and looked into his eyes. "I've missed you something powerful."

Abe's eyes smarted. "I've missed you too." He looked over his shoulder at the door to the horse pen. "I should go."

Sister Franklin shook her head adamantly. "Not at this hour. It's past dark. Where will you spend the night?"

Abe's mouth worked as he sorted through the dilemma. He hadn't thought that far ahead when he'd stormed out. All he knew was that he wasn't leaving without both his new chestnut and Shadow.

"Come over here, Abe," his mother said, and gestured to the narrow stairs leading to the barn loft.

Without a word, Abe sat beside his mother. She took his hand in hers and gently ran her hand up and down his arm as she once did to help him sleep. "Tell me more about your girl," she said. "Your letter only whet my appetite."

In spite of everything that had happened inside the house, Abe couldn't help but smile at the thought of Lizzy. His mother noticed and leaned close, her eyes lighting up.

"She must be something special."

"She is," Abe said. Images of Lizzy went through his mind—the curve of her cheek, the smell of her hair, the way she laughed.

"What is she like?"

"For one thing, she has read nearly all of your books," Abe offered. "And she's let me read hers."

"Sounds like a woman after my own heart," Sister Franklin said, then added with a grin, "and yours."

"And she's got a lot of grit," Abe said, still in the habit of talking about her without using her name, as he had with Joshua up at the quarry—as if his mother wouldn't approve of the match either.

"Grit? How's that?"

Abe paused, picking his words carefully. "Her parents . . ." How could he say this right?

"They disapprove because you're a Gentile?" she asked after a pause.

Abe nodded. "But that doesn't matter to her. Or to me."

He waited nervously for her response. She had always been a believer. Would she too think that he and Lizzy didn't belong together because he wasn't baptized?

"You plan on marrying her then?"

"I do," Abe said with a firm nod.

Again his mother rubbed his forearm as she thought. Abe wished he knew what was in her mind. The toe of one of his boots began tapping as he waited for her to speak. Her approval meant more than he had expected it to.

"Have you . . ." she began, then paused.

"Have I what, Mother?" Abe asked.

She pressed her lips together in thought. "You know I've never imposed my beliefs on you, although I always hoped you'd embrace the gospel."

A ripple of shame went through him. The desire to learn about those things had never entered his heart. As a child he had lumped anything religious with Brother Franklin's view of the world—and of God—and he wanted to get as far away from all of that as he possibly could.

"Have you ever thought about coming to meetings?" she asked.

Abe knew she meant much more than that. She also wanted him to read scriptures, to pray, to "get wet" in the waters of baptism.

"Maybe someday, Mother," Abe said. "But now when I think of God, I picture a mean, angry man with a belt in his hand."

Her brows knit together. "Like your father."

"Like Brother Franklin," Abe said, gently correcting her.

The back door slammed, and Abe stood up sharply. "He's coming," Abe said, hearing the thud of Brother Franklin's heavy boots stepping toward with barn. "I'll go."

But his mother stepped in front of him and placed a hand on his chest. "You will do no such thing."

She turned to the barn door just as her husband entered. He paused at the door, catching his breath. "Get out," he said to Abe. "And leave my horse here."

"I'll gladly leave," Abe retorted. "But I'll be taking both of my horses with me."

Brother Franklin took a heavy step toward Abe as if he wanted to fight, but his face was pinched and red.

"Stop!" Sister Franklin ordered. "I will not have you quarreling in this way. My son will not travel in the cold of the night with two horses to care for."

"Two horses?" Brother Franklin yelled. He gripped his arm for a moment, then steadied himself against the wall. "Two?"

"Two," she said firmly. "It is only just. Even you can't argue that."

"The devil I can't," Brother Franklin said, pointing a round finger at Abe. "I can get him put into the jail for stealing my animal." He glared, breathing heavily.

Abe felt a sliver of pity for the man, who looked to be bone-tired and in pain. But before Abe could decide whether to say or do anything, his mother broke in.

"And if you send my son away, I will tell everyone within twenty miles why Abe had to rescue his own horse—and why he was compelled to leave it here in the first place." Now her face was flushed and hot.

The three of them stood in silence while Brother Franklin contemplated what would happen to his reputation if his wife carried out her threats.

"Don't think I won't do it," she said, her mouth in a hard line. "You know I'm not the timid young thing I used to be. I won't lie down and take such folderol anymore."

Abe put an arm around her, this time not even trying to keep a smile from his face. He never imagined she would stand up to her husband in this manner. But maybe a good part of it was because

Brother Franklin wasn't as strong anymore, and carrying the load for both of them had made her a stronger woman.

Brother Franklin's hand went to his chest, and he inhaled with shallow breaths. He grunted in disgust and opened his mouth to surely say something rude and insulting, when he drooped against the wall and closed his eyes, pain twisting his face. Hand clutching his chest, he groaned.

"Mary, help me," he said, his voice scratchy, his eyes pleading.

Sister Franklin's stony expression softened, and she flew to him. But he collapsed before she could reach him. "Bart? What's the matter, Bart?" She knelt down and lightly slapped at his unconscious face, his eyes back in his head.

"Abe, get some water," she called. "Quick!"

In a flash Abe ran out to the well and filled a bucket, then returned, finding a nearby cloth to soak with the water. He handed over both, and she quickly went to work dampening the rag, wringing it out, and mopping his face with it.

"He's breathing," she said quietly, but with a tone of fear.

Abe put on his hat and headed for the door. "I'll fetch a doctor."

"Help me bring him inside first," his mother said. "Please? He's so uncomfortable out here."

"Of course." Abe returned and slid his arms under Brother Franklin. The old man was heavy, and Abe grunted with the effort. His mother led the way into the house, holding open the front door and arranging a pillow on the bed for her husband. As Abe laid him down, Brother Franklin opened his eyes. They narrowed as he looked around.

"What happened?"

Sitting beside him, Sister Franklin smoothed a blanket over his form and shushed his concerns. "You've had a bad spell. Abe is going for help right away."

With surprising force, Brother Franklin's hand shot out and grabbed Abe's wrist. "Get out," he said. "I don't ever want to see your face again."

Abe looked from him to his mother, unsure what to do. "You need a doctor—"

"Get out! And leave my horses." Brother Franklin's energy spent, he turned his head and tried to breathe easier.

Sister Franklin looked at Abe and nodded sadly. He backed out of the room, somehow knowing he would never step inside it again. *The stubborn old coot. He could be dying right now, yet his only thought is to get rid of me.*

His mother followed him out and closed the door behind her. "Will you still get a doctor?" she asked him.

Looking into her eyes, he couldn't say no. "Of course I will."

"Thank you." Her eyes were misty, and she sniffed. He made a move to leave, when she took his arm, making him turn back questioningly. "And when you leave, be sure to take both of your horses."

Abe leaned over and kissed her cheek. "I will, Mother."

CHAPTER 21

Lizzy became fast friends with Helen King following the sister's first visit. Although there was nearly six years in age difference between them, Lizzy didn't feel it. Perhaps it was because Helen's husband, Billie, was only three years older than Lizzy. Regardless of the reason, the two women found a true friendship together.

When the harvest was in and the air turned crisp, Lizzy went to the King home more often, and there she and Helen would talk while working on clothing for the temple workers, Helen stitching shirts while Lizzy knitted socks.

The King home was modest, but clean and inviting, and as Lizzy sat in the kitchen before the stove, she wondered if she too would have a home like this to care for someday.

"How long have you been making clothing for the temple?" Lizzy asked.

Helen looked up in thought. "Honestly, I don't remember. Must be coming on a year and a half. It was something I decided to do right after the cornerstones were laid. Billie was insistent that we contribute all we could to the building of the temple. I've been making socks and other clothing, and whenever Billie can, he works up at the sawmill in the canyon."

"Is that where he is now?" Lizzy asked, realizing she hadn't seen Billie that day and it was reaching candlelighting time.

Helen nodded wistfully. "I miss him when he's gone—so does little Andrew—but I can't begrudge him the time he spends as an offering to the Lord." She lowered her work, and her voice took on a soft tone as she looked to her feet where her son played with wooden blocks his father had probably made. "Billie reminds me to think on what it will be like to take Andrew to Temple Hill one day and to tell him that his parents sacrificed their time and means to help build it. I hope my son will be willing to give such an offering of his own someday."

Lizzy thought about Helen's words, and the two women lapsed into comfortable silence. While Lizzy focused on working the heel of a sock, Helen lit a handful of candles so they could see their work better, then settled back into her chair.

But the heel wouldn't cooperate because Lizzy was too distracted to give full attention to her knitting.

"I hope I don't sound impertinent," Lizzy said, half wishing the moment the words escaped that she hadn't even said that much. "But how can you be so confident in your offerings? You sound like you've never questioned whether you would give to the temple."

Helen looked up, surprised. She considered. "I suppose I never have. When you know it's the right thing to do, it doesn't enter one's mind to question, does it?"

Lizzy pretended to be counting the stitches on her knitting needle, figuring out the next place to decrease a stitch for shaping the heel, all the while envying how simple the matter of faith was to her friend. "Did you pray over it?" she asked.

Helen shook her head. "There wasn't a need. Like I said, it was clearly the right thing to do. We've already received blessings for helping with the construction, and I'm sure we'll continue to."

Lizzy's brow drew together. "Do you pray then?" She shook her head, trying to clarify her thoughts enough to communicate them to Helen. "Of course you do. What I mean is do you ever pray—alone, about something you just don't understand or something you need?"

Helen's mouth softened as she began to understand Lizzy's under-lying concerns. "I have offered those prayers many a time."

"Have you . . . received answers?"

"Oh yes," Helen said. "Although not always in the way I expected." She paused for a moment, reliving experiences. "There was a time I worried I would not marry. All of my schoolmates were married and having children well before I was. I yearned to have the same blessings."

"And you prayed?" Lizzy prompted.

"Yes, I did," Helen said. "I went out to a meadow behind our fields and knelt down. And I stayed there for a long time. That was the first time I didn't just pray. I waited, and I listened for an answer." She smiled. "I felt a bit like Enos as I knelt on the hard ground so long. My parents were beside themselves when I finally came home."

"Had you received an answer then?" Lizzy asked. Her heart sped up at hearing the story. She wanted so badly for the heavens to hear and answer prayers for those who lived today, not just for those pulling handcarts.

With a sentimental expression in her eyes, Helen nodded. "I did. And I knew it was an answer, because it wasn't what I had expected." She looked up at Lizzy. "I thought it would be, 'Yes, you will be married,' or 'No, you will die an old maid.'"

"Then what was your answer?" Lizzy asked.

Helen chuckled to herself. "That it wasn't time for me to know, but that I shouldn't worry about the future because it would all work out in the Lord's due time."

That didn't sound like much of an answer to Lizzy, but she didn't say so. To Helen, it had been the answer she needed.

"The important thing I learned that day is that sometimes listening for the answer is as important as offering the prayer."

Lizzy finished the stitches on one needle, turned the work around, and began the next row. "You are a good woman, Helen King," she said.

With a laugh, Helen said, "I know many women more valiant than I will ever be."

And I am not one of them, Lizzy thought to herself. She was grateful for Helen's openness; Lizzy couldn't discuss these things with her mother as one woman to another.

The back door groaned open. Before Helen could react, Andrew stood up and raced for the person standing there, then squealed.

"Daddy!"

Helen's face lit up. She left her work on the kitchen table and went to her husband's side. "You're home early," she said in a voice filled with joy.

He leaned down and kissed her forehead. "I came back with the last team instead of staying the night. Had a hankering to see my family."

Lizzy stood and gathered her things, unwilling to intrude. Billie noticed her and said, "Hello, Lizzy. It's nice to know Helen isn't all by herself when I'm gone. Thank you for spending time with her."

"It's my pleasure, Billie," Lizzy said as she reached the door. "To be honest, I come for purely selfish reasons. Helen is a joy to be with."

Billie turned to his wife, his eyes filled with love. "She sure is."

With a flush on her cheeks and a smile curving her mouth, Helen looked down and smiled shyly.

Lizzy bade them good night and walked home by the light of the moon. The night air was getting colder, and she was glad she had brought her wool wrap. But as she walked, her thoughts turned from the chill outside to the warmth of the King home. She stopped and turned around to look at it, a dark, receding shape, and sighed.

Would she ever be worthy of such of life? Of such a husband, a family? Would she ever have the calm assurance that Helen had about seemingly everything?

Listen, Helen had told her. *Pray and then listen. And the answer might not be what you expect.*

* * *

Joshua's visit was the first of several as the crisp days of autumn made way for winter. Lizzy grew to anticipate their long talks together in spite of the occasional look from Joshua that sent her heart beating faster. She refused to entertain the feelings such moments conjured. After all, it was *Abe* she had given her heart to months ago. Joshua was only a chum. *He had to be.*

This year Lizzy was surprised to realize she didn't hate the coming of winter. Usually she disliked the cold and snow, but last year had been especially hard spending it as guests in the Webster home. Now everything was different. First of all, her family would celebrate Christmas together under their own roof. And without being so crowded in a small space, they had spent more time together in the last six months than in the previous year. Not that the Sullivans didn't love the Webster family and enjoy being with them, but somehow Lizzy suspected that time alone within their own four walls would bring her own family closer together.

Then there was the fact that Lizzy's collection of books was growing. And even better, she and Abe were allowed to see each other every other week and exchange books. Granted, her mother still made it very clear that she felt wary about the relationship, but she no longer lectured Lizzy about it. Having Joshua visit at least as often as Abe seemed to put her mother in a better disposition, although Abigail and Lizzy rarely talked of the future, for which the latter was grateful.

One day in early January of 1879, Lizzy stopped washing dishes to watch her mother work while she mulled over some thoughts. She wasn't ready to seriously contemplate the realities of marrying Abe and leaving her home. As long as there was a chance of her mother accepting him someday, she held onto the possibility—although she had to admit that the prospect was unlikely. Then again, Abigail invited Abe inside on particularly cold days, and sometimes to join the family, although that was infrequent. She felt she loved Abe, but something had changed. A part of her missed the thrill of meeting in secret, of finding an excuse to sneak out of the house to join Abe at a predetermined spot.

Though it was weeks ago, she also often thought of her conversation with Helen about prayer. Marriage was certainly an issue worthy of it, Lizzy was sure, but she wasn't ready to pray about it. What if, by some chance of fate, her prayer *was* answered? And what if the response was, "No, don't marry Abe"? She might not be able to follow that counsel. Having Abe in her life was the spark of excitement she had been looking for ever since reading Shakespeare's sonnets. Could she give that up?

Lizzy noticed how her mother had seemed weak and tired lately. She had taken to resting throughout the day, something she rarely used to do. That afternoon, as Lizzy watched, Abigail suddenly stopped, put her hand over her stomach, and closed her eyes hard.

"Mama?" Lizzy put aside a plate. "What's wrong?"

Abigail took a deep breath, swallowed, then opened her eyes and answered. "I tried not to hope," she began, her eyes drawn.

Lizzy's heart leapt, and she reached for her mother's hands. "Oh, Mama, are you . . . ?"

Abigail managed a weak smile and nodded. "I think so."

"When?"

"Fall. Frankly, I'm getting so old I didn't think it was possible anymore." She looked at Lizzy, her eyes glistening. "Oh, Lizzy. I am so torn. What if I lose this one too? I don't know if I could bear it. But even so, the thought of holding a baby again . . ." Lizzy pulled her mother close in an embrace.

At the sound of jingling bells outside, they both looked up.

"I wonder who that could be," Abigail said, wiping her eyes. She went to the other room, peered through the window, and laughed. "Lizzy, come here."

"Who is it?" Lizzy asked as she joined her mother. When she pulled the curtain aside and looked out, she smiled broadly at the sight of Joshua standing beside his sleigh and his mare, a dark brown beauty with ivory fur above its hooves.

Lizzy went to the front door and opened it. "Joshua, what are you doing out there?"

He grinned, took off his hat, and tipped his head formally. "I came to request the presence of the young lady of the house."

Lizzy laughed. "It's getting dark. And isn't it cold?"

"Nope," Joshua said with a shake of his head. "I've got hot water bottles and a thick blanket. And besides," he added, gazing at the sky, "we've got nearly a full moon and a clear sky. We'll be able to see for miles. Come on, Beth. Let's go for a ride."

"I'll get my coat and boots," she said excitedly.

Minutes later, Lizzy and Joshua sped down Main Street, noses red with the crisp night air. But between their coats, hats, blanket, and the hot water bottles at their feet, they kept quite warm.

"Where shall we go?" Joshua asked several minutes into the ride.

Lizzy shrugged. "You decide. I'm simply enjoying the view." She breathed deeply. "It's so beautiful driving at night . . . so smooth, quiet. Much nicer than a clunky wagon, isn't it? I'm glad you thought of it."

"It occurred to me that it's probably been some time since you had an enjoyable evening drive."

She nodded. "Last winter we rode into town occasionally, but this year I've walked almost everywhere, even to the dances at the hall." Lizzy eyed Joshua. "I haven't ever seen you at any of them. Why not?"

Joshua shrugged. "I've been pretty busy working on the house."

"Is it almost finished then?" Lizzy asked, adjusting the blanket.

"Not yet. I'm living in the barn for now. It's pretty cozy. I don't have many animals to live with yet, so I don't think I smell too bad, do I?" He lifted his sleeve close to her face for her appraisal.

Lizzy laughed and pushed the inoffensive arm back. "Of course you don't."

They passed a young couple walking closely to each other, and Joshua nodded to them, then turned back to Lizzy. "I'm hoping that by the end of the summer I'll have enough of the house finished to live inside. Would you like to go see . . . ?" His voiced trailed off, and his brow furrowed.

"What?" Lizzy asked.

He pressed on. "Would you like to see what I've done with the house? I know it's not the home you grew up in, but . . ."

Lizzy swallowed hard and looked away. She hadn't been back to see the remains since the day her parents returned from Salt Lake City, but not one day had passed that she hadn't thought of it. She had known, of course, that Joshua had been fixing it up, had probably built much of his new house, but she always pictured the farm the way she last saw it, black wood, twisted metal, and ashes.

The horse had slowed down. Joshua flicked the reins to get it going again. "I'm sorry, Beth. I shouldn't have—"

"Let's go." In an odd way, the sound of the pet name only Joshua used gave her strength. She nodded with determination.

"But—"

"Let's go," Lizzy repeated. "It's been nearly a year and a half. I . . . I'd like to go back, if only to see your work on it."

Joshua eyed her intently. "Are you sure?"

She linked her arm through his. "I'm sure."

He placed his hand on top of hers and squeezed it with reassurance. Joshua turned the sleigh around, and they drove in silence the rest of the way, hearing nothing but the sleigh gliding on the snow and the horse's jingling bells. Bright stars and a full moon showed through the dark sky. As they rounded the final corner before the homestead, Lizzy closed her eyes and sucked in her breath. When she opened them, she saw the moon lighting up the frame of an unfinished house where her home had once stood. It was the same size as the old house—and the same shape, Lizzy suddenly realized.

Joshua stopped the sleigh in front, and she stared at the structure.

"It looks . . ." She turned to Joshua with questioning eyes, unable to finish.

Joshua turned to face her, excitement etched on every feature. "I'm building the house just the way it was. Do you like it?"

The structure was nowhere near finished, but there was enough for her to imagine the rest, to remember what had been. Lizzy's hands came to her mouth as tears sprang to her eyes. She turned and put her arms around his neck. "Thank you, Joshua," she whispered. "This means so much."

"I hoped you'd like it," he said quietly, holding her close.

CHAPTER 22

After that first evening sleigh ride, Lizzy and Joshua rode together regularly, often stopping at the old farm. Even after being apart for months, it felt natural to be together again. Sometimes, when the snow wasn't too deep, they got out and Joshua showed Lizzy around. Other times they stayed bundled in the warm sleigh and talked. Joshua told Lizzy about his dreams for the house, often asking for her opinion about housekeeping or things such as curtains and furniture. She readily gave advice, enjoying re-creating her old home and improving it, even if at times she had a twinge of guilt wondering what Abe would think if he knew about her evening rides with Joshua.

Aside from thoughts of Abe, her only reluctance came in contemplating who would be lady of the house. She couldn't imagine who would take that place, and she resented the woman, whoever she was, for living in and caring for the house that Lizzy had helped create. A few times she actually found herself thinking about being the mistress of the house herself, of sitting before a fire with Joshua and talking as they ate hot rolls smeared with fresh butter.

She always drove such thoughts from her mind. Joshua was a great friend, surely, but nothing more. It was natural for such thoughts to feel comfortable.

But they certainly weren't her idea of romance.

"You still haven't taught me the peacock call," Lizzy said one night, keeping her thoughts from the future Mrs. Joshua Sorensen.

Joshua grinned. "That's right. You want to learn it now?"

"Consider me your pupil," Lizzy said, settling herself into the sleigh.

"Remember," Joshua said with mock seriousness, "this is something between you and me. No teaching the secret call of the peacock to anyone else. And no using it except to call one another. Do you promise?" He held up one hand in the air.

Lizzy followed suit. "I promise to never use the ridiculous peacock call for any purpose other than summoning my fellow birdcaller, Joshua Sorensen."

"Very good," Joshua said, a silly grin toying with the corners of his mouth. The solemn tone vanished, and his regular self returned. "You use the back of your throat," Joshua began, and continued to explain how to make the call.

Lizzy's first attempts sent them both into peals of laughter. "It sounds like some poor tortured animal," she said.

"Keep trying. It's tricky, but I'm sure you can do it. Here. Listen to me do it again."

They spent at least a quarter of an hour in the sleigh, heedless of the cold, as Lizzy tried to mimic Joshua's call.

"I'll never get it right," Lizzy finally said. "I'm hopeless."

"No," Joshua said, but the playfulness in his eyes left, replaced by something warm that sent a thrill through Lizzy. "You're nothing of the sort."

* * *

One evening near the end of February, Lizzy curled up on the sofa and read her latest loan from Abe, *The Diary of Samuel Pepys*. Matthew came in the back door and barreled through the kitchen without taking off his boots and coat.

"Lizzy, there's going to be a big dance on Friday! At the hall!"

The book clapped shut as Lizzy sat up, her face aglow. Here was one more beacon of light shining through to create a less bleak winter, one more thing making life from the previous year pale in comparison. Of course Abe would be there. And she was quite sure that in addition to the quadrilles, lancers, and polkas, that a few waltzes would be played, even if Brother Lindsay didn't provide the music. After all, a big dance like this one would have a real band. And she and Abe would easily manage to work in a waltz in spite of her mother's disapproval of that particular "form of wickedness," as so many parents called it.

Friday afternoon was devoted to getting ready for the dance. Lizzy had to wear her brown silk, which was still the only thing she had that would be appropriate for such an event. But she spent much of the evening on her hair. She finally settled on pulling it back into a chignon at the nape of her neck and adding a cream-colored ribbon to it. In the end, she felt quite pleased with the final result, although she wished for some yellow spring flowers to tuck by her ear to finish off the look.

When she arrived, Lizzy searched the dance hall for any sign of Abe. He wouldn't be hard to find, she knew, not with his dark coloring contrasting with everyone else in the room. There was no sign of him yet. She walked the crowded perimeter of the hall, enjoying the music played by "Siv" Jeppson's orchestra, which consisted of a piano, a couple of horns, and a few stringed instruments. The dance floor was filled with couples. Several young men asked her to dance, and she willingly complied, but always looked for Abe between each one.

At quarter to eleven, nearly time for the intermission, Abe still hadn't arrived, and she worried over what might be keeping him.

"Beth!"

She turned to see Joshua pushing his way through the crowd. Her face lit up, and she crossed the distance to meet him halfway. Joshua took her hands in his and held them out, surveying her.

"You look beautiful," he said. "I mean, even more than usual."

Lizzy smiled with pleasure. She gave a mock curtsy. "Why thank you, sir. But what are you doing here? You never come to dances."

Joshua put her hand through his arm and walked to the edge, near the table where drinks were served. He shrugged. "I just had a hankering to see my girl, that's all. Thought you might be here." He leaned close and brushed her cheek with his lips. When someone walked by and called Joshua's name, he looked over and waved, for which Lizzy was intensely grateful. Her hand went up to the spot he had kissed. It almost burned. Had anyone else seen that? What would they think?

Her mind turned topsy-turvy. Did she understand correctly? Had Joshua called her "his girl"? Was his kiss that of a brother or a beau?

She thought back to all of their evening rides. Had that been his way of courting her?

If so, *what* had she done?

She felt light-headed as, for the first time in months, Lizzy let herself remember her mother's words about Joshua. *"He told us himself . . ."*

The polka finished, and a waltz was announced. Lizzy licked her lips and wrung her hands as she looked around again for Abe. No sign of him. She wondered what Joshua thought of waltzes. Would his opinion of her change if he saw her dancing one?

Joshua turned toward her and held out a hand, a mischievous look in his eye. "I hear the waltz is scandalous. But it's a truck of fun. Care to?"

Lizzy hardly believed what she was hearing, but as Abe was still nowhere in sight, she gladly went along. "Is that a dare?"

"If a dare is what it takes to dance with you."

Lizzy laughed and took his hand. "I don't know whether I should be more shocked at your asking me to waltz or at the fact that you know how."

Joshua led her to the floor, and Lizzy glanced around to see if her mother was watching. She hoped to avoid the inevitable lecture about the evils of the waltz and the reputation of a young lady—especially when she had every intention of dancing at least one more waltz with Abe. But on the other hand, since Joshua seemingly could do no wrong, seeing him waltz might convince her mother to feel differently about the dance.

Joshua turned around. Lizzy placed a hand in his and rested the other on his shoulder. He wrapped his hand around her waist, and Lizzy held her breath at the warm pressure on her lower back. The two of them had never been close this way—it was different from any embrace they'd shared over the years. She could feel his breath on her neck, smell the lye soap he had used to scrub for the evening. She stole a glance at him, and he looked at her, the edges of his mouth rounding upward. They began swaying to the music.

The crowd seemed to disappear as Lizzy glided around the room, feeling strangely at home in the crook of his arm. She was just aware enough of the crowd to keep some distance between her and Joshua. *That* would cause a sensation among the gossips of the community.

When the music ended, her cheeks felt hot and her heart beat rapidly, but not from exertion. As Joshua lowered their hands, he leaned in and whispered, "Thank you for the dance." Before pulling away, his lips brushed her cheek again, sending her heart beating faster. She looked up at him, and as he turned to lead her off the floor, she saw him differently than she ever had. She could no longer pretend that she saw him as a schoolmate. Joshua was a grown man. And a handsome one at that. The thought gave her butterflies. But she shook her head, chasing the thought away.

Abe, she reminded herself. She loved Abe. She had for more than a year. And she had all but promised herself to him.

That's when her gaze fell on Abe standing at the edge of the crowd. Arms folded, he stared with an expression that said he had seen Joshua's kiss.

Her heart sank into her stomach as Abe stared at the two of them in disbelief. She looked from Abe to Joshua frantically, feeling a tightness around her head, making it hard to think.

It's not what it looks like, she wanted to say. *He's just a good friend.* But even if she could have said the words, she wasn't sure if even *she* believed them just now.

"Abe!" Joshua called. He broke into a huge grin, walked over, and patted Abe's shoulder. "It's so good to see you! It's been months. I want you to meet Beth, the woman I told you all about at the quarry."

Abe's jaw was set tight, his eyes filled with confusion. Lizzy swallowed hard. "You two met at the quarry?" she asked, her voice as weak as her knees.

Abe wasn't looking at Joshua anymore. He gazed instead at Lizzy. Joshua's eyebrows went up as he noticed the tension. He looked between Abe and Lizzy, unsure of what was going on. "Have you . . . met?" Joshua asked.

Absolute panic swept over Lizzy. She wanted nothing more than to erase the evening, to go home—to escape the moment and remove it from memory.

Abe swallowed hard, then broke his stare and turned to Joshua. "Your Beth . . . is the girl I told you about."

Joshua's face went pale as he looked from Abe to Lizzy and back again, trying to digest what he had just heard. Both men's eyes blazed.

What had they told each other? Lizzy wondered. Did Joshua know about the plans she and Abe had for the future? What had Joshua told Abe about their friendship?

What had she gotten herself into?

She turned away from the hurt expression on Joshua's face. "You don't understand," she began, not sure herself which man she was speaking to or what possible explanation would pacify either of them.

But before another word could be uttered, a man rushed in from outside, a thick layer of snow covering his coat. He hurried through the crowd, which hushed and parted as he made his way to Brother Butler, who was in charge of the festivities. The unknown man's brow was furrowed, his face red, his breath panting as he spoke animatedly. Brother Butler nodded to the man in understanding, then raised his hands to quiet what little noise remained among the dancers. Lizzy took a step away from Joshua and Abe, relieved to no longer be the focus of their attention.

"A severe snowslide in the canyon caught a wagon team from the wood camp," he announced. The crowd murmured in shock, and Brother Butler waved his hands to quiet them.

"Of the seven men on the wagon, five managed to escape. All of the animals are buried. As are . . . as are Brothers King and Osterholdt."

A gasp went through the room, and Lizzy's heart nearly stopped.

"Poor Neph," a woman near Lizzy cried, using Brother Osterholdt's nickname. "What will his family do?"

"Doesn't he have a baby girl at home?"

"That's right," the first lady answered. "Born just last fall, my husband told me, and named after her mother Jacobina. And three wives, too. Such a shame."

A convert from Denmark, Nephi was one of the workers who had agreed to be apart from loved ones for a time to work on the temple, so Lizzy didn't know any of his three wives or his baby daughter. They were in Idaho waiting for his return. When the news reached them, how would they go on? Lizzy's hand covered her mouth and she tried not to cry. Both men weren't much older than she was. Was Helen here tonight? What about their little son?

"We need every able man for the rescue effort," Brother Butler said. "Right away."

A flurry of conversation erupted, followed by men racing to their coats and hats, including Joshua and Abe. Women fetched coats for their men as the orchestra packed instruments. Within minutes the hall was nearly empty. Only a few women were left behind, each stunned at the news.

As Lizzy retrieved her coat, her mind racing, she noticed Helen King standing in a corner. One hand over her face, her other arm holding her son, she stifled sobs and cried, "Please, God, Billie's so young. Don't take him yet. He was working on Thy house."

Lizzy stepped toward her, wanting to give some comfort, then stopped, unsure what she could possibly do or say that could help. "Can I . . . walk you and Andrew home?"

Helen looked up, tears streaking her face. "Oh, Lizzy. What are we to do?"

Lizzy closed the gap between them and pulled Helen close. "We are going to pray and we are going to hope until we hear word. Maybe those five aren't the only ones who got out. You'll see. When the rescue party gets there, they'll find Billie waiting for them, stomping around to keep warm and not a bit worse for the wear."

"You're a brick, Lizzy. I . . . I hope you're right." Helen tried to smile through her tears as she brushed Andrew's hair out of his eyes and then pulled his little head close. "I didn't want Billie going up to the wood camp this early in the season. I knew it wasn't safe until the weather warmed up, but he insisted. He was so anxious to get back to work on the temple." She wiped at her eyes and choked on her breathing.

"Come on," Lizzy said. "I'll take you home."

But Helen spied someone over Lizzy's shoulder. "Oh, Mother King!" Lizzy stepped to the side to allow Helen's mother-in-law to come through. Andrew squirmed in discomfort, and Lizzy took him in her arms to let the mother and wife of Billie King weep together.

As she held little Andrew, Lizzy couldn't stop her own tears from falling. She held the tired, young boy close and rocked him side to side. "God can't take your papa," she whispered. "You need him too much."

* * *

The rescue efforts continued all day Saturday and Sunday, with men volunteering from across Cache Valley to dig through the snow. Since eight feet of water had frozen under the slide, they worked in constant danger of getting caught if the snow shifted again.

Little else but the two missing men was thought about in town throughout the weekend. Both days, groups of women, children, and a few men could be seen climbing up the hilltop in the fifth ward to look down into the canyon for any sign of the searchers returning with word. Sunday morning Lizzy climbed the hill with her mother, Jimmy, and brothers. They trudged up the hill silently, and Lizzy tried not to think of the procession as a funeral, but she couldn't imagine the two men surviving since Friday night under all that snow.

As she gazed out at the canyon, which looked pristine and white, she choked back a sob. It was so unfair. The teams had gone up the canyon in spite of the weather because the men were so eager to work on the house of the Lord. And then tragedy struck. It was devastating, especially to Helen and little Andrew. Why would God allow such a thing to happen? Weren't the temple workers protected? She thought of how quickly James Quayle's hand injury had healed, how Hugh McKay's fall should have been fatal, yet how soon he returned to work. Everyone said that those two men had been preserved through God's power.

Helen had expressed faith that the Lord would continue to bless her family for their offerings. *Then where was God when Billie and Neph needed help?* God had abandoned them. Just as He had abandoned so many other people.

Lizzy turned away and headed back down the snow-covered hill, alone.

* * *

A few days later Lizzy went to Christiansen's Store for her mother, and as usual, those visiting inside discussed nothing but the accident and the search party. Those were about the only topics anybody talked about anymore. Lizzy stood with her back to the group as she decided between fabrics, listening hopefully for some good news.

"I heard they found both Neph and Billie," a woman said. Lizzy caught her breath. She turned around expectantly.

"That's right," a man answered.

"I don't suppose they were . . ." The woman's voice trailed off, and Lizzy wanted to finish the question for her.

The man opposite shook his head. "No, and by the looks of how they were found, neither of them had a chance."

Lizzy's stomach grew tight. She put her hands over her middle and braced herself.

"They found Neph crushed against the riverbank," the man continued. "They say he looked as if he had been trying to climb out."

Lizzy looked away, closing her eyes tightly and willing away the picture his words had put into her head.

"What about Billie King?" someone else burst in.

"They found him facedown in the river. It seemed he stood on the backs of his team. To get on top of the slide, maybe."

Lizzy wanted to yell at them. They all seemed sincerely interested, but not particularly upset. Did it really matter what Billie King's frozen body looked like when it was discovered? She didn't want to know the details—couldn't see why they seemed so fascinated in hearing them. Didn't they understand? Didn't they realize that Helen King, practically a newlywed, was now a widow? That she had a child not much more than a year old who would never know his father?

Lizzy ran out of the store, sugar forgotten. She tore across the street and collapsed against the wall of the unfinished tabernacle. Hands over her face, she trembled. It was too horrible. Too tragic. She couldn't listen to any more of it.

* * *

On the second day of March, a joint funeral for Brother Nephi Osterholdt and Brother William L. King was held. The Sullivan and Webster families attended, some of the last to squeeze into the building in honor of the fallen brethren. In all, at least fifteen hundred people paid their respects.

During the service, Lizzy looked over the crowd in search of either Joshua or Abe. She hadn't seen or heard from either since the night of the dance, but assumed both were involved in the search parties. With the bodies recovered and properly buried, there would no longer be an easy excuse for why she hadn't seen either of them.

What would she say when she finally saw Abe? Then again, explaining to Joshua would be doubly hard. As her family filed out of the building, she caught sight of someone with dark hair and looked a second time to see if it was Abe, but the person was gone.

Lizzy's thoughts returned to the tragedy in full force when she saw the four widows standing near the door. Nephi's three wives, Jacobina, Bena, and Biana were holding fast to each other's hands and, last of all, to Helen King's. Helen greeted mourners, her eyes filled with pain, though she kept a stoic expression as she accepted condolences from friends as well as perfect strangers. It would be a relief for her to go into a private spot and cry, Lizzy thought. When she reached Helen, the two women embraced, and Helen sniffed, keeping the brimming tears at bay with all her strength.

"Thank you for coming, Lizzy," she began shakily. Then the two friends clung to one another, and Helen burst into tears, both women crying into each other's shoulders.

* * *

The Sullivans went to the cemetery to witness the dedication of the graves and see the monument created for Neph and Billie. Lizzy thought it fitting that her father and the other masons had fashioned the monument out of sandstone quarried for the temple.

The rest of the family piled back into the buckboard to go home, but Lizzy didn't move. She kept staring at the graves. Her father came up behind her and placed a hand on her shoulder, making her close her eyes tightly.

"It's time to go," he said quietly.

"I can't," Lizzy said. "Not yet. Go on without me. I'll walk home."

"It's so cold—" he began, but Lizzy shook her head and ran into some nearby trees. Who cared about the snow? Billie and Neph had been stuck under it for days, had died from it. How could she even think of worrying about getting a little chilled?

From her spot in the pines, she watched her family drive out of the cemetery toward home. That's when she burst into tears again.

"What am I going to do?" she said aloud in a strained, whispered voice. "Father, if You really are there, You have to help me. I see miracles one day, then heartbreak and tragedy the next, and none of it makes any sense. I've asked for help before. Why have You never heard me?"

She fell to the ground, caring nothing for her dress or the snow scraping against her legs. Hands cradling her head, she sobbed. "If none of it is true, there's no reason for me to stay here. I might as well leave and start a new life with Abe. But if You really are up there, if You really care about your children—if You know and care about *me*—then maybe I can find a reason to stay with my family and follow their wishes."

Lizzy wept a long time in the snow, following Helen's advice and listening for an answer—perhaps the burning in her chest she had heard about so many times, a feeling of overwhelming peace washing over her, *something*. But after at least half an hour, she still felt nothing but exhaustion and searing pain behind her eyes. Her heart heavy, she finally stood, hardly able to feel her feet for numbness, and stumbled across the snow to the road home.

CHAPTER 23

Over the next several days, Lizzy tried to keep her mind on her daily tasks, to not think about Billie and Neph, her miserable prayer in the trees, or the fact that, like all her childhood prayers, it too had gone unanswered. Instead she focused on more practical things, or at least made an attempt to look at matters of the heart with a practical eye.

She hadn't seen either Abe or Joshua during the search, which was understandable—nearly every man in the city was occupied with the tragedy. But several days after the funerals, they still hadn't contacted her. Surely they were both upset over what had happened at the dance. Not surprising, she told herself as she trudged through the muddy yard from the chicken coop. And it was just as well. Not seeing either of them would give her time to assess the situation and decide what to do about it.

Because I'm certainly not getting heavenly help. The thought dropped into her mind suddenly, and she wiped it away, refusing to think about her pathetic prayer and how she had begged for help from above, only to be given silence.

Abigail watched Lizzy as she came inside with the basket of eggs, eyeing her daughter's bright pink cheeks. "It's not that warm out yet. Didn't you wear a wrap?" she asked, mixing batter in a bowl. Then she noticed the muddy trail of footsteps Lizzy had made from the back door, through the boiler room, and into the kitchen.

Lizzy's gaze followed her mother's. She picked up one foot and then the other, then wiped a hand across her forehead. "I'm sorry, Mama. My mind must have been elsewhere." She took off the boots and proceeded to clean up the slick brown muck, hoping her mother wouldn't ask what she had been thinking about.

She picked up the boots and pushed the back door open so she could scrape the mud off them. Once again her thoughts turned to the fix she had gotten herself into. She had to see Abe so she could explain. For one thing, he needed to know about her friendship with Joshua. But even as she tried to compose a speech explaining it to Abe, she found herself figuring out how many days had passed since her last sleigh ride with Joshua.

She now knew without a doubt that Joshua had feelings for her. And for a brief moment at the dance, she had wondered about her own heart. *What* was she to do?

Waltzing with Joshua had been exhilarating. She couldn't deny the flutter in her stomach when he kissed her cheek, that she felt something she had never experienced before. There was no escaping that she viewed Joshua differently now, as more than the awkward boy who used to pull her pigtails and race her home from school.

The snow had almost lost its hold, she realized suddenly. Sleigh rides were no longer possible. When the roads dried, would Joshua come calling in his buggy?

Lizzy scraped her boots against the bricks, then struck each one hard against the wall. Getting the mud off them was as good excuse as any to express her frustration. She dropped them and closed the door, her hands coming to her face as she turned away, hoping her mother wouldn't see the bitter emotion.

* * *

Several days later, near the middle of March, Abigail decided it was warm enough to sit on the backyard swing to do her mending, which sat on the ground behind the house. A brisk breeze kicked up, and Abigail tucked the blanket around herself better. Her belly bulged under the cover now, and the regular movements of her baby inside were a daily comfort.

David sat beside her, reading a book, a small quilt draped across his legs. She glanced over at him, pleased at how he was finally growing—nearly two inches in the last six months. He had a persistent cough, but it was nothing to worry about, the doctor had assured the family. Abigail hummed a hymn softly to herself and smiled periodically at the sounds of play coming from the fields behind the barn as the boys let out their spring fever. They would surely return covered in mud. *No matter. Let them play before the hard spring work begins.*

Abigail finished the patch on the pants and laid them aside. As she reached for the next item in the pile, a shirt with a torn sleeve, she heard someone approaching. Figuring it was one of the boys, she returned to her needle. When the footsteps stopped, Abigail looked up.

For an awkward moment, she and Abe stared at each other without saying a word.

"Hello, Mrs. Sullivan," he said, his voice cracking slightly. "Hello, David."

"Hi there," David said quietly, pulling his blanket higher.

"I don't recall you and Lizzy having arranged a time to meet," Abigail said bluntly as a reminder of the rule. She didn't like Abe talking to David, either. Abe glanced up at Lizzy's window. Abigail looked too and saw the lace curtain swaying slightly.

"Mrs. Sullivan, I know I should have talked to you first, but I assure you, Lizzy doesn't expect me. And I really need to speak with her."

Abigail pursed her lips and raised her eyebrows.

Abe stuck his hands farther into his pockets. "It's a—a matter of a personal nature."

Abigail sucked in her breath, then laid her work in her lap and clasped her hands together. "It's *personal?*"

What could he mean? Abigail couldn't help but jump to thoughts of matrimony between the two, and her heart ached. Lizzy would miss so much if she married outside the faith. Abigail couldn't believe for one moment that marrying this Indian boy would make Lizzy truly happy.

"I just need to . . . discuss something that happened at the dance," Abe said.

After a moment of consideration, Abigail said, "Very well. But only for a few minutes." She stood and led him into the house, through the kitchen, then motioned for him to have a seat in the parlor. "She'll be down in a moment."

Holding his hat between his hands, Abe nodded. "Thank you, Mrs. Sullivan. I won't be long."

Abigail went upstairs and knocked on Lizzy's door. "You have a visitor."

The door opened a crack. Lizzy didn't seem excited. "Who is it?" she asked, then saw the look on Abigail's face and knew it could only be Abe. She came downstairs and joined him in the parlor.

While she was tempted to stay in the kitchen where she could hear them talk, Abigail went out when David called for her. His cheeks were rosier than normal, and a quick press of her hand told her that he had a slight fever. She sat beside him, and he leaned his head against her, unable to climb into her lap now that her belly stuck out too much. She covered him once again with the blanket and kept an ear open to sounds from the house.

With the door closed, and both the boiler room and the kitchen between her and the parlor, she couldn't hear anything. She had a mind to prop the door open. After all, what would the neighbors think if they knew her daughter and a young man were alone without a chaperone? But she couldn't bring herself to leave David's side. She stroked his hair and rocked the swing.

David lifted his head and smiled at her. He had recently lost his two front teeth, and he looked much older now with large adult ones poking through his gums.

"Thanks, Mama," David said, putting his head back down. "You're the best medicine."

* * *

When Lizzy appeared, Abe found himself twisting his hat in his hands; he hadn't ever felt so awkward around Lizzy, but after the dance . . .

"Hello, Abe," Lizzy said from the doorway. "I've been wondering when I'd see you again."

Abe turned to her. She wore his favorite dress, the navy one with small peach-colored flowers all over it. She crossed the room and sat beside him on the couch. They sat together awkwardly, neither knowing how to start the conversation.

With a glance toward the door, Lizzy said, "I think Mama has been hoping that I'd given up our friendship," she said with a nervous laugh.

As Abe reached for one of her hands, he realized his own was trembling. "Is that what we have, Lizzy? Just a friendship?"

"Oh, Abe. Of course not," Lizzy said, putting her other hand on top of his. "You mean much more to me than that."

His heart began beating again, but his throat stuck as he tried to swallow. "Then may I ask exactly what Joshua Sorensen means to you?"

"I suppose I should have told you about him long ago." She withdrew her hand and shook her head. "I'm sorry, Abe."

"How do Joshua and I both fit into your life?" he asked, voice low.

"You have to understand that Joshua and I have been close since our early school years. He's always been a great friend, but never anything else."

Abe let out a deep breath, one he hadn't realized he'd been holding. "I thought he had stolen your heart," he said with a shaky laugh. "It sure looked that way when he . . ." Abe couldn't say the words *kissed you,* but when Lizzy flushed, he knew she understood his meaning.

"You don't mean that *I* looked that way, do you?"

Abe shrugged. "I was so surprised to see Joshua with you that I'm not sure what I saw anymore. At the time I thought you looked at him . . . well, the way you've looked at me sometimes. It made me powerful jealous. I didn't like it one bit."

Lizzy leaned forward and kissed Abe's cheek. She sat back. "There. Now I've given that kiss back to you."

Abe smiled in relief, but then his brow furrowed. He looked into her eyes, trying to see what was behind them. "Lizzy, there's something I don't think you understand about Joshua." Abe thought back to the quarry, to the late-night talks he and Joshua had discussing their girls back home. Their *girl,* he corrected himself.

"He loves you," Abe said.

"Of course he does, as a friend. I love him too, in a way." But Lizzy seemed to be trying just a little too hard to convince even herself. She had to know that Joshua had deeper feelings for her.

"No, Lizzy. It's not like that. Joshua *loves* you. He told me all about his girl at home, how he had loved her for years and had plans to marry her and make her happy in the house he built for them."

Lizzy's eyes went wide, and she flushed hot. "He—he told you—those things?" she began to stammer.

Abe took her hand and pressed it between both of his. "I just wanted you to understand. He's serious. And I need to know if you return his feelings."

She shook her head and hugged him. "How could you ask something like that?"

Abe closed his eyes and breathed deeply, wishing she had said words that left no doubt, like, *No, Abe. I don't love Joshua. I love only you.*

But it was him she held now, he reminded himself. He was the one she was risking her family's approval over.

"I don't know what I'd do if I lost you, Lizzy Sullivan," he murmured.

* * *

While Abe was inside with Lizzy, Abigail fidgeted, surely disturbing David. At least she wasn't doing the mending. In this state she wouldn't be able to make any decent stitches. To her relief, Abe emerged not ten minutes later. He touched his hat and nodded once more.

"Good day, Mrs. Sullivan," he said, then headed for the street. He stopped and turned back, pulling a tattered book from his pocket. "I meant to loan this to Lizzy. May I give it to her?"

Abigail reached for the volume. "I can give it to her," she said.

Abe hesitated a moment before handing it over. "Thank you, ma'am," he said with a final tip of his hat. "It's a special book to me. I appreciate you taking extra care with it."

She watched him retrace his steps toward the front of the house and wondered where his home was from there. A moment later

Abigail heard the sounds of Sophie's growls, followed by Abe backing up, his hands raised. Sophie's ears lowered as she moved forward. Abigail couldn't help think that even the dog recognized danger when she saw it, avoiding thoughts about how Sophie had behaved the same way when their family arrived at the Webster home.

Abe kept moving away. "Don't worry," he said to the dog. "I'm not going to hurt you."

"Sophie, come here," Abigail called, rescuing Abe. She had to call a second time before Sophie moved to Abigail's side.

"I'll go the back way if you don't mind," Abe said. "That animal obviously doesn't want me to go out front." He went toward the barn, then around the building and disappeared from sight. Abigail scratched Sophie's neck and let out a sigh, looking at the book Abe had brought for Lizzy to read. *Rasselas.* Whatever that was. She wiped the cover with her apron as if it needed some kind of cleansing. One hand dropped to her side, and she rubbed her forehead with the other.

"Lizzy, Lizzy," she murmured. She looked down at David. She tucked the blanket around him as Sophie trotted off. With a deep sigh, Abigail headed inside the house and found Lizzy just as she reached the base of the stairs.

"Lizzy."

She blinked and looked over. "Yes?"

Abigail held out the book. "He meant to give this to you." She still couldn't bring herself to say his name.

"Thank you." Lizzy took the book. "This used to be his mother's," she said, and flipped through its pages. "Well, I suppose all his books used to be his mother's. But this one is special to him." She lifted the book to her face, as if breathing in the smell of the pages. Abigail never could understand her daughter's fascination with the printed word, and wondered what influence it had on the girl as Lizzy held the book to her chest and headed for the stairs.

"Would you tell me what you talked about?" Abigail asked before she could leave.

Lizzy turned around slowly. "What do you mean?"

Abigail picked stray threads from her skirt as she spoke. "He said he had something of a personal nature to discuss with you. What was it?"

Lizzy seemed to peer into her mother's eyes, as if she truly wanted to tell her everything in her heart but didn't dare. As much as Abigail wanted to hear her daughter's inner thoughts, she knew as well as Lizzy did that if those inner dreams included an Indian Gentile for a husband, the girl would hardly confide something like that.

"We talked about Joshua," Lizzy said quietly.

"What did you say about him?"

Lizzy shrugged. "That he and I have always been friends."

"And now?"

Mother's and daughter's eyes locked for a moment, and Lizzy said, "I don't know."

"And Abe? How do you feel about him?"

Lizzy looked down at her hands, as if she were unwilling for her mother to read the truth in her eyes. Abigail wanted to reach for her chin and lift her face, but instead Lizzy wiped both hands across her cheeks, sniffed, and turned to the stairs. "I'd rather not talk about this right now."

As she began up the stairs, David cried from somewhere outside. Thoughts about Abe and Joshua were put on hold as mother and daughter turned to race outside. Just as David entered the house, they reached him.

"David!" Abigail's voice rose in anxiety. "What's wrong?"

Without an answer, he spun around and ran past his abandoned quilt to the barn, Lizzy and Abigail following close behind. Just outside the door they found Sophie on the ground. David wrapped his arms around the dog's neck, her fur moist with his tears. "Something's wrong! Help her, Mama. Please!"

Lizzy managed to urge David away from the dog and into her arms while their mother checked Sophie, who lay motionless. Leaning down, Abigail put her hand on the dog's nose, feeling for breath, her hands pressed on the animal's chest and abdomen. Several seconds passed, but she detected nothing. She finally pressed her ear against the dog's chest. When she heard no beat, she closed her eyes and bit her lips together before sitting up and facing her son. "I'm so sorry, David. She's gone."

"She can't be," he said, bursting into a new round of sobs. "She's my best friend. And she's only a few years old."

David fell into his mother's embrace, and she rocked him back and forth, her own tears mingling with his. Sophie had done for David what no doctor or medicine could do. Abigail owed her son's life to the dog. She turned to the furry body and stroked Sophie's head.

"Sweet thing," Abigail said. "She was a good friend, that's certain."

"Do you have any idea what happened to her?" Lizzy asked.

David sniffed hard and shook his head back and forth. "That's the strangest part," he said, his voice quavering. "Nothing happened. She walked out of the barn looking fine, then she stiffened up, shook, and fell over."

Abigail's tearful face hardened. "That sounds like just like what happened to the Turners' dog when—" She stopped, then glanced backward through the barn door. She stood up, lifted her hem, and marched inside. "I thought so."

Lizzy and David came inside to see her pointing to a spilled mess on the floor.

"It was rat poison," Abigail said. "Lizzy, I hope you know what this means."

Her brow furrowed, and she shook her head. "No, what?"

"That your Indian friend did this. He poisoned Sophie."

Lizzy's jaw dropped open as if her mother were joking, but Abigail had never looked so somber. "Mama, that's a ridiculous notion."

"Is it? He was here just a few moments ago, wasn't he? Sophie all but attacked him. He left by way of the barn and probably wanted to get rid of her. He could have easily entered the back door and dumped out rat poison beside her food dish without anyone seeing him. It was only a matter of time before Sophie went in there."

"But Abe *couldn't* have done this, Mother," Lizzy insisted. "He isn't that kind of person. David, you know Abe wouldn't have done this, don't you?"

Abigail pulled David close and shook her head. "Don't bring your brother into this. He has just lost his dearest friend. And don't try to protect that boy." She rocked back and forth, holding David fiercely. When she spoke again, her voice was scarcely a whisper, but the force behind it was unmistakable.

"But now I see what kind of man he really is. Abe Franklin murdered Sophie," she said, for the first time uttering his name. "I will never tolerate him on our property again."

She lifted her index finger and punctuated her next sentence with it. "If I ever see him on our property, so help me, I will chase him off with your father's rifle." Her voice rose several notches.

All color drained from Lizzy's face. Abigail nodded to herself. Maybe now Lizzy would understand that this family's values were not to be ignored so long as she lived in this house.

"Mama, please—"

"He will never be welcome in this house again. Never."

"But he didn't do anything—"

"Do I make myself clear?" Abigail was speaking at the top of her voice now.

Stunned, Lizzy closed her eyes, anger burning through her body. She wanted to scream, yell, and argue, but her mother's tone showed she was beyond reason. For a moment Lizzy just stared at her mother, mouth gaping open, unable to find any words to say in response to her mother's unreasonable ultimatum.

Abigail repeated herself, this time stabbing her finger toward Lizzy. "Do I make myself clear?"

"Completely," Lizzy said, unsure how her voice was remaining so calm. "But don't think for a moment that it will stop me from seeing him."

With that she stormed out of the kitchen and up the stairs, then slammed the bedroom door behind her.

CHAPTER 24

Lizzy sat on her bed in a stupor for much of the afternoon and into dusk. How could she convince her mother that Abe was innocent? Her mother was too blinded by emotion to be swayed by logic. She realized it would be very hard to continue her relationship with Abe now. Not impossible, but more difficult than ever. It occurred to Lizzy once that she should be working, that her mother would surely fetch her at any time, especially when supper needed preparing. But her mother never came.

Lizzy heard the clinking of dishes in the kitchen and knew the family was eating, but she didn't go down. She had no stomach for food right then.

When the family finished and the dining noises turned to ones of evening banter, Lizzy heard the back door open. She looked down from her window to see David making his way to the barn. His head hung low, and his feet stepped heavily. The sun had set, but it wasn't yet full dark. Lizzy watched David's shadowy form go inside the barn.

To Sophie.

A hand went to Lizzy's mouth. She had been so involved with her own sadness that she had forgotten about David's loss. He was surely saying good-bye to his beloved pet and needed that private time.

But several minutes later, he still hadn't emerged. Lizzy opened her window to call for him, and make sure he was well, but before she could, she heard the sound of sobs and cries.

Without another thought, Lizzy raced down the stairs and outside to find her brother. Even from the doorway of the barn she realized it was too dark to see much inside.

"Da—"

But her call was cut off by the sound of the same pathetic cries coming from somewhere behind the barn. Lizzy hurried through the dim structure and out the back door, looking around frantically for her brother.

When she emerged, she saw him by the orchard. She stopped, unable to move. David held a shovel in both hands and was fiercely hacking at the hard springtime soil. Each effort produced significantly less than a full shovelful of dirt, and the hole was pitifully small. He had dirty tears streaking his face, and he sobbed each time he pushed the shovel down into the ground. Sophie's body lay beside him on a burlap sack.

David bordered on hyperventilation as he tried again and again to dig the grave. In despair, he let the shovel fall from his hands, and his knees gave out. He dropped to the ground and wept.

Lizzy spurred herself into action and flew to his side. She scooped him into her arms, and he clung to her, sobbing into her shoulder uncontrollably.

"I can't do it," he cried.

And she knew he meant more than the grave. He had lost his best friend. How could he go on? She rocked back and forth, unable to find any words of comfort.

"I'm sorry," she managed to say. David burrowed deeper into her arms, his entire body shaking with grief.

They sat that way until darkness surrounded them and stars began poking through the black sky. Finally David was able to speak.

"Can you help me?" he asked quietly.

Lizzy nodded. David slid off her lap as she stood and picked up the shovel. She put the tip into the ground, put her foot on top, and heaved against it with all her weight. She pulled it back to loosen the ground, then dumped the soil to the side and began again.

David watched for several minutes, then went back to the barn for a second shovel. Together he and his sister dug the grave for Sophie by the light of the stars.

After nearly half an hour, with breath heavy and a quick heartbeat, Lizzy put an arm around David's shoulders. "Will that do?"

She could feel David nod.

They lay their shovels aside, then went to Sophie's still form. David knelt down and looked at her. His hand hovered over her face, as if he wasn't sure whether he should give her head a final stroke of farewell.

After a moment's hesitation, he patted her head and leaned in. "I miss you already," he said, his voice tight. Then he gripped the edges of the sack, and Lizzy helped drag the dog toward the hole and gently place her into it. As they reached for their shovels once again, the back door clanged open, and they both looked over.

"Lizzy? Are you out here?" It was their father. "Do you know where David is?"

"I'm here," she called. "By the orchard. With David."

"They're both out by the orchard," Richard called back into the house, then let the door slam shut. He walked around the barn and found them. "Your mother thought David had gone to lie down for a nap and just discovered he wasn't inside. She nearly had a fit looking for him."

"I'm fine, Papa," David said, although even in the darkness Lizzy could see his gaunt face and hollow eyes. "We're giving Sophie a proper burial."

Richard reached them and looked into the hole, where the dog lay pitifully stiff in the bottom. "I was going to help you do that first thing in the morning."

"I know," David said. "But . . ."

His voice trailed off, and he didn't finish the thought. Lizzy knew what he meant. He couldn't wait until morning, not when his heart was breaking. He couldn't leave Sophie lying on the ground rather than laid to rest.

Richard cleared his throat. "You did a right fine job," he said, gesturing toward the grave.

"Thanks, Papa." David's voice was scarcely audible. He looked up at his father with pleading eyes. "Would you say a prayer over her?"

"I would be honored," Richard said. He took off his hat, wrapped an arm around David and another around Lizzy, and the three of them stood at the edge of the orchard, heads bowed, as he spoke to the heavens.

* * *

Lizzy walked the distance from their home on Main Street to the stores on the south end. Spring had come fully. With the snow melted, the dirt roads were dried enough for wagons and buggies to move along without getting bogged down in mud. She could also walk without soiling her hem before reaching the wooden sidewalks.

In the weeks since Sophie died, Lizzy's mother remained as steadfast in her decision as ever. If Lizzy and Abe were to continue their relationship, it wouldn't be on Sullivan property. Once her mother even implied that if David ever had a relapse, it would be Abe's fault, since Sophie couldn't help him get well. She had seen Abe only once since—for less than five minutes by Christiansen's Store to tell him about her mother's decision.

She felt as if a heavy ball were in her stomach. *We can still meet,* she reminded herself. *It will be just as it was before Mama ever found out about us.*

For some strange reason, the thought held no thrill of expectation. When she'd first told Abe, she hadn't stayed long enough for him to respond or for them to arrange a time and place to meet again. Somehow she knew that a chapter had closed, that she couldn't rebel against her mother the way she had over a year ago. Not after the pain Sophie's death had caused. Abe hadn't had anything to do with it, Lizzy was certain. But she had no way of proving it, and until then she could not bear to bring even more pain upon her family. She would no longer invite Abe to the house. And she knew that even her meetings with him elsewhere would be fewer than before, because each time she left for one her mother would relive Sophie's death.

Ironically, in spite of Lizzy's sadness, the thought of following her mother's wishes made Lizzy feel more like a woman than before when she'd defied them.

"It won't be the same," she told Abe. "I thought we had almost won her over, but now we're further away from that day than ever. I'm sorry, Abe," she had said. "You don't know how sorry." Then she ran away before he could say anything more to make it worse. She couldn't bear to stay and listen to his efforts at comforting her, his assurances that they would turn her mother's heart yet. Now Lizzy lifted her face to the sun, needing the warmth, as if it could ease the chill in her heart.

And she thought of Joshua, who hadn't come to see her since the dance nearly two months before. What would she do without either of them? The thought was more than she could bear. With an added ache, she wondered what Joshua's house looked like now that it was no longer surrounded by snow. What improvements had he made on it? Was he close to moving inside? She wondered if Joshua had set his eye on courting someone else.

Passing ZCMI, she neared a man just outside Cardon's Furniture Store. He was hitching up a dark brown mare with white fetlocks. Joshua and his horse. She had to speak to him. The coincidence was positively providential, as Sister Webster would say. Lizzy hurried to him, holding her skirts, wracking her brain for something to say. He pulled on the knot in the rope to make sure it would hold. Stepping inside, he reached up to remove his hat as Lizzy called to him.

"Joshua!"

He paused to look over his shoulder toward the voice, then froze when he saw her. "Joshua," she repeated when she got closer and reached for his arm. The look of surprise that crossed his face was replaced with one of sadness.

He tilted his head and touched his hat. "Hello, Beth. Nice to see you." His voice was as formal as if she were a mere acquaintance. It pierced her heart, but she supposed it was no less than she deserved. She groped for something to say, a way to approach the subject they had surely both been thinking about for weeks.

"How have you been?" she asked pathetically. *I've been miserable.* "I've missed our rides."

Joshua looked at the store, then down at his hat and shrugged. "Been pretty busy with the house and all." He glanced at Lizzy, who waited for more. "Besides, weather isn't real suited for sleigh rides anymore, is it?"

He attempted a weak smile, but Lizzy could feel his detachment in every word, every movement. She forced herself to speak the words that clung to her tongue.

"I'm . . . I'm sorry about what happened at the dance." She stopped, realizing that the problem was so much more than one eventful night. "I'm sorry about everything."

Joshua still didn't look in her eyes. His lips pursed slightly as he ran his finger along the edge of his hat. "You mean about being Abe's girl—and not telling me about it?"

Her mind raced. What could she say? Yes, she was Abe's girl? That was the truth, wasn't it? And yet . . .

When she didn't speak, Joshua walked past her, into the furniture store.

"Are you buying something for the house?" she asked, following him into the dim light, desperate to keep the conversation going.

Joshua nodded. "I need a wardrobe and a bed. I suppose I could make them, but I haven't had that much time, and—"

"Joshua, I—you—" Lizzy stammered. Somehow she needed to apologize, to explain. But all she could muster was, "Would you like help picking them out?" She immediately regretted the words. After all that had happened, all she could give was a ridiculous offer to help choose housewares?

Joshua turned to her. He glanced around as if making sure no one else could overhear them, then stepped into a corner, pulling her there with him. He lowered his voice, which was husky with emotion. "Beth, when you helped me pick out curtains and rugs and all those other things, I thought . . ." His voice trailed off, and he coughed awkwardly. She held her breath, half afraid of what he was about to say. "I thought you were the woman I would enjoy all those things with. I suppose it was foolish to think you might feel the same way."

He shifted his weight uneasily, but then he looked Lizzy in the eye. "A few times last winter I thought I saw . . . *something* in your eyes. I felt it between us. Can you tell me you didn't feel it?"

Lizzy found herself unable to speak. Her mind returned to the thrill that went through her at the dance when she twirled across the floor in his arms, of the flush when he kissed her cheek. "I—I don't know," she stammered.

Joshua breathed out deeply and searched her face. His eyes looked red, and Lizzy could hardly stand to look into them and see the hurt she had caused. "I love you, Beth. I always have. There. I said it."

The words sent Lizzy's heart knocking against her chest, and her cheeks suddenly burned. But Joshua's gaze penetrated so deeply that she had to lower her eyes. She was so confused. If she kept looking into those eyes, Joshua would surely read her very soul.

And what would he find there if he did? She didn't know anymore. Emotions welled up inside her, too many to sort out or to know what she thought—or felt—or could possibly say.

Joshua went on. "I'm sorry. I never imagined saying it this way. But why did you think I bought your family's farm? I wanted to give your home back to you, to care for you and be by your side for the rest of our lives. But since you don't feel the same, I'd rather you didn't pick out anything else for the house. As it is, I can hardly look anywhere without seeing your touch."

He waited only a moment for a response before turning around and striding away. Lizzy opened her mouth to call him back, but stopped, not knowing what to say. In a daze, she left the store. She steadied herself on the hitching post beside Joshua's horse. It nuzzled her, and Lizzy stroked its face.

"What should I do?" She said to the animal. "What can I say to him?" She couldn't deny what she had felt those moments in the sleigh and on the dance floor. But what about Abe? Surely what she felt for him outweighed whatever flutters Joshua gave her. She shook her head to clear it, but it didn't do much to quell the waves of emotions clashing inside her.

* * *

Lizzy pressed butter into molds one afternoon as her mother sat at the table with her feet up, taking another one of her more frequent rests. Lizzy knew that her help would be especially needed until her mother felt better. They figured the baby would arrive sometime in October.

Jimmy came downstairs carrying a book in one hand.

"Aunt Abigail, can Lizzy read to me today? It's been almost a week, and if we don't read more soon, I'll forget what's happening in the story." He looked very serious about the matter.

Abigail glanced toward Lizzy, who had nearly finished with the butter. "Sure, Jimmy," she said, taking the paddle from Lizzy's hand.

"You aren't feeling well. Are you sure?" Lizzy asked.

"I'll be fine," Abigail said, then turned to her nephew. "But Jimmy, I'll need Lizzy's help again in about an hour."

"Thanks, Aunt Abigail." Jimmy clapped his hands together. "Come with me out to the barn. I know a perfect spot for reading!"

He gripped her hand and nearly pulled her off the chair. She ran after him, trying to keep up. Jimmy entered the barn and pointed to the stack of hay bales in the corner which Richard had bought from the temple stable's excess.

"See? If we put one of these on the floor," he said, moving over to grab a bale, "I can sit on it and lean back to rest like this." He did just that, then folded his arms, a silly grin on his face, showing how pleased he was with himself. As Lizzy crossed to him, Jimmy stood suddenly and pulled another bale down. He placed it beside his and patted the top. "Here. You sit on that one."

Lizzy complied. She took the book from Jimmy, one she had borrowed a second time from Abe. Jimmy lay back again, this time with his hands locked behind his head and his eyes closed to listen. She laughed to herself as she opened the cover. He could be rather dramatic at times and could never sit still for long, even during a story. Within minutes he would be picking at hay or playing with whatever the latest diversion was in his pocket, be it a rock or a handful of marbles.

"Chapter seven," Lizzy began. "'The harder Tom tried to fasten his mind on his book, the more his ideas wandered.'" Rather fitting, she thought, considering who she was reading to. She smiled to herself and went on.

Lizzy read chapters seven, eight, and nine, one more than she had intended when they'd come out. "I need to see if Mama needs me now."

Jimmy sat up in a hurry. "You can't stop with the dead man and the coffin," he said. Apparently he *had* been listening. "You just can't! I have to find out what happens next. I just have to." He looked around for a way to prove his intent to her. "I won't even play with the wheel." He clasped his hands together and placed them in his lap.

She glanced from Jimmy toward the barn door, then down at the book in her hands. "Fine. But only one more chapter. *One.*" She held up a finger for emphasis. Jimmy nodded eagerly.

"Chapter ten," Lizzy said, and already Jimmy was picking pieces of hay out of the bale. He pulled some out, then fiddled with the pieces between his fingers. Lizzy eyed his latest entertainment, then sighed and continued. "'The two boys flew on and on, toward the village, speechless with horror.'" She paused when she noticed Jimmy fingering something in his pockets.

"What are you playing with?" she asked.

He turned away slightly. "Nothin'. Just . . . just some little pieces of wood."

Lizzy went on, deciding not to pay any more attention to Jimmy so she could get through the chapter and back inside to help with the chores. She didn't look up over the next few pages, not until Jimmy stood, screaming. Lizzy turned in surprise, her expression changing to shock as she heard the hay bale he had been sitting on crackling. On the floor were the charred remnants of a dozen matches.

"It hurts, it hurts!" Jimmy yelled. He ran, flames crawling his side.

Already the smell of smoke brought a choke of fear to Lizzy's throat and sent her heart beating wildly. Images of her burning home returned instantly. She shoved those thoughts from her mind and chased after Jimmy.

"Stop running," Lizzy yelled after him as he ran blindly through the smoke. She beat at his arm and back to quench the flames, but Jimmy would not keep still. He flailed about, twisting this way and that, and finally knocked her to the ground. She landed with a thud, his strength far too much for hers. She stood, searching through the smoke for Jimmy. The fire had spread fast to one whole side of the barn and kept growing. An orange blaze engulfed the hay where they had been sitting moments before.

"Jimmy!" Lizzy screamed into the haze.

He came back into view, the flames spreading to his torso. He shrieked in pain, and the dry straw on the floor sprang to life in flames as he passed. Before he could disappear again, Lizzy grabbed a saddle blanket and threw it over his shoulders. Thick smoke burned her eyes and choked her breathing as she pounded on his body. Jimmy's only response was a low moan. Her heart raced with a fast, heavy beat, feeling like it would jump out of her chest at any moment.

With his flames extinguished, Jimmy's back looked red and black, and his shirt had burned away. Lizzy put her sleeve over her mouth to make breathing easier and looked around, trying to gain her bearings and find the door. Her ears pounded with the sounds of burning and crackling wood as she prayed someone would notice the fire. But it might already be too late to save the barn.

"Let's go!" she yelled, pulling Jimmy along toward what she thought was the door. He put so much of his weight on her small frame that she could hardly walk. She glanced up to whisper a prayer, then gasped at the sight of the rafters engulfed.

"Hurry!" she choked.

Jimmy no longer spoke, and with her next step he got suddenly heavier. His eyes rolled back. In a panic, Lizzy slapped his cheek. "Jimmy, come on. Don't stop."

He opened his eyes just as a beam broke free and crashed to the ground in front of them. Jimmy eyes widened in fright, and he broke away.

"Jimmy!" Lizzy's voice ripped from her throat in terror as he disappeared from sight.

She looked around for him in vain. But her mind was fuzzy, and she couldn't get enough air into her chest, which burned with each shallow breath. A coughing fit wracked her body. She took a tentative step forward, feeling the ground with her toe.

The smoke stung her eyes, and since she could no longer see clearly anyway, she closed them tightly and reached to feel her way. She gasped for air, heat pressing her from all sides. Where was Jimmy? Where was the door?

Lizzy felt as if the smoke were smothering her, and she gasped for air. Her body was just too weak to move any farther. Her knees buckled beneath her, and she fell to the ground.

As she lay there, she fought the blackness threatening to take over. Out of the haze, Abe's face came into view. "Abe?" she said, voice cracking.

He scooped her up and ran through the burning doorframe. After putting her down at a safe distance, he beat out her flaming skirts. Lizzy grimaced as he did it, but gasped deep gulps of fresh air, then choked and coughed the smoke from her lungs.

"How do you feel?" he asked.

"Jimmy . . ." she gasped, reaching toward the barn.

Abe's eyes went wide. He studied the blaze for only a second before plunging back into the barn. Lizzy raised up on her elbow, still coughing, and waited to see any sign of Abe and Jimmy. She heard the sound of another beam crashing, and put up her hands as if to block it. Tears coursed down her cheeks.

"God, if You're there, save them. You must. Save them both."

Abe finally emerged, half carrying, half dragging Jimmy's limp form. Lizzy's arm collapsed, and she fell back to the ground with sobbing relief. She closed her eyes and surrendered to the darkness around her as commotion and shouts began from all sides.

CHAPTER 25

"Lizzy? Can you hear me?"

At the sound of her mother's voice, Lizzy's eyes strained to open. She tried to sit up and became sharply aware of searing pain in her hands. She cried out and dropped back against the pillow.

Where was she and what had happened?

She strained to think through the haze of her mind, finding no memory of coming into the house or lying on her bed. The only image she had was of collapsing on the grass after . . .

The barn. As the memory washed over her, she caught her breath, which sent her into a coughing fit. Her throat felt raw, as if the smoke had eaten through it. A damp cloth stroked her forehead, and as the coughs gradually subsided, Lizzy was able to feel the relief of the cool rag.

"Mama?" Lizzy whispered, causing sharp pains to shoot across her throat. Her eyelids felt like lead, but she managed to open them anyway. It took a moment to focus on her mother's face, which looked tired and haggard.

"How do you feel?" Abigail asked.

"Hands hurt," was all Lizzy managed. She swallowed hard to relieve the horrible dryness. "Here too," she added, reaching up to her neck with a bandaged hand. But touching her throat sent a shock of pain through her fingers and up her arm. Grimacing, she rested her hand back on the bed.

She heard liquid pouring from a pitcher, and moments later her mother appeared with a glass of water. "Here you go." She gingerly put her hand behind her daughter's head and helped her raise up enough to drink. Lizzy's lips were cracked, her mouth parched, and as the water passed over her lips and down her throat, it cooled and soothed each surface.

Feeling much better in spite of her hands, which throbbed, Lizzy lay back and thought of the fire, of the terror of being trapped in the blinding smoke and the heat, of falling to the ground and hearing Abe's voice. Her heart jumped. *Is Abe hurt?*

"How is he?" she croaked. As soon as the words came out, she realized that her mother would assume she meant Jimmy, and was ashamed she hadn't thought of him first.

"Jimmy . . ." But Abigail's voice trailed off. She brought her fingers to her lips as she looked away, emotion choking her voice.

"Mama?" Lizzy swallowed to moisten her throat. But even as she spoke, she knew the truth.

Abigail looked back but slowly shook her head. "He wasn't breathing when Abe brought him out. We did everything we could, but . . ." She pressed a handkerchief to her eyes.

Lizzy stared at her mother in shock. Surely it wasn't true. She had seen Abe carry Jimmy out of the barn. He would be fine.

But her mother kept shaking her head. Jimmy was dead.

For a moment Lizzy lay there, staring at her mother in shock. It couldn't be true. It couldn't. But the sorrow in Abigail's face made the reality sink in. Suddenly Lizzy wanted to scream at God, to pound the bed with her fists, but all she could do was lie there, turn her head, and cry. Guilt washed over her. Could she have done more to save Jimmy? Every second of those terrifying minutes in the barn came back, the smoke, the heat, the darkness. As she relived it all, she began coughing, sending more tears from both eyes from the pain.

"He's dead?" Her voice cracked miserably.

Eyes misty, Abigail said, "I'm so sorry."

Lizzy turned her face away. If it hadn't been for Abe, she would have died too.

Abigail wiped her eyes and cleared her throat. She adjusted the quilt, as if to help make Lizzy warmer, but probably to keep her hands and mind occupied so she could control her emotions.

She glanced over her shoulder at the door. "Abe has been staying here as he recuperates. He's still too weak to go home, but he's doing better."

Lizzy's eyes shot open, and she suddenly felt weak with relief. Abe was alive. And here, in her house.

"The doctor agreed he wasn't strong enough to be moved," Abigail went on. "And after all, it's the least I can do for him after he saved my first child." She ran her hand along Lizzy's cheek. "I have something to tell you." Her eyes moved back to the quilt, and she hesitated. "I—I was wrong about Abe."

Lizzy's heart beat quicker, but she didn't dare speak. Her mother went on.

"He couldn't have poisoned Sophie. I see that now. The bag must have been knocked off the shelf. It wouldn't surprise me if Jimmy did it and forgot to mention it or—or if after Sophie died he didn't dare." Abigail's brow furrowed, and she sniffed. "The fact is, Lizzy, most men wouldn't have the character to run into a burning barn like Abe did, let alone twice." Her voice caught, and she coughed to even it out. "In risking his own life, he saved yours and did his best to save your cousin's. For that I will be eternally grateful."

Lizzy nodded, confused by the gratitude and sorrow warring within her. Where was God in all of this?

* * *

By the light of a candle, Abigail sat at the kitchen table with a sheet of paper before her. The only words she had managed to write on it were the date and *Dear Louisa.*

How was she supposed write to Louisa what had happened to her son? Abigail's sister had never returned to Utah since leaving all those years ago. Thinking back on the time her family was baptized, Abigail realized that Louisa probably hadn't been fully converted; she wasn't yet ready to take on the covenants that membership in God's kingdom would require.

Louisa never had been the same after her husband and baby died on the trail. Later, when Jimmy had his accident, she became a broken woman. At the time, it tore at Abigail's heart that her sister would leave. Now, almost twenty years later, Abigail could see that it shouldn't have been a such surprise.

Abigail had often wondered if her sister ever thought about Utah more than to send packages. Did she wonder about her son? Worry over him? Louisa never mentioned the Church or the gospel in her brief letters. Edward's family had never converted, and knowing Louisa, there was slim chance of her being involved in the Church where she was.

Abigail put the pen down and rubbed her eyes with her fingers. What could she say in the letter? Should she bare her soul and shower sympathy, despite the fact that Louisa may or may not feel the loss? Would it give Louisa guilt if she didn't feel Jimmy's death keenly? Would Louisa prefer a brief note with the bare facts?

She continued to stare at the paper by the golden glow of the candle, unsure what to say, how to begin. A noise sounded by the door, and Abigail looked up. It was Abe. He leaned against the doorframe for support, his left arm in a sling.

Abigail stood and went to his side in a hurry. "Are you well? You shouldn't be up yet."

"I'm feeling stronger," Abe said.

"Let's go back to your bed in the parlor," Abigail said, unconvinced. "I can bring you some water if you like." She tried to reach for his arm and lead him away, but he stepped into the kitchen instead.

"Truly, I'd prefer to sit out here for a spell. But thank you, Mrs. Sullivan."

He gingerly walked to the kitchen table and sat down. Abigail was used to looking at the swelling burns on his face, but the sight still made her wince. She could only imagine his pain as she went to the bucket of well water and ladled him a mugful.

"Thank you," he said, then took a long drink.

Abigail reached for the pen again, then stopped, suddenly aware of an audience. If she couldn't decide what to write alone, she certainly wouldn't be able to write with a virtual stranger across from her.

"What are you writing?" Abe asked.

Pushing the page aside, Abigail shrugged. "A letter to my sister."

His eyebrows raised. "Aunt Louisa?"

"That's right," Abigail said, surprised he knew the name. "Has Lizzy told you about her?"

"Quite a bit actually," Abe said. He went on to explain how Lizzy looked forward to the packages twice a year, and how she read to Jimmy largely out of duty to her aunt.

Abigail wondered if he knew that Lizzy had almost gone to live with Louisa. Probably. Lizzy apparently told Abe almost everything.

"Does she know yet?" Abe asked, nodding toward the letter. "About Jimmy, I mean."

Abigail pursed her lips together and shook her head. "That's what I'm trying to do now. But I don't know how."

Abe's brow furrowed. "I'm sorry I didn't save him."

Leaning over, Abigail stunned herself by putting a hand on his shoulder. "Abe, you have nothing to apologize for. You risked your life twice by saving Lizzy and then trying to save him. I couldn't ask for more."

His eyes brightened, and he smiled. "Thank you, Mrs. Sullivan."

"If anything, I am the one who owes you an apology. I misjudged you rather harshly, I'm afraid." Abigail's voice cracked. Saying the words was so much harder than *thinking* them. Abigail Sullivan wasn't a woman who was wrong often—or admitted to it easily when she was. But something in her middle told her it was time to make this right.

"I suppose my daughter has inherited my stubborn streak," she went on with a laugh. "We tend to lock horns when we feel strongly about an issue. And—and I regret feeling about you as I did. I was wrong. And I'm sorry."

Abe stared at her in amazement. "You don't know how long I have hoped to hear those words," he said quietly. "Thank you, Mrs. Sullivan. Thank you. You're a good woman."

With a shake of her head, Abigail sat back in her chair. "Now don't misunderstand me. I think you're a fine man and a tribute to your parents. But . . ."

Nodding, Abe finished her sentence. "But I'm still a Gentile and you would prefer a Saint as your daughter's beau."

"Yes," Abigail said. "I hope you understand."

"Perfectly," Abe said. "Although I wish I could change your mind."

Abigail had to chuckle. "Crazier things have happened. I suppose I won't say 'never' about even that. After all, I said it once and look where it got me—here I am sitting in my own kitchen enjoying the company of a Lamanite."

* * *

Lizzy stayed in bed for nearly a week. She yearned to get up, frequently insisting that she had the strength, as there was little to occupy her time. But each time she tried to move around, her burns would throb. Just holding a book and turning pages with the tender tips of her blistered fingers was simply too painful. And needlepoint was out of the question.

Instead she lay in bed from dawn until dusk, staring out the window and thinking about Jimmy. She still had a hard time comprehending the reality of his death. Jimmy had been a part of her life as long as she could remember. Another brother. An older brother in body, a younger brother in mind. She remembered their many hours together, reading to him or teaching him to read, to spell, and to write his name. She thought of the hailstorm that had frightened him so much, and his humorous misunderstanding of what she'd called it. To have him gone so suddenly, without warning, and without being able to say good-bye . . .

"Lizzy?" came a voice from the door.

She turned her gaze from the window and saw her mother.

"How are you feeling?" Abigail asked, crossing over and sitting at the foot of the bed.

"Better," Lizzy said, grateful that her throat was no longer quite so raw.

"Are you hungry?"

"No," she said with a shake of her head. She was tired of broth and other liquids, but her throat still hurt too much for any other foods. "How's Abe?"

"Good," Abigail said. "He'll be going home today. Would you—like to come down to talk with him?"

A spark of hope erupted inside Lizzy, and a smile broke across her face. "Mama, you approve of us then?"

Abigail hesitated before answering. "I must admit that I've grown to like him during his recovery. But—" She sighed. "But that doesn't change the fact that you should marry in the faith."

Lizzy closed her eyes and looked away.

Abigail changed the subject. "Your father just finished eating. He'll be up in a minute to carry you down to the parlor."

When her father lifted her into his arms, Lizzy winced, surprised at the pain. Although he walked down the stairs carefully, she was relieved when he set her on the couch and tucked a blanket around her.

"Thank you, Papa," she said as he left.

He paused at the door and winked at her. "Just you get better."

When she saw Abe, Lizzy's stomach leapt with excitement. He slowly crossed the room and sat at the foot of the couch. He wore a sling to support a broken arm. The left side of his face was red and puffy, and blisters covered his cheek. She flinched at the sight.

"I'll be fine," Abe assured her before she could ask. Lizzy couldn't see his other burns, but she had been told his back and shoulders had gotten the brunt of his injuries. He hurt as much as she did, judging by how he sat so still, perched in his seat.

A knock sounded on the back door, and Abigail excused herself to answer it. Abe made the most of the moment alone and skipped over greetings and pleasantries. "Your mother has taken a real liking to me. I think she might accept me into the family now."

"I already talked to Mama about that," Lizzy said. "As much as she admires you, she still says I must marry in the faith. She was quite adamant about it."

"I know. Listen, Lizzy. I've been thinking." Abe bit his lower lip nervously. "I've been to a few Mormon funerals. Like the one for King and Osterholdt. Almost everyone was there. And I've been listening to your family talk about Jimmy living in the spirit world. There's something so—I don't know, so real about it all, as if you all just know that's the way it is. A couple of times as your parents talked of him, well, it wouldn't have surprised me to see Jimmy himself standing in the back of the kitchen listening to it."

Lizzy smiled to herself. She knew that discussing Jimmy in the spirit world had been a great source of comfort for the family. Her parents especially seemed to take solace in the idea that Jimmy's limitations were gone now, that his mind was whole again.

Abe began picking at some lint on his sling. "It's got me thinking. I might not understand you folks or believe in prophets and angels and such, but it's done me good to see the way you Mormons treat each other and view death—so hopeful-like. And considering how your mother has taken a real liking to me—we talked about it the other night and she even apologized and said she was wrong and . . ." His voice trailed off, and he tried again. He placed a hand over her bandaged one and looked into her eyes. "I suppose what I'm saying is that if your parents would accept me wet, I'd be willing to do it for you."

Lizzy turned to him, her eyes narrowing with curiosity. "What are you saying?" she asked, hardly daring for the answer.

Abe blew out heavily, looking at the pattern of the braided rug on the floor, then raised his head and faced Lizzy square-on. The tips of his ears were bright red. "I'm saying that if it means we could be together, I'm willing to be baptized."

CHAPTER 26

Joshua had purposely avoided seeing Beth and her family ever since the dance, and with the exception of that day at the furniture store, it had worked. His trips to Main Street were few and far between nowadays, which explained why he didn't hear about the fire until nearly a week after it happened. He was pricing seed at Christiansen's Store when two women, one behind the counter, the other looking at bolts of fabric, began chitchatting.

"Too bad about the Sullivan fire," he heard the first say. "When is the funeral?"

Funeral?! Joshua whirled around and stared at the women. Never had a single word sent such panic through him. He nearly raced over to interrupt the conversation when the second woman responded, "Tomorrow morning. What was his name again? Billy?"

"Jimmy," came the response, and Joshua suddenly had to grab the counter to keep his melted-butter knees from giving out. *Jimmy is dead?*

He turned to the women and demanded, "What about their daughter?"

The ladies' eyebrows went up. Clearly they didn't appreciate his eavesdropping, in spite of the fact that they talked so loudly it was impossible not to hear them.

"Is their daughter well?" Joshua asked again.

"I believe so," the older of the two women said. "Although I heard she was caught in the fire too."

Joshua breathed out a sigh of relief. "Thank you," he said, then left the store without a thought to the seed he had come for. He went home in a daze, wishing he could comfort Beth, wondering if she had been burned in the fire and if so, how severe her burns were. An urge came over him to race over to their house to see her, but he controlled it and drove home instead. He wasn't sure whether Lizzy would want to see him after their last meeting. He had practically pushed her out of his life that day. Did he still have the right to invade hers after that? The thought was painful, but not nearly as much as the idea that she was injured and hurting. At least he could go to the funeral tomorrow and pay his respects to Jimmy.

That night he stared at the ceiling of his barn, feeling cold and lonely even though it was May. Somehow the winter nights were much more comfortable out there when hopes of a future with Lizzy kept him warm. He had often imagined hearing her squeaking peacock call outside, summoning him. A few times he had wakened in the night, thinking he had heard it, but only the regular nighttime sounds of crickets met his ears.

Soon his house would be ready to live in, but the thought held no expectation for him any longer. It would be nothing more than a place to live.

How he missed Beth. He closed his eyes tightly, refusing to think about the past months. In spite of his efforts, each moment that had given him so much hope replayed itself in his mind, driving him to distraction.

He ran his fingers through his hair. It wasn't as if he could do anything to comfort Beth when her was heart set on Abe. Joshua couldn't help notice that Abe looked like the heroes in so many of the books Lizzy had read over the years. Why couldn't she content herself with books where the characters acted sensibly? Couldn't she see that life was more than flowery speeches made by strange beaus with dark, brooding eyes? Couldn't she see that he, Joshua Sorensen, could make her happy if only she would give him a chance?

He knew he didn't fit into the mold. But he also knew he had seen more, had *felt* more than friendship from Beth on several occasions. She just couldn't see it. Or admit to it. He often relived those moments when her eyes, her touch, her tone had given him the first real shred of hope that one day she might be his. Rolling over, he cursed the night-time three o'clock hour when such worries haunted a person.

At least there was one thing he could do. He closed his eyes and prayed for her.

The following morning he went to the funeral. He arrived early, and as he was about to take a seat toward the back of the chapel, he heard some movement in the entryway. Peering around the corner, he saw the Sullivan family in the foyer. Beth and her mother were embracing. Beth's back was to him, her hair pulled into an elegant knot. He wondered about the extent of her burns. What if her face had scars? He knew he would love her no matter how she looked. But how did she feel about her appearance? Perhaps it would be a chance to prove his love.

He wondered if Abe would care about a scarred face. No. Joshua had to admit that Abe was a respectable man. The fact that Beth was beautiful would be like cream poured over a bowl of peaches—a pleasant addition, but not necessary.

As he stepped into the foyer, Abigail Sullivan caught sight of him.

"Oh, Joshua," she cried, coming toward him, arms outstretched. "I'm so glad you're here."

She gave him a crushing hug, her growing belly only slightly in the way. "Thank you for coming," she whispered into his ear.

Joshua pulled back, still holding her hands. "Of course I came, Sister Sullivan. You've been like a second family to me."

Abigail's fingertips came to her lips. "We should have invited you to be part of our family prayer today. I'm so sorry we didn't."

Joshua touched her arm softly. "I feel honored that you would think of including me." He looked around at the rest of the family members. "Did Jimmy's mother come?"

Abigail shook her head. "No." Her eyes had an emotion behind them that Joshua couldn't quite read, and he guessed there was more to the story than that. From what he knew of Jimmy's history, he guessed that his mother couldn't bear to face the death of the son she had abandoned over fifteen years prior.

He glanced over and saw Beth, who had brought her handkerchief to her eyes. He still couldn't see her face, but her hands were in bandages—evidence of the fire. As he waited for her to look over at him, he hoped this meeting wouldn't be awkward or stiff like their last. When her eyes finally stopped on him, she crossed the distance and threw her arms around him, burying her face in his shoulder.

"Oh, Joshua," was all she could say.

He held her tight, tears springing to his own eyes as he felt her grief, her trembling in his arms. He breathed deeply and looked at the ceiling to ward off his own emotion. "I'm so sorry, Beth."

She cried harder, as if she had been holding her emotions in for days and finally had released the floodgates.

Joshua guided Beth into the chapel for the service. He had planned to sit toward the back, but she wouldn't let his arm go. She clung to him as if her life depended on it, so he found himself sitting on the front row with the Sullivan family. Once seated, Joshua put his arm around her protectively and cupped her bandaged one gingerly in his so as not to hurt her burns.

"It's not fair that I made it out and he didn't," she whispered in a choking voice. "I should have tried harder."

The bishop rose to begin the service, so Joshua leaned close and whispered, "It's not your fault. It's a miracle that anyone survived."

"Thank you," she said, but her heart wasn't in it.

Joshua looked over his shoulder at the congregation; each pew was filled, and a few people even stood in back. He saw Abe walk in, pause, and look for the family. After spotting the Sullivans, he moved down the aisle, then stopped short when he saw Joshua sitting beside Beth, who had turned her face away as she dabbed at her tears. Abe stared at the two of them for just a moment before settling in the pew across the aisle where the twins sat.

As Abe took his seat, Joshua squeezed Beth a little tighter and pressed his lips against her forehead. He didn't know what the future held, but for this moment, she was his.

* * *

Abe stood in the boardinghouse stable with Shadow. His left arm still rested in the sling, and while his burns weren't entirely healed, at least day-to-day movements didn't hurt so much.

The horse whinnied with pleasure as Abe brushed her neck. "I've missed you too, girl," he said. "Believe me, I didn't stay away because I wanted to."

Abe stood in front of Shadow and leaned back to examine the sides of her face, then behind her ears, where her sores were healing nicely. In another few months when the fur grew back completely, it would be hard to tell she had ever been the miserably tortured animal he had found in Brother Franklin's care. As Shadow nuzzled Abe's neck, he sucked in air between his teeth and took a step back. As much as he welcomed his animal's affection, one side of his face was still sensitive.

"Easy, girl. I'm not quite myself yet."

"But you look good," came a voice from the door.

Abe turned to see Joshua. The horse brush paused midair, and Abe's hand lowered to his side. The two men stared at one another for an awkward moment.

"Hello, Joshua," Abe finally said.

Stepping beside Shadow's stall, Joshua said, "She's beautiful," and put his hand out for her to smell his scent.

"Thank you," Abe said, and turned to brush Shadow's back. What could he say to Joshua? They had been so close at the quarry, sharing their hopes with one another. *Hopes about the same girl.* He looked over at Joshua.

"Neither of us knew," Abe said, breaking the silence. "And neither of us should feel guilty for—for what happened. I know how much you care about her."

"And how much you do," Joshua said. He stroked Shadow's nose and let out a cynical laugh. "Look at us now. Completely at her mercy."

Abe chuckled along with Joshua, but couldn't find an answer right away. He and Lizzy had discussed their future together. She was willing to marry him, she said, even if it meant disappointing her parents. Joshua couldn't have received a similar assurance about his future with her. But Abe refused to say anything that would wound his friend.

"I suppose she's got her work cut out for her, doesn't she?" Abe answered, putting on a grin. "How can she pick between two great men like us?"

Joshua laughed aloud. "No hard feelings, then?"

"No," Abe said. "I can hardly blame you for loving someone like Elizabeth Sullivan, can I? We should be amazed more men aren't falling over their feet to win her heart. Besides, you're the one who convinced me to pray for the first time in my life. How can I harbor a grudge over that?"

After a final brush stroke down Shadow's flank, Abe put the brush on a shelf. Joshua followed him out of the stall, and Abe closed the half-door behind them.

"Thanks for coming," Abe said. "I'll always consider you a friend, no matter what happens. I wish I had been man enough to come see you first." Abe put a hand out, and they shook.

"You take care of that arm," Joshua said, nodding. He turned to leave, and murmured something under his breath. Abe it thought sounded like, "And take care of her, too."

* * *

A couple of weeks later, Lizzy carried a bundle of flowers as she walked into the cemetery—a few lilies, but mostly Jimmy's favorite wildflowers. She walked past Billie King's and Neph Osterholdt's graves, paid her respects to her baby siblings who had passed on, then turned to find the fresh grave where Jimmy had been laid to rest.

Her father had bought a piece of stone from the temple to use as a monument. Under the rounded top he had carved a willow tree with long boughs almost reaching the ground. Below the image were the bare facts of Jimmy's mortal life, "James Frederick Wadsworth (Sullivan). Born February 20, 1855. Died June 5, 1879."

It was strange to see his name written as "James" instead of "Jimmy," although she thought it fitting that her parents and Aunt Louisa had agreed that "Sullivan" belonged on the headstone as much as his "real" family name.

At the bottom Lizzy read aloud the inscription her mother had chosen. "Now protected in the arms of his Lord." The willow tree was supposed to symbolize that security.

Now protected . . .

The statement implied that in life he hadn't been protected. Well, in many ways that was true. His accident as a child handicapped him for the remainder of his life. And his manner of death—Lizzy shuddered at the memory. He certainly hadn't been protected then, either. She wondered if she would ever be able to feel the warm coziness she once had before a roaring fire. Too many times now she had experienced the horrifying power behind the heat.

It had been weeks since she'd last picked up a book. Just turning the pages brought thoughts of smoke and Jimmy crying out in fear and pain. Lizzy would probably never find out what happened to Tom Sawyer.

She knelt before the new headstone and placed her small bouquet at the base. "I'm so sorry," she whispered to him.

The swish of grass moving sounded behind her, and Lizzy realized someone was there. She didn't want to say anything else, not until her privacy was regained. But the footfalls only came closer. She finally turned to look over her shoulder and saw Joshua. He stopped.

"I don't want to intrude."

She shook her head and motioned for him to join her. "You aren't."

Joshua sat on the ground beside her, and together they silently took in the gravestone.

"I'm sorry," he said.

Lizzy gave a wan smile. "I said the same thing to Jimmy a moment ago." She gazed at the birth and death dates, reread the inscription, then shook her head.

"It all seems so wrong for him to be gone like this," Lizzy said.

He leaned forward and brushed aside a stray weed that had landed by the headstone. "Death never does make any sense," he said. "That's what makes it so difficult for those left behind."

For a moment, Lizzy half wished it were Abe sitting beside her so she could freely speak her mind. Joshua wouldn't understand her conflicted emotions. At first she didn't answer him, unsure what to say. Finally she decided to speak anyway and let him think what he would.

"You always have an answer for everything, don't you?" she asked, the bitterness in her tone surprising even her.

"What?" Joshua looked at her, brow furrowed. "What do you mean?"

The hurt look in his eyes immediately sent regret shooting through her. "I'm sorry," Lizzy said. "Somehow I can't—" But her voice cut off midsentence. Saying to Joshua what she had been unable to put into a letter was nearly impossible.

"I lack your faith," she said simply.

"Faith about what?" Joshua asked, sincerely perplexed. "I don't have any inkling why Jimmy's life wasn't spared, if that's what you mean."

Lizzy turned to him full-on. "I have never heard you question or doubt or struggle—"

Joshua raised his hand to interrupt her. "Just because I haven't spoken of my concerns doesn't mean they don't exist."

Lizzy rocked back. "Then your faith has been tried?"

"Of course it has," Joshua said. "Many times." His eyes got a far-off look to them, and he turned away, making Lizzy want to know what he was thinking.

"How have you been tested?" she asked.

Joshua took a long time to answer. He pulled up a few blades of grass and began breaking them into pieces. "I—I have had—a hope—for a long time," he stammered. "Something I have always considered to be a righteous desire."

When he didn't go on, Lizzy prodded, "And?"

Joshua glanced up at her, then at the shredded grass. "And many times I've wondered if I will ever receive the blessing I've prayed for."

Lizzy was too occupied with Joshua's faith to consider what he was referring to. "What if you never get it?"

His head came around suddenly, and his face grew pale. "What do you mean?"

"What I mean is, will you still believe in God? No matter what?"

"Of course I will," Joshua said, his voice registering relief. He brushed his hands together, and the pieces of grass drifted away in the breeze. "It's not as if the Lord is some childish dream I've imagined for myself. I know He's real. I've had dozens of moments that have proven it to me. I can't reject those witnesses whether or not my prayers get the answer I'm hoping for."

"But how can you be sure?" Lizzy asked. Joshua didn't seem to be disappointed in her lack of faith. She was relieved that he hadn't turned his back on her or talked with a patronizing tone as if to a child. And she suddenly realized that this was the first time they had ever discussed such matters.

"I can be sure," Joshua said, "because I can. I can't explain it better than that. I suppose it all returns to the scripture that says we receive no witness until after the trial of our faith."

A wistful smile crossed Lizzy's face. "I suppose one must have faith for it to be tested." Joshua looked up into the sky, at the puffy clouds. Then he looked over from the corner of his eye. "I think you underestimate yourself, Elizabeth Sullivan. You haven't allowed your faith to be tested and proved, but you have faith nonetheless."

"You think so?"

"Absolutely."

They lapsed into silence for several minutes, then Lizzy spoke again.

"I'm glad you came," she said. She looked up at him and smiled. "And I'm glad you don't think I'm a heretic for questioning."

Joshua laughed. "You're no heretic. More like a follower of Moses."

"Oh?" Lizzy asked, perplexed. "How do you figure that?"

He shrugged. "Moses once said he wished every person would seek after their own revelation so he wouldn't have all the work. The way I see it, that means he welcomed questions, as long as the people went to the Lord with them."

Lizzy nodded to herself. "I like the idea of following Moses." She grew quiet again, then asked, "But the issue remains, if we turn to the Lord with our questions, will He answer us?"

Reluctantly, Joshua shook his head. "No, at least not always in the way you expect. I imagine some of my questions won't be answered until the next life or later."

Not until the next life? But that's so far away. "Like why Jimmy had to die now," Lizzy said.

"Exactly," Joshua said.

After another moment of silence, Lizzy rearranged the flowers and stood up, wiping dirt and grass from her skirts. "Will you walk home with me?"

Joshua stood and held out his arm for her. "I'd love to."

Together they strolled through the streets, agreeing without words to abandon the topic. As they walked, Lizzy eyed Joshua and smiled to herself. He hadn't seemed a bit shocked at her confessions. And apparently she wasn't a heretic. But she wondered what he'd prayed about for such a long time.

* * *

As her time grew near, Abigail began looking more drawn and tired than ever before. The weeks since the fire had taken a toll. Through it all, her middle swelled with her unborn child. Her back ached nonstop, and the heat was becoming a strain. She couldn't move easily to do the regular chores, and her feet had swollen so much that her shoes pinched, making every step painful.

One afternoon she collapsed on a kitchen chair and sighed heavily. *I feel so much older carrying this child,* she thought. *I suppose I am. But please, Lord, let me keep my baby.*

Lizzy came down the stairs and into the kitchen. She held a washrag in her hand and headed for the counter. "Are you feeling all right, Mama?"

"I keep telling myself, this too shall pass. Only a few weeks left. I can do anything for a few weeks." She watched Lizzy dip the cloth into the bucket of water on the counter and wring it out. Lizzy strode across the kitchen, half hiding the cloth. She leaned down and kissed her mother's cheek.

"I'm glad you're taking a break," Lizzy said. "You need your rest." With that she headed toward the stairs again.

"Lizzy," Abigail said, calling her daughter back. Lizzy stopped at the stairs and slowly turned around.

"Yes, Mama? Can I get you something?" she asked, an awkward look on her face that Abigail couldn't quite read.

"What is that cloth for?"

Lizzy stared at the damp rag in her hand. "It's nothing, Mama."

Abigail stood to follow Lizzy. "If I didn't know better, I'd think that someone upstairs is feverish."

"Mama, please rest." Lizzy crossed to her mother and gently urged her to the chair. She sat opposite Abigail. "You seem so tuckered out of late, and I didn't want to add one more burden to your shoulders. David just seems a little peaked, so I thought I'd take care of him and not worry you any."

Abigail pushed back from the table, but before she could stand, Lizzy shook her head. "I'm sure it's nothing serious. David hasn't been ill for a long time. He'll be fine after a good night's sleep. Let me care for him so you can rest."

Abigail's eye narrowed. She looked up toward the second story. "Will you call me if he needs me? If he asks for me? If he gets worse—"

"I promise, Mama. I will."

Abigail relaxed and patted Lizzy's hand, trying to smile. "Very well, then. I'll rest for a bit. Thank you, Lizzy."

* * *

When dawn turned the windows into squares of gray, Abigail awoke, feeling better than she had in days. Her growing size made sleeping much more difficult of late. But she had gotten to bed quite early last night. Lizzy had insisted on it.

David. She remembered him with a jolt. How was he? She tried to get up quickly, even with her swollen belly, then dressed and put her hair up, for once forgetting to wash her face in the basin as she went out.

She stood a few steps from the foot of David's bed, which was pushed against the wall in the cozy room at the head of the stairs. He slept peacefully but took shallow breaths that were too far apart for Abigail's liking. Lizzy lay curled up at the foot of the bed, one hand protectively resting on David's foot through the quilt. A chair stood beside the bed, and signs of Lizzy's all-night vigil were sprawled on the floor—several books, a small bowl of water with a cloth, and a glass. The poor girl had probably barely fallen asleep herself.

Abigail walked across the old braided rug. She peered into the next room, where she could see the twins still sleeping, then turned to David. His hairline was damp with sweat. Abigail touched his forehead. It burned with heat. She closed her eyes and breathed in, praying silently that his illness would be brief and simple; then she leaned down over her bulging middle and kissed his hot cheek.

* * *

The sun was heading for the western horizon as Abe walked along Main Street. Ever since the funeral, he hadn't seen much of Lizzy. She hadn't contacted him much, and it didn't feel right for him to intrude on the family when they were still mourning Jimmy's loss. He reached over and rubbed at his left arm. The bone had healed fine, although the arm wasn't quite as strong as the other yet. Being unable to work for several weeks had robbed him of money, too. No matter. He still had a nest egg.

As he walked along, Abe missed Lizzy. He couldn't help but think about that fateful morning so long ago when he'd stumbled across Lizzy's path and they'd made arrangements to meet in secret for the first time. She had been on her way to mail a letter back then. His brow furrowed at the thought. Who had she been writing to? She hadn't mentioned anyone by name, and at the time he had assumed the recipient was one of her girlfriends. Suddenly Abe realized the truth. *Joshua.* She had been writing to Joshua all along, long before the quarry.

He instinctively walked toward the post office, not expecting to find anything there, but needing to think through—to relive—the past. He had picked up a letter from his mother only four days ago and hadn't planned on checking again for two more weeks at least; she generally didn't write more than once a month.

His boots clunked against the wooden sidewalk as he walked, remembering that day with Lizzy. Every detail was still vivid in his mind. He could even remember the dress she wore, the way she had her hair. Before he knew it, he had stepped inside the post office and was asking for his mail.

"You got a letter this morning," the postmaster said, and slid an envelope across the counter.

Abe's brow furrowed as he picked it up and looked it over. It was from his mother. But why had she sent a letter so close to her last one? Was something wrong at home?

He quickly tore into the envelope and pulled out two sheets of paper, one folded into fourths and yellowed with age, and the other one white and small with one fold and penned by his mother's even hand. He opened her letter first.

My Dearest Abe,
Sister Hutchings came by the other day. Apparently she was cleaning out some old trunks to prepare for her daughter's wedding and came across something she thought we would want to have. To say the least,

it was a surprise to me. I didn't tell your father about it. His constitu-
tion isn't what it used to be, and I didn't want to upset him. Then
again, he would probably just gloat if he knew. But I felt it belonged
to you. And you have it in case you ever do decide to exercise faith
and believe on the Lord.

All my love,
Mother

The short note didn't explain more, so, filled with curiosity, Abe unfolded the other paper and read it. His eyes widened, and he almost laughed with the shock of seeing his own baptismal certificate.

He had been *baptized?* When? He looked at the date—four months after his assumed eighth birthday, probably a few weeks before he became a Franklin. By whom? He searched for the name. *Bishop Raymond Carter.*

Abe's head came up, and he stared at the window by the post office door, trying to remember. He could find no memory at all. Then again, he had tried to forget everything about his life with the Hutchings family. It was even worse than life with Brother Franklin. The entire family hated him there, not just one ornery man. Abe scratched his head. *Baptism?*

His mind turned back to his last days at the Hutchings farm, something that felt strange after all these years. Now that he thought of it, there was one day at the river with lots of other people gathered around. The water was cold when he stepped into it, and he almost fell on the slippery stones. An older man reached for him so Abe wouldn't go all the way under—until the man said a quiet prayer and then deliberately dunked him. He suddenly recalled that it had made him so all-fired mad he would have tried to dunk the man back if Sister Hutchings hadn't come to the riverbank for him with a warm blanket in her arms.

Now he shook his head with a chuckle, understanding what his eight-year-old mind hadn't comprehended. No one told him what was going on, what the significance was, what it all meant.

A corner of the certificate was bent, and Abe smoothed it out, reading the words once more. It was strange to see his name written as *Abraham Michael Hutchings,* a person Abe thought of as dead.

The baptism is just as dead, he thought. *It means nothing to me, so it means nothing to God.*

But a possibility suddenly dawned on him. Would this change things with Lizzy's mother? He *wasn't* a Gentile or a heathen—and he had proof.

"Thank you," he said to the postmaster, then left the building with a lift in his stride and plans to tell Lizzy soon—very soon. *This just might change everything . . .*

CHAPTER 27

Over the next several days, Lizzy and Abigail took turns caring for the household tasks and staying at David's side. Twice Abe came by, but Lizzy sadly turned him away because of the sickness in the house and her overwhelming duties.

Neither Lizzy nor her mother mentioned that David looked worse than he had in years. They didn't discuss what his pale face, fever, or chills might mean. David tried to put on a smile for anyone who came up the stairs, but he crumbled under the pain at times, whimpering and wishing for the hurts to go away. His alert times were becoming less frequent as he slept more and more and had increasingly difficult nights.

Sometimes, even when he was awake, he didn't seem to be fully conscious of his surroundings. He would murmur unintelligibly or moan. More than once Lizzy felt sure he was trying to talk to someone who wasn't there, and she feared he was delirious. Soon he stopped eating much of anything; it was all Lizzy and Abigail could do to get him to swallow a little broth and some broken bread.

One afternoon as she sat beside David, Lizzy heard the stairs creaking behind her.

"How is my boy?" Abigail asked, directing the question to David, but both women knowing that Lizzy would answer if he wasn't coherent.

"Mama, he's so much worse. I'm afraid . . ." Lizzy turned to her mother, eyes red and swollen. Her hand came to her mouth.

Abigail sat at the base of the bed and checked on her son, who stared at the ceiling blankly. She turned to Lizzy. "He needs another priesthood blessing."

Lizzy thought back to all the other times David had been administered to—the last was just days ago—and how the blessings didn't seem to do a thing for him. She wished Sophie were alive and could snuggle close to David, bringing him back from wherever he was.

Being in the upstairs room all day also made Lizzy lose all sense of time. "How long until Papa comes home?" she asked.

"Not for a couple of hours." Abigail put her hand over her belly and held her breath.

"Mama? Is something wrong?"

The moment passed, Abigail breathed out, then smiled. "The baby's time is coming soon, that's all. My body is getting ready."

Mother and daughter sat in silence for a moment and watched David.

"This time is different with him, isn't it?" Lizzy said, so quietly that she could hardly hear her own words.

Abigail reached for Lizzy's hand and squeezed it, her eyes growing misty. Perhaps it was something in David's eyes, which no longer had the constant spark. Perhaps it was something else. But both felt that David's influenza wasn't just another one of his many illnesses.

"I need to get supper started," Abigail finally said, but without conviction, and neither moved, as if they might miss something if they spent a brief moment away. David didn't seem aware of anything around him. Mother and daughter sat there watching his chest rise and fall almost imperceptibly. Abigail wiped his brow with the damp cloth, and Lizzy stroked his hand.

Lizzy noticed they were out of water and forced herself to the kitchen for more. To her dismay, she discovered the bucket empty, and she had to go out to the well. She hurriedly filled the pail, losing much of the contents as she raced back. She refilled the bowl and glass, then rushed to her mother's side. She stared at David's chest. Not seeing any movement, she gripped her mother's shoulder until his breathing started again with a staggered intake of air.

Abigail pressed her hands to her face for a moment. "That is just how your Uncle Edward sounded before he passed."

"Mama, don't say that," Lizzy said, her voice breaking.

But Abigail didn't answer. Instead she turned away, clenching her teeth as she put a hand across her belly again.

"Mama?"

Abigail glanced at the clock, not answering for a moment. "It's just the strain and heat causing the pains," she said, clearly trying to reassure her daughter. "I'm sure I have another week or two before the baby comes."

"Lizzy," came David's weak voice.

"What is it, David?" Lizzy dropped to her knees beside him and reached for the cup. "Do you want some water?"

"I want Sophie." His voice cracked, and his eyes were still closed. "Sophie makes me feel better."

Lizzy and Abigail exchanged anguished looks. Was he delirious? What could they do to help ease his discomfort?

"Here," Lizzy said, setting the cup on the nightstand. "Let's read." She picked up the worn copy of *David Copperfield* lying on the floor beside the bed. Her throat was tight with emotion, and it was hard to speak the words, but she forced herself to read about David Copperfield's childhood friend Emily.

David didn't seem to notice. He moaned periodically, but he seemed unconscious for the most part. Lizzy hoped that if nothing else, her voice was soothing for him.

An hour later, Richard came in through the back door. "Hello . . . ? I'm home," he called. Then, "Abigail, Lizzy. Where are you?" He came up the stairs. "Is everything all right?"

Lizzy glanced over as he entered. "Sorry, Papa. We meant to get supper ready, but we've been so worried about David that we haven't done much else today."

"David is far more important than boiled potatoes," Richard said, squatting beside the bed and holding his son's hand. "How's my little man?"

When David didn't respond, Richard sighed. He patted David's hand and stood. "Tonight after the chores are done, I'll see if Brother Owen can come over and help me administer to him." Richard looked at his wife, his eyes registering alarm. He grabbed her hand and eased her onto a chair. "How close are they?"

Lizzy hadn't been paying much attention to her mother, and only now noticed Abigail gripping the sides of the chair and closing her eyes, pressing her lips into a white line.

The book dropped to Lizzy's lap. "It's time?" she asked. "But you just said it would probably be weeks yet."

The contraction subsided. Abigail lifted her head and opened her eyes. "About five minutes," she said, answering her husband's question. "They started after breakfast."

Richard made mental calculations. "Do I have enough time to fetch Sister Johnson?" The midwife lived four miles away.

Abigail nodded. "I think so, if you hurry."

Richard looked ready to bolt, but stopped long enough to gingerly kiss his wife's forehead. "I'll be back as soon as I can. Just hold on." He glanced at David and hesitated just a moment before reaching down and tousling his hair. "I have to go, son. I'll be back soon."

Richard barreled down the stairs and out the door. His voice carried through the window as he yelled instructions at the boys to get the horse and wagon ready.

"I'll go lie on one of the twins' beds," Abigail said. "I want to stay close to David." She took the bed that had its head against the same wall as David's, which allowed Lizzy to sit in the doorway and watch both patients at the same time.

"What should I do now?" Lizzy asked. She could hardly think at all, but she couldn't just sit still, either. On her mother's suggestion, she gathered several clean sheets and some towels. Lizzy suddenly remembered a pot of water she had boiled earlier that day and never used for the laundry, something she had forgotten about earlier when David needed a drink. "Do you need water?" she asked.

Her mother nodded.

"I can reheat the laundry pot."

With a shake of her head, Abigail said, "It doesn't need to be warm."

Minutes later, Lizzy returned with the pot of lukewarm water and placed it near the foot of the bed. She glanced at the stack of towels and sheets, nervously wiped her hands on her dress, and wondered what else she could do. She finally settled her chair in the doorway between the two rooms, alternately watching David's chest rising and falling and holding her mother's hand through the pains. And then she waited.

The prospect before her was terrifying. Abigail's face screwed up in pain as another contraction came on, and her head fell back onto the bed. Lizzy steeled herself, determined to be strong. She waved some flies from her mother's face.

"Everything will be just fine," Lizzy whispered, her voice suddenly strong and confident. "Papa will return any moment with Sister Johnson."

For nearly an hour, Lizzy whispered about happy memories through the contractions, anything to keep her mother's thoughts off her anguish: Christmas, Abigail's last birthday and her surprise gift of a new dress, moving into the new home . . . Between contractions she could turn back to David and monitor his breathing. Then another contraction began, and Abigail's grip tightened on her daughter.

"You can do this," Lizzy said, wondering where her own strength was coming from—and where her father was. Shouldn't he be back by now? Her mother's face twisted in agony; this contraction was the worst so far. Lizzy nearly cried out, wishing she could take some of the hurt away. Not any too soon, it subsided, and Abigail sighed shakily, and collapsing on the pillow, eyes closed.

Lizzy checked on David again, and was startled to see his face gray. Something heavy gripped her heart as she watched his chest, willing it to rise. It didn't. She jumped to her feet and reached for her brother's shoulders.

"David, breathe. Now, David," she cried, shaking him. "You can't leave us. Not when Mama's having a baby. Not now! We need you. Breathe, David, breathe!" She slapped his cheeks, then put her ear to his chest, straining to hear his heartbeat. He gasped for air, and Lizzy shakily lowered herself beside him, catching her breath in relief.

"Lizzy!" Abigail's voice startled her.

"What is it?" she asked, hurrying to her mother's side.

"It's coming! Now."

"Already?" Lizzy ran to the window and looked out, but saw no sign of her father's wagon on Main Street. She froze and swallowed hard. "I . . ." She glanced at the water, soap, and other supplies. Without any instruction or knowing why she did so, she washed her hands and arms as thoroughly as she could. As she toweled herself dry, a single word came to her mind.

Pray.

If there ever was a time she needed divine help, Lizzy knew this was it. She squeezed her eyes closed.

Father, please help me. Please. Mama needs it. David needs it. I can't do this alone.

Of all the prayers in her life, this might have been the shortest, but it was also the least selfish and most sincere. She couldn't help her mother and David without aid, and at that moment she wanted nothing more than to help them.

She discarded the towel beside the basin of water and turned back to her mother. "Tell me what to do," she said, sitting at the foot of the bed. She pushed aside all thoughts of panic, determined to do her best.

Abigail positioned herself, grimacing with each movement, so Lizzy could better assist. Long moments passed before another contraction ended and Abigail asked, "Do you see the head?"

"Not yet," Lizzy said, but braced herself for the moment anyway. Somehow she was able to steady herself and think clearly. "Now what?"

"Now I'll push. When you see the shoulders, ease the baby the rest of the way."

Lizzy braced her position and nodded. "Ready."

Abigail, her expression riddled with anxiety, waited for the next contraction, then began to push. Her face turned red, every muscle registering anguish. Lizzy ripped her gaze away from her mother's to turn her attention to the emerging baby. Her mother pushed hard, moaning at the pain, then collapsed on the bed in exhaustion to wait for the next contraction.

Lizzy found herself breathing heavily, her hands shaking. "Mama, are you all right? Is something wrong with the baby since it's not coming yet?"

Abigail, eyes still closed as if gathering her strength for the next push, shook her head so slightly that Lizzy almost missed the movement. "I pushed for five hours with you," she said. The faintest hint of a smile crossed her face at the memory.

"Five hours?" Lizzy's heart thumped even harder at the thought. She glanced toward the window. Her father would certainly be back with the midwife before this was over.

Abigail leaned forward, getting ready for the next push. "But Hannah took only six minutes," she said, her voice breathless. She took a deep breath and braced herself. Lizzy recognized this as her cue and got into position.

"It's coming!" Lizzy said, almost unable to believe it.

The only answer Abigail gave was a cry of anguish as she pushed through the worst pain of the entire experience and brought the baby into the world. Lizzy gently eased the baby out just as her mother had instructed—head, shoulders, body. The tiny red bundle of arms and legs slipped into Lizzy's hands. Caring nothing for the moisture and blood all over her dress, she stared at the baby, joy coursing through her.

"It's—it's a girl," she said with awe, then looked up. "Mama, you have a little girl."

"A girl?" Abigail choked out. She pushed herself up on her elbows to see better. "How—how is she?"

"Perfect," Lizzy said, eyes smarting again. "Pink and perfect."

Abigail smiled and let out a sigh of relief and joy. But she couldn't completely relax quite yet. "Clear the nose and mouth so she won't choke on the liquid," she said, her breathing ragged.

Lizzy held the baby at a slight angle so the liquid wouldn't go into the lungs and grabbed a cloth to clean the nose and mouth. The baby's weak noises gradually increased and soon became insistent wails. At the sound, Abigail finally lay back in relief. She instructed Lizzy to tie some string in two spots, a few inches apart on the cord, then to cut between them with scissors. Surprised at her own calm, Lizzy carried on as if she had assisted in a dozen births. She washed the baby, wrapped her in a blanket, and placed the baby in her mother's arms, amazed at the tiny, wriggling being.

As Abigail took her new daughter, the lines of pain and worry in her face softened. Lizzy wondered at the change in her mother as she stroked the baby's cheek. Her mother looked at least fifteen years younger. Lizzy sat there, trying to take in the miracle she had just been part of, something so much deeper and more profound than she had ever experienced. The day Sophie's puppies were born paled in comparison.

Lizzy looked out the window for her father, but saw no sign of the wagon yet. She retrieved some clean clothing for her mother. As she stripped the sheets from the bed and gathered the soiled sheets into a pile, her mother nursed the baby for the first time and talked to her as if she could understand. Perhaps she could, Lizzy mused.

As Lizzy headed for the door to take the sheets out and get some new bedding, she eyed David's chest. She stopped midstride.

"Is everything all right?" Abigail asked peering over her shoulder through the doorway. Both women stiffened and waited, then let out a sigh of relief when the rattling breath began again. Abigail sat up and made a move to stand.

"No, Mama. Lie down," Lizzy said, dropping the bedding to coax her mother back to the pillow. But Abigail shook her head.

"I may not have another chance to say good-bye, Lizzy. Please let me do it now."

Lizzy's face drained, and she stopped protesting, though everything in her being wanted to scream out that David wasn't dying, that there was no need to say good-bye.

Abigail gingerly walked through the doorway to David's bed. Her eyes narrowed with grief, every part of her struggling with the pain of what was about to happen. She stroked his cheek.

"Good-bye, my little boy," she whispered, a shiny tear falling onto the sheet. "I will always love you. Take care of your brothers and sister in heaven." David did not respond. Abigail held the baby in her other arm. "Here's your new baby sister. Straight from above."

David's eyelids flickered slightly. His lips moved, but no noise came out. He took a labored breath, then whispered, "I'll watch over her from heaven too."

Another rattling breath sounded, and a moment later David managed, "If Joshua asks, say yes."

Then nothing. His body went limp.

Lizzy straightened and began to shake David's form. "Breathe, David! Breathe! You can't go now. Breathe!"

He would breathe again, she determined. He had to. Her head fell to his chest, and she listened for his heartbeat. Only then did she realize the truth. She stayed there, her head on his chest, as sobs wracked her body. Images of young Richard lying on his deathbed returned, along with the horrible pain it brought. Not again. She could not bear it again.

Father, please don't take him. Please make it all better. She cried out in agony and exhaustion, so engulfed in her own misery she was scarcely aware of her surroundings. Then slowly, so slowly she hardly noticed when it began, she felt a warmth at the crown of her head. It spilled down to her shoulders, gradually but completely filling her body, down to its very core. Her sobs eased and she lifted her head. She looked around—at David's body, at her mother—and didn't see what she was looking for. But she could feel . . . something . . . beside her. Almost as if David stood there and rested his hand on her shoulder.

Lizzy looked at her mother, whose cheeks were shiny with tears. She had experienced her son's last moments, knowing through each labor pain that he could be gone at any moment. How did she endure it? Lizzy stood and wiped her face, then gazed at David. His body no longer looked the same; it looked empty. The realization gave her the strength to reluctantly draw a sheet over his face. She turned back to her mother, still feeling the presence beside her, and together they wept.

* * *

Later that week Lizzy stood in the parlor and held baby Caroline close as she looked on David's frail body in his casket. He wore his Sunday best, and Lizzy herself had combed his hair the way he liked it, as she had done so many times before he went outside to play. The funeral would be tomorrow. She pressed the baby close, breathing in her scent.

So many emotions ran through Lizzy that she couldn't name them all; it was both all-consuming and confusing at times. She often didn't even know why she was crying. Having experienced birth and death so close to each other had had a sobering effect on her outlook. She had spent hours contemplating what it all meant.

She patted Caroline's sleeping form and unconsciously began swaying side to side, watching the baby's even breaths, her angelic round face, her tiny features, and her little mouth making sucking motions even in sleep. This little person had to have existed before. Caroline couldn't have simply come into being that fateful day when Lizzy delivered her into the world.

It was as if David had waited for Caroline's arrival before making his departure. But Lizzy couldn't accept that he was gone forever, that his contagious grin and laugh had disappeared with his heartbeat. Yet, in spite of her sadness over David's passing, as she thought back on it, the actual moment had felt natural, as if he had simply walked into another room.

She thought of David's sparkling eyes and rosy cheeks, then looked at his pale face, so different now. With his spirit gone, he no longer looked like himself. Emotion built in her chest and caught in her throat.

Oh, David. Dear little David. Where are you? she thought. *Why did you have to go?* She looked at the body again. A shell, a tabernacle. That's all it was. And she knew it. David wasn't there anymore.

I had to go because my mission was complete. The thought came to her mind forcefully. *I'll be waiting for you, my own Lizzy-Beth. The Lord helped you bring our sister into the world, just as you asked. You know He loves you, don't you?*

Joy coursed through her, and she smiled through her tears. She had felt him beside her at his death. She felt him now, and she realized he was right. "I *do* know it. I do," she whispered into the baby's ear. "God heard me pray. Me. And He answered. I didn't even see it at the time."

She kissed Caroline's tiny head and looked at her. "David would have been the best example for you to follow, but he's gone now. I'll have to do."

And now she *could* fill that role. All because of a brief moment, which told her that she could trust the principles she had been taught all her life.

My own Lizzy-Beth. She remembered the words that had come to her mind. From David. Death wasn't the end. It all made sense. Birth, life, death. Each element fell into place, and standing over them was the love of a Savior. She had finally felt it. She could no longer doubt that He loved her, Elizabeth Sullivan.

Only one thing would make her peace complete—sharing it with the person who knew her heart. She had an urgent need to tell Joshua everything, to share her innermost feelings about the experience with him. He would understand as no one else possibly could, because he had felt it too.

Her pulse quickened as she thought about seeing Joshua and telling him about her experience. She had to go see him. After hurrying to her parents' room, she laid Caroline in her cradle near their resting mother, then ran out to the new barn. She saddled the horse, her fingers shaking so much that she could hardly manage the buckles, but she finally mounted the horse and brought it around.

Her father came in to milk the cow as she was about to ride away. "What is it?" he asked, concerned.

"Nothing to worry about, Papa. I just need to talk to Joshua." Lizzy couldn't contain a grin. Once again, conflicting emotions got the better of her as she fought her grief over David, yet rejoiced in her newfound faith.

Minutes later she was galloping up Main Street, counting the minutes until she could speak with Joshua. A flutter went through Lizzy as she remembered his arms around her at the dance the previous winter. His arms were so strong. So safe.

* * *

Joshua was working in his barn, cleaning a stall so he could put down new straw for his horse. His forehead glistened with sweat, and puffs of steam rose into the crisp autumn air from his breath. At the creak of the door, he looked up. When he caught sight of Beth, his shovel stopped midair. Her face was flushed and filled with emotion. He lowered the shovel to the ground and stepped toward her, worried that something might be wrong.

"Beth?"

At the sight of her smile, he relaxed and sighed with relief, resting his hands on the shovel's handle as he took a break, his breathing heavy. Suddenly she ran the length of the barn and threw her arms around him, all but pushing him over. With a laugh, he caught his balance on the edge of the stall, preventing the both of them from falling to the ground in a heap.

"What's that for?" Joshua asked, pulling back. His heart was racing, and it was no longer because of the work.

"I had to come tell you," she said. "Of all people, you would understand it. There isn't anyone else I wanted to see in the whole world."

Not anyone else? Not even Abe? Joshua thought. *What does she want to tell me? Do I dare hope it's something more than—* But he cut off his thoughts there. "What is it?"

"Can we go somewhere to talk?" she asked, looking around the barn. Her eyes lit up. "How about the hayloft?"

With a chuckle, Joshua shrugged. "Sure, why not. It's been years since we did that."

The two of them climbed up to the loft, which awakened memories of when they were children. Joshua led the way, and when he got to the top, he turned around and reached for her hand. He gently helped her the rest of the way, and when she stepped up beside him, he didn't want to let go.

And to his surprise, Beth didn't seem to be in any hurry to reclaim her hand. He led her to a perfect spot, and they sat together, the smell of sweet hay and sweaty animals around them. They sat like that for several moments. Beth seemed intent on her thoughts, and he was too happy to want the moment to end.

She finally looked up and squeezed his hand. Her eyes were glittering with emotion. "Something has happened, Joshua. And it's so wonderful." A tear escaped one eye, and Joshua reached forward with his free hand to wipe it away. Her cheek was so soft. Only her smile kept him from unduly worrying. These were happy tears.

She went on to tell him about the most sacred experiences of her life. Of David's final breaths, of her anguished prayer, of Caroline's birth, and the wondrous moment when she knew it was all true.

"I never thought that death could bring anything good," she said. "And, of course, I wish David hadn't died. But somehow his passing has changed everything." She lowered her head and twisted a piece of hay in her lap. "Do you remember what we talked about by Jimmy's grave?"

"Of course I do," Joshua said, thinking back to that day. It was the first time Beth had shared the spiritual side of her heart with him, a day he would always treasure.

Beth looked up into the rafters. "I think I know why it took so long for me to have an answer to prayer."

"Why's that?" Joshua asked. The quiet of the barn lent a sacred air to the moment as Lizzy spoke.

"I was always demanding an answer, insisting on one." She wore a wan smile. "But the Lord doesn't work that way, does He? He couldn't answer until for one moment I was truly humble. I couldn't have endured those hours without help, so my plea was urgent, but it wasn't angry or selfish, or any of the other things my prayers had been before."

With a smile, she looked over at Joshua. "I think Moses would be quite pleased with me." She looked at her lap, and her voice lowered. "Thank you for believing in me, Joshua."

He raised her chin so he could look into her eyes. There was something different in them. He had never before seen the woman who looked back at him now. "I always believed in what I saw, even if you couldn't see it."

Her cheeks flushed at his touch, and his heart began beating hard at the sight. For a charged moment they gazed into each other's eyes.

With a cough, she cleared her throat nervously and looked away. "I suppose it was silly of me to race over here, but I just had to tell you."

"I'm glad you did," he said, watching how the sun filtered through the roof, and the dust danced around her hair like a halo.

"I've questioned for so long, wondered whether I mattered to God—or if He existed. It's strange somehow for all that to be changed. I feel a peace I've never known." She touched her heart, then reached over and touched his. "You've known all along, haven't you?"

Joshua hesitantly put a hand over hers. "Not always. And even after I knew, my faith has still been tried." In an instant his thoughts were cluttered with images of the quarry, the dance, the funeral. Where did he and Abe fit into all of this? He couldn't tell Lizzy exactly how his faith had been tested. Maybe someday. Did he dare hope?

Beth leaned over and put her head on his shoulder. He wrapped an arm around her.

"I'm glad you've had your witness," he said huskily, squeezing her tight.

CHAPTER 28

It was warm, just past the hottest hours of the day, when Lizzy ventured out of the house and down Main Street by herself. In one hand she clenched Abe's note, one he left earlier that day asking to meet her on Temple Hill Friday evening at sunset. They hadn't seen one another in weeks, and now that the prospect lay just two days away; Lizzy knew she had to sort out her thoughts and make some decisions.

Without any thought of a destination, she walked down Main Street several blocks, then turned up toward Temple Hill. At the top, she stopped by the base of the grand structure, walls growing taller each day, the scaffolding surrounding it protectively. She stared at it, a multitude of memories from the place washing over her: the day Brother Webster first brought the family to see the site, watching her father work, Brother McKay falling to what should have been his death, and one memory overshadowing the rest—the cornerstone ceremony when she first saw Abe.

Abe. Her heart battled against itself, and her hand gripped his note tighter. What was she to do? Over the last several days she had realized what her feelings for Abe were mostly about—a thrill that, while exciting and romantic like her daydreams, was nothing to base a life on. If Abe had been a typical Mormon boy, she'd asked herself, would she have felt the urgency to become his friend? The answer sent a wave of guilt over her. *No.*

More than once Abe had mentioned how grateful he was to her for seeing beyond his heritage. But had she really? Hadn't she actually been chasing an exotic hero that Abe's heritage made him into? She shook her head, ashamed at the thought.

But had it all been an act, nothing more real than the circus performers they had watched that first day together? Lizzy couldn't accept that thought, either. Her feelings for Abe had been real. Immature, perhaps, but real.

With a deep breath, she continued past the temple stable and beyond. She and Abe used to walk these same streets together, and at each corner a new memory faced her. Before she knew it, she had reached the Webster farm. In a strange way, this place felt like home. Her eyes traveled from the house to the rows of trees and the grove where she and Abe met so long ago, where everything began.

A compulsion to see the trees again overtook her, and she walked toward them. As she entered the grove, her hand went to her throat, and she fingered Joshua's chain. She stopped and slowly walked in a circle, looking around her. No one was about. And the trees shielded her from the road as well as the house.

The place brought more thoughts of Abe to the surface. It was here he had first kissed her hand, where they had first exchanged books, where she had tied the yellow dishrag as a signal for him. After all the months they had spent together in secret, Lizzy had all but promised Abe her heart and her future. She couldn't bear the thought of sending him away and breaking his heart after that. She looked up at the blue sky, the patchy clouds, and wondered aloud. "Perhaps if he received a witness of his own and was baptized. Perhaps then we could be happy together."

She paused, half hoping for an answer from the air around her. All was quiet and silent—and somehow reverent. Lizzy suddenly dropped to her knees, bowed her head, and clasped her hands together. *This will be my second sincere prayer*, she thought, and knew she needed an answer to it almost as urgently as she needed help before.

Eyes squeezed shut, she bared her soul to the Lord and pled for help to know her own heart and what to do. Tears ran down her nose and dropped onto her hands. The damp ground was soaking through her skirts. And still she prayed.

She expressed gratitude for the blessing of having had Abe enrich her life. She asked whether his conversion would make them equal and happy partners.

But as much as she tried to keep her mind focused on Abe and the problem at hand, she couldn't prevent images of Joshua from entering her thoughts. Joshua. Dear Joshua, who understood her like no one else ever could.

Her eyes opened at the sudden realization. *I love Joshua.* More than she had ever thought she loved Abe, more than she had ever before understood what love was, she knew this now. He was part of her very being. He knew her and understood her heart. And that moment she knew, without any agonizing prayers about it, that she could happily spend the rest of her life with Joshua. If he would have her.

She shook her head. Even if he wouldn't, she now understood what genuine love was—and that she and Abe wouldn't have what they needed to make a happy match.

* * *

Friday evening, right before sunset, Lizzy wrapped her shawl around her shoulders and picked up *Rasselas* to return to Abe. With all the events over the last several weeks, she hadn't found the time or motivation to finish it until now, when they would be meeting—for what she knew would be the last time.

As she opened the back door to leave, the crisp autumn air greeted her and she hugged the book close against the cold. A few blocks down Main Street and her nose was red, but her body was warm with the exercise. She continued down the street, biting the corner of her lip in thought.

So much had happened since that fateful day of David's death and little Caroline's birth that it felt like another lifetime since she'd last seen Abe. She hardly recognized her former self, the girl who had once met him in secret and enjoyed the pure excitement of it. She thought again of her prayer in Brother Webster's grove, of the clear answer and her determination to follow her heart.

Her hands gripped the book tighter. *Rasselas*—a book about the nature of happiness. It was Abe's favorite, the one book he treasured beyond any other, which was why he hadn't lent it to her until recently. Ironic that of all times she could be reading about the nature of happiness, it would turn out to be when she was on the cusp of changing her life. And now that she had made her final decision, one she believed would offer her the greatest chance at happiness, she would hurt Abe. Deeply.

She recalled their discussions about religion. Those were the moments she had felt most close to Abe, as if they shared a common vision. But even on those points she had changed and was continuing to change. Everything that had once held them together seemed less important—less compelling as reasons for building a life together.

She didn't have all the answers to her questions—and doubted she would ever have them all—but that didn't matter so much anymore. She finally knew that her Heavenly Father was watching, that He knew her and loved her. Getting the answers wasn't so urgent. She could spend a lifetime learning them now that she had the most important answer of all.

Would Abe understand that?

If they had a conversation about prayer today, what would it be like now? Lizzy smiled. *Very different, that's what.* This would be one more thing she couldn't share with Abe, and the one most significant and dear to her heart.

She paused at the base of Temple Hill and looked at the growing structure and its scaffolding. The walls were beautiful and strong. Someday she would go inside them and receive the blessings she had heard so much about. She took her first step up the hill and trudged along the steep slope, knowing that each moment brought her closer to facing Abe.

Thank heavens Joshua hadn't yet found someone else. With him everything was different. But would he accept her love now after everything that had happened? She didn't know, but it was that hope that would help her get through what was coming.

Abe met her at the base of the temple walls just as the sun had begun to set. His eyes lit up at seeing her, and Lizzy noticed the burns on his cheek. They looked much better now. She hoped for his sake the scars wouldn't be very noticeable when the wounds healed. Before she could say a word, Abe broke in.

"Perfect timing," he said, eyeing the sky. "Follow me."

He led her up the south scaffolding on the interior of the temple. She knew the building was far from complete, or dedicated, that men of all walks of life worked there every day, but it still felt strange going inside the temple. These might be planks of lumber they were on, but she could reach out and touch the stone walls, sacred walls. The thought crossed her mind that they were trespassing, that perhaps they should turn back.

But then she glanced down and realized how high up they were, and, with a nervous flutter in her stomach, she stepped closer to the stone and reached for Abe's arm to steady herself. She tried not to think about the distance she would fall if she slipped. Dozens of times she had seen workers pass each other on the scaffolding ramps, often pushing loaded wheelbarrows. The ramps were plenty sturdy, she reminded herself. A young woman her size would hardly break them. But the height was enough to make her stomach twist anyway.

When they reached the top, all such thoughts evaporated. They stood at the southwest corner of the temple by one of the towers, with the city and valley spread out below them.

"Oh!" Lizzy said, the sight taking her breath away. "It's so beautiful."

"Look," Abe said, pointing at the sunset. The deep purple at the horizon gradually gave way to pink and then a blazing orange which splashed across the sky and valley. An evening breeze wafted past them, and Lizzy breathed it all in. She gazed out, feeling as if she were a bird in flight as she looked down.

She leaned forward against the wall, the book under her arms. "It's what heaven must look like," she whispered, unwilling to speak loudly, as if doing so might shatter the moment.

"I was thinking the same thing," Abe whispered. Lizzy glanced at him. He wasn't looking at the sunset, but at her. He took her hands in his and turned her to face him. He seemed nervous, and for a moment she worried he was ill.

"Are you feeling well?"

"I think so. I'll know for sure in a moment." He motioned toward the sunset. "Every time I'm with you, this is what it feels like. I never want it to end."

The light fluttering in her stomach turned heavy. She placed her left hand over it, leaving her right hand in his. She had known for some time this was coming, and until recently she had been so sure she would be with him. But everything had changed, and as much as she cared for Abe, her greatest desires no longer rested with him.

He fished in his pocket for a piece of paper. "I have something besides the sunset to show you," he said, unable to contain a grin. "Look at this."

As Lizzy took the paper from his hands, he got down on one knee and gazed up at her. She scarcely had time to read and comprehend the baptismal certificate before Abe spoke.

"Lizzy Sullivan, will you marry me?"

"I don't understand," Lizzy began, her brow furrowed as she read and reread the paper.

Abe pointed to his name. "There. See? I'm not a Gentile. My mother sent that to me recently. I didn't remember ever being baptized, but I was."

Lizzy couldn't answer. Everything she had planned on saying had up and left her mind.

"Don't you see?" Abe pressed. "Your parents will surely accept me when they know I've been baptized. They can't object now."

Her eyes grew misty as she lowered the paper. "Oh, Abe."

"Will you marry me?" Abe asked again.

"Oh, Abe," Lizzy repeated, this time with a slow shake of her head. She turned back to the sunset, which now lacked the thrill of only a moment before. "I can't."

"Why not?" Abe asked, standing, looking at the certificate. "This is real. It's proof. My last name is different now, but it's still me."

"I know." How could she make him understand? Had she not experienced it herself, she wouldn't understand either. Mere membership in the Church wasn't the important thing anymore. That had become clear the moment she yearned to share her deepest feelings with Joshua. She couldn't do that with Abe.

"Are you still worried about your parents? Your mother likes me now, remember? I don't think she'd object to a 'Lamanite' marrying her daughter anymore."

She shook her head and sighed. "This has nothing to do with either of my parents."

Abe searched her face, confused. "I thought you loved me. You know I love you. That I'd do anything for you. We could still go to California, if that's what you want."

"Abe." Lizzy shook her head. "Something happened after David died, and now I understand . . ." Her voice trailed off. She gazed into Abe's eyes, hoping to find a glimmer in them, some indication that he would be able to accept what she would say.

"Now you understand *what?*" A hurt tone replaced the soft one of a moment before.

"Everything," Lizzy said helplessly.

"Such as?"

"Such as all the things my parents—"

"So this *is* about your mother," Abe interjected, looking away.

Lizzy shook her head vehemently. "No, no. This has nothing to do with her. It was my decision. After all these years I understand what she's been telling me. Abe . . ." She touched his shoulder, and he looked at her. "I have a testimony now. I *know.*"

She waited for his response, but Abe's blank stare told her that he didn't register the significance of her words. Lizzy went on. "I understand now why my parents were so concerned about my marrying outside the faith." She turned to the rock walls of the temple, and her hands traced the rough surfaces her father had worked on. Her voice lowered as she thought of David looking down on her, counting on her to be part of their family in the eternities.

"I want my family to be together for all times. I want to be married in a temple."

Abe breathed out in frustration. "But we can do that together, Lizzy. I'm a bona fide baptized Mormon, remember?" He held out the paper as if having to prove it all over again.

"Oh, I know. I know. And that's all I would have cared about before, when it was my parents who worried about whether I married a man who believed. But it's different now. Now *I* care whether I marry a man who believes as I do."

She took the paper, read it again, and turned it to him. "Does your baptism mean anything to you?"

Abe hesitated, but finally shook his head. "No. Not like you mean. I might as well have jumped into the river for all the good it did me."

"And if we married," Lizzy said, touching his arm, "we wouldn't be partners. Not really. We wouldn't be *equally yoked,* as the Bible says. That's what I need . . . that's what I didn't know I needed."

Lizzy looked down at *Rasselas,* which she still held, and opened it to one of the last pages. "It's like it says here close to the end, 'The choice of life is become less important; I hope hereafter—'"

"'—to think only on the choice of eternity,'" Abe finished. He let out a strained chuckle. "I never thought you would use *Rasselas* against me." He took the book, his jaw working in thought. "What if—what if I read your Book of Mormon and start praying and coming to meetings—and I truly start to believe? Then would you marry me?"

Lizzy stared at Abe, speechless. Her eyes misted up, and she finally shook her head. "I'm so sorry, Abe. No."

He turned away. "Joshua," he said under his breath.

"Abe—" Lizzy started, then stopped, because she had no idea what she would say. She couldn't deny it. She did love Joshua.

"Think about it, Lizzy," Abe said, staring at the waning sunset. "And be honest. Can you truly say that Joshua still means nothing more to you than a school chum?"

He looked over his shoulder, and their eyes held for a strained moment. Lizzy tore her gaze away, not trusting herself to speak. But she knew her eyes had already betrayed her heart. She had hoped to spare him this.

Abe nodded. "I thought so. Ever since Jimmy's funeral."

She turned back to him again. "What do you mean?"

"I watched you," he said with a shrug. "Joshua comforting you, the way you let him hold you. I tried to imagine me doing it, but I couldn't. You two have a bond that we don't. I hoped I was wrong about it and tried to convince myself that Joshua just happened to be there when you needed someone. That if I had shown up first it would have been my shoulder you would have cried on, but now . . . now I know better. You love him, don't you?"

She tried to restrain a cry at the sight of Abe's obvious hurt, but she no longer tried to deny what he had said. He was right. Abe could never have given her the comfort she needed that day. And he could never have rejoiced with her at the things she had experienced after David's death. He no longer understood her, because she had changed.

"Joshua and I have known each other for so long. He knows my heart, and I know his." Tears streamed down her cheeks as she tried to explain. "I'm so sorry, Abe . . . because I did love you." *In a way.*

Abe's face softened, and he put an arm around her. "I wish I could show you that love is enough. I could make you happy. I know it."

Lizzy put her hand against his chest and urged him back. "Abe, don't."

The hope in his eyes faded at the expression of determination on her face. He lifted the yellowing paper to eye level and gave a cynical laugh. "To think I was so sure this would make a difference . . ."

Leaning over the wall, he tore the paper into shreds and watched the pieces drift away against the backdrop of what remained of the sunset, only a few fading streaks of color.

"I think I'll hate sunsets after this," he said, quietly.

He turned to Lizzy one last time and softly kissed her cheek. It sent the butterflies in her stomach into a frenzy.

"Good-bye, Lizzy."

He turned and headed down the ramp, leaving her behind to stand against the cold, gray stone as the light faded.

CHAPTER 29

The late-October sun beat down in warm rays as Lizzy drove the wagon down streets toward Joshua's house. On the bench beside her lay a quilt she had begun months earlier. It had lain untouched for many weeks as her burns healed. As soon as her fingers permitted, she'd spent countless hours finishing it. The quilt was intended for Joshua as a housewarming gift.

Shading her eyes against the sun, she drove westward, then lowered her hand when she turned north. She reined in the horse for a moment and gazed at the house. It looked awfully close to the original. Joshua had gone to a lot of effort to make it so. He had even planted a few shrubs in front that matched the ones of the original Sullivan home. If it hadn't been for the fact that it looked so perfect, so new, she could have believed she had traveled back to the summer before her family lost their home.

She could picture Jimmy and the twins romping in the yard, imagine herself milking the cow in the stable out back, hear her mother's humming floating through the window as she canned fruit. With a click of Lizzy's tongue and a light snap of the reins, the horse moved on.

After pulling the wagon behind the house, she tied the horse in the shade of a newly planted tree. She hopped down and lifted the quilt out, then stopped and considered the situation, trying to decide exactly how to go about this. With a deep breath to steel herself, Lizzy stepped toward the house.

It would be odd to knock on the back door, as if she were knocking at her family's home. She thought again about what Joshua had said in the furniture store, how he had built it in hopes that she would be the woman who would make it a home. Did he still feel that way?

Instead of raising her hand to the door, she took a few steps back, closed her eyes, and made the peacock call as best as she could. It sounded pathetic, she knew, and she cringed at the noise coming from her mouth.

Joshua opened the door, a curious look in his eyes. He grinned at the sight of her. "I thought I heard some poor bird crying for me."

"I told you I'm hopeless," she said, attempting a smile. She swallowed hard. *This is it. No turning back now.*

"Come in," he said, opening the door farther to let her through.

She flushed, every inch of her feeling awkward. The quilt seemed to weigh twice as much, and she just knew she would trip. "Thank you," she said, stepping inside.

Joshua led her into the kitchen, where she looked around her in awe. The last time he had shown it to her, the place had looked so different. Now the walls were painted, the floor freshly sanded, the rooms furnished. It could still use a feminine touch like her own, she reasoned, but it really did feel like a home now.

"It's wonderful," she said, hugging the bulky quilt.

"Thank you," Joshua said. "Can I get you something to eat? I don't have any cookies or cake, but I bought a fresh loaf of bread today. I tried making some bread myself, but it might as well have been stone."

"Yes, thank you," Lizzy said with a laugh, even though her stomach felt too queasy to eat. She placed the quilt on the table and sat beside it. As Joshua fixed her a slice of bread and slathered butter on it, her stomach churned with anxiety. In years past she and Joshua had no trouble filling the time with conversation, but today she could hardly get out two words. And it would take more than that to do what she had come for.

"There you go," Joshua said, placing the bread in front of her—on one of the earthenware dishes she had picked out months ago.

"Thank you." Was that the only thing she could say? She stared at the bread and swallowed hard, trying to get up her nerve. She finally pointed to the quilt, as it was an easy and obvious conversation topic.

"I made this for you. Hoped it would keep you warm when winter comes on."

Joshua ran his hand across the pattern of interlocking links. "It's beautiful. Thank you. This must have taken months."

She couldn't answer at first. Joshua turned back to the cutting board to get himself some bread, when she finally blurted out, "I was hoping I could add one more thing to your home."

Joshua nodded as he spread butter on his slice. "The quilt is the perfect addition to the house. It means a lot to me."

"I didn't mean the quilt," Lizzy said, feeling her cheeks and ears growing hot. She began studying the toe of her boot. "Don't get me wrong. I'm glad you like it. But there's something else."

"Oh?" Joshua placed the bread on a plate and looked around the room. "What did you have in mind?"

Lizzy gulped hard as Joshua took the chair beside hers. Her hands trembled uncontrollably, and she clasped them together under the table in an attempt to still them. *This is not how it works in books,* she thought, her heart pounding in her chest. *Elizabeth Barrett Browning would be rolling in her grave if she saw me now.* Lizzy finally dared a look into his eyes.

"Are you still missing . . . a *lady* for your home?"

Joshua gaped at Lizzy for a moment, his jaw slack. "I . . ."

His confused expression sent panic through her. Of course his feelings had changed. She'd been silly to expect him to still have the same ones he had months ago, especially after everything that had happened with Abe. For all she knew, he'd had his eye on someone else and saw Lizzy once again as an old schoolmate. Her fingers went to her forehead absently as she fought to think.

"I'm sorry. I should go." She stood and hurried toward the door. "I'm glad you like the quilt. Good day."

Joshua shoved his chair back and got to his feet in time to grab her arm. "Beth."

She stared at the floor, humiliation drenching her like water. His touch on her arm practically burned into her skin. Closing her eyes tightly, she took a deep breath, willing herself someplace else.

Anywhere but here.

"Don't go," Joshua said.

But she couldn't move anyway; her feet already felt rooted to the floor. If only she could run away and never return. Or at least take back the last five minutes.

She felt a movement and opened her eyes to find Joshua kneeling before her. Her heart stopped at the sight. Joshua's hand was the one trembling now. She held her breath, her mind a blur. *This doesn't mean . . . it couldn't mean . . .*

"Beth. My Lizzy-Beth. I love you. I've always loved you."

What did he call her? *Lizzy-Beth.* She had heard that name only one other time, in the parlor after David died.

"Will you marry me?" he asked. "I'll make you happy. I know I will."

Lizzy's heart began beating again—twice as fast as normal—and for the first time since coming in the door, she found the use of her tongue. "Of course I will, Joshua."

He stood and pulled Lizzy into his arms. She held him tight, his strong arms encircling her. "I love you, Joshua," she said into his ear. "And I want nothing more than to be your wife here in this house for the rest of my life."

When they parted, Joshua tentatively leaned down. No longer having to be content with a peck of friendship on the cheek, he gave Lizzy a proper kiss on her lips. She returned the kiss willingly, feeling something much more powerful awakening inside her than she had ever experienced. It was new and all-consuming, yet so familiar at the same time.

Too soon, Joshua pulled back and stroked her hair. She closed her eyes at his touch.

As he put his hand on her cheek he whispered, "Is it true? Are you really mine?"

She leaned closer into his arms. "I'm completely yours. Forever." She looked up at him, a sheepish smile curving her lips, and she lifted a finger at him. "But don't you dare tell anyone I nearly proposed to you."

Joshua put his head back and laughed out loud, then kissed her soundly again and held her close. "Your secret is safe with me, my own Lizzy-Beth."

EPILOGUE

Three Years Later—August 1882

Abe took a break from his work with the plasterers for the midday meal. He knew most of the other workers at the table by name, but he didn't know many personally, so he tended to keep to himself. After all, hadn't he learned the hard way that, as an Indian and a Gentile, he didn't fit in here? Of course, there was also the fact that one side of his face was still scarred enough to draw attention. And pity. It was hard to tell which stares were at his burns and which were at his Indian skin. Not that it mattered. The fact remained that some of his isolation was his own fault. There was a time he would have tried to make friends with the men he worked with, but no more.

After Lizzy said good-bye to him on the temple walls so long ago, Abe had gone to Idaho for work. The pay wasn't good and the winters were colder, so two and a half years later he'd returned to Logan and now worked with the plasterers. But he still wasn't content. Just being there each day reminded him of Lizzy. Had she changed much over the years? Word had it that she and Joshua were expecting their second child now. Once he had seen her going into the general store on Main Street. She had carried a brown-haired child on her hip and chatted with another woman. The sight sent Abe's heart beating at a crazy speed.

Ever since, he'd avoided going anywhere he might run into her, from community dances to Christiansen's Store. When he had to buy something, he planned the trip for the early morning hours when she would be least likely to shop. Seeing her would be too painful. He doubted that he would ever let himself give his heart away again.

"I shall henceforward fear to yield my heart to excellence, however bright, or to fondness, however tender, lest I should lose again what I have lost." He often quoted the line from *Rasselas* to himself. It expressed his emotions perfectly. And it was particularly fitting, he thought, that it came from the same book Lizzy quoted from when she pushed him out of her life.

But as frustrated as he was, he couldn't be angry at Lizzy. And when he took a hard look at how it all turned out, he was glad she made the choice she did. Chances were good he *would* have made her miserable. He knew now what he couldn't have known then—that loving her wasn't enough. Abe wasn't so selfish he would wish to have Lizzy as his wife even if that wasn't what she wanted.

She was happy with Joshua. That's what mattered.

But staying close to her was making him miserable. Next payday he would leave for California and start anew. He had enough money. He had saved plenty—money that was supposed to have gone to making a home with Lizzy. First he would see his mother in Salt Lake City and coax her into coming with him. Brother Franklin had passed on two years before from heart trouble, something Abe shed no tears over. Without a husband to care for, his mother might be willing to start a new life in California.

With a bite from a thick piece of buttered bread, he gazed out the cookhouse window. The temple towers were across the street. Images of that last night with Lizzy jumped into his mind before he could stop them.

He remembered the baptismal certificate, how he was so sure it would change everything. Until that last night she seemed to want the same things he did. What had happened? She had gotten a "testimony," she'd said. But that wasn't the whole story. She also loved Joshua more.

Abe stabbed his fork into a piece of apple pie. He glanced out the window toward the eastern side of the temple, a structure he was helping to build but didn't care for, at least not the way Lizzy and her family did.

And when it was finished, he wouldn't be allowed to go inside.

Of course he knew all that, always had. But the realization struck him suddenly. Every morning he walked inside the walls and worked all day. And that evening so long ago he had even climbed up to the top of the scaffolding with Lizzy. He bit off a chunk of pie thoughtfully. Suddenly the temple represented all that Abe had lost when Lizzy left his life. He glanced over at Richard Sullivan, who sat eating near the door. Mr. Sullivan caught Abe's gaze and nodded in recognition, then returned to his meal. Abe looked down at his plate. Lizzy's father always had been kind.

A conversation at the same table interrupted his thoughts. "You're really going to do it then?" Josiah Smith asked, clunking his glass on the table.

"Of course," said William Davis, a plasterer. "We're going to make the inscriptions after we eat. Of course, they'll be inside the walls. Maybe no one will ever find them, but no matter. We'll always be a part of the temple."

Another man piped up, one Abe thought was named Sam. "What do you plan to write?"

Davis shrugged. "Our names, some of our happenings, you know, things that might be interesting to folks years from now."

The men's words planted an idea in Abe's mind. A slow smile crossed his face.

After lunch he followed them to the spot where a few of the plasterers had gathered. William Davis had already taken his turn, as had Josiah Smith, who wrote his name, hometown, and *mudmaker*. Clayton stepped forward and wrote a few lines, including, "John Tayler is the President" and "Wilford Woodruff is the president of the twelve and is 72 years auld" and something about the laws against polygamy. He finished by adding his own name, the date, and his birthday. He stepped back and surveyed his addition, then nodded to Sam to take his turn. Then they noticed Abe standing several feet away.

Abe stepped forward. "Could I—would you mind if I added something to the wall?"

The other men looked to each other. Clayton shrugged, and they all silently nodded in agreement. When Sam finished, he stepped aside to make room for Abe, who reached high above the others' writing. Instead of recording his name or a date or a current fact, Abe inscribed his initials, each letter nearly a foot tall and in fancy, calligraphy-style script.

When he finished, he took a step back and looked over his work, then nodded to himself. *AMF. Abraham Michael Franklin.*

"Thank you," he said, handing the writing tool back to Williams and feeling much better. He surveyed the letters again with satisfaction, knowing he would always be a part of Lizzy Sullivan's world whether she knew it or not.

Lizzy *Sorensen's* world, he corrected himself. He hoped Joshua appreciated his prize.

Abe absently wandered around the temple, eventually coming to the bottom of the stairs leading up the southwest tower. He climbed them, and at the top he looked over the city, barely able to make out the new house Joshua had built on the old Sullivan land. He closed his eyes and turned his head away from the sight of their home. On one hand the image was painful, but strangely peaceful on the another. If only he could have been the one. At least she was content in her life. He could leave, never to return, as long as he knew that Joshua would take care of Lizzy.

Against Abe's will, he thought again about their last night. He could almost see Lizzy as she stood beside him and said she loved Joshua more, that she couldn't be with him.

Now, picturing his initials inside the walls, he couldn't hold back a smile as he whispered, "But I'll always be with you. And you'll always be part of me."

Author's Notes

I have had a love of Logan and its temple since I was a child. My grandparents, August and Frieda Miller Luthy, raised their family of eleven children in Logan, and my grandfather worked as a temple groundskeeper for several years. My parents were married in the Logan Temple, as were my husband and I. Several years ago, my parents' copy of Nolan P. Olsen's book, *Logan Temple: The First 100 Years*, caught my eye. Because of our family connection with the temple, I borrowed the book and read it, enthralled with the rich stories and heritage of the temple and the people who worked on it. I couldn't get the images out of my mind. Later I reread the book, this time taking meticulous notes and creating a master chronology. Soon characters and a story began forming, demanding to be told. This book is the result.

My grandparents' home stood at 870 North Main in Logan. Although their home was built decades after the story is set, I used the old Luthy home, which I spent many happy hours in as a child, as my model for the home the Sullivans bought from Sister Mills. A Central Park fast-food establishment now stands in its place.

To the best of my knowledge, the historical details of Logan, building the temple, and so forth are accurate. Quotes from Church leaders at the cornerstone ceremony were taken directly from Brother Olsen's book. A circus really was the same day as the laying of the cornerstones, and a little boy named Joseph was heard to complain about the length of the services, as described. Other factual details include Sabbath eggs for the temple fund, the eclipse and rockslide at the quarry, the stonecutting shed, Old Jim, and many, many others. If it sounds unbelievable, chances are it really happened. Some facts I used and elaborated on, such as a pair of silver sugar tongs known to have been donated to the fund, which I attributed to Abigail Sullivan. Any errors are entirely my responsibility.

I used many cultural details from the period as well. For example, a number of Latter-day Saints between 1850 and 1870 purchased Native American children in an effort to "save" them, be it spiritually or from the slave trade or other harm. According to a paper written by Brian Q. Cannon, prices varied between twenty-five dollars and forty-five dollars, or consisted of goods like weapons, ammunition, livestock, food, and clothing. Parents who bought and indentured Native American children were bound by law to clothe, feed, and educate them from age seven to sixteen. The situation described with Abe's adoption (being sold by his mother as she fled her husband with another man) really happened with a child adopted by Christopher Arthur and his wife. In some cases the families didn't fully accept their new family member, particularly if the child didn't embrace the religion. (See "Adopted or Indentured 1850–1870: Native Children in Mormon Households," *Nearly Everything Imaginable: The Everyday Life Utah's Mormon Pioneers,* Brigham Young University Press, 1999, 341–357.)

All the literature mentioned during this period is accurate. The reader may note that Aunt Louisa tends to send Lizzy contemporary literature, while Abe's mother had mostly older works in her collection. Although books were quite scarce in the decades before the story is set, at this point they were much more readily available, and novel reading began to be more culturally accepted.

According to the NASA Goddard Flight Safety Center, eye damage will not occur during the few seconds or minutes of a *total* solar eclipse, which is why Joshua and the other men were able to look directly at it. Partial eclipses of any kind, however, *will* result in permanent eye damage.

Due to the length of the temple's construction and constraints on how much time and information the story could cover, I reluctantly left out large portions of the fascinating history of the temple. I also took a few liberties as follows:

Scofield, the site of the coal mine in central Utah where Joshua goes to help George build a home, was settled two years later than in the novel.

Although I didn't find a firm date, Truman Angell probably decided to even out the towers of the temple a bit later than mentioned. According to Olsen's book, this was a decision based solely on aesthetics; the temple simply looked more proportional with even towers.

The details surrounding the King and Osterholdt tragedy are accurate, including how their bodies were found, the community finding out about the accident during a dance (which they really held that late at night), and the facts about Billie King's widow and son. However, the accident took place in 1880, a year later than in the novel. In my first draft I invented details about Billie King's wife and child. Interestingly, when I went in search of their real identities, I discovered I had picked the correct gender and age for his child and even selected his wife's real name. However, Helen's home life and background are purely fictional.

Finally, the details surrounding Hugh McKay's fall from the temple walls—including landing with the rock on him, standing up immediately afterward, and his miraculous eleven-day recovery—happened about a year and a half later than I placed it, six months *after* the King and Osterholdt tragedy, not before. Otherwise, all dates and events are, to the best of my knowledge, accurate.

On October 1, 1976, the Logan Temple closed for renovations. The inside was completely gutted, leaving a stone shell. A new, modern interior was then constructed. During the demolition, the handwriting of several different people was discovered on the plaster of one wall. Recorded were names, dates, and current events, some of which are included in the novel. Topping the other writings, in elaborate foot-high letters, were the initials *AMF.*

Who or what *AMF* was remains a mystery.

ABOUT THE AUTHOR

Annette Luthy Lyon has been writing for most of her life. While she's been successful in magazine, newspaper, and business writing, her true passion is fiction. She graduated cum laude from BYU with a BA in English, and served on the Utah Valley chapter board for the League of Utah Writers for three years, including one year as president. She has received several awards from the League, including a Quill award and two Diamond awards. Annette and her husband, Rob, live in American Fork, Utah, with their four children.

ABOUT THE AUTHOR